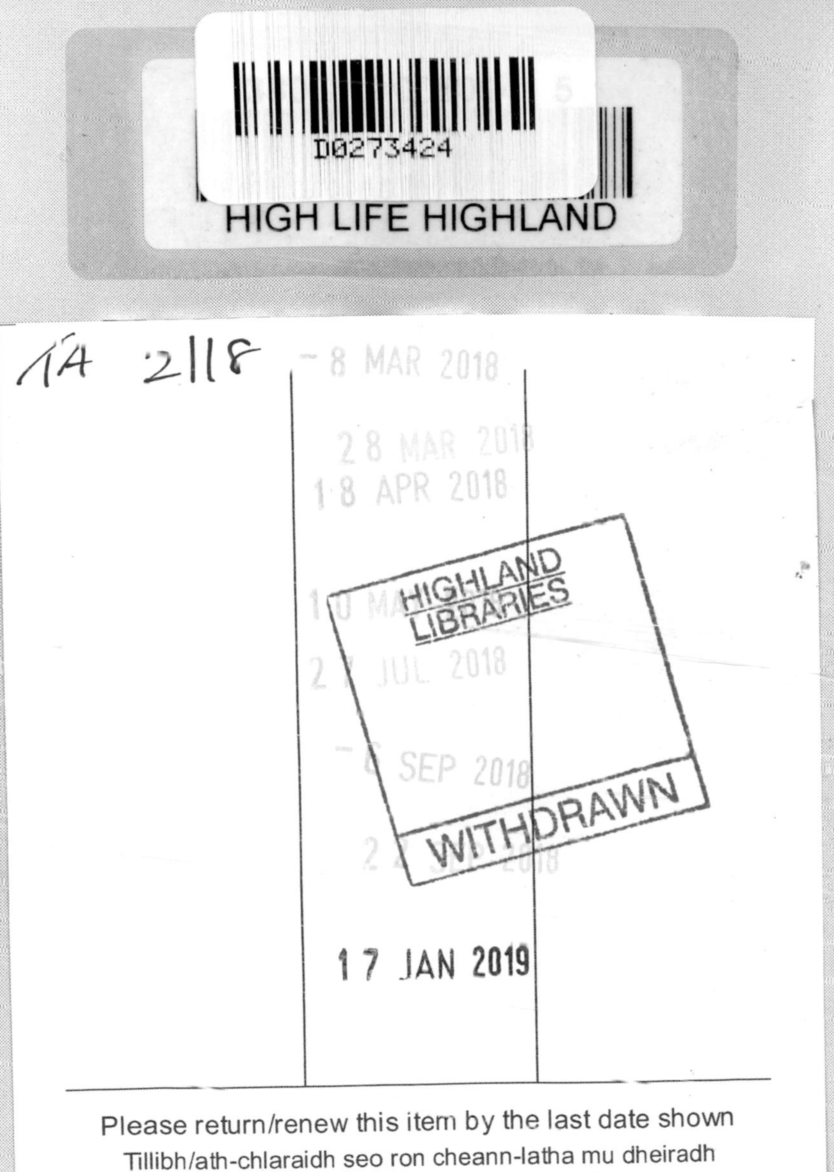
D0273424
HIGH LIFE HIGHLAND
TA 2|18
- 8 MAR 2018
28 MAR 2018
18 APR 2018
HIGHLAND LIBRARIES
WITHDRAWN
27 JUL 2018
- 6 SEP 2018
17 JAN 2019

HIDDEN PASTS

CLIO GRAY

Urbane
PUBLICATIONS

urbanepublications.com

First published in Great Britain in 2018
by Urbane Publications Ltd
Suite 3, Brown Europe House, 33/34 Gleaming Wood Drive,
Chatham, Kent ME5 8RZ

A CIP catalogue record for this book is available
from the British Library.

ISBN 978-1-911583-19-6
MOBI 978-1-911583-21-9
EPUB 978-1-911583-20-2

Design and Typeset by Michelle Morgan

Cover by Michelle Morgan

Printed and bound by 4edge Limited, UK

urbanepublications.com

THE SCOTTISH MYSTERIES SERIES

BOOK 1 – DEADLY PROSPECTS

BOOK 2 – BURNING SECRETS

BOOK 3 – HIDDEN PASTS

CONTENTS

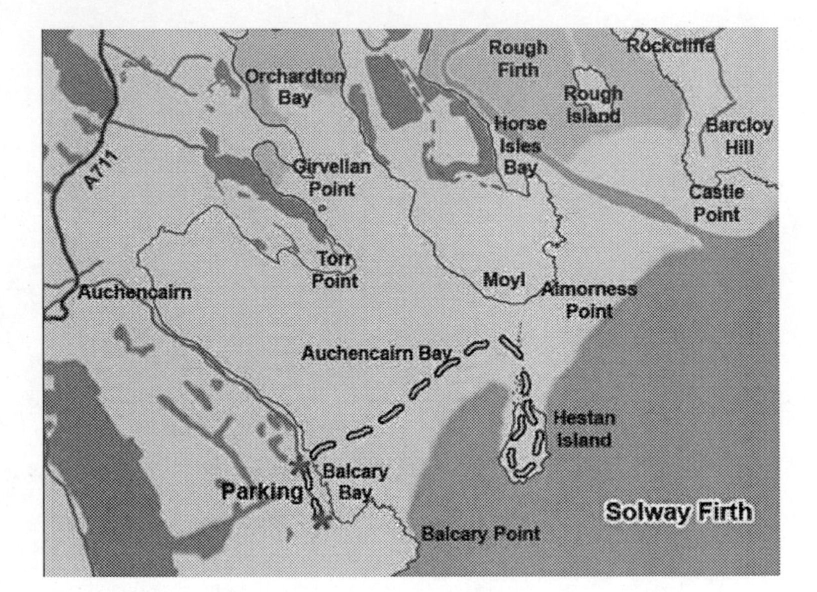
Rough
Firth
Rockcliffe
Orchardton
Bay
Rough
Island
Horse
Isles
Bay
Barcloy
Hill
A711
Girvellan
Point
Castle
Point
Torr
Point
Moyl
Almorness
Point
Auchencairn
Auchencairn Bay
Hestan
Island
Balcary
Bay
Parking
Solway Firth
Balcary Point

PREFACE

1833, GENICHESK, CRIMEA

The farmhouse the men had been directed to outside of Genichesk was a mean-looking building – barely more than a shack – timbers falling away from its roof, the fields about the homestead unkempt, overgrown with purple larkspur and pink-flowering peach shrubs that would never bear fruit. The air was rank with marsh-stink and stagnant water rising up from the Putrid Sea: a skinny lagoon marooned between the northern shores of the Crimea and the landlocked – though freely flowing – Azov Sea, separated from its freshness by the isthmus of one hundred kilometres of sandy shingle called the Arabat Tongue. A more dismal place they'd none of them ever seen, and no more functional looked the barn that was adjacent to the house, that was even more dilapidated. As they advanced upon the door of the farmhouse they tallied up their duty here.

'This is a badger's arse of a farm, if I ever seen one,' grumbled the first man. 'Can't think of anywhere them Tatars are less likely to have anything stashed.'

'Maybe that's the point,' said the second of them, speaking softly. 'Stick it all where no one'll ever look…'

''Cept we're looking now,' pointed out the third, the youngest, eyes wide and blue even in the gloom of the gloaming.

'Only 'cos they was tattled on...'

'Sssh!' warned a fourth, as he took a few more paces towards the overgrown yard.

'What're y'hearing?' asked man number two, cocking his head, hearing the faint sound of a child crying.

'Ah, Jeez,' number one came back. 'That's all we need. A crying bairn fit to break all our bastard hearts.'

'Quiet!' commanded their nominal chief, on account of him being the only native Russian speaker. 'Get out to that barn and take a look, before we do anything else.'

His companions did as commanded and pulled back the creaking wooden doors of the creaking wooden barn.

'Load of potatoes and grain,' said number one, sniffing at the stack of pallets and walking away, rubbing a nervous hand through his scant and youthful beard.

'Don't think so,' said another softly, lifting off the first two pallets, pulling away the dirty sacking to reveal the spines of leather-bound books and folios. 'It's what we thought, though have to say it seems criminal to burn the lot of them.'

'If them Russians wants 'em burned then that's what we're gonna do,' the bearded man retorted, eyes glancing into the cobwebs that hid in the corners like enemies. 'Only a load of rubbish anyway and a grand fire them'll make. Might actually get warm for once in this shit-hole of a country.'

He scuffed his boots into the dirt and closed his eyes, thinking of home, wishing he'd never left. No grand adventure this, not like he'd been promised.

'If you think they're rubbish then you're a bigger fool than I thought,' said the leader of their cadre coming in behind them.

'That's the combined libraries of all the Tatar leaders in this district.' He whistled lightly as he approached the pallets and laid his fingers on the books within their crates. 'And I for one am not going to be party to their destruction.'

'That's mutiny...' grumbled the bearded man, not unaware of the smiles the others exchanged.

'Insubordination, maybe,' corrected their leader, 'but mutiny's an entirely different thing.'

The bearded man cursed and spat.

'Don't matter what you call it; you're going to get the lot of us shot.'

'Then go home back to Scotland,' his leader spun on his heel and fixed the man with a hard stare. 'That'd be called desertion in our neck of the woods, and that really would get you facing the firing squad.'

'Enough,' intervened the soft-voiced man. 'I'm with the boss on this one. What about you?' he asked the youngest of their four-strong cadre.

The lad's blue eyes sparkled, the dimples in his cheeks deepening as he smiled.

'I'm in. So what's the plan?'

It took them most of the night to get the books out on a couple of rickety wheelbarrows they found at the back of the barn, got them stashed in the pit they'd dug a few hundred yards away in the middle of a copse of withered birch, lined and covered with tarpaulin before topping the lot off with the turf they'd carefully removed at the start, scattering on leaves and branches to complete the disguise. Back in the barn, they filled the emptied crates with straw and the scant supplies of winter vegetables from the first pallets, all except the top two that they repacked with books: some duplicates and those considered least worth saving.

During all the while they worked, the folk in the farmhouse never came out to see what was going on; assuming they'd heard, which possibly they hadn't, for not a lamp had been lit the whole while they'd been here, the only signs of life being that child crying right at the start and the movement of a few scrawny goats bedding down in their wattled pen to the side of the farmhouse, laying down on the bare earth that was all scuffed up, right down to the roots of the grass that was apparently all they had for food.

'Bit of a rough place,' the youngest soldier, Archie, commented as he tipped his cap back, looking around him in the dim light of the fire they'd made on the other side of the barn from the copse where they'd buried their loot. 'Them goats don't look like they'll last out the winter.'

'Should've had 'em slaughtered months back,' said the bearded man, 'when 'em still had a bit o' meat on their bones.'

'It's a sad place, right enough,' said the softer voiced man. 'Strikes me that mebee them folk inside can't look after themselves, let alone their farm.'

The Russian nodded sadly. It had taken him a while to get used to these foreigners speaking, but he was well educated, fluent in English, the reason he'd been given this little lot to look after in the first place.

'You've got that right,' he said. 'These borderland places always gets it in the neck. A century ago this whole area was a Khanate, liberal and rich as cream…'

'What's a…Khanate?' asked Archie, leaning forward, face lined with concentration and smoke. Too excited to sleep, and not much time anyway until morning came.

'Remnants of the Mongol Expansion,' he was informed. 'A protectorate of the Ottoman Empire; very tolerant back then and the wealthiest part of the whole of Russia. And this isn't the first

book cremation my countrymen have carried out to try to weaken them. It's a bit of a miracle there's any Tatar books left at all. When we first invaded, a hundred years back in the 1730s, we did exactly the same – the Khan's archives and libraries burned to the ground.'

'But why? Why would they do that?' the younger man creased his brows, trying to understand. Where he came from, Dundrennan on the west coast of Scotland, knowledge was something to be aspired to, not destroyed. The Russian shrugged, rubbed his hands together and held them out to the fire, leaving another of the Scotsmen to answer for him.

''Cos knowledge is powerful,' Kerr Perdue said quietly, gazing into the flames. 'Take that away, take away education, and what've you got left?'

'This is all a load of shit!' the fourth man interjected, flapping at his beard to put out a couple of random cinders that had burrowed their way in. 'Who needs history? And who needs books? Give me a steady job, couple of cows, bit of pasture and what the hell is there to complain about in life?'

'You'd find complaint about anything, Gabriel. Don't you ever stop?' Kerr argued, soft no more and about to say harder when the Russian held up a hand.

'They're coming,' Kheranovich said quickly, and they all turned their heads in the direction he was pointing, seeing a line of men outlined against the glimmer of dawn in the eastern sky, at their lead the unmistakeable silhouette of Captain Tupikov, his large bulk heaving from side to side on his steed.

'OK, men. This is it,' Kheranovich said, standing up, kicking over the fire, the others getting up with him. 'Remember what I said before: say nothing, do nothing except what I tell you. No way they can find out what we've done and when we get out of this, well, there'll be good pickings for all...'

CHAPTER 1

COTTAGES, COPPER AND LIGHTHOUSES

Kerr Purdue woke on his narrow bed and stared up into darkness. The wind outside was strong, coming in spasms, the wooden walls of his shelter juddering, the sea arhythmically breaking on the south side of the island. He wasn't frightened by the dark, the wind or the sea. The small square of his lighthouse had been battered by winter storms for years and was still standing, though occasionally the carbide lamp atop would shift in its bolts and chains. What feared him was what the coming day would bring and what it would spell out for him and Merryweather. The rain began suddenly, loud and insistent against the small windows built into his adjacent workshop, clattering like hail against the glass. It stopped as swiftly as it had begun, desisted for minutes and then began again, as if a small boy was out there gathering ammunition from the pebble-strewn land, only able to attack several handfuls at a time.

He eased himself from beneath his counterpane, a quilt stuffed with the down of the eider ducks he saw so often out there in the firth: great rafts of them floating and preening side by side before slipping – neighbour following neighbour – beneath the waves.

He loved the sound of them, the ragged choir of rising oohs and chucks that were so very human, so very like a gaggle of elderly maidens wondering what was going on. Yet another reason not to leave this island, as if any more were needed. He'd been compiling a list of all he would miss, not the least being those he was hearing now: the wind, the rain, the sea; the faint shaking of the wood about him; the unsettling soft booms that came from the mines when the wind funnelled in and met itself again on the way out; the beating of birds' wings as they came in from the Solway to settle on the quieter waters of the estuaries of the Urr and Auchencairn Bay; the loud churring on summer evenings of the nightjars – called wheel birds hereabouts, on account of them sounding like cartwheels constantly jarring over stones.

The list got longer every day.

He swung himself off his bed, changed his thick cotton long-johns for fresh, put back on his shirt and trousers and laced up his boots, thinking of what Merryweather – who was not nearly so cheery as his name implied – had said the day before, when the two of them were informed that the copper mines had been bought out from under them, representatives of some unheard of European corporation already arrived at Balcary House, ready to be taken over next low tide.

'They'll chuck us out on our ears, you see if they don't,' had been Merryweather's first reaction. 'They'll ditch us soon as they can sneeze,' he'd grumbled on. 'They'll stick their own man on your light, take the wage and let everything else go to hell.'

Kerr Perdue closed his eyes, for Merryweather was probably right. The wage Kerr got from upkeeping the light was exactly the same as the rent paid for his little homestead, him and Merryweather the only occupants of the island, the two of them scraping by as best they could, with a bit of crofting and coppering;

Kerr adding a bit more to his income with his birds, Merryweather with his woodcarving. Christ knew what they'd do when they were kicked off Hestan, and today was the day they'd find out how soon that was going to be.

The rain was at it again, flinging itself against the windows and walls of shack and workshop. He felt for his oilskins hanging on the hook – no light in here, no glimmer – and pulled the trousers over his boots, flung on the jacket, pushed up the hood. No time to brew a pot of tea or stick a hunk of bacon into the pan, his time dictated by the tides as they pulled back from the Solway to reveal the Rack – a black mussel bed extending three quarters of a mile from Hestan almost to the point at Almorness, where the Company men would be waiting. No deviation from that shell and shingle track from there to Hestan, not unless you wanted to be sucked down by the sand and mud, and only an hour and a half once over before you got back again, before the tides swept in again and covered the Rack – and anything on it – with the speed of a greyhound coursing a hare. And his duty to bring them in safely, no matter the bad tidings coming with them.

Kerr cracked open the door of his little lighthouse shack and went out into the dawn, no need of a lamp, knowing every inch of this tiny island – barely a square mile in extent, knowing it like others know their children's faces – and didn't hesitate as he strode away into the unborn day. The track led down towards a small cottage half a mile distant that he and Merryweather had erected thirty-odd years before, and wasn't surprised to see a lamp bobbing up and down inside its windows, for Gabriel would be as worried as he was, both sewn into the fabric of this island as lichen into a tree.

He rubbed at the stubble about his neck, the only outward sign of his agitation, looked out towards the east and saw the narrow

shine of cloud, the low spread of light kept dim by a thick grey roll of cloud. He shook himself to get some warmth into his limbs and headed on for the sparse shell causeway, heard the sounds of the many birds hunched upon the edges of the island – in every crevice of every inlet, ledge and cave – heard them beginning to wake and shake out their feathers, untuck their heads from beneath their wings, unfolding themselves into the coming day. He saw a stray duck sitting a few yards ahead of him in the heather, the graceful curve of her neck, the black bead of her eye, the slight shine of one single green feather amongst the tawny rest. It was odd she'd not moved at his approach, for usually such birds would hie and fly at the slightest disturbance, and odder still that she didn't up and go as he moved closer still. Once upon her, he had the reason: the bird was dead, and not long since, still in full rigour, held upright by a small tussock against which she must have leant for support while she breathed her last. The perfection of the bird made him catch his breath as he nudged it with his boot. The beak was the colour of polished tortoiseshell with black smudges at either end, the faint run of blood from her nostrils serving only to enhance the shine of the rest. She'd most probably been night-flying, he thought, maybe upped by the single fox family that inhabited the island, run into one of the pulley cables from the mines; a quick hit, stunned and downed, no hope of getting up again. He studied her a few moments more before taking the knife from his belt and kneeling down in the heather, and with one swift movement separated the head of the bird from its body, took it up and tucked it into his pouch, wiping the blade of his knife upon the heather before moving on, the beheaded bird toppling onto her side as he went.

He didn't get far, halted by Gabriel Merryweather who was high-tailing it across the heather towards him. Kerr sighing briefly

in irritation. He and Gabriel got on well enough, for two men who had voluntarily stranded themselves upon the island for the specific purpose of not wanting to get on with anyone, passing the occasional evening together when the isolation got too much, sessions that routinely ended by them drinking more than they should have and starting to argue before one or other of them chose to stagger off to their respective home.

'Wait up! Wait up!' Gabriel was shouting and so Kerr did, though indicated by his stance, by the stamping of his boots, that he was in no mood for company. 'Wait up!' Gabriel said again, coming to a ragged halt a few yards from Kerr.

'Let's not go over all this again,' Kerr started. 'You know there's not a damn thing I can do about…'

'It's not that,' Gabriel said, hands on his knees, getting his breath back. 'It's not that all. It's that I think someone was in number three last night, caught a glimpse I'm sure.'

'They can't be here already,' Kerr argued. 'I've to them this morning. You know that as well as I do.'

'T'weren't them.' Gabriel shook his head. 'Couldn't ha'been. Just a singleton, I'm certain. But it was wicked stormy, like you knows, so didn't check it then, but checked not half hour since, and them's still there. I can hear 'em, Kerr.'

Kerr looked over at Gabriel Merryweather, the light beginning at last to shine, to make shadows, the rain falling again, the wind buffeting the two of them as they stood legs akimbo on the track. He glanced over towards the copper cove and doubted Merryweather's story, for what the blazes would anyone be doing over here at all, let alone in number three? He worked number one shaft and Gabriel number two, but number three was all boarded up, being saved for a rainy day, and not this one; not any, if they could help it, given what they knew was inside.

‘It’ll just be one o’ the foxes,’ he said shortly, ‘getting out o’ the rain. And anyway, what do you want me to do about it?’

Not much time to waste, the dark meander of mussel causeway already emerging from the sands and not long to be shilly-shallying.

‘We’ve gotta go see,’ Merryweather insisted, lifting his lantern, storm-shuttered, but enough light for Kerr to see how pale Gabriel’s face was, the slight sheen of sweat on his forehead. Kerr Perdue sighed, but he could spare a few minutes. Merryweather was too gutless to do this on his own.

‘Come on, then,’ Kerr commanded, and off he went, heading away from the track towards Copper Cove and the bluff that came down from the hill into which the mine workings burrowed, going straight for number three, slowing as he closed on it, creasing his brows, for Merryweather had a point. Something was wrong – the large boulders the two of them had rolled across the opening had been levered back and the sheets of corrugated iron removed, held down on the ground by a few rocks, the water gathered between the metal ridges shining in oily pools. A crowbar lay to one side and a yard of steel lever was leant against the larger boulder, slick with rain. Kerr approached quietly and with caution, bent down a way and gazed into the dark throat of number three, seeing nothing, but hearing a faint scraping coming from deep inside.

‘Hey there,’ he yelled. ‘What d’you think you’re doing? This here’s private property and copper’s not a free-for-all!’

The scraping stopped, but no one replied. Kerr didn’t move, cocked his head, listening hard.

‘Hey there!’ he repeated, stopped from saying more by the undoubted strike of a pickaxe against stone. ‘What the…’ he muttered, hunkering down, ready to crawl inside, see what the hell was going on for himself. Another few frenzied strikes of the pickaxe and then a dim kind of rumbling, a sort of stuttering

in the rock where he'd braced his hands against the sides, Kerr Perdue falling on his backside, boots kicking on the ground to push himself out.

'You've got to stop that!' he shouted, his scrambling feet revealing the rope on the shaft floor that was presumably attached to the ankle of the intruder. He grabbed it up and pulled, felt it tighten and tug against his grasp, and then that rumbling again, louder now and dust beginning to feather up the tunnel towards him.

'You've to stop! Right now!' he yelled, pulling frantically at the rope. 'Merryweather!' he called, needing aid, needing to haul the interloper out one way or another, because he knew that whatever was going on in there had the roof destabilised, about to collapse. There were a few seconds of tortured groaning as the rotten wood props sagged, resisted briefly and then gave way completely, followed by the unmistakeable sounds of crumbling earth and rock, Perdue momentarily rocked back on his heels, a chittering flap of pipistrelles darting expertly by his head, followed immediately by a huge swirling ploof of dust and grit flying up the shaft and out into the morning, covering Kerr Perdue head to foot.

'Jesus! What's happening?' came Merryweather's querulous voice, although it was obvious. Perdue righted himself, grabbed Merryweather's lantern, got it unshuttered with shaking fingers.

'Gotta get in there,' Kerr said, breath coming too fast, the grit from the fall catching at his throat, feeling Merryweather's hesitation behind him, shuffling from foot to foot. 'Godsakes, man,' Kerr growled. 'Get a hold of that rope and don't pull till I say.'

Gabriel Merryweather was suddenly down beside him, rancid tobacco-laden breath rasping in Kerr's ear.

'We should just leave it. Ain't nothing to do with us.'

Kerr blinked, eyelids scratching, vision blurring, anger boiling

up in him like water in a kettle.

'Can't bloody leave it,' he growled. 'There's a man down there and Christ knows...'

A ghastly moan came from the tunnel towards them both: terror-laden, agonising, gut-clenching with its intensity.

'Gotta go in,' Kerr repeated, ignoring Gabriel, grabbing the crowbar, and off he went, lamp before him, shaft-walls no longer trembling but plinking down small loose stones here and there that knocked against his arms and legs as he crawled his way along its length, heading into the bowels, into the heart of Hestan and what they both knew lay at its core.

Chapter 2

Arrival At Balcary

'Can't think why they're sending us on down here,' Brogar said, a little grumpily and not for the first time.

'Well, we were sort of on the spot,' Sholto offered, smiling as he surveyed his companion who was leaning on the rails of the boat that was carrying them from Fort William all the way down the side of Scotland almost into England. 'It won't be for long, and remember there'll be real mines there for you to explore,' Sholto added, knowing Brogar's penchant for scrambling into the depths of the earth, such as he'd not done for a while.

'Well, there's that,' Brogar replied, somewhat mollified. 'But I'm no negotiator, Sholto. What the hell do they expect me to do?'

'Beat down the opposition with your fists?' Sholto asked. 'Get a better price?'

Brogar barked out a laugh.

'Ha! Alright. You've had your fun. But really, what's the point?'

Sholto shrugged.

'It won't be for long. Fitzsimons will be here from Edinburgh soon enough to take over.'

'And you think he'll be running to get here?' Brogar asked with

sarcasm, Sholto tilting his head at the validity of the question. They'd met the lawyer a couple of months previously, an Edinburgh man through and through, both knowing his intense dislike of anything approximating countryside, Fitzsimons pronouncing Ardnamurchan – from where Sholto and Brogar had just come – as the worst backwater he'd ever been too, and couldn't get out of fast enough. Sholto had to concede that Brogar had a point. No way would Andrew Fitzsimons be rushing down-country to Galloway, he'd stall his journey, stop at every town and centre of civilisation he could before he made it to yet another backwater that might prove worse than the last. Their conversation was interrupted by their young assistants, Gilligan and Hugh, racing up the deck towards them, elbowing each other as they skidded to a stop beside Brogar and Sholto, eager to get their words in first, Gilligan being the faster.

'Never guess what we've just learned,' he said, 'only that this Balcary House we're heading for was built for smugglers!'

'Not for smugglers,' Hugh added pedantically, 'but by them. Three men called Cain, Clark and Quirk, who all came from Manxland.'

Sholto looked down at Hugh, his face as serious as always, his personality not in the least changed or embittered by the fact that one of his eyes was now blind as the moon, and just as pale.

'Do you mean the Isle of Man?' Sholto asked, who could equal any pedant going.

'Oh Jesus!' Brogar interrupted. 'Not smugglers! Not again. Had my fill of them.'

Gilligan was happy to enlighten his hero.

'Nothing like it was up north,' he explained. 'Down here they call it Free Trade. Been going on for a coupla hundred years, apparently. All on the up and up, and them three men as built the

house? Well, they were a proper business. Built the house with five-foot-thick walls and a cellar that could hide two hundred men on horseback, if they needed it.'

'And that's on the up and up?' Brogar commented wryly.

'They were on Mull, mostly,' chipped in Hugh, exchanging a small smile with Sholto, both sticklers for the truth. 'Brought in a lot of agricultural changes that made everyone's lives the better.'

'And what's your source for all this information?' Sholto asked the two boys, who didn't demur, piping up together the same answer.

'Man at the helm!'

They looked at each other and took a tacit decision that Hugh should go on first, Hugh being the wiser and more sensible of the two.

'We was asking all about the history of the place, just like you do,' Hugh said, casting an admiring single-eyed glance at Sholto, who acknowledged the compliment and allowed the boy to go on. 'Well, he says this place we're heading for is just the best and the most mysterious place we'll ever go to. Told us all about the Ghost Trees and the Tower at Orchardton that's supposed to be haunted, and the Barlocco caves…'

'There's one called Black and one called White,' Gilligan put in, unable to stop himself. 'The Black'uns huge, hundred feet wide and fifty high and you can sail right into it, even at low tide.'

'Perfect place for smugglers,' Hugh added, smiling broadly, his own encounter with lesser smugglers apparently not dampening his enthusiasm for the adventure such tales implied.

'And did they tell you anything at all about the place we're going?' Sholto asked. 'I mean anything about the island itself?'

'Cor, yes!' Gilligan answered quickly. 'An' it's nothing like we seen up at Ardnamurchan. This one's green as new beech leaves in

spring,' he added, quoting the helmsman's words exactly, 'and got a rock on it that looks just like an elephant, though not entirely sure what an elephant is.'

'Big grey thing,' Hugh put in helpfully. 'Saw a picture of one once in one of Solveig's books. Got a nose that's like an extra arm…'

'Aaagh!' Gilligan responded, putting a hand up to his face and waving it about, almost falling over as the boat slew sharply to the east as they rounded Stranraer peninsula and pushed on towards Barrow Head. Drenched with sea spray from the sudden turn, Gilligan and Hugh sprinted off to check out this new development in their journey, leaving their masters alone.

'What do you think?' Sholto asked of Brogar as the two stood their ground, taking the spray, feeling its salt against their cheeks.

'Think like always,' Brogar said slowly, 'and that things might not always be what they seem, not where the Company's concerned.'

'What do you mean?' Sholto asked, brushing back the white streak in his dark hair, studying his companion closely. The scar that was so evident on the other side of Brogar's face was hidden now from Sholto, but he could see that his companion's shoulders had tensed as the boat changed direction, that he was holding his head a little higher, turning his face into the increasing wind.

'Just got a feeling, Sholto,' Brogar said, then turned and smiled brightly. 'Just a feeling is all.'

Sholto looked down into the waves, into the deep, dark churning of the sea, saw a couple of porpoises a way out to the left of them and the dark clouds funnelling with intent from the horizon in the west, feeling the rising of the wind. He was no sailor – far from it – but he recognised the signs, the shifting of the swell, knew that rain was coming, maybe even one of the storms so common on this coast at this time of year, and would be glad when they got to

where they were going and off the boat that felt as unpredictable beneath his boots as the shivering sands he'd been told were out there in the Solway.

'Never go out on them without a guide,' they'd been forewarned, 'and never believe anything is solid to stand on unless one of those guides has told you so. There's soft mud out there can suck you in, and channels you can't see, fast running burns that'll shove your feet out from under you. And whatever you do, never ever get caught out there when the tide's coming in or it'll swallow you whole, from bonnet to boot.'

A new landscape, one as unreadable as it was treacherous, and no wonder Brogar had a feeling when something so benign as mud and sand came with such embargo.

They arrived without incident, bad or otherwise, and were garrisoned for the night within the startlingly white walls of Balcary Bay House that was big as a palace. The owner, James Heron, was away on business in Manchester, but the young factor, Skinner Tweedy, was there to greet them, and could not have been more welcoming.

'You've to take every advantage we have,' Skinner told them, in a strong Lancashire accent he was taking pains to hide, shaking Brogar and Sholto's hands and bringing them all in, including Gilligan and Hugh who'd been about to do their usual and bunk down with the horses.

'I'll not hear of it!' Skinner said, rebuffing the boys' plans. 'You're all our most welcome guests, and we've more rooms here than in the entire village of Auchencairn,' – a slight exaggeration, but not much of one – 'and Mr Heron told me to take the best care of you. A big dinner's planned if you all want to make yourselves comfortable first. Comfort today, business tomorrow.'

Comfort be damned – Gilligan and Hugh had other things on their minds.

'Can we see down into the cellars, Mr Tweedy?' Gilligan asked for the two of them, Skinner Tweedy smiling broadly in response.

'Heard the tales already have you, lads? Might have guessed it. Captain Patterson's a worse gossip than three old women hanging out their washing. But come on then, let's get it over with.'

He led the boys away and took them down into the enormous cellars that didn't disappoint. Cavernous enough, thought the boys, to really fit two hundred horses side by side, though it held nothing more mysterious at the moment than sacks of potatoes, grain and peas, crates of apples, barrels of wine and whisky, shelves containing jars of pickles, jams, spiced oils, sloe gin – all the things any good housekeeper would provide, but on a much grander scale, like it was a shop and not a storeroom.

Up top, Brogar had been led to his room by a maid and looked about it with disgust. He hated luxury, and the idiocy that led men to buy places as large as this for no other purpose than to shout out their wealth; and he hated this room, with its massive silk-counterpaned bed and silk-covered cushions; would far rather have been led out to some barn to bed down on a couple of hay bales with a few blankets chucked over him to keep out the cold. He looked out of the window and could see the island they'd thankfully be going to at dawn the following morning. It wasn't quite as green as Gilligan had portrayed it, more grey in this sulky February afternoon. He estimated it to be about a mile square, a single rise at its middle, no discernible signs of habitation, at least not from this angle.

'Now that's more like it,' he said, as Sholto came in through the door.

'This place is a warren!' Sholto commented, before joining Brogar at the window. 'That it?'

'That it is,' Brogar agreed. 'And can't wait to get out there, though it's as odd a place for copper mining as I've ever seen.'

'From the reports the Company sent it's got three shafts going back into the cove.'

He pointed to the shallow escarpment that started halfway down the small hill and ran its rocky way to the shore.

'Must be something,' Sholto added, 'else they wouldn't be wanting to buy it up. Apparently half the world's copper comes from this country.'

'Not from this country,' Brogar corrected, geology his expertise, 'but from Sassenach England. Cornwall to be precise.'

Sholto raised his eyebrows.

'You suddenly feel patriotic?' he asked mildly, though he felt it too, this vague but growing identification with the land their families had been forced to leave – if on separate occasions – when the two of them were young. They'd felt it in Sutherland, and again in Ardnamurchan, both re-adopting their native tongue as if it had never left them, conversing now in English without a second thought, despite the other shared languages that were available to them. Brogar turned away from the window and looked at his companion, shrugging his shoulders.

'Maybe so. Maybe. Kind of gets under your skin, makes you think you want to be a part of it.'

Sholto was surprised. He'd only known Brogar five or six months, but never in all that time had he hinted at any need to belong anywhere. Quite the opposite, now that he thought about it. The way he told his tales of what he'd done, where he'd been and what he'd seen had always been told from the prospect of an outsider; someone who fitted in like a stone into an unmortared wall whilst he was there, but a stone that would soon roll out again and go its own way.

‘What’s changed?’ Sholto asked after a moment, Brogar going to his bed, flinging open his kit bag, taking out nothing but his binoculars and returning to the window.

‘Nothing’s changed,’ Brogar said, a little brusquely, bringing up his binoculars to hide his eyes, studying the escarpment, the dark arches of the shafts. ‘Ignore me,’ he added, handing the binoculars over to Sholto. ‘Guess coming back to the homeland just has a way of seeping into a person’s bones.’

Sholto took the binoculars and took his look, sweeping the glass over the edges of the island, resting momentarily on what appeared to be the entrance of a cave and a slight shift of the shadows that suggested something was moving inside. Just like something was moving inside Brogar Finn.

‘I think I can see that rock, the one Gilligan was on about,’ he said, by way of distraction, ‘just to the left of the cove.’

Brogar took the glasses back and leaned forward.

‘Curious,’ he said, a definite note of interest in his voice. ‘Some form of erosion. And it really does look like an elephant.’

‘You ever seen one? A real live one, I mean?’ Sholto asked.

Brogar brought the glasses down and turned a serious face towards his friend before breaking into a grin.

‘Do you really need to ask?’

‘Not even you’ve seen everything,’ Sholto countered, Brogar laughing shortly, slapping Sholto hard on the back and flinging the binoculars onto the bed with one graceful movement.

‘No one can ever see everything,’ Brogar said, ‘but what I don’t want to see more of is this damned house. People who buy monstrosities like this should be shot on the spot. Christ knows, I’d shoot them myself if I’d bullets enough and a place to run afterwards where no one would find me.’

Sholto’s turn to smile, happy the real Brogar was back again.

'If anyone knows such a place, that would be you.'

Brogar grimaced into the large mirror that was hung in an ornate gold frame on the wall, tugging at his collar to loosen it, rolling his broad shoulders in his jacket.

'Got that right, friend, and don't you ever forget it.'

They ate and drank well, all sat at a table the size of a barn door, Skinner Tweedy eager and attentive to his guests, his face animated and alert, having an irritating habit of rubbing his fingers through his clipped brown hair so that it stuck up in tufts, making him look like a startled grebe.

'Well, the history of the island's this,' he said, in answer to Sholto's question, Skinner not usually a book learning man but one who'd been drilled in this little bit of history specifically to provide this information to his guests. 'Used to belong to Dundrennan Abbey way back, mostly used for trapping fish. You can see the remains of the Monks' Pool over there at the other end of the causeway. Went from them to the Earls of Nithsdale after the Dissolution, though the resident monks were allowed to stop on at the Abbey until they popped their clogs. Then it went to a family from Duncow at the start of the 1800s, and from them to the Herons along with the rest of the Balcary Estate...'

'Are there caves over there?' Hugh asked, swallowing the last of his baked fish and about to stand up to hand his plate over when he was blindsided by a girl with long pale fingers whisking it away, making him blush when she inadvertently touched his hand in doing so.

'Ah,' Skinner said, 'you boys obviously know your stuff! Island's riddled with 'em, loads of inlets and crags and two big caves worth the mention. Only don't try to get to them unless tide's out or you'll likely get drowned, like Daft Annie.'

'Who's Daft Annie?' Gilligan put in, sitting back in his chair as a rack of venison was put in front of him, attention momentarily diverted as he wondered how he was supposed to eat it. Back at Solveig's he'd have picked it up with his fingers and got straight at it, but there were a load of knives and forks to left and right of his plate that presumably he was supposed to use. Skinner saw the confusion and led by example, took the rack up and tore it apart, dipping a bit of meat into the rich juniper gravy and shoving it in his mouth.

'Get stuck in,' Skinner said, his Lancashire accent deepened by the several glasses of wine he'd already imbibed. 'No need for airs and graces, not wi' me. Mr Heron, now, that'd be different, but not wi' me. Food's just food far as I'm concerned.'

Everyone took him at his word and shoved the shiny cutlery aside, excepting the spoons needed to scoop up the buttery potato mash soaking in the sea of gravy.

'Daft Annie,' Skinner went on, 'just a story really. Simple lass from Auchencairn, and there's a load of simple lasses there, believe me. Well, there's some bad rocks on southern end of the island she's supposed to have put there as stepping stones to get her over. Drowned, of course, as daft lasses will be. Said to haunt the steps. Ooooh ooh!'

He gestured, holding up his arms, pretending to be the ghost of Daft Annie, making Gilligan giggle.

'Think maybe I saw her in the big cave earlier,' Sholto said, filling up his glass, getting into the mood. 'Saw shadows moving, just before the sun went down.'

'Aye right,' Skinner looked over at Sholto and winked. 'That'd be her. Never left the island, like no one does, specially not if they dies there. Like Perdue and Merryweather would if they had their way. But don't worry,' he added hastily for the Company men, 'they'll

be long gone by the time your lot get here, and good riddance to bad rubbish.'

'I thought the place was uninhabited,' Brogar broke in, clattering a bone down onto his plate, Sholto looking up sharply, knowing how Brogar always saw the human angle, no matter what the Company thought. A trait he'd admired from the first.

'Well, only them two,' Skinner answered, his cheeks bright with drink, misunderstanding the situation, Sholto wincing as the man brushed the tips of his greasy fingers through his hair after the briefest touch of them to a napkin.

'But two there now, all the same,' Brogar stated.

'Kerr Perdue looks after the light,' Skinner said, a little of the cheer gone out of him. 'Not that it's much of a light, just one he's rigged up himself and can't hardly be seen two yards out. Gets a pittance from Trinity House for it. An' him and Merryweather scrape away at the mines, but like I said, they'll be good and gone within a few weeks. Heron's been looking for a way to get shut of them for years.'

'But what'll they do when they go?' Hugh asked, like the caring lad he was, Skinner Tweedy swivelling his head towards Hugh.

'What the hell's it to do with you? You've never even met 'em!'

All gaiety gone, turning on a sixpence from a man happy to entertain guests like he was Lord of the Manor for a day, to one unmasked, who'd drunk too much and said too much, aware he'd somehow overstepped the mark but not exactly how.

'Get this stuff cleared, Esther,' Skinner commanded, clicking his fingers to summon the young maid with the long fingers who'd been hovering in the corner of the room, Sholto having a sudden contempt for the man, looking over at Brogar who clearly felt the same.

'So answer the lad, Mr Tweedy. What will those two men do?' Brogar growled, Skinner Tweedy narrowing his eyes, refilling his

glass clumsily, spilling a little of the dark wine so that it spread out on the white tablecloth like a pool of blood.

'Ain't nothing to do with me,' he said eventually, rubbing his nose, taking a slim cigar from the small metal case lying to his right, lighting it ostentatiously from the nearest candle. 'Heron wants them out, as do your lot, so don't you be worrying about the details.'

He leant back into his chair and smiled, certain he'd the upper hand, certain of his place in the grand scheme of things, that all was going well.

Gilligan and Hugh went completely still, their gazes switching from Skinner to Brogar, whose fists were bunched on the table either side of his half-emptied plate, thumping one of them hard and fast onto the wood a second later so his pushed-aside cutlery jumped and plinked.

'I'll be worrying about the details, Mister Tweedy,' Brogar said slowly, imbuing the word 'Mister' with unmistakable sarcasm. 'That's precisely why I'm here, and you'd do well to remember it.'

Tweedy blinked through the smoke coming from his cigar, his neck beginning to colour above his collar at the unmistakable challenge in Brogar's voice, the girl Esther arrested in her task of removing Tweedy's plate by the power of Brogar's words, hanging at Tweedy's back like a second shadow, uncertain whether to insert herself into this tense conversation or not. She knew all about Skinner Tweedy, how he shone like the sun one minute and was mean as a cornered rat the next. It was the boy with the blind eye who came to her rescue, scraping back his chair and standing up, bringing her his plate.

'Here you go, miss,' Hugh said, 'I'll fetch the others to you in a minute.'

Gilligan was not to be left out and up he went too, clattering his plate down onto Hugh's as Esther held it in her outstretched

hands. Brogar smiled, but it was not a good smile, as anyone who knew Brogar Finn would have known. Skinner Tweedy was not one of them, and didn't understand what was going on.

'Well done, boys,' Brogar said, 'and well done Esther,' the girl jumping slightly at the mention of her name. 'I think we're done here, don't you, Sholto?'

Sholto tipped his head, got to his feet.

'I do,' he said, Brogar following suit, getting up, blowing out the candle immediately in front of him, leaving Skinner Tweedy at the head of the table, uncertain how everything had gone so wrong.

'New negotiations in the morning, Tweedy,' Brogar said, the Mister long gone as he headed for the door. 'New negotiations.'

Skinner Tweedy stayed where he was, suddenly alone, the visitors gone through the door to their bedchambers and Esther disappearing fast as she could back to the kitchens, all a-twitch with what had just happened and how the hated Skinner Tweedy had just got his comeuppance, even if he didn't know it himself.

Which he didn't, not until he woke up the next day and remembered what had gone on the night before.

'Oh shit,' he mumbled, grimacing at his reflection in the mirror as he tried to shave himself with cold water, bad soap and hands that were none too steady. 'Oh shit,' he muttered again, as the enormity of what he'd said and done blundered into his mind, that somehow or other he'd endangered the sale of Hestan Island, and hardly any time to make things right before James Heron returned from Manchester; and how if the sale fell through because of him then he'd undoubtedly be sacked, and without this job, without the reference he'd need if he left it, he was going to be as up the creek as Merryweather and Perdue.

CHAPTER 3

OVER THE RACK

They were away the moment the first glimmer of dawn came into the sky, the girl Esther tapping on each of their respective doors a half hour earlier, bringing cups of tea and a small breakfast of toast and kippers none had much stomach for, Gilligan and Hugh wrapping theirs in the napkins provided, neither liking waste. By the time the boys got down to the courtyard, Brogar was already there, face dark and dangerous, nothing forgotten from the night before. The revelation that buying out the copper mines, and therefore the island, meant depopulating it by even so few as two had not gone down well, nor that the Company had neglected to tell him about it.

'Everyone ready?' Skinner Tweedy asked, attempting a joviality he didn't feel as he came out to join them, his face a little bloated, his throat scratchy and dry, head feeling too big for his body. He knew he'd overdone it the night before, but had regained his confidence. After shaving and dressing and having a couple of cups of tea he was back on track. He'd rechecked the documents available to him and they all substantiated the claim that the charter of sale had already been drawn up between the Heron family and Lundt and

McCleery's, the possibility of further bargaining a mere formality. Nothing that this Brogar Finn could do to derail it, no matter his stupid and unwarranted concern for Merryweather and Perdue.

They got started in near silence, Skinner having to fetch Brogar from the sands where he'd been studying several pebbles, putting them in his pockets, but all soon trotting off down the lane along the bay from Balcary to Auchencairn, around the bay and up to Torr Point from where the sand was solid enough to take them over to Almorness, the deep gully going all the way from the Rack to Almorness and on down to Orchardton now drained of water. There were quicker ways to get to the island, going direct from Balcory across the bay being one, skirting the water as it slunk away from the sands, intercepting the Rack and on up the Rack to the island, but there weren't many men had the nous to try it, who knew the lay of the sands well enough. Kerr Perdue could have done it, three planks of wood strapped to his back in case any of them sank in the mud, but that would have meant him coming over the day before and that he'd flatly refused to do. It was also possible to bring in a boat at high tide and allow it to be grounded in the mud as the water ebbed, but it wasn't easy to get far enough in or be sure you'd get out again, and no way to know if you could walk from boat to shore without getting swallowed up by the sands. The only folk who risked it were the luggers who took the copper ore out to the bigger ships waiting to take it down to Swansea to be processed, and that only happened a couple of times a year, and only by people who really, really knew what they were doing and had been doing it a long time.

Skinner Tweedy nodded off a couple of times while his horse plodded on and on the long way round, shaken awake at the last when they were in sight of the shallow shell causeway emerging that led over to Hestan, blinking to clear his eyes because he

thought he could see someone running over the Rack towards them, barely waiting for the waters to recede as he pounded on, boots crunching on the mussel beds without care of any damage he might be doing them; a sight so unusual that Skinner Tweedy called everyone to a halt, going the last way on his own.

'Might be an odd tide,' he said, by way of explanation, though he doubted it, being as well acquainted with the waters' running as anyone was around here.

'What the hell?' he shouted, as soon as Kerr Perdue was in hearing distance.

'It's bad!' Kerr answered, as he clattered over the last few yards. 'Been a fall, a man injured!'

'Merryweather?' Skinner asked, for who else could it be?

Perdue stopped at the Rack's end, water lapping at his boots, and Skinner could see the wide panic in his eyes, the shaking of his head.

'Not he. Dinna ken who, only that he's still in there, and cannae get him out.'

'What's going on?' Brogar came onto the scene, loud and large, keeping his horse in perfect control, looking down on Kerr Perdue for answers, Kerr looking up, swapping eye-lines with Skinner Tweedy and this stranger, but not for long; Kerr seeing in Brogar Finn the command Skinner lacked.

'Went into number three,' Kerr said, trying to get his breath, get his words sorted. 'Don't know who or why, but started going where he shoudn't'ha and whole thing's collapsed on 'im. Don't think he's got much longer if we don't get him out.'

Brogar was down from his horse in an instant.

'Take me,' he said, Perdue hesitating a moment, looking up at Skinner Tweedy and seeing nothing there except a quick nod of his head, and so away he went, back over the causeway, Brogar on

his heels, wanting to overtake him but reining back, remembering what he'd been told about this place, about the causeway of mussels and shells, about only stepping in the footprints of those who'd gone before.

Sholto, back on the foreshore, was of a more even mind.

'Got a doctor hereabouts?' he asked Skinner, Skinner grimacing before he answered.

'Sort of. Well yes, there's Tuley in Auchencairn and, as it happens, most likely just down the road on account of the Reed woman being about to croak.'

'Well, go fetch him,' Sholto said sharply, wondering why the man was being so obtuse, Skinner lifting an eyebrow and giving Sholto a look he found hard to interpret, before turning his horse and heading back the way they'd come, speeding up once he was off the shore and back on hard land.

Gilligan and Hugh were off their horses in a trice, smiling discreetly as Sholto dismounted with as much grace as a man can muster when he routinely gets tangled in stirrup and reins before getting both feet square on the ground.

'Right,' Sholto said, brushing himself off, glad the lads hadn't outright laughed at his usual display of incompetence with horses, skills he still hadn't got the hang of.

'There's a tie post over here,' Hugh piped up, Gilligan leading the animals away to join his friend. The two of them had the greatest respect for Sholto and his book learning, but when it came to tying knots or other practicalities they'd not trust him farther than they could spit.

Sholto took the time to study the causeway over which Brogar and Kerr Perdue were fast disappearing. The Rack, as Skinner Tweedy called it, wasn't at all what he'd expected. No neat line extending from point A to point B, rather a snagging ribbon that

wound from left to right and back again, black as coal, looking thin and unstable, though at least the water was receding fast, revealing more of the Rack even in the few minutes that had passed since Brogar had set out upon its back.

'Should we go?' Hugh asked, coming up beside Sholto.

'I think we should,' Sholto replied, 'but mind what we've been told. Keep to the centre of it, to the highest point. And don't go jumping off to cut corners. And Gilligan,' he added, Gilligan leaping to his side, body twitching, ready for the off. 'You've to keep Hugh beside you, and I mean right beside you. Hugh's not used to having just one eye, not yet, and what he sees is not what we see. Alright with that, Hugh?'

'Alright with that, Mr Sholto,' Hugh replied, and glad for it, for in truth he was having a few difficulties adjusting, not that he'd mentioned it to anyone, least of all to Gilligan.

So off they went, the horses snickering behind them, pushing each other for the last of the grass they could munch at while they waited to be of use again; Sholto, Gilligan and Hugh setting out over the Rack, boots at first trepidatious but gaining confidence as they went, the waters of the Solway seeming to part from them as they'd done for Moses crossing the Red Sea even if – as certain scholars had it – it was no more than a sea of reeds. The speed with which the sea retreated was astonishing, one yard of sand revealed with every step they took, so that by the time they'd got two thirds across the causeway there was nothing but mud and sand stretching out all about them, as if the sea had never been there at all.

Brogar was at the opening of mine number three, Kerr Perdue by his side readying the couple of lamps Merryweather had fetched from his cottage.

'So how far in does it go?' Brogar was asking, Perdue and Merryweather exchanging a brief glance that didn't escape Brogar.

'Near sixty feet – twenty yards – last count,' Kerr Perdue said quickly. 'And guess that man's deep in as he can go.'

'Sixty feet in?' Brogar said. 'That's nothing. And all on the level? No ups or downs?'

'No big uns,' Perdue confirmed, a little awed that this man had arrived on the island only a few minutes previously and was already preparing to disappear down number three in search of a man he didn't know, and who most likely was already dead. 'Slopes up a bit,' he added, 'to help drainage and that.'

'Got it,' Brogar said, nodding with approval, testing the harness he'd rigged from a couple of bits of leather and rope that had been lying about the mine entrances, grabbing up the lever and crowbar presumably left by whoever was in there, also supplied with a pickaxe Perdue had helpfully provided.

'What're you gonna do? Merryweather asked, jittering nervously, Brogar standing there before him all geared up, tools tied to his back, big grin on his scary face, look of madness – as Merryweather perceived it – in this newcomer's eyes.

'Going to go in,' Brogar said, 'and you said there's a rope tied to the man's foot?'

'There is,' Kerr Perdue agreed, Kerr still as a stone, though he was nervous as Merryweather. 'Tried bringing him out with it, but no good. He didn't want to come at first and then, well, too late.'

'All set then,' Brogar said, going down on hands and knees, and in he went.

Sholto and the boys made it across the Rack, Sholto dithering briefly at its end, his brief look through the eyeglasses the night before not enough to make a decision as to which way to go. But

Gilligan was ahead of him.

'It's this way, Mr Sholto,' he said, heading to the right, 'can hear voices.'

Sholto tilted his head, hearing nothing, but didn't doubt Gilligan's younger ears and followed on behind, pleased to see that Gilligan was still holding Hugh's hand to guide him over the strandline of slimy bladder wrack and kelp weed, the scatter of driftwood and detritus left by the tide.

Like brothers, he thought, *or more like twins*, recalling a meeting of the Linnaean Society back in Trondheim when someone had been lecturing on the incidence of dual germination in nature: two nuts in one kernel, two fruits growing from a single centre, conjoined animals growing from the same fertilized egg, born of a piece, attached by skin or bone at head or hip or back.

'Certain societies,' the lecturer had informed his audience, 'believe human twins to be an abomination and will destroy one or both at birth. Some venerate them, especially if they're male; others see them as a complementary duo of such perfect balance they are assumed to be invincible to the natural order of the universe, and so sacrifice them for the greater good.'

Sholto smiled, glad they lived in an age of reason, that people like Gilligan and Hugh existed to show the rest of the world how to look after one another when they have no one else.

'Hey look! D'you think that's the elephant rock thingy?' Gilligan suddenly shouted, pointing with his free hand, Hugh turning his head fully so he could see it too.

'Gotta be,' Hugh agreed with enthusiasm, once he'd got his seeing eye in the right direction, 'but no time to look at it now. We've got to find Brogar first.'

And find him they did, for a few steps later they turned into Copper Cove and on the escarpment above them they saw Brogar,

standing outlined in the morning sun, adorned with some kind of belt and a load of tools at his back, saw him duck down and start crawling away from them, out of sight.

'Anyone down here?' Brogar asked, though not loudly, once he was twenty or thirty feet in. The tunnel was dark as a badger's burrow and as narrow. He could see from his sparse light that the shaft was correctly propped, but also that the props were old and none too strong, dust falling from between their intervals, bat guano covering the section of the floor he was crawling over, the stink of it in his nostrils, in his clothes. Some folk hated bats and hated their smell even more. Not so Brogar, who came across them often in his sojourns beneath the earth and was well acquainted with their comings and goings, admiring their ordered society, their caring, their apparent altruism in feeding the old and sick in anticipation of another doing the same for them when their time came.

'Alright down there?' Brogar heard Kerr Perdue's voice echoing down to him, its strength absorbed by rock and moss so it sounded like a whisper in a cave. He didn't answer, but gave a couple of tugs at the rope about his own ankle even as he traced the wriggle of the other rope with his fingers. Perdue had been right. Whoever was at the other end of this shaft hadn't gone in willy-nilly, but had obeyed the usual rule of miners going into spaces they would find it hard to turn around in, a lifeline that could tug them out in case of emergency, though apparently on this occasion no one had been at the other end, at least not in time.

'He's in there?' Sholto asked, as he clambered up from beach to cove, Kerr Perdue nodding anxiously, indicating the rope he was holding in his hands.

'Dunno why he's bothering,' grumbled another man, who was sitting on a nearby boulder sucking at his pipe, smoke billowing up like the tobacco was cut with dried heather flowers, which it was. 'Gotta be a thief,' he continued, 'one way or the other. No reason he'd be down there any otherwise.'

'That's Gabriel Merryweather,' Perdue said to Sholto, as if Merryweather wasn't listening. 'Grumpiest man in all the world.'

Perdue shot Merryweather a glance and Merryweather shifted his pipe, waved it from his mouth an inch or two.

'Got that right, and with good reason,' he said. 'And still don't know who you lot are nor what you're doing here. And that man down there? Well, take my word for it. He's dead and gone as…'

'We'll not speak of that,' Perdue put in sharply, Merryweather shifting his stance on the rock but taking the hint, shoving the pipe stem back into his mouth and shutting up.

'Anything?' Perdue asked again, calling down the hole into which Brogar was apparently burrowing.

'Best not distract him,' Sholto said quickly. 'And if there's been a fall already then best not make any more noise than's necessary.'

Perdue heeded the warning, would have been saying the same himself in any other circumstances but felt a guilt that he was not the one down there instead of this Brogar Finn he'd only just met.

'He knows what he's doing,' Sholto added, noting the look of chagrin on Perdue's face.

'Done it a million times!' Gilligan put in, dragging Hugh up the short slope behind him.

'Well, maybe not a million,' Hugh qualified as he got upright, got his balance, let go Gilligan's hand and took a careful one-eyed look about him. 'So what you got here? Three workings, three shafts? But this one looks like it was all boarded up until recent.'

Kerr Perdue shifted his gaze to the two boys who'd come up and clustered themselves about Sholto and, more specifically, at the boy who'd just spoken, the only one of this new crew who'd noted the anomaly.

'We don't work this one,' he said shortly.

'And why is that, Mr Perdue?' Sholto asked, catching Hugh's meaning, seeing for himself that it was obvious this shaft had, until very recently, been boarded up.

Kerr Perdue might have answered honestly or might not have, but at that moment the rope attaching him to Brogar twitched and he switched his attention away from the inconvenient question.

Inside the tunnel, Brogar had got as far as he could go, the way ahead blocked by fallen rocks. He put down his lamp, un-roped his tools, then started at the rocks with method and care, lifting each one and placing it along the tunnel's sides before moving on to the next. Some needed the pickaxe, crowbar or lever to get them shifted, but it took Brogar less than a half hour to uncover a foot, rope still attached, then one leg, and the second crooked up beneath a torso, and a few minutes more to scrabble away everything else from the prostrate figure who was completely covered over in grit, eyelids thick with it, exposed skin grey with the fallout from the collapsed roof, hunched over on himself, back curled above his head, hands tucked in against his chest.

'Here to get you out,' Brogar said, putting a hand below the man's chin, lifting it, brushing away the dust, assuming he must still be alive for plainly he'd attempted to raise himself into this awkward posture instead of being completely flattened on the ground. He blew on the man's face, slapped his cheeks lightly, rewarded by a groan, a flicker of movement beneath his fingers.

'Don't move,' Brogar advised. 'Don't know what might be broken. Hold still and we'll soon have you out.'

'Oh Jesus, oh my Lord,' a voice croaked out of the ghastly grey throat pulsing in the dust beneath Brogar's fingers. 'Is that you, Frith? Jesus, please tell me it's you.'

'It's me,' Brogar said quietly, giving the man what he needed to hear. 'Can you feel your legs? Your arms? Don't move them, mind, just tell me if you can feel them.'

'I…think…I…can…but, oh but Christ, that hurts. Oh man, that really hurts.'

'Alright then,' Brogar said. 'That's enough. I'm going to leave you for a few minutes, fetch a board to bring you out.'

Gilligan, on Perdue's say so, had climbed up top of the cove to the small mound above, the highest point on the island.

'Someone's coming!' Gilligan shouted down, good view from where he stood of the Rack and the mainland beyond, two figures making their way over, movements measured but clean and fast.

'Thank God,' Perdue murmured, feeling two pulls on the rope that meant for him to haul Brogar out.

Brogar emerged a few minutes later, dragged out on his stomach, easing his neck as he came clear.

'No room to turn a mole in there,' he said happily, getting to his feet.

'He alive?' Perdue asked, blinking as Brogar slapped his hands against his thighs, sending up a cloud of dust.

'He is,' Brogar replied. 'And conscious. Thing now is to get him out. We need a board, a piece of wood…'

'Corrugated iron do?' Perdue asked, indicating one of the rusted sheets that had previously been covering the mine's opening.

Brogar went down on one knee and studied it, tested its strength.

'It'll do,' he said, 'but we'll need a bit and brace to punch a couple of holes in, get some ropes attached.'

No sooner said than done, Perdue going to a small sea chest outside number two – his own workings – and retrieving the tool.

'Folk are coming,' Gilligan said, jumping down into the cove beside them. 'That Skinner Tweedy and a woman, by the looks of it.'

'Lord preserve us,' muttered Merryweather from his rock, shaking his head dolefully. 'That's all we need.'

'She's good as any,' Perdue said sharply. 'Better than her husband, anywise.'

Merryweather carried on shaking his head.

'Bloody women. Came here to get away from them, them and their...'

'That'll do, Gabriel,' Perdue cut him off, turning to Sholto and Brogar, holding up his hands. 'Hope you don't mind, but Hazel Tuley's what we've got around here far as doctoring's concerned.'

'You've a female doctor?' Sholto asked, surprised but intrigued. 'That's very...unusual.'

'Aye, right enough,' Perdue said, keeping his head down, holding the iron sheet while Brogar went at it with bit and bore. 'She's not a doctor exactly, more like the doctor's wife, but take it from me, you'd rather have her with you than him, in extremity.'

Sholto nodded, not that he knew the circumstances, but he'd known strong women before and didn't doubt their capabilities.

'I'll go meet them, shall I?' Gilligan broke in, not liking to stay still for very long.

'Away you go,' Sholto smiled, wishing he had the boy's energy, and away Gilligan went, though Hugh stayed by Sholto's side.

'So what's the plan?' he asked.

'Far as I can see, it's this,' Sholto said, watching Brogar cast bit

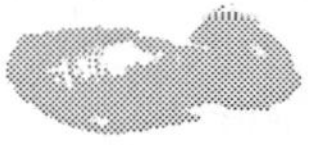

and brace aside, threading ropes through the holes he'd made. 'Brogar'll go back in, push the metal below the man inside, and then we'll pull him out.'

'He's going to be in awful pain,' Hugh said quietly, rubbing at the corner of his dead eye, the pocked scars on his cheeks, remembering how bad he'd felt after he'd been shot full in the face and carried off another island far from here. Sholto put his hand on Hugh's shoulder.

'We've got to get him out, Hugh. Can't do anything for him while he's still in there.'

'Ken that,' Hugh said. 'Just wish we had something to make the going better.'

'And we have,' both Sholto and Hugh looked up, unaware they'd been overheard, saw Kerr Perdue's grim face break over with a smile. 'Got laudanum and chloroform up at the workshop. Can you wait a few minutes?'

'I can,' Brogar said, 'but make it quick.'

And quick Perdue was, leaping up the cove and over the waist of the island to his workshop, back within minutes.

'This should do it,' he said, breathing hard, handing Brogar a small vial. 'Already mixed. Should be right enough to knock him out for a little bit at least.'

'So who are we going over for?' Hazel Tuley was asking Skinner Tweedy as they hurried across the Rack. She was a small woman, late fifties, grey hair pulled back from her face in a severe bun that bobbed at the nape of her neck. Skinner Tweedy, naturally, hadn't told her anything other than that she was summoned and was going a little too fast for her to easily keep up. Just the way with men like him, she knew, who didn't think women should be anywhere but the kitchen, the hearth or the bed.

'Don't know his name. Just that someone's stuck in the shafts,' Tweedy answered shortly, irritated to have this woman at his side instead of the proper Dr Tuley, though he knew perfectly well that the proper Dr Tuley wasn't exactly right in the head. Depression, was what everyone said, meaning he was a drunk of the first order, only person able to fill his shoes being his wife; but just because she knew her stuff didn't make it right, not to Skinner Tweedy and not to many others hereabouts.

They got to the end of the Rack to find the boy Gilligan waiting for them, who at least wasn't quite as annoyingly judgemental as his semi-blind friend, and Skinner asked him flatly what was what.

'They're bringing him out now,' Gilligan said. 'Got to get him out on something flat, but Brogar's already gone and done that.'

'Do we know if he's any bones broken?' the woman asked, Gilligan looking up at her rather severe face, her blue eyes reminding him strongly of Solveig's over in Sutherland, where he and Hugh had spent the first part of their lives.

'Don't know, Miss, but Brogar says he's awake, so that's gotta be good.'

'You're quite right, young man,' Hazel Tuley replied, Gilligan liking her from the off, 'that's got to be good.'

'So let's get on with it,' Skinner said brusquely. 'No time to be wasting.'

Hazel and Gilligan looked at each other, Hazel rolling her eyes, making Gilligan giggle, Gilligan grabbing at the doctor's bag she had in her hand and taking it from her.

'Think it might be bad,' Gilligan confided to Hazel as Skinner Tweedy strode on ahead, glad to leave the two of them behind, his hair sticking up into the morning.

'Ever seen an angry heron?' Hazel asked, as she walked beside Gilligan, moving quicker now she'd been relieved of her heavy bag.

'Only just now!' Gilligan replied, catching Hazel's meaning, looking at Skinner's back. 'He got some kind of stick up his arse, or what?'

'Or what,' Hazel Tuley replied easily. 'Thinks he's better than all the rest. Thinks he's better than you and me, for starters.'

Gilligan snorted.

'He ain't a patch on Mr Sholto and Mr Brogar,' he said with undisguised contempt. 'Things them and us have seen? But that man Tweedy? He's going to spend his whole life seeing nothing but hisself, and that's a fact.'

Hazel cast a quick glance at her young companion, admiring his astute interpretation. Never before had Skinner Tweedy been put down so well, and if ever a man needed putting down – in every sense of the word – it was Skinner Tweedy.

Chapter 4

Out Of The Shaft

Brogar was back in the shaft, pushing the makeshift stretcher before him, taking care not to tangle its lines with his own. All the way down, he could hear the injured man murmuring and sighing, carrying on some incoherent conversation with himself, or maybe with the imagined Frith. Once beside him, Brogar got himself placed, squeezed the injured man's nostrils together without explanation, pouring Perdue's mixture down his throat as he opened his mouth to take a breath. The effects were not instantaneous and the man let out a wretched volley of groans as Brogar pushed the iron sheet beneath his body, leaning over him in the confines of the shaft to place his head gently onto its end. They heard it outside, that low moaning of an animal in pain that came up at them like the wind blowing over bottlenecks. Kerr Perdue ground his teeth, clutched at the ropes he had ready, Sholto behind him to take the strain. Gabriel Merryweather was still as the stone on which he was sat, pipe gone out, making no move to remedy it, thinking back – as no doubt Perdue was – to another time years back when they'd heard the same noises, standing helpless outside until they'd ceased.

Deep inside, Brogar had the man laid out as best he could and manoeuvred himself back onto the floor of the shaft, his head at the stretcher's end, testing the ropes that had been pushed through the punch holes, lifting them over his shoulders to keep them free. Once all was in place he put his hand down to his own rope tied about his left ankle, and gave it three tugs. Time to see if his plan would work. He'd never been happier in his life.

'Three tugs,' Perdue pronounced, glancing over his shoulder towards Sholto. 'All ready?' he asked, a sheen of sweat on his forehead despite the early morning cold.

'Ready,' Sholto answered. 'Boys?'

'Ready,' Gilligan and Hugh replied in unison, a notable absence from their rescue mission being Skinner Tweedy, who was standing to one side, looking out across the bay towards the white walls of Balcary House, wondering why the hell anyone was bothering with any of this. Man dying while illegally entering a shaft? None of his business, far as he could see. More on his mind was the fact that he was supposed to get these Company men to sign the papers Heron's lawyers had drawn up for them, and what would happen if one of them died trying to rescue the idiot who'd no right being down the bloody shaft in the first place.

'On my mark,' Perdue said.

'On your mark,' Sholto agreed.

'After three, then,' Perdue said. 'One, two, three,' and then the four of them gripped their hands to the ropes in the order Brogar had commanded, and pulled.

Brogar came out first, right leg laid upon his left, arms stretched out in front of him to keep the sharp edge of the iron stretcher from his face. It had caught him a couple of times at the start of their trip,

ripping a few ragged gashes across the bridge of his nose and lower forehead, but soon as he was out he was up, the stretcher coming on behind him, rattling and jiggling on the stones Brogar's body had not already cleared in his wake. Hazel Tuley was ready, bag open as she knelt on the ground, getting several nested pewter kidney bowls filled to the brim with distilled water and iodine, a wad of cleaning lint in her hands. She was so concentrated on the neat emergence of the corrugated iron with its victim shovelled on its surface that she didn't immediately notice the wreck of Brogar's face.

'Oh my!' she exclaimed, when she looked up at him, about to offer congratulations on the success of his extrications, seeing the blood coursing haphazardly down his face, soaking into the plentiful stubble about cheeks and chin and dripping off onto his boots. 'Let me see to you first,' she said, about to rise, cleaning materials at the ready.

'Stop, woman,' Brogar said, his mouth breaking open in what he assumed was a reassuring smile, though it only worsened matters as the blood went down into his mouth and stained his teeth.

'I will not stop,' Hazel remonstrated stoutly. 'I'll have at you, young man, whether you like it or no.'

And so she would have, had not Brogar placed a hand on her shoulder and pushed her gently away.

'I can see to myself,' he informed her, 'but this man can't.'

Hazel Tuley held Brogar's gaze a moment, arrested by the determination in his eyes and possibly – although she was at a loss to account for it – amusement too.

'On your head be it,' she said tersely, moving instead towards the prostrate man.

'Quite,' she heard Brogar say behind her, and couldn't suppress a smile. That boy had been right, Skinner Tweedy was not a patch on his Mr Brogar, whoever he might be.

'You said he was conscious earlier?'

'He was,' Brogar said, 'but Perdue's concoction has done its business. Might be an idea to check for broken bones while he can't feel it.'

Hazel dipped her head and did just that, went over arms and legs, wrists and ankles, before turning the man onto his back and checking up and down his spine from neck to coccyx.

'Feels like some ligaments torn in the left elbow, two clean snaps of lower right leg, one to the fibula, another to the tibia two inches below.'

'Will he be alright, Miss?' Hugh asked softly, kneeling down beside her, placing his hand upon the man's brow, noticing what she had not and that his eyes were flickering beneath their sediment of dust and grit.

'He will,' she said. 'But we need to get him stripped, cleaned and splinted. The leg might be complicated. It will have to be completely immobilised, of course, but we can only do that when we've got him to the surgery. What's your name?'

'Hugh,' Hugh replied, Hazel glancing over at him, at the concern in the half of his face she could see.

'Do you know who he is?' she asked. 'Is he a friend? A relation?'

'No, Miss,' Hugh answered honestly. 'Never clapped eyes on him. Thought maybe you or Mr Tweedy did, seeing as you're both from around here.'

Hazel took in this information, wondering why she'd not thought of it herself. Certainly she didn't know this man as he was presenting to her now, but then everything about him was dusted over, every crevice of his face crusted with grime and grit.

'Take the first of the bowls,' she commanded, handing Hugh a wad of lint. 'Can you set to washing off the dirt on his face,' she

asked, 'while I cut off his breeks, get some splints onto his leg. And Mr…Brogar, was it?'

'It is,' Brogar said. 'What can I do?'

'Well, if you can manage to get enough blood out of your eyes so you can see straight for half a minute,' Hazel said, 'then I'd be obliged if you or your companions could find me several straight lengths of wood about a foot long. I can pull these leg bones back into place while he's still semi-conscious, and once we get him back to Auchencairn I have plaster of Paris that will set his breaks tight and right.'

'Plaster of Paris?' Sholto spoke up for the first time since Brogar and the patient had been dragged from their shaft. 'Isn't that rather experimental? Some Dutch military's man's invention?'

Hazel cast her blue-eyed gaze towards yet another person here she didn't know, but would not be cowed. Let them think her a woman, let them think her unsuited to her husband's calling, but by God let them not think that she didn't keep up with what was going on in the world of medicine.

'Experimental, yes,' she admitted, 'but one Antonius Mathijsen has many times proven the worth of and, if you think you can do better, sir, then have at it.'

'Oh for Christ's sake, enough!' Skinner Tweedy put in, no longer standing on the sidelines but coming in for the kill. Gone for good the affable man Brogar and Sholto had first encountered, the two of them staring at him and his interruption with undisguised antagonism.

'He's a man's got caught in a mine-fall in a shaft he shouldn't have been in in the first place,' Skinner went on without regard. 'Fix him up quick as you can, Mrs Tuley Doctor or whatever you call yourself. And don't believe for a second that I won't have him in court soon as he can stand, broken legs or no. This has all gone

on far too long. No one's here for this, least of all me and certainly not you. And by you, I mean Finn and McKay,' he added, glaring at Brogar and Sholto. 'You're only here to get some papers signed, not to start interfering with local matters that don't concern you. And I'm telling you this, Rack's going to start covering over soon, and I for one am not going to be stuck out here on this bloody island for much longer, so best make fast and get your plans together for you've maybe an hour before you'll be well and truly grounded.'

'Now hold on a second,' Kerr Perdue said, taking a few steps towards Tweedy. 'You've no cause to speak like that.'

'I'll speak however I find, Perdue,' Skinner cast back at him. 'And you'll not be here much longer to tell me any different, not you or your gargoyle over there.'

Merryweather blanched as Skinner Tweedy shot him a look, but didn't retort, no more did Perdue who shook himself, fists clenching, before turning away, thunder on his face, teeth grinding so hard his jaw began to ache, walking off several yards so he didn't clock Skinner Tweedy right there and then. He was out of earshot when Hazel chose her moment to lock her patient's leg bones back into their proper places, a short gasp escaping the man's lips, Hugh stroking his forehead gently, dipping lint into the water and carrying on getting away the worst of the dust, taking special care over the man's eyes.

'Frith,' the man murmured. 'Where's Frith?'

'Who's Frith?' Hugh asked softly, Hazel lifting her head, twitching her nose.

'An unusual name,' Sholto commented, Hazel suddenly aware the man with the stripy hair and a face like a priest was standing at her shoulder.

'Could be Frith Stirling, over at Dundrennan,' she offered, 'which would probably make this her brother Charlie.'

Good enough for Hugh.

'Charlie?' he asked, placing a new piece of dampened lint across the man's forehead like a compress.

'Where's Frith?' was all Charlie, if indeed it was he, could say, sucking air in across his teeth as Perdue's anaesthetic began to wear off, the pain and bad memories of the accident coming over him in waves.

Brogar arrived back with a few pieces of spare planking and held them out to Hazel.

'If he's here, then so is she,' Hazel said enigmatically, 'but first things first.'

She hated to agree with Skinner Tweedy, but he had a point.

'We've to get him across the Rack and back to the surgery and we've no time to waste. The gully will already be filling. Charlie,' she spoke a little louder, 'I'm going to lift your leg now, get it splinted. Hugh, can you elevate his foot, keep him still?'

Hugh could, and did just that as Hazel deftly placed one piece of planking to the calf, another against the shin, the de-trousered leg looking like a badly prepared joint of meat – skin pale, goose-pimpled, hair horrent, blotched over with bruises and beginning to swell – Hazel wrapping the splints tightly together with gauze.

'If it's quick you need, then I've an idea,' Brogar said. He'd washed his face in a pool of rainwater trapped in a rounded rock but was still brushing an irritated hand across his forehead and nose to stop the last of the dripping blood. 'Won't be comfortable,' he went on, 'but won't be slow.'

'Anything,' Hazel said. 'And quick as you like.'

Hugh grimaced with every groan. They'd done as Brogar had advised, Gilligan racing across the Rack fast as he could, returning with one of the horses, boy and animal galloping back with abandon

across the mussel and shingle beds, lips pulled away from their teeth with the thrum of their going, Charlie Stirling soon hitched up on his metal stretcher to the horse and dragged back over to the mainland, another large dose of Perdue's anaesthetic shoved down his throat before he undertook the worst journey of his life.

'I don't like it,' Kerr Perdue said just before they left. 'You've not much time. I should go with.'

'Nonsense, Mr Perdue,' Hazel was adamant. We've time enough.'

'I'm not sure,' Kerr prevaricated. 'What about the gully?'

Hazel tutted impatiently. 'You seem to forget that I've lived here long enough even if I wasn't born here, and if I say we've time, then we've time.'

She was right, but only just, the gully Kerr had worried about already halfway full, strong with the push of the sea as it was funnelled in long before the rest of the tide, Hazel biting her lips, heart thudding, her plan having been to skate across the sands to Torr, but with the gully filling this fast they'd never make it, only thing to do being over it and to Almorness a few hundred yards the other side.

'We've got to go over and we've got to do it now,' she called, trying to sound confident and in charge. 'Hugh and Gilligan, can you manage it?'

Sholto looked dubious. That water was raging between its bounds but Hugh was already slipping down the gully's sides, yipping with the cold, the swiftness of the current almost tugging him off his feet, arms tucked about the horse's neck to keep it calm as he pulled it down the slope and veered them both through the water, clambering up the other side after several tortuous minutes, Sholto having no choice but to follow, as did Hazel, the three of them keeping the tin stretcher aloft, Sholto feeling the bump of Gilligan at his side, the water getting higher with every second, his

breath coming hard, the cold severe, the push of water strong and getting stronger, standing his ground at the other side and pushing at Hazel to shove her upwards. A few more minutes and they'd have been done for, swept away on the bore, Sholto just managing to grab Gilligan before he went under and propelling him up what remained of the bank, Gilligan returning the favour and pulling at Sholto's arm until the two of them scrambled across the trackways left by the blunt end of the stretcher and grounded themselves on Almorness moments before the gully filled to its gunwales and the sea began spilling over its sides, creeping across the mud, the Rack behind them covered completely, nothing between them and Hestan but water, and more of it sneaking and snaking through sand grooves and licking over the mud, inch by inch, foot by foot, yard by yard.

'Thank God!' Hazel whispered, wiping sweat from her brow, eyes bright with panic, skirts heavy with the sea. 'I should never have risked it. I should have bought Perdue with us. I thought at least Skinner Tweedy would have waited to give us a hand…'

'No worries, Missus,' Gilligan panted, rolling himself over in the heather, getting his breath, tide mark right up to his neck.

'Thank God it was calm, or else…I never should have…' Hazel began, interrupted by Sholto who was frightened and chilled to the core.

'And where is that bloody Tweedy anyway?' he blustered, raising his voice as he very rarely did, placing a hand on his chest to calm his heart.

'You alright, Gilligan?' he heard Hugh's soft voice behind him.

'Very nearly almost! And blooming fine!' Gilligan replied merrily, exhilarated by the adventure. 'My turn to almost drown this time round 'stead of you!'

'Got that right,' Hugh said with a smile. 'Now you ken how it feels.'

'Like a mouse being dropped down a drain!' Gilligan said, through chattering teeth.

'Like a fly in a puddle,' Hugh countered.

The boys' easy banter cheered Sholto, the shaking in his legs beginning to desist. He'd always known the sea had no care of anyone, but that had been a damn close thing.

'How's he doing?' he asked of Hazel, his voice back to normal, his mind refocused on the task at hand as he watched Hazel bending over her patient on the stretcher.

'Still knocked out, which is a blessing,' she said. 'But we've got to get him back to Auchencairn. We'll have to go right round Orchardton now the gully's overfilled. I thought we'd have time to cross over to Torr...'

'No use worrying about it,' Sholto said, shivering in his soaking clothes, 'but maybe we can get some proper transport. A wagon, maybe?'

Hazel looked up at him, Sholto silhouetted against the calm blue sky, the pale round circle of cloud-hazed sun above his left shoulder and saw a similarity between them, a solidarity of dependence, that each would rise after even the darkest of nights.

That bloody Skinner Tweedy, as Sholto had so astutely labelled him, was long gone, departing soon after Gilligan's wild run back over the Rack, disgusted with the entire rescue operation. By the time Hazel had co-opted the use of a wagon to take her and her charges to Auchencairn, Tweedy was leading the three empty horses across Orchardton Burn, well on his way home. Whatever was going down on the island was none of his care; and none of the Company men's either, but if they chose to bury themselves in the mire of it then that was up to them. More time for him to right his own wrongs, check all the documents in the office, make sure that

his speaking out of turn about Merryweather and Perdue wasn't going to stick any spokes in any wheels. He didn't know much about the older Heron's history but he knew enough from James that it would've been just like the old man to have salted some ancient document somewhere to give his friends the right to stay on Hestan as long as they chose. Not that James had ever found it, nor Tweedy either – not that Tweedy had the entire run of the estate's papers. But he did have some access to the accounts and knew how most of its money had been falling through the cracks the last few years before James had taken over the reins from his father. Which was precisely why Skinner had been drafted in from the outside: a man after James's own heart: no loyalty to the links of land and place the older Heron had espoused and allowed to rule him; Perdue and Merryweather mere stones strewn on their mutual path to progress, a path this company of Lundt and McCleery's had supposed already cleared.

Brogar had no idea of the drama Sholto and the others were undergoing. He'd elected not to cross over to the mainland for several reasons: firstly that Skinner Tweedy meant to get Perdue and Merryweather off the island, presumably with the Company's connivance, and he meant to find out why; secondly that Perdue and Merryweather were keeping something from him about the shaft they'd just rescued their casualty from; and thirdly because if Hazel's Tuley's deductions were correct – and he'd no reason to doubt them – then the man just dragged over the Rack was named Charlie Stirling and had a sister named Frith who was possibly still here and could cast light on why her brother had been in a closed up, unstable, copper mining shaft.

Quite enough to engineer a lockdown, and no better way than for the sea to do it for him.

Brogar rubbed his hands as he and Perdue lingered, feeling the frisson of something odd going on here, something not quite right, Perdue looking back over the Rack the others had departed over.

'I shouldn't have let them go,' he said. 'At the very least I should've gone with them.'

'What's the worst that could happen?' Brogar asked, with the innocence of someone who doesn't know the Solway Firth at all.

'That they all drown,' Kerr said, holding a hand to his forehead, trying to make out how far they'd gone, but they were lost to him, the skirr of raindrops held in the air without falling obscuring his view.

'Surely not,' Brogar countered. 'It's what, a mile at most?'

'Three quarters,' Kerr said immediately, 'but the dangerous bit is at the other end. She'd have wanted over to Torr, get that man back to her little hospital...'

'So what's the harm in that?' Brogar asked, still not understanding.

Kerr Perdue put his hand down by his side and led Brogar on, away from the cove. Nothing he could do about any of it now, only the guilt gnawing at his stomach like he had a rat in there trying to get out, a small voice in his head telling him that by not going over with Hazel Tuley, by not pushing this Brogar to go with them – strong as an ox as he obviously was, and had to be the Company man – he was only trying to save his own skin, his and Merryweather's. Having Brogar here captive until the next low tide was something good, a chance to get over his point of view, put in his tuppence worth, invoke the older Heron's clause. But that rat and that voice kept on niggling, making him wonder if those skins might not be worth the price.

He looked over his shoulder as they reached the top of the island, saw the majesty of its isolation, Hestan placed on the horizon of

the tide like a marker boulder that said *no more, and no further,* the sea pouring in towards the enormous bays of Auchencairn, Balcary and Orchardton. The sea that never left the back-end of the island, always lapping there, always eager at low tide to get back in, recalling the great whumps of waves that came against the island's farthest side when the water was at its angriest, crashing over Daft Annie's Steps and flooding through the caves.

Yet more memories to add to the list when he was gone from here; like the maniacal scuttle and dip of the oystercatchers and redshanks as they ran along the briefly revealed sands about the inner shores of the island before the tides came in again; the angry downpour of gulls that went at his head in the breeding season; the stink of guano that overtook the rocky crags at the other end of the island where they bred their young.

He felt sick to think he might not be here to see another season through; not be here in the next couple of months when the spring returned, witness the great gatherings on the flats of swans and geese as they got ready to return from wherever it was they'd come from. He looked out over the great expanse of mud and sand that divided him from other human beings, the low haze of rain waiting to fall, the pinks and greys of a mackerel sky up above reflected in the wetness of the bay; felt a great urge to weep for all that he – and Merryweather with him, curmudgeonly old tic that he was – might be about to lose.

Salvation was what he wanted, but no idea how it could possibly come about.

CHAPTER 5

SETTING LIMBS, SETTING BOUNDARIES

Salvation was on everyone else's mind as they arrived at Auchencairn, carefully lifting their stricken patient from his rusty bier into the Tuleys' tiny hospital: a small, functional room, wide windows with open blinds covering the whole of one wall, below which was a small desk and an instrument cabinet, four narrow, neat-sheeted beds opposite so patients could gaze out into the sky; tucked away behind pulled curtains at the far end of the room was the operating area – a marble-topped metal cupboard-stack that could be adapted into birthing table or mortuary slab as was necessary, and it was here they deposited their burden.

'Thank you,' Hazel said, letting out a breath, glad they'd got the man back in one piece and without breaking any more bones as they'd hurtled across the Rack. Thankfully the man had been unconscious ever since, Hazel's administration of morphine doing the trick, his chest rising and falling in regular rhythm. She glanced up at the wide-faced clock on the wall. Nine thirty-four. Far too early for her husband to be abroad, which was a blessing.

'I'll need to hose him down, get rid of all the dirt,' Hazel said, taking up a pair of scissors and clipping away the remainder of

her patient's clothes. 'Hugh, do you mind operating the pump? It's just the other side of this wall. I'll push out a small metal rod from here when I want you to start, and pull it back when I want you to stop. I'll need to do it couple of times, once for his torso, once for his legs.'

'Righto, Missus,' Hugh said, straightening his back, smiling full on at Hazel who creased her brows as the morning light filtered down onto his face, observing at close quarters the deep and recent pockmarks in cheeks and forehead, the foreshortened nose, the white moon of his blinded eye.

'Thank you,' she managed, turning to Sholto the moment Hugh, and Gilligan with him, had scampered from the room, finding the pump, standing at their station ready for action.

'What happened to him?' she asked, as she carefully peeled away cloth and stitch, Sholto taking them from her, putting them in a bucket that lay nearby, checking for anything secreted in cutaway pockets or hiding places.

'We had a bit of a time of it up at Ardnamurchan,' he answered. 'A run-in with smugglers, Hugh taking the brunt of it. But he never complains, just gets on with things, always putting other people before himself.'

'I've seen that in him,' Hazel said, Sholto studying Hazel Tuley as she paused briefly at these words before carrying on her snipping and removing, Sholto admiring the deft efficiency with which she was going about her task, the way she pulled so gently on her patient's clothes, easing them out from under him as if he were awake and conscious.

'I don't like to presume,' Sholto added, 'but you seem very good at your job, Mrs Tuley. Maybe there's something you can do for Hugh that we can't.'

Hazel stopped her ministrations and looked up, unsure whether

or not she was being mocked. Instead of answering, she put out a hand and pushed a rod in the small metal plaque in the wall just above the operating table and took up the hose that was lying on the bricked floor about the table, on which the presumed Charlie Stirling was laid out. A few seconds later, the hose began to bulge and gurgle and out of its end came a jet of water, Hugh and Gilligan grand at their job as always, feet pressing down rhythmically on the pump pedal to keep the water flowing evenly, Hazel directing it expertly over the body on the table, washing away every last speck of grime and dust. Once done to her satisfaction, her patient's skin pale as the inside of an oyster shell – apart from the livid bruises that patched stomach, arms, chest and back – Hazel pulled the rod in again and Hugh and Gilligan ceased their pumping.

'So, is this Charlie Stirling, then?' Sholto asked.

'I think it might well be,' Hazel said, 'although I don't know the family well. I've met Frith a few times, but her brother and mother only once and a long time ago.'

Something was nagging at her, like sheep's wool caught in thorny briar, but she couldn't quite put her finger on in.

'He certainly has her aspect,' she said. 'Straight blond hair, narrow nose, square jaw, wide teeth, and yes,' she tugged up one of her patient's eyelids, 'blue eyes. They're fraternal twins, you see. Him and Frith.'

'And what do you know about the family?' Sholto asked, intrigued.

'Not much,' Hazel answered, still wondering at that lost memory, something she knew she knew but couldn't quite grasp. 'Like I said, I don't know the family well, but from what I recall they arrived with their mother at Dundrennan in the late fifties, poor wee souls.'

'Why poor wee souls?' Sholto asked, looking down at the man

on the table, noting how young he looked, now he'd been sluiced and cleaned like a gutted fish, and was maybe a couple of years shy of eighteen.

'Well, they arrived without anything but each other, the children barely out of the cot. No money, no baggage, no husband or father, and the mother hardly had a word of English. Had to wait until the bairns grew before she could communicate properly. But she'd some connection to the chapel at Dundrennan,' Hazel said abstractedly, beginning to unwrap the splints, lay them aside, taking away the last of the rags about her patient's waist and groin, unmoved by his youthful nakedness. 'Worked there as housekeeper, cook and cleaner for the Minister,' she added, pushing out the rod again, Hugh and Gilligan at the ready, taking it easier this time, knowing Hazel would be washing down the man's legs and wanting to make that laving as gentle as they could. Hazel noticed the pressure of the water had slowed and asked Sholto a question to staunch his own.

'So how did you come by Hugh and the other boy? Whose name, I'm sorry, but I've forgotten.'

'Gilligan,' Sholto replied. 'Hugh and Gilligan. The two of them grew up together up in Sutherland, and are pretty much the only family each other has.'

'Except they now have you,' Hazel said slowly, pulling in the rod, the water ceasing, Hazel straightening up, placing a hand to the small of her back. 'We really need to get this gypsum cast on,' she said, looking directly at Sholto as if about to be challenged. Sholto smiling, holding up his hands.

'By all means,' he said. 'I'd be really interested to stay and watch. To help if I can. I think this plaster of Paris invention could be of immense use.'

He was thinking of Brogar. How he'd got away the past two decades – given all the scrapes and hard places he'd been in –

without breaking every bone in his body was a mystery to Sholto. But if or when it happened, Sholto meant to be as well-equipped as he could.

Hugh came back into the small hospital room, Gilligan on his heels.

'All done? Did we do it right?' Hugh asked.

'You did it perfectly,' Hazel answered, flashing the boy a smile, casting a brief professional look over his face, wondering if there really was anything she could do for him, though she rather doubted it. Blind was blind, after all, and nothing she could do about those scars. She did notice though, as Hugh came across the room, the careful way he moved, that his depth perception wasn't all it could be, and maybe there was something she could do about that.

'Well, let's get to it,' she announced, glancing once again at the clock on the wall, dreading that her husband would soon be up and come down and demand to take over. He wasn't a bad man, not by any means, but had become a bad doctor and a bad husband, a man stuck in the past. All to do, Hazel knew, with the sinking of the SS *Arctic* on which he'd been ship's doctor when it left Liverpool on the twentieth of September 1854, Bill heading off for America to join another ship bound for the Crimea to do what he could in that dreadful war, her going on afterwards as one of the Nightingale Nurses. But Bill had never got over his experiences in the war, which served to pummel all idealism out of him and never a good word to say about any of it since, including Hazel's part in it.

'That Nightingale woman is doing nothing! Nothing!' had been a frequent refrain back there on the shores of the Black Sea, once reunited with his wife. 'You've got to tell her, Hazel. She needs to understand the importance of hygiene, cleanliness and sterile

circumstance. Without it she's just another woman holding the hands of men she's unwittingly condemning to death.'

Their marriage a hard road ever since.

'This gypsum thing is garbage!' he'd ranted at Hazel, when she'd proposed it as a possible advance in healing broken bones and correcting deformities like club foot. Hazel not bothering to answer. She knew his primary objection was not the fact that plaster of Paris might be a good thing, but that Antonius Mathijsen had pioneered it during the war in the Crimea, anything to do with it – Hazel included – being henceforth tainted goods. But Bill wasn't here, not yet, and Hazel had the help of Sholto and his boys and took full advantage.

'Hugh,' Hazel asked, 'can you get the gas lit over there on the stove?'

She regretted this immediately, not that Hugh objected, but to ask a lad with depth perception problems to light a match and put it to a burner was not the most tactful thing she could have done, but Hugh had Gilligan together got the task completed, Sholto lifting two filled kettles to the burners to get them boiling.

Hazel's patient was beginning to stir, not yet awake, but she quickly fetched a towel and dabbed him dry, got a blanket folded over him from mid-thigh to neck, a gesture Sholto appreciated, for no one wanted to wake to find themselves stripped and vulnerable, strangers gawking at all you'd got. She next fetched her tins of pre-impregnated bandages, hoping she'd prepared them well enough, it being quite an art – from cutting the bandage lengths from a roll of muslin, removing three strands from the weft on either side so they didn't catch in the soaking, the passing of the bandages through the superfine gypsum powder and rubbing it into the meshwork.

Not too much, not too little, and the rolling up of them took

skill – too loose and the plaster would fall out, too tight and the water wouldn't get through evenly.

Hazel had read her manual of instructions carefully, had practised and practised until she'd got it just right. But this was the first time she was going to put her knowledge to the test on a real live person, and she felt a pulsing at the corner of her eye as she opened her sealed tin, hoping to God no moisture had got in and ruined her handwork – it hadn't – checking the bones of her patient were still in place – they were – gently laying felted wadding along his damaged leg to allow for the expansion of the skin caused by swelling, and easier removal of the cast later on.

Lastly she tested the temperature of the water in the buckets, nodded, took a deep breath and began.

Into the buckets she gently dropped several rolls of bandages, waiting for the bubbling to cease before lifting them out with care, squeezing them from the edges in to rid them of excess water, turning to her helpers.

'You need to lift his leg up and hold it completely still. Charlie? Are you with us?'

Charlie was, his blue eyes open and flickering around him with concern. He was groggy, not understanding what was going on, Hugh coming up beside him and taking his hand in his own.

'Don't worry, Mister. Mrs Tuley's going to fix you up now. You've bust your leg good and proper but hold still, and she'll have it done it no time.'

Charlie slid his watery eyes towards Hugh, tears trickling from their corners.

'Not going to leave you,' Hugh said softly, 'gonna be right here all the time.'

Gilligan standing at the ready and, at a nod from Hazel, lifting Charlie's thigh as Sholto raised heel and ankle and kept them

steady, Charlie sucking air in over his teeth as the last warm nuzzle of morphine slipped away with the movement. Hazel worked quickly, unwrapping her moistened bandage rolls with steady fingers, working from top to bottom, thigh to ankle, and then back up again, using seven rolls in all. Hazel massaging the layers the one into the other as if she'd done this a hundred times before instead of never.

Once finished, her patient subsided into sleep and Hazel screwed up her eyes, rubbing her fingers to her temples, scraping them through her hair, leaving white streaks all over her face.

'No offence, Missus,' Hugh commented, after this brief outlet of her agitation. 'But you looks like you've had a party with pot of paint.'

Hazel didn't react for a moment, then caught her reflection in one of the windows as she moved away to wash her hands, saw a scatty bedraggled ghost in the glass and began to laugh a little shrilly, her throat tight, tears pushing at eyes and throat. She couldn't believe she'd actually done it, carried it off, and was ashamed to show her weakness.

Sholto came over to her, offered her a towel.

'You've done a good thing today, Mrs Tuley,' he said softly, 'a really good thing. I hope you'll teach me how to do it myself.'

Hazel took a sharp breath in through her nose and swallowed hard, sniffing as she wiped the towel roughly over face and eyes.

'Thank you,' she said, once she'd got her composure back. 'I've only ever tried it on chair legs before,' and that was enough to start Hugh and Gilligan giggling.

'Bet you've got the straightest chair legs in all the country!' Gilligan said.

Sholto too was smiling.

'I've never seen the like,' he said easily, 'but I like what I see.'

And Mrs Hazel Doctor Tuley, fifty-seven years of age, hardened veteran nurse of the Crimea, who'd been carrying her husband's ineptitudes for years, had a blush over her cheeks like a sunset over Hestan.

The Crimea be damned, she thought a little headily, at least something good had come out of it, and she herself had proved it this very day.

Chapter 6

When The Past Comes Calling

Brogar sat in Perdue's workshop, a pint pot of coffee clutched in his hands. He felt at ease here, with Perdue peeling spuds and neeps, adding them to a hunk of salted bacon that was already bubbling away in its pan.

'Be about half an hour,' Perdue said.

'Fine with me,' Brogar replied, nose twitching with the pepper that had been liberally slung in with the meat and vegetables, hunger growling in his belly. 'Great table,' he added, admiring the long slab of salt-whitened, smooth-edged driftwood cleverly slotted onto a sturdy frame.

'Need it for me by-line,' Kerr informed him, Brogar nodding, looking around the workshop – one wall taken up with tools neatly arrayed on evenly spaced lines of nails, functional and yet beautiful, like notes on a music manuscript promising great works yet to come. The other end of the table from where he was sitting was filled with melting-crucibles, crimping irons, lumps of copper-bearing ore, beakers filled with cleaning alcohol within which were an odd array of body parts that looked to be exclusively from birds: several skulls, a few complete skeletons

still with cartilage intact, a couple of fluffy white chicks, eyes not yet open. Also on display were sequences from large to small of blown eggs on sheets of bunched linen, a notched wooden rack holding an eclectic collection of beaks – the long, curved scimitar of a curlew, several bright red stabs of oystercatchers, a couple of gannets with their trademark white marked along the horizontal with a sharp black line, some tubenoses from fulmars, the grey-blue of a tufted duck with its distinctive black-hooked tip, the cheeky multi-coloured joy of a puffin. Brogar recognised them all, and was curious.

'So how'd you get all these?' he asked, Kerr Perdue shrugging as he stirred his pot, sipped his coffee, eased himself back into the day that had not exactly started on the normal.

'Kinda difficult at first. Rare to see a dead bird. Don't know where them all goes off to die. Guessing most of 'em gets tekked by bigger birds or rats and the like when them've got old or sick. But I has my ways. Loads of birds breed here and over on Rough Island too, and during the season some kick off, forget to feed, gets bumped off ledges by rivals and don't get it together in time. Some I just come across, like this 'un.'

He undid the pouch at his belt, suddenly remembering his find on the way over to Merryweather's that morning. He took out the duck's head and moved around the table, dropping it into one of the beakers.

'Female teal, I think,' Perdue said. 'Brown all over, single green hind feather in the wing.'

'I've never seen one up so close,' Brogar leaned forward to take his look. 'Almost like polished tortoiseshell.'

Kerr smiled deep within his beard.

'Just what I thought when I saw it. Strangest thing,' he said, 'just sat there it was, like it was asleep, but dead as last month's Sundays,

and the curve to its neck? Well, perfect, it was, just sat there in the heather, stiff as a board.'

'So what do you do with them all?' Brogar asked.

'Makes 'em into talismans,' Kerr explained. 'Gets 'em cleaned up and properly preserved and that, then fixes them into copper clasps. Do a good trade in the beaks and feet. Makes me a few extra coins. Ores-men fetch 'em down to Swansea when they come for the load twice a year, sells them on for me. Sailors like 'em. Gives 'em luck they reckon, when they're out on the sea.'

Brogar nodded, sailors being superstitious men, a different ilk from landliers, men who knew that if their boat or ship went down it didn't matter what god you believed in or how well you'd lived your life or how much money you had. Once in the water you were done for, and Christ help you if you could swim, for that was only going to prolong your dying. But birds? Well, most of them floated, most of them flew, some could dive right down into the depths and come out five minutes later, all properties any sailor would aspire to. Add in the copper – well known for relieving all kind of ailments – and you had the best kind of protection you were ever going to get.

'So what's the deal with the copper mines here?' Brogar asked, shifting tack, seeing Perdue's back stiffen as he turned away to the pot, began to stir it again.

'Don't know as how much Tweedy's told you,' Kerr said noncommittally, scratching his neck with his free hand.

'Nothing much,' Brogar said, leaning forward, elbows on table, chin in fists, fascination with bird beaks gone. 'Only let me tell you this,' he went on, voice hard, face set. 'I'd no notion folk would be chucked off this island by the sale of it and it's not a notion I hold with, and I'll fight tooth and nail with both the Company and Tweedy if I can wangle you a way to stay.'

Kerr Perdue left off stirring the stew. So he'd been right. Here was a possible ally, and maybe his one chance to take advantage of it. He turned and came and sat at the table opposite Brogar, filling up their mugs with the coffee that had been simmering on the stove.

'It's like this,' he began. 'We been working these copper shafts since late 1830s, me and Merryweather. Nigh on thirty year. Given free rein on it by Heron's father. Said we could carry on working it and living here long as we're able, unless the estate went out of Heron hands. But he's dead and gone, and son's not likely to honour the agreement. Scratched our names on a little piece of paper way back when, but if the island's sold then we'll be sent to buggery.'

Brogar cleared his throat, narrowing his eyes.

'So there's a contract, between you and the estate?' he asked, an idea ticking over in his mind.

'Suppose,' Kerr sighed. 'Must be something, or young Heron would've chucked us off years back.'

'Interesting,' Brogar commented, taking a mouthful of the over-boiled, over-brewed, bitter coffee that was dark as basalt and just the way he liked it. 'And you have a copy?'

'Aye right,' Kerr said. ''Course not, though wouldn't do to tell Tweedy or Heron that. Back then it was all word of mouth. Man's honour, shake of the hand and all that, never mind a scribble on a piece o'paper. An' even if we did it wouldn't save us, us not being lawyer men. But we's belong here, me and Merryweather. We're like the stones on it an' the birds on it. We're like a living breathing part o'Hestan. And thought we'd die here, like old Heron thought we would. Christ knows what us'll do if we're both kicked off this time o'life. We've no one, Mr Finn. No family, no one what'll take us in. It'll be a long hard road sees the two of us if we're chucked off now.'

Kerr Perdue shook his head, despairing.

'So what brought the two of you here in the first place?' Brogar asked. 'It's not exactly the most obvious place to end up in.'

Kerr didn't answer immediately, tapped his fingers on the table, took a sip of coffee and grimaced.

'We didn't exactly end up here,' he began, 'more like started. Went over to Sweden together to join up in the army when we was young, went to Russia…'

Brogar nodded.

'Not so uncommon. A lot of Scots in Sweden.'

'Aye,' Kerr Perdue agreed. 'Didn't exactly go well, not after a bit.'

Brogar raised his eyebrows but Perdue didn't seem inclined to go on.

'Something happen? Man's honour, shake of the hand, and all that?' Brogar suggested, Kerr twisting his lips, raising half a smile.

'Kinda,' he said. 'Sort'o thing that goes way back an' can't be undone.' He raised his head and looked directly at Brogar. 'But a bargain's a bargain and shouldn't be broken, like us being here. All of a part. It's like we're custodians. Old Mr Heron knew that, knew all of it, an' we've still a task we're not yet at the end of.'

Brogar's face remained impassive but he was surprised by this declaration of fealty to some past pact, some task undone. He sensed a tale, a story with a kick in its tail and wished Sholto was here to puzzle it out of the man with the delicacy he couldn't do. Instead, Brogar blundered and shut him down.

'And it's to do with shaft number three?' he asked slowly, Kerr Perdue unable to stop the quick shift of his head, the horrible thought that the man he'd taken as an ally might be the exact opposite.

'Why would you think that?' he blustered, standing up, going to his pot, declaring it ready, getting out two bowls, ladling in some tatties and neeps, hoiking out the salted bacon joint onto a large

platter and placing it on the table, picking up a vicious looking knife and beginning sharpening it on a soap stone. Anyone other than Brogar would have taken this as a direct challenge and pursued the matter no further, but not him. He merely smiled and leant back in his chair.

'Because I know men,' he said lightly, 'and I know mines, and I've seen the reports of the copper veins on this island and know full well that number three is on the wrong trajectory. So what was that man in there really looking for, Mr Perdue? And what is it you're not telling me?'

Charlie Stirling was awake. He'd been shifted from the operating table in Hazel Tuley's tiny hospital to one of the beds and was feeling like hell: throat dry and scratchy, the bruises on his back and chest hurting like he'd taken a tumble down a God almighty long set of stairs, his broken leg gently pulsating with pain but immobilised by a swathe of solid bandages.

'I can't stay here,' he mumbled, trying to shift himself off and get himself upright, stopped by a small hand held against him and a small voice coming out of nowhere, but a voice he recognised and trusted, though he'd no idea why.

'You're not to move,' said Hugh, jumping up from the seat beside Charlie's bed. 'Mrs Tuley says it's gonna to be at least twelve hours before everything's set good and hard, but not to worry, Mr Charlie, Gilligan's already away to the carpenters to fetch you some crutches.'

Charlie frowned but subsided.

'Have you some water?' he croaked, Hugh at the ready and immediately thrusting a beaker towards his charge, Charlie glugging the water down, not sure he'd ever tasted anything so fine in all his life.

'Can you tell us anything about why you were where you were when your accident happened?' Some of Sholto's and Brogar's curiosity rubbing off on Hugh.

Charlie stopped his drinking, looking over for the first time at the small boy who had placed the beaker in his hand.

'You're…who?'

'I'm Hugh,' Hugh answered brightly, 'was there when Mr Brogar dragged you out. Everyone thought you were a gonner, but not him. He's a real first-class person, is Mr Brogar. Got me saved too.'

Charlie coughed, put down the beaker on the cabinet beside the bed, placed his hands to his ribs.

'Feel like I've been squashed in a mousetrap,' he said, screwing up his face in pain and concentration. 'I can't really remember…I was…over on Hestan…down the…but where's Frith? Where's Frith?'

Charlie's voice had risen to the heights but Hugh patted Charlie's hand to calm him.

'Is she your sister?'

'Well, of course she is! But why isn't she here? I told her to wait…oh Jesus! I told her to wait! How long have I been here? She's in the cave! The big one on Hestan! Oh please tell me you've got her out of there! Oh please tell me…'

'Time to take a look at number three,' Brogar said, pushing away his plate after mopping it clean with hunks of coarse grained bread ripped from a rough-heeled loaf. He'd stopped asking Kerr Perdue about his secrets – they had a way of coming out their own and he could wait. Instead he started thinking out loud. 'He must have come over yesterday. No chance over the sands or your Rack this morning, not without any of us seeing.'

'Suppose,' Kerr agreed, without enthusiasm, starting to clear the

table, uncomfortable at Brogar's previous prodding, his deductions about the mine, already having decided he'd offer no more up.

'And then there's the girl Frith,' Brogar added, taking out a toothpick and sliding it between his teeth. Kerr Perdue stopped his clearing and looked over at Brogar.

'The girl Frith?' he repeated. 'What's she got to do with anything?'

Brogar swung to his feet and studied Perdue, running swiftly through the sequence of events earlier that morning.

'It was just after you'd squared up to Tweedy,' he explained. 'Mrs Tuley thought the man we dragged out might be the girl's brother, Charlie, from...Dun...well, Dun somewhere or...'

He stopped speaking as he watched Perdue's face – or as much of it as could be seen between beanie and stubble – drain of blood.

'Oh my God,' Perdue whispered, his voice taken over by the clattering of the plates he'd been holding as he dropped them without caring into the trough used as a sink. He shook his head, body braced as his mind raced towards some terrible conclusion Brogar couldn't fathom, then suddenly ran for the door, grabbing a looped coil of rope as he went.

'Come on!' Perdue yelled, flinging himself out into the late morning. 'She'll be in the cave and water's rising and she'll not know...oh dear God...she'll not know...'

Brogar was perplexed, but not slow to follow, and couldn't stop a small smile twitching on his lips as his adrenalin began to pump.

Here we go again, he thought happily, and by Christ it felt good.

Hazel Tuley retired back into the interior of her house after her ministrations to Charlie Stirling were at an end, happy that Hugh had volunteered to stay with him and that Gilligan was off getting him a pair of crutches made. She'd invited Sholto with her, and they

were both sitting at her table tucking into a meal she'd whipped up from some cold rice, a few hard-boiled eggs and some smoked fish, when she heard a banging on the floor up above her.

'That'll be my husband, Bill,' she said quietly to Sholto as both raised their heads at the commotion. 'There's maybe a couple of things I should tell you about him before he comes down.'

Sholto wiped his fingers on the serviette provided and looked at Hazel with curiosity. He'd not missed her slight wincing as the upstairs noises had begun, nor the worry that tugged at her lips as she mentioned her husband's name.

'You've no need to explain anything to me,' Sholto said, 'not if you don't want to.'

Hazel shook her head.

'It needs saying. It was all a long time ago now, but Bill…well… he just can't forget it. Slough of despond and all that.'

She rubbed her hand over her face before going on, Sholto still and attentive, eager to understand.

'He went off to the Crimea before me,' she began, quietly and quickly, wanting to get out as much as she could so that Sholto wouldn't judge her husband too harshly, as others had done and still did. 'Left Liverpool on a steamship to America, on the SS *Arctic*…'

'I know about it,' Sholto interrupted, for indeed he did, and knew too that it hadn't ended well. 'Big fog came down somewhere in the North Atlantic,' he continued, 'iron-hulled ship from France…'

'The *Vesta*,' Hazel put in, too surprised to volunteer more.

'The *Vesta*,' Sholto agreed, seeing the report of the accident lying neatly upon his desk in Trondheim in black and white. 'Iron-hulled *Vesta* crashes into the steamship *Arctic*, but all seemed fine. No breaches, so both chugged on upon their way. But all wasn't fine…'

'Not fine at all,' Hazel added sadly, the scenes her husband had put inside her head making her shiver. The incident had ruined Bill, shredding him from the inside out.

'No,' Sholto said, caught up in the story, reading from that report as if it was there in front of him. 'The *Vesta* sustained no damage, being iron-hulled and sturdy, but the *Arctic* didn't fare so well, ploughing on under full steam until it began to list and then sink and down went the lifeboats…'

'And down went the lifeboats,' came another voice, stopping both Hazel and Sholto in their tracks as Bill Tuley – shambling and badly shaven – came in through the open door, Hazel standing up immediately.

'Oh Bill,' she said, but Bill Tuley made no notice, came and sat down at the table, sitting in Hazel's abandoned chair, staring straight into Sholto's eyes.

'And into the lifeboats went the crew,' he continued in a monotone, 'and no one listened to the ship's doctor, who shouted himself hoarse. No one listened to him as he yelled and fought and kicked and told them there were places aplenty and time enough to get the passengers into the lifeboats. But no one listened. No one listened.'

'Don't do this, Bill,' Hazel said, sitting herself down beside her husband, taking his hand, Sholto shocked at the man's aspect, the pallor of his skin, the sweat upon it, the intensity of his eyes, as if he was not in the present at all but rising up like a spectre from those old news reports Sholto had been so blithely quoting.

'But they didn't listen to their doctor,' Bill went on. 'They started rowing away like there was no one else in the world that mattered but them; they rowed away and left their captain and all those women and children to go under. Three hundred and fifty,' Bill whispered, great globules of tears falling as he lowered his head

almost to the table. 'Three hundred and fifty,' he whispered, 'left behind as they rowed away and still rowing half an hour later through the detritus of baggage and bodies left scattered like bloated wheat-heads across the water...'

Bill Tuley laid his head down, back heaving, banging his fist impotently upon the tablecloth, sending a serviette ring rolling onto its side across the surface towards Sholto.

'I'm so sorry,' Hazel said as she put an arm across her husband's back. 'He just can't leave it; sees it every night, wakes up in it every morning.'

Sholto stretched out his long fingers and stopped the serviette ring rolling any further, laying it down gently on its side, rubbing his fingertips upon its upper rim, trying to imagine what it must be like to be trapped in that small circle of history in the fog of the North Atlantic, bodies bumping against the lifeboats as Bill and his companion crew rowed on.

'And you were the ship's doctor,' Sholto stated quietly, Bill looking up, wiping his nose on his sleeve, taking deep breaths, blinking tears from red-rimmed eyes.

'I was,' he whispered, 'but those damn bastards didn't listen to me, and I couldn't make them...didn't stop them...feared they'd chuck me overboard, which makes me a worse coward than all the rest.'

Sholto nodded, but saw more than that; saw a man who'd climbed into the shell of his own self-loathing and forbidden himself from coming out again, no matter what it cost him, including the wife who'd stood by him all these years, taken up the slack, was most likely the better doctor of the two of them by now. And hated the waste of it, saw a little of himself buried in that husk, saw a person who needed kicking out of the ordinary and being told exactly what was what in order to become what he could be.

'She'll be in the Great Cave,' Kerr shouted at Brogar as they ran from his workshop across the island, the opposite way from the mine workings and the Rack, heading to the west. 'Can get down to it from the top,' Kerr panted, fear knotting his muscles, making it hard to run. 'Bit of a scramble but we've got to do it, else she'll be drowned!'

'Hold up, hold up!' Brogar hooked an iron fist about Kerr's arm, dragging him to a stop, Kerr's limbs shaking and fighting against the interruption, itching to get on. 'Hold up!' Brogar commanded. 'What the hell is going on here? I need to know, Kerr, and you've to tell me, and right now.'

Perdue tried to wrench his arm from Brogar's grip, shouting into the wind that was coming in strong from the north-west, bringing a load of sleet in with it that slapped Kerr's dark hair flat down upon his forehead below his woollen cap, catching in the rough bristles on his chin.

'If that was Charlie Stirling down the mine,' he yelled, 'then they must've come over the Rack last night, else we'd've seen 'em. Means Frith'll be in the cave like when they was kids, but she don't understand the tides, nor that this 'un's a big 'un. She'll think she's safe at the back but she ain't!'

Enough for Brogar, who released Perdue, and a few minutes later they were standing catching their breath at the top of a short stump of cliff, rocks sprawling down in every direction, sea crashing about its base pushed on by the wind, the thin white line of its shallow breakers and bore already two miles inland and long past Balcary and Almorness Point and touching Torr, remorselessly filling in the blanks between Hestan and Auchencairn, heading for its farthest point which lay at the very end of Orchardton Bay.

'How in hell are we going to get down?' Brogar asked, but Perdue was ahead of him.

'We ain't. You're stopping right up here, but I'll need you to anchor the rope, be ready to bring the girl up if she ain't already done for.'

He unhooked the rope coils he'd been carrying, threw one end at Brogar who immediately got the gist and tugged it about his wrists and shoulders, Perdue nodding once in approval.

'Don't know what kind o'man you really are,' he said, 'but you's a strong one, I ken that already, so you hang on and I'll get meseln down and you start pulling her up the moment you hears me shout for it.'

And then he was heading for edge of the cliff and chucking himself over, back down towards the sea, dropping so quickly that all Brogar saw was the top of his woollen hat disappearing.

'Well hoorah for that,' Brogar muttered under his breath as he found a rock against which to brace his feet, get his ropes properly tied. He'd've been glad to be the one to chuck himself out over the cliff in search and rescue, but for once he'd been supplanted by another man of action who'd got there first, and faster.

Bill Tuley had gathered himself enough together to be able to sip at a small cup of coffee, pick at some of the fish dish Hazel pushed towards him.

'You really can't blame yourself,' Sholto said, Hazel astonished when her husband didn't immediately rile up like he usually did when she'd said those same words to him a thousand times down the years. 'Bad things happen to good people,' Sholto went on mildly, 'I've seen it a hundred times. Or not a hundred,' he qualified, hating to be inaccurate, 'but many, many times. I've only just begun working out in the field, Dr Tuley, but before that, and for almost two decades, my duty was to read all the reports coming in from Company of men like Brogar Finn, my colleague,

who your wife has not long met. The *Arctic–Vesta* clash was only one of them, one of our own going down with the rest, first woman in Sweden to qualify as a doctor and heading the same place you were to do what she could. A good person, a forerunner, lost before she'd the time to prove herself. But I can tell you right now that worse things have happened to other people, people I've known. People murdered horribly for no other reason than that they were in the wrong place at the wrong time.'

Sholto paused, looking over at Hazel and then at her husband, whose head was still bowed but moving very slowly from side to side, looking up, gripping his fork like a weapon, Sholto thinking it a crime that a person could be so wounded by his past that he couldn't function properly fifteen-odd years later.

'My point is this,' Sholto ploughed on. 'Good people get put in bad situations all the time, but if they're wise enough, strong enough, they'll put that situation to their advantage and not…'

His counselling session was interrupted by Hugh suddenly bowling through the door, miscalculating the distance in his haste and knocking into the table before he'd time to stop himself.

'Sorry, Missus,' Hugh apologised, 'but your patient's going a bit mental out there. Keeps asking about his sister. Can't hardly keep him on the bed an' I knows…'

'It's alright, Hugh,' Hazel on her feet immediately. 'Let me come see. We've got to keep him still if he's to patch up properly.'

She left, with Hugh on her heels. Silence then, Sholto unsure whether or not to follow, playing the with napkin ring, liking the certainty of it in his hand.

'That boy,' Bill said, lifting his head to look at Sholto, 'what happened to his face?'

Sholto was surprised Bill had even noticed but was glad of it, saw a way forward.

'One of those good people I was telling you about. Shot with a musket a few months back,' he said, staring over at Bill, 'almost died, lost the sight in one eye, still adapting.'

Bill nodded, closed his eyes.

'Wish I could shake everything off like he's done,' he said dully. Enough for Sholto, who stood up. It was obvious Bill Tuley was suffering deeply from his past experiences, but depression never sought out company, and company – Sholto included – had a tendency to leave whenever it was about.

'He's not shaken it off,' Sholto said a little brusquely, pausing as he realised he was still holding the napkin holder and turned to put it down again. 'He's just getting on with life, thinking on other people instead of himself.'

He took a few steps towards the door, but wasn't quite finished. He didn't like to be cruel, no more did he like to see a man as ruined and self-absorbed as Bill Tuley. Hazel deserved better.

'He's young and resilient,' Sholto added, 'but an example we'd all do well to emulate. So think on him, Dr Tuley, when you next look in the mirror, the next time you wake up from your nightmares. Because those nightmares are just nightmares; he has them, you have them, but he's the sense to leave them back in the night where they belong.'

CHAPTER 7

RESCUE, AND REALISATION

Perdue was down the cliff, salt spray lashing at his face, driven on by the wind.

'Frith!' he shouted, as he hauled himself across the slippery boulders separating him from the large triangular entrance to the cave, feet losing purchase on the seaweed that was amassed on them, between them, slipping across the wet kelp and bladder wrack.

'Frith!' he shouted again as he closed on his goal, sweat cold on his back, swearing when he saw the water rampaging up the gully between him and the cove, crashing against its narrowing rocks. Nothing to do but take his chance, make a leap. His boots caught the opposite side but not enough to save him going in, his world suddenly hugely cold, dark and salty as the water closed over his head, hands scrabbling for a crevice finally found, pulling himself out with difficulty, clothes waterlogged and heavy, beanie lost, bobbing along the surface like a dark, malevolent jellyfish. This cave on his list of memories not to be lost once he left Hestan, but not like this.

He shinnied and clawed himself over the last of the boulders, got his feet onto the sand of the cove, sea up to his thighs, wading

forward, body bent against the push and suck of it, finally getting himself inside the cave and onto shingle not yet taken.

'Frith,' he sighed with relief, for there she was, sat cross-legged at the back, blond hair poked up with the wet of the spray even that far in, hair she always clipped short – no matter the convention – so she and her brother looked more alike. She was hiccupping with the cold, lips almost blue, clothes tugged tight about her. 'Gotta get you out, girl,' Kerr said, marching towards her, dripping with every step. 'Water's on the rise, and going to swallow you whole if we don't leave right now.'

Charlie was still trying to get to his feet when Hazel and Hugh arrived.

'Back on that bed immediately, young man,' Hazel commanded, as she flung open the door linking the mini-hospital to the house.

'Told you so,' Hugh added brightly, scampering up behind her, blundering into one of the beds before righting himself.

'I've…got to…find out about…Frith…' Charlie said through clenched teeth, but he stopped his useless task of getting upright, having realised his damaged leg couldn't take the weight, the pain of trying more than he could bear.

'There's a time for everything,' Hazel stated, coming over to him, gently pushing him back onto the bed, swinging his leg up and on to it, pleased to feel the bandages hardening beneath her fingers; plumping up his pillows, straightening blankets. 'And I'm guessing you've now discovered that your leg isn't going to be taking you anywhere soon.'

'Too right,' Charlie murmured, face white, glistening with his meagre efforts.

'Let's give you a bit of something to make you more comfortable.' Hazel went to a cupboard and took out some a bottle of morphine mix.

'But what about Frith?' Charlie managed, after she'd forced him to take a swallow.

'Frith will be fine,' she said. 'There's folk over on the island know she's there and will be looking after her.'

She lied with ease, but not with an easy conscience. She'd no idea whether Frith was all right or not, but it wasn't going to do Charlie any favours to know of such doubts.

'Ooh, wait a minute!' Hugh said, taking up his familiar seat at Charlie's side. 'We could maybe Morse code Mr Brogar! Back in Sutherland, Mrs McCleery had an actual machine, but I'm sure I heard them talking about it once, how it was all done with lights and that.'

'A very good idea, Hugh,' Hazel said, smiling encouragingly at her patient.

'Not just a good one,' Sholto interrupted, stepping through the door, 'but a great one. Well done, Hugh! Where would we be without you?'

Hugh beamed a smile, though not at Hazel or Sholto but at Charlie Stirling.

'Didn't I tell you before that my Misters were the right kind of stuff?'

'That you did,' Charlie said, weaker now, his previous efforts – as well as the morphine – taking effect. 'But you'll tell me the moment you hear about Frith?'

''Course I will!' Hugh supplied happily. 'Won't we, Mr Sholto?'

'That we will,' Sholto said, already turning away, wondering why he'd not thought of such a simple method of communication before, why he'd not set it up with Brogar when Brogar had decided to wait out the tide. Twelve and a half hours between one low and the next, so Brogar not able to get back over to the mainland until the following morning. Worth a go, he thought, predicated on

Brogar being of like mind and looking out for any signal he could send. It would mean returning to Balcary House, not necessarily a bad thing, apart from it requiring another meeting with Skinner Tweedy, for surely Balcary was the closest point from which such a signal could be sent and reciprocated from Hestan.

'I've got her!' Kerr Perdue shouted, having launched Frith about his shoulders like a side of lamb as he waded through the waist-high water, heading to the south side of the cave, the gully now overflowed and impassable. He wasn't at all sure Brogar could hear him, the wind crashing waves against the boulders, vibrations from them hammering against the rocks and the sides of the cave and juddering up through his boots, jarring his bones. He'd salt and sand burning in his eyes, but he got him and her a few boulders up and felt a tug at the rope he'd tied about his waist and unknotted it with freezing, unwieldy fingers, looping it about Frith.

'Charlie was supposed to come back for me,' Frith whispered, terrified by what might have happened to Charlie and what might have happened to her. She'd waited in the cave for her brother but had never known the tide to creep in so fast and subtle up its way, had always thought the back of it to be safe and dry, had been thinking for the past few hours she should have got out sooner, that Charlie should have been back hours since; maybe climbed her way up the cliff, but by the time she'd thought of doing so it was far too late.

'Dinna worry about that now, lass,' Kerr said, getting his knots tied. 'Just you concentrate on getting yerself upward. Man up top will take the slack if you's slip.'

'But what about you, Mr Perdue?' Frith asked, voice small against the slap and hammer of the waves behind them, looking

at her rescuer standing fast against the stones like he was made of them, made of Hestan.

'Be right behind you,' he said. 'Up you go, lass,' he stuttered, teeth and body aching and sluggish with the cold, hooking his hands below her feet, shoving her up as far as he could. 'Take it slow, feel for leverage with your hands. I'm right behind you; been up and down these cliffs a thousand times, so not to worry.'

But worried he was. Getting up that short length of cliff was going to be a task and no mistake, best idea being to get himself out of the way of the waves and hang fire until Frith was up top and Brogar could chuck the rope back down to him. Ah Jesus, but he looked out over the mudflats, at the tide surging forward over the sands, far past Torr now, filling up Auchencairn Bay, well on down towards Orchardton, well on down and heading for its end. Top of his list this sight would be, and never had he seen it from this angle, right down in it, on its eye-line, gulls going mad up above him with the wind and his disturbance, raft of velvet scoter out there on the waves, bobbing up and down like they'd nowhere else to go and nowhere they'd rather be, load of geese flying low over Balcary heading for the fields of the farms beyond, the strange glistening hanging like a wide rainbow over the feet of Bengairn, an illusion given by the sleet and the sun behind it like it had been placed there just for him to see, like he might never see another moment so perfect, thought occurring to him how easy it would be to let go of all those memories, lose himself in his list, turn himself away and fling himself into the water, let it take the last of him, the very last of him, for God knew what the hell was going to happen after this.

Gilligan was back from the carpenter's, chattering loud and incessant as a starling the second he entered the house.

'Got there like you said, Mrs Tuley, and what a place he has! Coffins lined up against the wall like he's expecting the next plague, and all sorts of bits and bobs of wheels and that, but says he'll be at making the crutches first priority and …ooh…sorry… who are you, then?'

Gilligan had been speaking as if Sholto and Hazel would be precisely where he'd left them, at the table, brought up short to find only a man he'd never seen before. Bill Tuley's hand was clutched about a fork, body completely still on the outside but not on the in – a strange sensation creeping through him as if an army of worms had gone on the march beneath his skin, Sholto's words about leaving nightmares to the night burrowing their way deep inside him, apparently knowing their way, triggering one reaction, one emotion after another, giving him the first glimmer of hope he'd had in fifteen years that he was not as dead as the people he'd left behind in the North Atlantic, that maybe there was a possibility he could claw his way out after all. He needed to see that boy Hugh again, knew it without knowing why, and then – as if conjured by his thoughts – there he was.

'Thought we heard your voice,' Hugh was saying as he came back through the door from the hospital, Sholto with him, Hazel staying behind to see to Charlie.

'Was just saying to…well, to whoever this is,' Gilligan started up, 'that I've just come back…'

'Wait on,' Hugh interrupted his friend. 'We've had a grand idea! Remember all that Morse code stuff back in Sutherland?'

Gilligan moved his lips to left and right, trying to remember.

'Can't say as I do,' he admitted, but Hugh was having none of it.

'Course you do! That telegraph thingy Mrs Solveig hooked up between Helmsdale and Brora?'

'Oh aye,' Gilligan replied, though he was still mystified.

'Hugh's had the brainwave that we can use the same kind of code to communicate with Brogar on the island,' Sholto put in. 'Only trouble being that I can't quite remember all Morse's dots and dashes.'

'Actually it wasn't Morse,' Bill Tuley unexpectedly broke in, holding his head up, wobbling though it was like a dandelion clock in high wind with the strain of trying to appear normal. 'It was Joseph Henry, his mentor, who invented it. And I can help you, if you'll wait a moment,' he added, getting to his feet, face blanched as if he were about to be sick.

Hazel stopped short to hear her husband speaking in the next room, more astonished when she heard him go up the stairs and the soft scrape of him dragging out his army box from beneath their bed. The battered metal suitcase held his uniform and medals, his service record, a roll of surgical instruments – the leather stained black with blood, the few books and bits and pieces brought home with them from the Crimea. Her heart was drumming like a swan's wing inside her chest. The first time he'd had the courage to even look at the damn thing, let alone open it, in all this time and though – Lord knew – she didn't wish harm on another human being, she blessed the fact of Charlie Stirling's accident bringing Sholto and his boys to her door, blowing in like a healing breeze through the house she and Bill had been trapped together in for far too long.

The rat's tail of the rope came down the cliff to Perdue, his lifeline, so paralysed by the cold wetness of his clothes and the bitter wind that he'd been teetering on the brink of being done with it. He was shaking so hard it was difficult to noose the rope under his armpits but he got it done, looking up to see Brogar's broad face peeking over the cliff, the blood from the cuts on his nose oozing with the effort, lying on his stomach to see what was taking so long.

'You ready, Perdue?' Brogar yelled, Perdue nodding spasmodically, Brogar seeing immediately that Perdue was not ready at all but as frozen up as if he'd been buried in snow

'Keep there a moment! Get the knot tight as you can,' he shouted down. 'Soon have you up…'

Brogar straightened himself, took his large knife from the sheath sewn into the side of his trousers, jammed it into the earth, hammering it home with a rock, expertly fixing a hitch line about its handle to give him more pulling power.

Down below, Perdue was jerked into action by Brogar's first hard tug lifting him momentarily off his feet. His entire body shivered as he turned himself with difficulty and put his hands to the rocks, found himself heaved upwards, concentrating on breathing hard, grasping tussocks of grass, shoving his boots on small ledges, Brogar sensing the rhythm of his climbing and speeding him on. Ten minutes later, Kerr was creasing himself over the top of the cliff, Brogar's strong hands hauling the other half of him out onto the heather.

'Gave us a bit of a fright,' Brogar panted. 'Sent Frith back to the house for blankets and anything warm. Soon have you up and going.'

He slapped Perdue hard across the shoulders, partly from exuberance, partly to keep the man awake. The sleet of a sudden hardened into hail, Brogar lifting his face to it, smiling wildly, savouring the lash and sting of it on his skin.

'Christ, but doesn't the world constantly surprise?' he asked of no one in particular, Perdue hunched at his side like some demented gargoyle, finding the words so incongruous, so contradictory to the situation, that he couldn't help himself, started laughing, wheezing like one of those night rails that were so near the top of his list.

Bill started off up the stairs but hung a moment at the door, taking deep breaths, steeling himself to do what he meant. He'd been listening to the chattering of the two boys all the while he'd been going up to the bedroom and now was staring at that battered suitcase, wondering if he could really do this and get it open.

'We could make a big bonfire,' Gilligan was saying, Bill imagining the small damaged Hugh shaking his head as he offered his objections.

'Not going to work. We need summat that we can shutter and open, real quick like.'

'Some kind of lamp, then?' Gilligan came back. 'But ain't it going to need to be an awful big 'un?'

Bill closed his eyes, took a deep breath, put out his fingers and unclipped the clasps of the case. The lid sprang open immediately, as if it had been waiting for this moment, and the smell that came up to Bill made him gag: damp and mildew, the awful hint of old and stale blood.

'Mebbe we could use Gilligan's bonfire but use a mirror?' Hugh was saying, ''Cos surely if we got it in the right direction we could cover and uncover it right quick?'

'Or a sheet of metal!' Gilligan put in excitedly. 'Used to see the sun shining off that sheep pen roof back in Sutherland, didn't we, Hugh?'

'That's right!' Hugh was enthusiastic. 'Right blinding it was, when everything was at the right angle.'

Bill opened his eyes and looked down into his suitcase. Everything for him hadn't been at the right angle for years, and he was beginning to understand how much it had cost him. How much it had cost Hazel. He placed his hand on the folded up uniform, felt the cold metal of his useless medals pinned below the pocket. It occurred to him only now that Hazel had no suitcase, no

uniform, no medals, despite having done as much as he had out there to help the broken and dying men dragged from the lines. He shook his head to get rid of the images.

'I think you've got it, boys,' he heard Sholto saying. 'We've got to get over to Balcary and light a fire on the beach with driftwood. We've to find a sheet of metal. There's a blacksmith's in Auchencairn. We'll need to ask. Then we add a piece of sackcloth with a bit of string so we can lift it up and let it fall and, once we've got the angle right…it'll work. I'm sure of it!'

Bill had heard enough. They were all so positive, so looking on how to get things done that their enthusiasm was contagious. He picked up the little book he'd come to fetch, closed the lid of the metal suitcase and abandoned it, giving it a sharp kick to head it back beneath the bed. Sometime soon he'd open it again, with Hazel next to him, go through it properly, maybe even read the diary he'd kept of his time over there. Or maybe just give it to Hazel, let her read it for him. He stayed a few moments, standing there, a hazy memory coming back to him of his wife scribbling in her own little diary by a lamp in the tent they'd shared.

'Oh God,' he whispered, as the enormity of his self-imposed obsession came in at him from all sides. *How is it that I've forgotten she was there with me? That all I saw, she saw?* His own wife, Hazel, always keeping such meticulous records of every one of the patients she'd ever treated. If ever there was a diary to be read it would be hers, not his. Not Bill Tuley's, who was beginning to understand that he was the most selfish man ever to walk the earth.

CHAPTER 8

LIGHTS, DOTS, AND DASHES

'Warmer now?' Frith was asking solicitously of Kerr Perdue, who was piled in his bed in the small room below his light, a kerosene heater going full blast, Kerr having managed back to his workshop and being stripped of his clothing by Brogar, Kerr's fingers unable to work at all by then. He stopped short at the removal of his long johns in front of Frith, who blushed a merry red and went off voluntarily to make sure the heater in Kerr's sleeping cabin was up to scratch and his bedding piled high with all the blankets she could find.

Once Kerr was despatched to bed, Brogar and Frith sat companionably in the workshop, Frith reheating the remains of the bacon stew, taking it through to Kerr Perdue to find him soundly asleep, still shivering below his blankets.

'So you came here last night at low tide,' Brogar stated, once the girl was sat down and comfortable, none the worse for her sojourn in the cave, more concerned about Perdue than she was for herself.

'Aye,' Frith answered, shy and quiet, finding this stranger intimidating with his huge build, his face scarred from forehead to chin, but knowing to him be a good man, else why would he

have hauled both her and Perdue up from the cave when he could have just left them to die there?

'Big thing to stop out overnight on the island and have no one see you,' Brogar said with admiration, Frith dipping her head, a quick smile as she recalled she and Charlie huddling together beneath their canvas sheet with only a couple of candles for light and heat; such intimacy between brother and sister with their newly learned secret, kept hidden from the rest of the world.

'What I don't know is the why,' Brogar went on. 'You obviously know Mr Perdue, so why did you and your brother have to do anything on the sly?'

Frith cleared her throat, cheeks pale but endearingly dimpled, just like her brother's.

'We just wanted something of our da,' she said quietly. 'We heard about the island being sold and couldn't bear that he'd be left here all alone.'

'How d'you mean?' Brogar asked, no further along with the tale.

'Well, he's in number three,' the girl stated baldly. 'Got trapped in there years back and Charlie, well he couldn't stand that someone would come barging in and clear him out like he was load of nothing, nor me neither, come to that.'

Brogar frowned, this hardly explaining anything.

'So your father worked the mines with Merryweather and Perdue?'

Frith nodded assent.

'So why all the cover-up?' Brogar was completely perplexed. Men died in mines all the time, but certainly his co-workers would know about it, and the mines' owners too. So why would they leave him in there? He pinned Frith with a stare that was rarely ignored, but Frith was hanging her head, not looking at Brogar. Nor answering. For in truth she didn't know. This had

been Charlie's big idea, not hers; and he'd been infuriatingly vague about it all.

'I need to get word over to the mainland,' Brogar said, suddenly rousing himself, realising it must be almost three o'clock and the afternoon dark with the clouds coming in from the north; no chance of getting over the Rack later that night – even he'd wanted to – not with Perdue out of commission. There was Merryweather, of course, but Brogar had sized that man up in a moment and wouldn't trust him farther than he could spit: a man who'd taken no part in the day's drama, hadn't even bothered to come see what had transpired because of it, nor been there to help when Perdue needed it most.

'Where's Charlie?' Frith raised her head, looking over at Brogar, the thought simmering in her for a while, unable to decide whether or not to ask, whether or not Charlie would want it, no idea of what had happened to him earlier. 'He'd not have left me there, not if he'd been able. Not unless he's hiding out too, but that don't seem likely.'

Brogar weighed his options. A hysterical girl he didn't need, but this Frith seemed self-possessed and able, so he decided to tell her straight, get her on side.

'He had an accident in the shaft,' he said, 'but he's fine,' he added quickly. 'Over on the mainland with Mrs Doctor Tuley and in the best of care.'

Frith paled, steadied her back against the chair, but didn't panic, instead concentrated on what Brogar had said previously.

'So you're needing word over? Assuming we can't get back over in the dark?' she asked without need of answer. 'Will we know how Charlie is then?'

'We will,' Brogar smiled, and despite the crease of the scar that lent Brogar's face a continual look of menace, Frith could see beyond it.

'Well then,' she announced, 'we could use Mr Perdue's light, if someone's the other side to see it.'

'Someone'll be there,' Brogar answered, 'at least if I know Sholto, and I believe I do.'

Sholto and Gilligan soon had a merry little fire going on the foreshore of Balcary Bay, Hugh standing further down, trying to pinpoint the best angle for the sheet of metal Bill had conjured up from a small shed near the house.

'Used the best of it to make the operating unit in the hospital,' he said to Sholto's admiration, an admiration Bill shook off. 'Don't thank me for it. That was one of the dark months when I flung myself into doing anything and everything except my proper job. Hazel was the one drew up the plans and specifications, got the details right.'

Hazel had come out of the hospital to see what the sudden flurry of movement was all about; seeing her husband out of the house was such a shock she couldn't take another step, and when he came out of the shed brandishing his sheet of metal his face was so alive she could have cried. Did cry, going back into the hospital and closing the door, unwilling to break whatever spell Sholto had cast on her Bill, tears running freely down her face, hand held hard against her throat to stop the sobs, not wanting anyone to hear her, especially not when Bill left with the others for Balcary, an event so astonishing she could hardly get her breath.

'You alright, Missus?' Charlie had been so quiet she'd forgotten he was there. She sniffed, rubbed her fingers beneath her eyes, got herself back together.

'Quite alright, thank you,' she said, letting out a long held breath.

More than alright, she was thinking, a mad smile upon her face,

aware that somehow the world had changed, turned a corner, might be taking both her and her husband to a better kind of life.

'So what's this light of Perdue's run on?' Brogar was asking Frith as she led him from the workshop to the small square box of Perdue's sleeping quarters, noting the rungs that had been built into one of the walls, that the roof was flat and strong, designed specifically to take a man's weight.

'Don't know exactly,' Frith said. 'Was rather hoping you could figure it out. Don't want to wake Mr Perdue unless we absolutely have to.'

'Quite right, young Frith. Nothing like a challenge,' Brogar replied, launching himself up the rungs and onto the roof, Frith scampering up behind him, not wanting to be left out.

'Ingenious!' Brogar said as he studied the lamp that had been bolted into the wood. 'I've seen plenty of these used down mines but this one, well, it's far larger than I'd expected. See here, Frith?'

Frith followed Brogar's pointing finger, watched him opening various parts of the lamp to reveal its innards.

'It's in three sections,' he explained, 'water in the chamber at the top, calcium carbide in the base, the chamber in the middle carrying the burner. When the water is dripped through the adjustable valve onto the carbide it produces acetylene gas and the gas is then burned to produce the light.'

Brogar began fiddling with the valve, getting used to its settings, in luck because the lamp had been recently primed: enough water up top, enough carbide below, everything ready for the go.

'There's been loads of ships wrecked around Hestan,' Frith said at Brogar's side, eager as he to see how the light was put into action. 'Folk sometimes miss the Firth of Clyde in a storm and come into

the Solway by mistake, or get wronged by thinking Orchardton or the Rough are really the way in towards Dumfries.'

'I can well believe it,' Brogar said, as well he could, 'but Perdue put this light up on his own?'

'Guess so,' Frith wasn't sure. 'Think him and me da did it together.'

'Well, grand on them!' Brogar said. 'Look at the polish he's got on the reflector! I'm really very impressed. Shall we get it lit?'

Frith smiled, making the dimples in her cheeks all the more visible, not that Brogar noticed, intent as he was on getting everything right as he could before he set the light going.

'I can see a bonfire burning over at Balcary,' Frith said, having turned herself away from Brogar and the lamp, looking out towards Auchencairn as if Charlie might suddenly leap up and make himself know to her. 'And…ooh…look! Something's flashing!'

'You've got it!' Sholto said to Hugh as he shuffled about the sand with his sheet of metal, Bill Tuley coming alongside, squinting off towards the island.

'Not quite,' he said, 'a little to the left, Hugh, but only a little.'

Hugh did as commanded and, as he got himself repositioned, Gilligan began to jump up and down on the sand. They could barely see each other anymore, the afternoon become almost night, though it was barely past four.

'A light on the island!' Gilligan shouted. 'And it's flashing! Kinda dim, like, but can see it anywise!'

'Alright then,' Sholto said, straightening up from the fire. 'That's got to be Brogar. Is everyone ready?' Everyone was. 'Gilligan and Hugh, you're on lifting and dropping duty,' Sholto commanded, 'and keep that sacking sheet in place exactly as it is,' the boys eager and attentive, practising a few times to make sure they got it right.

'Bill, are you ready with your book? We really need help with what dots and dashes we need.'

'Ready!' Bill shouted back, exaltation in every movement because damn, it felt so good to be doing something practical and useful it seemed impossible he hadn't been able to do it before.

'Brogar's signalling,' Sholto had his eyes trained on the light on the island. 'Bill? I need your interpretation.'

Bill was at the ready, pen and notebook in hand, taking down every dot and dash as Sholto spelled it out to him.

'Frith…sa…fe…not… back…to…nigh…t…'

'Tell him that's fine,' Sholto said, 'and tell him Charlie's doing well.'

Bill nodded, staring intently at the relevant pages of *Army Life, and What Every Serving Civilian and Soldier Needs to Know During Wartime*, shouting out the relevant sequences of dots and dashes to Hugh and Gilligan, who hadn't quite got it down to pat, though enough for Brogar to get the gist, his own little helper – in the form of Frith – writing the letters down as Brogar sang them out.

'All…weel…Charie good…'

They were interrupted by someone stamping down the shingle, Skinner Tweedy's voice coming at them as he made the sand.

'So what's this little pantomime all about, then? Might have guessed it would be you lot.'

He was back to being affable again, which Sholto found a little disconcerting, but was polite in his reply.

'Brogar's going to be on the island for the night, too dark now to get back safely over.'

Skinner nodded.

'Sensible move. But if you're sending messages you might as well tell him that your lawyer friend, Fitzsimons, has been delayed. Just got word he'll be another few days arriving.'

Sholto wasn't surprised. Brogar had guessed as much and hadn't been wrong.

'Thank you,' he said. 'We'll let him know. Bill? Did you get that?'

'Got it,' Bill replied easily, squatting down by the fire, needing the light, getting his message out to Gilligan and Hugh.

'La…yer delay…d…few…da…s.'

If Skinner was surprised to see Bill Tuley with Heron's little band of visitors he made no mention of it.

'Impressive,' he said instead. 'Maybe you should tell your Brogar that he'll be missing out on pheasant tonight, for it's anyone's guess what muck Perdue and Merryweather will fling at him. They live no better than animals over there. And that light's a joke.'

Sholto frowned. How a man could be so friendly one minute and so barbed the next was beyond him.

'It seems to be doing a well enough job for us,' he informed Skinner Tweedy. 'Just one last message, Bill, and then we'll wrap it up.'

'Ready!' Gilligan shouted.

'Tell him we'll meet him first light and to bring Perdue with him. I've a couple of questions I need answering.'

These questions had occurred to him while they'd been at the Tuleys', to do with how long Perdue had been on the island, amongst other things. Like Brogar, he was uneasy that the Company's purchase of the island would been dispossessing Perdue and Merryweather of all they'd known for years, and Skinner being here had put a couple of ideas into his head about how to stop it.

'Meet you morning…' Bill spelled out the words. 'Bring Perdue… and Frith…' Bill added off his own bat, looking over at Sholto for approval.

'And Frith, of course,' Sholto smiled. 'Should've thought of that myself.'

They got an answering affirmative Yes: dash dot dash dash, dot, dot dot dot, followed by an intriguing sign off from Brogar:

'Mys…te…ris…ab…ond,' that had Sholto smiling. If there was a signal for an exclamation mark he'd no doubt Brogar would have used it, but there was not, and it occurred to him that Morse code – or Joseph Henry code, as Bill might have preferred it to be called – was all the poorer for not having it in its vocabulary.

Chapter 9

Old Tales, New Endings

Brogar might not have been about to dine on pheasant that night on Hestan Island, but he was happier where he was, preferring mucking about in the mire to fine dining any day of the week. Merryweather had turned up with a haunch of mutton that Frith was busily turning into something good, while Brogar and Merryweather sat at Perdue's table.

'So what's the what?' Merryweather asked, pouring Brogar a glug of spirits he'd made from heather and barley in his illicit still.

'Wasn't sure you'd much interest,' Brogar said, swilling the pale pink liquor around in his mug, 'what with you not showing up when we could've really done with your help.'

Merryweather cleared his throat, coughed up a glob of phlegm that he spat away onto the floor before tugging out his pipe and getting it lit, the uncommon stink of its smoke masked by whatever Frith was doing over on the stove.

'Never been one to stick me nose in,' Merryweather said, 'not when it ain't needed, and seems it ain't been needed this time neither.'

Brogar sat back in his chair and scratched his ear.

'Your friend, Perdue, could've died this afternoon. Went

headfirst into the sea while getting to the cave to fetch Frith out, and that's not your business?'

Merryweather had the grace to grimace, but wasn't intimated by this Brogar, not by a long chalk.

'Ken that now,' he said, 'but didn't ken it then. He's allus been a stupid fart far as being brave's concerned. Got up to his neck with it in th'army, and dragged me into it too, whether I liked or no. Which I didn't, by the by.'

Brogar took a slurp from his mug, pleasantly surprised by how good Merryweather's concoction proved to be.

'So let me take a stab at it, and you can fill in the blanks,' he said, Merryweather studying Brogar, but plainly Merryweather had had a few mouthfuls before coming over, his tongue just waiting to be loosened. 'You and Perdue joined up the Scottish arm of the Swedish army back, well, back when?'

'Early thirties,' Merryweather offered without hesitation. 'Young lads we was then, and plenty gone before us. Steady employment, bit of cash, them Swedes knowing better how to treat their soldiers than the English ever did.'

Brogar nodded. This much was true, Scottish soldiers being an essential adjunct to the Swedish army for hundreds of years, many making good, taking top rank and staying on, sons following in their fathers' footsteps, naturalised Swedes since the 1600s.

'So there was you, Perdue and Frith's father over there, and Heron too...' Brogar prompted, Merryweather letting out a huge puff of smoke and an unpleasant cackle.

'Heron too! That's a laugh! That came later. Nothing much doing in Sweden at the time, not since the Frenchies took over...'

'Jean-Baptiste Bernadotte, yes,' Brogar interrupted, tapping his fingers on the table, remembering his history lessons, quoting by rote. 'Avid supporter of the French Revolution and then Napoleon,

Governor of Hanover, invited by the Swedish Riksdag to take over from Charles XIII who was way past his best, to put it kindly. Bernadotte ruling until '44 as Charles XIV, family in monarchy ever since.'

Merryweather narrowed his eyes and looked at Brogar.

'You seem to know an awful lot about it.'

'As I should,' Brogar replied easily. 'Born in Scotland, but spent most of my life over the water. Excellent brew, by the way,' he added, taking another few sips, throwing Merryweather off guard. 'But the Scots and Scandinavians, we've always been close mixed. So what happened next?'

Merryweather was wrong-footed by these sudden changes in tack.

'Well, we was young,' he stuttered, 'wanted in the action, got an opportunity to skip over into Russia. Ye ken what they're like over there. Allus shifting borders, like a bloody bad game of Nine Men's Morris.'

Brogar was sympathetic.

'That seems about right. So where did you find yourselves?'

Merryweather puffed hard at his pipe, a deep crease forming across his brow.

'Aye well, didn't go too good, as luck would have it. Got stuck in Poland with them peasants and military all uprising and the Russians not liking that at all. All got a bit bloody, truth be told,' Merryweather scrunched up his face at the memories. 'Knocked ten bells out of us young 'uns. War looks like fun from the outside but from the in it's aye a different story.'

Brogar nodded.

'Always been the way. So why didn't you get out then?'

'Couldn't,' Merryweather said shortly. 'Was paid up members of the Ruskies by then, us all having taken a ten-year sub. But after

Wola, Heron saw a way to get us out. He'd connections see, being all high born an' that, and got us back to Tar…to the Crimea.'

'So you were stuck until when?' Brogar went on smoothly, affecting not to notice Merryweather's sudden correction, wondering what he'd been about to say. 'Early forties?'

'Aye,' Merryweather agreed quickly. 'Bit before. Least me and Perdue got out then, and came back here.'

'But not Stirling?' Brogar persisted, remembering what Frith had said about them all being tight back then, wondering whether Stirling had been tighter with Heron than the others.

'Archie was a bloody idiot,' Merryweather muttered. 'Took everything to heart and wouldn't let it go…both him and Kheranovich…'

Brogar looked over at Frith, but she carried on stirring her pots, apparently not mindful of what was being said, or maybe hadn't heard the undertone Merryweather had injected into his last words.

'So who's Kheranovich? And what do you mean by wouldn't let things go?' Brogar asked, but Merryweather had said his last.

'In no bloody way, an' no bloody business of yours anywise.' He stood up abruptly. 'Get the lass to bring us summat when she's done, but I've to be heading home, an' nothing more you're going to get outa me, Mr whoever the hell you think you are.'

Brogar didn't try to stop the man as he went for the door and tugged it open, flinging it back against the jamb, letting in some small scurries of the snow the sleet and hail had silently transitioned into.

'Informative,' Brogar said to himself as he got up and closed the door securely behind Merryweather.

'Everything alright?' Frith asked, alerted by the sudden departure of Merryweather.

'Everything just dandy,' Brogar replied. 'Any sign of food soon?'

'On its way,' Frith replied, happy to be helpful, happy to be here on Hestan, to know that Charlie was all right, that the sole man left at the table was a man she could count on and trust. She wasn't sure how she knew it, but she knew it all the same.

Over at Balcary, Sholto too was about to make several discreet enquiries. Gilligan and Hugh had been invited back to Auchencairn by Bill Tuley, who didn't want to let them out of his sight, worrying that his new energy and positivism would evaporate the moment they left his side.

'Might be able to get some exercises sorted to get Hugh used to having one eye,' Bill enticed them. 'Plenty men back in the field had the same problem…'

'It'd be right grand if you could stop him bumping into stuff,' Gilligan said, 'keep worrying he's going to catapult himself off a cliff or summat.'

He knocked a playful elbow into Hugh's arm, but wasn't exactly joking.

Bill smiled, surprised he'd managed to speak about being back in the field with such ease, without crumbling into a snivelling wreck like he usually did.

'It'd be my pleasure. And I'm sure that together me and Hazel can get some training plans in place.'

Me and Hazel, Bill thought, unable to remember the last time he'd put him and Hazel together in the same sentence.

'Alright with you, Mr Sholto?' Hugh asked.

'Alright with me,' Sholto was happy to agree. 'We'll come join you tomorrow when we've Frith and Brogar back from the island.'

And off they went, the sheet of metal Bill was carrying below his arm flashing brightly here and there as it caught the light of

the brands the two boys were carrying, the flames kept alive by a pot of grease Sholto had asked Skinner Tweedy to retrieve from the house.

'Quite the merry band,' Tweedy commented sarcastically as Sholto kicked sand over the remnants of the fire.

'Indeed,' Sholto answered. 'I hope you don't mind; it'll just me and you for that pheasant tonight.'

'All the more for us,' Tweedy said and began striding off for the house, Sholto having to run a few yards to catch him up.

'And while we wait for it,' he said, catching his breath, 'would you mind if I took a look at all the Company correspondence? I'd not ask normally, only now Fitzsimons is going to be late and Brogar's over on Hestan, I'll be kicking my heels a bit.'

'You can do what you like,' Tweedy answered. 'Nowt to do with me, and nowt needing hiding.'

Sholto tripped over a stone in the dark and swore loudly, partly at the stubbing his toes had got but mostly at Skinner Tweedy's infuriating changes of attitudes. The man was like those groups of knots that sped over the water at dusk, turning swiftly on the wing, under-feathers so white they almost disappeared in the fading light before flicking back into vision, revealing their darker side, and no way to predict when they would switch from one to the next.

Back at the house, Skinner Tweedy gave Sholto directions.

'Down that hallway and into the library,' he put a slight emphasis on the last word and twisted his lips in an odd kind of smile. 'Go right through it and out the other side and you'll find the office soon enough. Documents for the sale are all laid out on the desk ready for your lawyer feller, when he finally decides to turn up.'

Sholto was about to thank him, but Tweedy was already heading off to see to some errands of his own.

'You'll hear the gong when dinner's up!' he shouted back at Sholto, though didn't bother to turn his head, Sholto breathing a small sigh of relief that he was rid of the man, for a short while at least. He went down the darkened corridor, pushing open the door at the opposite end to emerge into a different world, the room aglow with a series of gas lamps on every wall where the space hadn't been taken up with books. Teetering on a sliding ladder, lighting the last of the lamps, was the girl who'd served them at dinner the night before, not that Sholto immediately noticed her.

'But this is magnificent!' Sholto exclaimed, glowing from the inside out, like one of the many gas lamps, as he gazed at the astonishing array of books and folios snug on their shelves, his unexpected entrance making the girl teeter on her ladder and sending it skidding a couple of inches to the left.

'I'm so sorry,' Sholto said, turning his head at the screech of the ladder on its rail, seeing her, blinking to bring himself back to the here and now. 'Esther, isn't it?'

'It is, sir,' she got herself down in a tangle of skirts, face pale as she blew out her lighting spill and made a clumsy curtsey. 'Are you needing anything? Can I fetch you tea or coffee? A glass of wine?'

'A glass of wine would be most welcome,' Sholto replied. 'But tell me, why are you lighting all the lamps in here when your master's not at home?'

'It were Skinner's…Mr Tweedy's idea,' she said, backing away to the door. 'Said he thought you looked a bookish type, if that's not saying too much.'

Sholto smiled in evident surprise, and couldn't have looked more bookish if he'd tried, his feet moving of their own accord towards the nearest bay of books, the library a complex warren of shelves designed to make best use of light from the wide windows during the day and gas lamps during the night.

'Skinner Tweedy said that?' Sholto muttered slowly, but didn't pursue the thought, his eyes already roving over spines and titles, pulling out first one volume and then another, Esther smiling and leaving him to it, retreating to fetch him his wine. Skinner Tweedy might be her most absolutely unfavourite person in all the world but it could never be said of him that he couldn't read people as simply and quickly as this man could obviously read books.

'He seems a bit touchy,' Brogar commented to Frith, once they'd made themselves comfortable at the table when she'd got back from delivering a good portion of food to Merryweather down the way. 'Is he always like that?'

Frith smiled.

'It's just his way,' she said. 'A bit private, like. Don't like getting involved. Never has done, never will; and don't like women, nor children, nor anyone really, come to that.'

'Well, he's found the right place to be living,' Brogar smiled as Frith ladled out two bowls of stew, the mutton falling away from the bone as she went at it with her fork, heaping Brogar's plate high.

'This smells good, Frith,' Brogar said, picking up his spoon and tucking in.

'Mr Perdue's got quite a bit of herbs and stuff,' Frith said shyly. 'Just got to know what goes together.'

'As you obviously do,' Brogar was appreciative. The girl could really cook. 'Tell me,' he asked between mouthfuls, 'you ever hear of anyone called Kheranovich?'

Frith put down her spoon and looked at Brogar with curiosity.

'Well of course. That's old Mr Heron. That was his name when he was back in Russia, long before he came here. Big friend of me da's. It's him what bought this whole place up and the reason me da brought me ma and us back here, else we'd never have left.'

Brogar's turn to still his spoon and look over at his dining companion.

'How'd'you mean? Where did you leave from?'

'We come over from Gen-i-chesk,' Frith explained, pronouncing the word slow and precise. 'That's a place in Russia. Well, not Russia exactly, or that's what me mam always said. "We're Tatars," she always used to tell us, "and proud of it."'

'Genichesk Tatars,' Brogar looked over at Frith with interest, 'water end of the Arabat Tongue by the Sea of Azov?'

'That's right!' Frith's eyes brightened. She'd never met anyone her whole life who'd ever heard of the place, let alone knew its whereabouts, not that she exactly knew herself. It had always been a kind of mystery, strange words conjuring up stranger fantasies: Genichesk, Arabat, Azov and the Putrid Sea. Places her mother talked about occasionally, giving her children an exotic adjunct to their past, Frith and Charlie using the unusual words to make up unusual stories, dreaming about what those places might be like. 'An' me an' Charlie,' she added, smiling up at Brogar, 'we're going to go back there one day. We was only tiny when we left but Mam's still got folk there what'll know us and see us right when we do.'

'*Not a hill, not a tree, not a stone*,' Brogar quoted the Dutch traveller who'd been to that area of the Crimea a couple of decades before Brogar had arrived to investigate the mud volcano at Kertch, that some folk rumoured had been throwing up diamonds, which of course it hadn't, although occasionally some mud volcanoes did exactly that.

Frith frowned.

'Me mam used to say that exact same thing. Like a proverb it was, local anywise, but she alwus said it weren't true.'

'She was right,' Brogar answered, taking up his spoon again, starting in at his meal with gusto. 'A vile calumny on a very unusual

and beautiful place,' he added between mouthfuls, 'if you discount the mosquitoes and the locusts. Those aside, that area of the Pontic Steppe is remarkably fertile. But what I find more interesting is when and why your dad – and Heron, or Kheranovich – were there. Do you happen to know anything more?'

Frith shrugged, picking at her meal.

'Dunno, not exactly. Ma and Da knew each other way back, but were only married early fifties, me and Charlie coming along a few years after.'

'Slap damn in the middle of the Crimean War,' Brogar said thoughtfully. 'Well, that's some kind of fit.'

But only some. What didn't fit was that half a word Merryweather had let slip, if by his truncated *Tar...* he'd meant Tatary, for he'd implied him and his fellow soldiers had been there in the early 1830s, not the 1850s. He needed to talk to Sholto. If it was possible that the combined histories of Heron-Kheranovich, Stirling, Perdue and Merryweather could supply ammunition for not getting the latter depopulated from Hestan then he meant to pursue it. He looked over at Frith, about to ask more questions, but noticed she'd hardly eaten anything despite him by now having consumed a good half of his enormous plate of food.

'Something troubling you?' he asked, Frith pulling a weak smile.

'Not really, just thinking about me mam, wishing she'd not died last year before having the chance to meet you...someone who's been where she's from. She'd have loved talking about the old country with someone who knew it. She was always so sad after me da disappeared, and always wanting to go home, not that she'd the means to.'

Brogar took a moment before replying.

'Well, I'm sorry I never met her,' he said. 'Hankering after the homeland is something I understand. My folk never forgot

Scotland after leaving, always talked about it, and it's been a bit of a discovery for me coming back. Kind of feel it here,' he added, thumping a fist to his heart. 'But tell you what I do know, and that's an old folk tale from where your mam was from. Do you want me to tell it you?'

'Do I!' Frith looked up, dimples deep in her cheeks as she gazed up at Brogar in unconcealed admiration.

'Very well then,' Brogar said. 'But first let's finish our dinner – and I want to see a bit of that mutton down your neck seeing as how you cooked it so good – and then we'll get ourselves about the fire and tell the story as properly as every story should be told.'

Sholto still hadn't made it through to the office. He'd sat down at a desk in Heron's library and was perusing several interesting tomes. Quite a few, he'd found, were in languages he recognised but couldn't read: Arabic, Hebrew, Farsi and Turkish amongst them. His grasp as a linguist centred on the Indo-European tongues, and he'd found a few volumes on the Crimean War in Russian and English he was keen to read more of, try to make sense of Bill and Hazel's experiences over there. He'd not known much about it before, but learned now that it had bizarrely originated as a territorial dispute between Russia and France about various possessions in the Palestinian Holy Lands, the Russians unhappy they'd not secured so many rights there as the French and, in retaliation, forcibly occupying several territories of the Ottoman Empire designed to give them reign over the Black Sea ports; which actions, like one tree falling in a forest that fells a second tree that fells a third, led to Turkey refusing to be subdued, declaring war on Russia, getting thoroughly drubbed at a battle in Sinope, which in turn stung England and France to join the Turks in order to keep the Russians out of the lucrative trading

posts of the Crimean Peninsula – that were a particularly valuable conduit from East to West and back again. So far so bad – a precise illustration of how wars were begun so unnecessarily, when all that really needed doing was people sitting down and thrashing it all out about a table.

Sholto closed those books and moved on to another that was far more interesting, at least to him. Badly bound, and with a scrappy illegible label half torn from its spine, like any decent bibliophile he was curious to know what it contained. Evidently it was a catalogue or inventory of some great library, presumably bought by Heron and incorporated into his own, for Sholto recognised a number of the listed titles on the shelves around him, those he'd previously noted as being in Eastern and Turkic scripts. They may have been outside his ken but, like a botanist capable of grouping one family of un-before-seen flowering plants from the next, so he grouped those books now. He creased his brows, concentrating first on the scrawly handwritten title page of the inventory from which the only information to be garnered was that the collection had been acquired sometime in the 1830s on Black Sea shores, before flipping carefully and slowly through its brittle pages, studying the tiny scribbles by one entry or another that indicated several volumes had been sold here and there and for how much. And some of the sums involved were quite staggering, many of them far more than a labourer might be able to earn during half a lifetime. Obviously whoever had compiled this inventory and sold those books knew what they doing, selling very specific volumes to very specific buyers and getting the very highest price for them. And he had a suspicion about who that might be.

He stood up and walked to the farther end of the library and out the other side and there, just as Skinner Tweedy had promised, was Heron's office – a small room tucked away to one side of yet

another long corridor – all the relevant documents to the sale of Hestan laid out upon the desk. Sholto glanced at those documents but didn't pick them up, instead went to the filing cabinets. All the drawers bar one were locked, but he riffled through the open one, finding various folders of correspondence to do with the running of the estate – copies of letters to creditors, to debtors, lists of annual outgoings and expenditures, sheep dipping details, veterinary bills, documents pertaining to markets and sales. He didn't find what he was looking for until he came to the last two folders – old and stained – containing a few letters signed by the older Heron, father to James, the present owner. Unmistakably the same handwriting as that of the inventory. He glanced briefly through the small stash and caught the corner of a piece of paper, pulling it out, perusing its contents, raising his eyebrows. He thought on that last message Brogar had sent him from the island: 'Mys…te…ries…ab…ound', and knew Brogar was right. Something more was going on here in Hestan, Balcary and Auchencairn than the mere sale of an island that might or might not have valuable resources of copper. He slid shut the drawer of the filing cabinet, rolled his shoulders and would have returned to his ruminations in the library had the gong not just then resounded about the house, summoning him to the dinner table. He smiled, looked out into the darkness beyond the study windows and thought on what was to come: another adventure, but so far no deaths, for which simple grace he was truly thankful.

Kerr Perdue was uneasy in his sleep, having one of his old dreams again, one that had never truly left him behind. He was outside the farmhouse again, Kheranovich pointing his finger, thin pink dawn scratched beneath a heavy roll of cloud; Tupikov getting closer, his men black sticks behind him; the only sounds the rustle of leaves

beneath Perdue's feet, the cough and spit of Merryweather in the morning and Kheranovich's voice, low and steady.

'Do nothing, say nothing. Leave it all to me.'

Not so hard for Merryweather and Perdue, who had a grasp of the Russian language but no fluency, always needing Kheranovich to interpret the finer points for them, Tupikov getting close and closer in the gloom: twenty yards distant, ten yards, five, then looming two heads above them with the elevation of his steed; the smell of leather and sweat and the lingering smoke from last night's fire; Perdue's shirt wet within his armpits as he lifted his hand in stiff salute; quick bark of Russian as Tupikov pushed himself up in his stirrups and down again, sending his stick men off to the barn, Kheranovich going with them, relaxed, unperturbed, proud smile on his face as he turned and gave them a merry wave, all going well, all going well, all going...

Kerr woke abruptly, skin clammy, a heaviness to his chest, blood thumping, a couple of herring gulls landing heavily on his roof, stumping about as they settled to their roost, faint noise out there in the night like the beat had escaped his heart – but only the familiar sound of waves booming and reverberating as they flowed into rock-traps and were released again, smashing into new waves eager to take their place. Only the waves, and the pile of blankets that was smothering him. No Tupikov, no barn, no whatever came next. Perdue pushed his arms free, rolled over, closed his eyes, and tried to will himself back to sleep.

CHAPTER 10

THE STORY

'So here's the story,' Brogar began, stomach full, him and Frith sitting around the wood stove, a cup of Merryweather's heather brew in their hands, the wind madly skirling about the corners of the wooden workshop, background noise of splashing sea. They might have been the last two people on the earth.

'There once was an old couple living on the shores of the Azov Sea, or the Surozke More as it's known in old Russian. They'd lived a good life, poor but always God-fearing, their only sadness being they'd had no children to look after them now they were nearing their end.'

Frith smiled, leaning forward slightly. All the lamps had been extinguished, the light from the open hatch on the stove jumping about Brogar's face, his voice deep and dark, like every storyteller's should be.

'And so they made a boy out of salt dough,' he went on, 'dried him off on top of a stove just like this…'

'But it was the Eve of Saint Nicholas,' Frith put in, excitement shining on her face, 'and he came alive!'

Brogar was taken aback.

'Well yes. That kind of steals away the moment, if you know the tale already.'

'Oh but no!' Frith said. 'Please don't stop! It's only that me mam used to start a story just like this…a boy made of dough who comes alive and goes on to do heroic deeds. Maybe you heard it the same place she did. Where did you hear it?'

Brogar took a sip of his drink and leaned back in his chair.

'I heard it where the tale began, on the shores of the Azov. And yes, the boy went on to do heroic deeds, but not at first. Not at all.'

Frith frowned.

'How not?'

'Maybe your mother only told you parts of the tale,' Brogar said, 'because it started badly, as many tales do.'

'Please tell me,' Frith said, her young face looking up at Brogar. 'It's so long since I've heard it.'

Brogar relented.

'Well alright. It goes like this: the boy came alive, just as you said. St Nicholas's gift to the old couple who'd never done anything wrong in their lives. But St Nicholas always has an edge to him, as you'd know if you'd ever lived in Finland like I have, for there he's not known as a kindly person but one who's inclined to exact retribution from folk who wish for more than they've already got. And the dough boy, who was given the name Kamyr Batyr, was so strong that he broke another boy's back with a bat when they were out playing in the snow.'

'Broke his back?' Frith whispered. 'Mam never mentioned that.'

'Maybe not,' Brogar went on, 'but that's how the tale must start, because that's when the boy was banished from the village, banished from the Azov, breaking his parents' hearts all over again. He walked deep and deeper into the dark forest he'd been told never to go into, smashing down trees with his bat as he went,

almost killing a man who was resting beneath them, another man who'd buried himself deep in the forest, who walked so fast he'd had to tie his legs together to slow himself down.'

'But that's terrible,' Frith interjected, shaking her head. 'I don't think this is the same story at all.'

'That's the thing about stories, Frith,' Brogar said, patting her on the shoulder. 'They change; get adapted to whatever is going on about them when they're told. As for Kamyr-Batyr, on he goes, the man with tied legs thrown over his shoulders like a goatskin; until they meet another man – very old, with a white beard, and a bald head black with frostbite. "Why don't you put on your cap?" they ask the old man, who is clutching his woollen hat in his hands. "I cannot," says the old man, "for when I do, a blizzard covers everything from left to right, from back to forward, and the whole land will be smothered in ice."'

'And then they meet the bowman?' Frith asked, hoping this was so, that the story would end well like it had when her mother told it.

'They do, Frith,' Brogar answered. 'They meet a boy so unnaturally gifted at shooting his bow he too has been banished from his home, his family fearing he's a changeling, and not of their own folk at all…'

Sholto entered the dining room. He wasn't much looking forward to spending an evening with Skinner Tweedy, but his stomach had got the better of him, and anyway he had questions now, about Merryweather and Perdue. He was surprised to find a man he'd not met before sitting at the head of the table.

'James Heron,' the man said, standing up immediately on Sholto's entrance, holding out his hand, Sholto moving forward, shaking it, ushered then to his seat by the maid Esther.

'You've a very interesting library, Mr Heron,' Sholto said, noting Skinner Tweedy's skewed smile at his words, wondering if he'd been deliberately stalled by it from going into the study.

'Not mine,' James Heron replied, a smile twitching beneath the dapper beard and moustaches that framed his broad and high-cheeked face, 'but my father's. Not for me, all those books,' he added, sitting down again, shaking out his napkin. 'I'm more at home talking beet yields and cattle, as Skinner has undoubtedly already told you.'

Sholto looked over at Skinner Tweedy but got no reaction; yesterday, Lord of the Manor, today deferential and unwilling to offer opinion.

'Still, it's a substantial collection,' Sholto said. 'Some very interesting volumes…'

'Bah! Let's not talk books,' James Heron interrupted him. 'Can't think of anything more tedious. Let me tell you instead about the greatest towns of industry the world's ever seen! Ever visited Manchester or Lancaster, Mr…McKay, was it?'

'Shol…' Sholto began, but was immediately cut off.

'Can't tell you enough about the textile mills there. Been hammering out an agreement on wool, and those clearances up north and in Cumbria these past decades? Well, they've done us a huge service. Thought it might knock down the price, but not a bit of it! We imported 100,000 tons of wool last year as a nation and exported less than half of that, so think how much shortfall there is to make up! Wool, wool and more wool is what's wanted, plus any flax for linen they can get their hands on. Matter of fact, I'm thinking of diversifying…'

Sholto scratched distractedly at his neck, got through the soup and the fish, all the while wishing he was out on Hestan with Brogar, for James Heron simply didn't seem able to stop talking.

'And human hair. Now there's another import I've been learning the facts on. Mostly from Germany and France. Come spring, the Paris merchants send agents out all over France to collect their wares. Women the country over cultivating their hair like others grow wheat or strawberries. Can you imagine! And factor in that a head of hair weighs on average eight to twelve ounces and, depending on its colour, is worth up to sixty shillings per pound; that in France alone they gather two hundred thousand pounds of the stuff every year – that's almost ninety tons – well, you see where I'm going. There's a hidden harvest all around us and only someone like me needed to set it in motion.'

James Heron was a man who, as Sholto's mother would have said – Sholto obscurely glad to have remembered the phrase – bummled and bullered, as raw-gabbed in his chatter as a tap you can't shut off. Not even Skinner Tweedy got a word in edgeways, and Sholto found out more than he wanted to know in the next hour and a half of their dinner about the wool industry and the industrial revolution going on in Manchester and Lancaster that was apparently making England the lynchpin of the world. Even when he actively stopped listening he couldn't help but hear the words, tried to distract himself by thinking on what he'd found in the study, then by looking over at Skinner Tweedy, at the way his head jerked ever so slightly forward when he speared his food with his fork in a way that reminded Sholto of a crow going at carrion, switching his gaze next to Esther who hovered like a vapour in the corner of the room until she was beckoned forward, Sholto moving his eyes politely back to James Heron every now and then. He was a handsome man, no doubting that, an impression bolstered by the confidence with which he held himself and spoke, every movement seemingly imbued with direction and intent. He was young, maybe twenty-five, everything about him clean and

determined, with just a touch of flamboyance – his suit threaded through with just enough blue that you only saw it when the light hit it just right, his lapels slightly wider than was usual, the buttons opalescent with mother of pearl, his tie a minor shade of salmon pink. All exactly, Sholto thought, as fitted his apparent personality. The only part of him not so ordered was his hair, which was blond and unruly, as if he'd forgotten to put a comb through it before coming down to dinner.

'And with the selling of Hestan,' James was droning on, 'we'll get enough of a cash injection from your Company, Mr McKay, to put some of these new ideas into action. They say German wool is the best, but I'm sure we can do better. And there's a great many estate fields we can convert to get flax growing on them. Get ahead of the game.'

Sholto groaned inwardly. No way he was going to get any of his questions shoehorned into this conversation, but thank God only the dessert to go and soon he could retire for the night.

'They met another man,' Brogar was telling Frith, 'your bowman, who could shoot out a lark's eye at a hundred paces.'

'And then the dough boy…Kamyr…' Frith was hesitant with the name, it not having featured in the tale before.

'And then the dough boy, Kamyr-Batyr,' Brogar finished for her, 'met the girl he wanted to marry, but her father was inevitably the king of some place or other, this being a story. And the king did the usual, setting Kamyr-Batyr an impossible task.'

'But it wasn't impossible at all!' Frith said.

'Well it was for most men, but not for Kamyr-Batyr, who had companions to see him through. "Let's see how fast you or your men can run," says the girl's father, Kamyr-Batyr agreeing, setting down the man with tied feet and slashing the ropes through with

a knife. And off he went, fast as a hare, but goes so fast he tires quickly and falls asleep.'

'Shot back into action by the bowman aiming an arrow to nick his hand!' Frith went on enthusiastically.

'Precisely so,' agreed Brogar. 'Fast man gets back going and wins his race, but the girl's father is not content, and absolutely doesn't want Kamyr-Batyr – a peasant from nowhere – to be his daughter's husband and locks them all up in a barn and sets fire to it, a horrible end for anyone.'

A shiver seemed to go round the room, the two of them involuntarily hunching their shoulders against it.

'But it's not the end,' Frith said slowly, 'at least it wasn't the end in ma's tale. Does yours end differently?'

'Not at all,' Brogar confirmed with a broad smile, 'because all that needs to be done is for the old man to put on his cap on so down comes the blizzard and down comes the snow and down comes the ice across the entire kingdom. Gist is that it puts out the fire, everyone is saved, and Kamyr-Batyr gets his girl.'

Frith stared into the open stove, watching the flames teetering over their partially consumed logs, caught by some unexpected wisp of draught.

'But what happened afterwards?' she asked, gazing intently into the fire. 'Were they happy, the two of them? They didn't even really know each other, did they? And especially not the girl, who never got a say in the matter. And what happened to the rest of them? Did the runner have to tie his feet together for the rest of his life? And what about the old man's frostbite? Did he ever get better?'

Brogar looked over at Frith with curiosity. He'd told many a tale about many a fire, most of them – unlike this one – having truth at their core, but no one had ever looked so far beyond the tale's end. It struck him as very odd that she could empathise so deeply with

characters from a far-fetched fairy tale.

'What do you think happened?' he asked, leaning forward to catch her words.

'Think that maybe it ended badly after all,' Frith said very quietly. 'Think nothing's ever the fairy tale it seems.'

Brogar moved back with astonishment.

'Now why would you say that?' he asked, caught between a frown and a smile. Too old for her years she seemed, too old by far.

'Because she's right,' came another voice, the two of them looking up to find Kerr Perdue standing at the door that he'd opened a crack without them noticing, the source of that shivering, that sudden wisp of wind; Kerr having woken in his bed cold and alone and in darkness, the fire and lamp having burned themselves out, suddenly in need of company, light and warmth.

The night outside was utterly dark, the snow having ceased, glimpses of stars beyond the clouds. He'd made his way towards the workshop with practised step and heard them talking as he'd approached and recognised snatches of their words leaking into the outer world, listening intently to the last part of the story, feeling the echo of it in his bones, closing his eyes, leaning against the jamb, pulling his blanket about his shoulders.

'Because she's right,' he'd said on the exhalation of a long held breath as he came inside and closed the door behind him, thinking now that maybe it was time to tell his own tale, and what came afterwards.

CHAPTER 11

OLD MEMORIES, NEW ENEMIES

Merryweather finished the last scrapings of the stew Frith had brought him, burping loudly, shoving the dish and spoon into the sink, pushing viciously at the pump that brought salt water from the Solway into his home. But let them wait. He wasn't going to clean them now. He'd other things to think about, like how much he'd let slip to that bloody interloper up at Perdue's. Nobody was supposed to know anything about what had happened back then – all part of the pact – and that bloody girl being there? Jesus. What had he been thinking? Thinking nothing, was what. All these years on the island, just him and Perdue, never mattering what was said between them. Got to be a habit, he supposed, opening his mouth without thinking. He screwed his face up in frustration, felt something moving in his beard. Another bloody louse that would need combing out in the morning. Lord, but things had got so complicated. Maybe it was best for them all that young Heron was selling everything out from under their feet. Maybe it would undo everything that had been done, or maybe find what they'd never done. That would be a laugh to curdle all their stomachs. He wondered briefly if James had the least idea

what his father had been about, but it seemed unlikely. He'd always been a straightforward child, hands on, practical, liking anything mechanical or animal; and had grown into a straightforward man whose only interest lay in the estate and the farms, doing more to build it up in the several years since his father had died than old Heron had done in all his years here. But then old Heron had other reasons for settling in this neck of the woods.

Merryweather stood by the window, lamp in hand, the darkness a visceral weight all about him. He looked towards Copper Cove and thought how much darker it must have been for Archie Stirling when he'd died there. He hung his head, closed his eyes. He'd never really thought on it before, how Archie must have gone when the ill-built props had collapsed, just as Kerr had warned might happen.

'You can't use that wood, Archie,' he'd advised. 'Them's green and not cured. You'll need to leave them to dry before you get them in.'

But of course Archie hadn't listened, like Archie never did. Always one to rush in without thinking forward ever since he was a lad, just like when he'd put his grand proposal to his friends.

'We've to get over to Sweden!' he'd announced one morning, not long after him and Perdue had turned seventeen and Archie almost there too, never mind that by then they'd all been apprenticed for several years – Merryweather to the smithy, Perdue to the carpenters, Archie to the leather works – and would be earning good money if they only stayed the course.

'But it'll be grand!' Archie assured them. 'Loads of men gone on before us and a guaranteed ladder to the top. Think on it, lads: a proper career in foreign lands, and all the adventures we'll ever need.'

Merryweather screwed up his eyes hard, feeling the tears coming, because yes, they'd had adventures, but adventures

Merryweather for one would rather have done without. If only they'd stayed, if only they'd picked Archie Stirling up that wild morning and chucked him into the sea, told him where he could stuff his grand ideas and to leave them to the life they were meant to live. But they'd not done that. Like idiots, they'd allowed the smiling, beguiling Archie to lead them on, like when they were kids: over the Abbey walls to nick some stone to build a proper den that had promptly collapsed with the weight, knocking Archie senseless; putting out snares for rabbits and getting it wrong so Kerr almost lost a thumb; getting into Matheson's orchards to pinch some apples and plums – and Jesus, the drubbing they'd got from that. Couldn't sit down for a week; but never learning, not him, not Kerr, always taking Archie seriously, following him all the way to Sweden and into Russia, and from Russia to Poland where they'd witnessed the worst men can do to other men, and been forced by necessity to do the same. All because of Archie, the Pied Piper of Auchencairn, who could lead you into situations you couldn't get out of.

Merryweather thought on the years of calm that had come over him and Kerr once Heron had got them out, brought them home, years when all they did was hard but regular: building the cottage, working at the copper, keeping themselves together by the crofting and egg collecting, the carving and the birds; years undisturbed and unremarkable. Until Archie had burst once again into their lives and changed everything, like he seemed to do wherever he went, like he couldn't stop himself, like he was a river that was constantly bursting its banks and had no notion of what it was to be easy and slow.

He thought on the young bundles of storm petrels they used to hoik out of their burrows with hooked sticks, how they'd thread some of Archie's leathering-needles with a wick and push the point

from gullet to tail, set the wicks burning, the little birds so filled with fat they burned and spat like the best kind of lamps until all that was left was a little pile of feathers and bones. Archie all over that was – both the doing and the being – quick and inventive, a bright light leading the way until he burned himself out far too young, the wood giving way and breaking his back, splintering his bones, the weight of Hestan falling in on him and snuffing him out.

The son being hauled out of shaft number three this morning had set the memories in motion again, giving Merryweather a horrid itchy feeling in his teeth and gums. No hiding their Archie now, not with the younger one apparently knowing all about it. How he knew, Merryweather wasn't sure. Certainly not from him or Perdue, keeping quiet all these years so Archie's wife and kids wouldn't lose their army pension. Not that Merryweather cared directly about Archie's family, and certainly not the wife, for – to his way of thinking – this was pretty much all her fault. If she hadn't been greeting so piteously back in Genichesk the night they'd shifted the books they wouldn't even have known she existed, and they wouldn't have watched out for her when Tupikov gave his orders, wouldn't have cared a farthing about him burning down the barn and the farming family with it, her included; and Archie's heroic actions would never have come to pass, would never have been given the opportunity to bind him and Kheranovich together heart and soul until the end of their respective lives.

Merryweather shook his head, put down the lamp, took out his pipe and stuck a fresh plug of tobacco into the bowl. In a few weeks – maybe even days – he and Perdue would be chucked off of Hestan, and in an odd way he was relieved. Christ knew what either of them was going to do but at least it was an end, and an end, at the moment, was all he wanted. He'd always hated knowing

Archie's bones were still down there where they'd left him and he shivered sometimes, out of nowhere, having the unpleasant feeling that Archie was still here, standing just out of sight behind his shoulders so he could never catch sight of him, turning as he turned. Like tonight, for instance, when he'd stumbled back over the oft trod path from Kerr's workshop to his cottage, drunk and angry, his light as tottery as he was, glancing to left and right to keep to the path, his heart missing a beat when he got too close to Copper Cove and was certain – absolutely certain – he'd seen Archie there, coming out of shaft number three, Archie unbending suddenly, staring up at him as if he'd weight and form, as if he'd heard Merryweather. Merryweather had stood several moments on the lip of the cove, shining his lamp in that direction, blood pulsing wildly, before turning quickly away.

Shaking his head.

Because it couldn't have been Archie.

How could it have been?

Even so, he was tired of thinking it might be so, tired of looking at shadows the wrong way round, like they were always coming back at him.

He'd sobered up with the walking and the food, and made a decision. He'd go to Kerr in the morning and agree to what Kerr had occasionally mooted down the few years since Heron's death, which was simply to tell the story, get everything out in the open and let happen what would happen. He picked up his lamp again and sucked at his pipe, heard a noise outside and a tentative knock at his door. No doubt Frith, bringing more stew, or maybe even Kerr himself, which would be a blessing; no chance for Merryweather to waver.

He managed a small smile. He'd told that interloper from the Company over at the workshop that Kerr had been the fart who

took them both where Merryweather had never wanted to go, but that had never been true. Fact was that Kerr had provided him the only real stability he'd ever known. Him and Kerr, always him and Kerr trying to hold out over Archie's maddest ideas. Him and Kerr over there, him and Kerr back here on Hestan. Not all bad. Not bad at all. Merryweather aware he'd always been a grumpy sod, but Kerr knew that too and understood, saw through it somehow and offered a kinship that managed to move beyond it.

He opened the door, expecting Frith or Kerr or even Archie's wretched ghost, but it was none of them and he was so surprised he couldn't speak, and no more did his visitor speak to him, but took a sudden step inside, catching Merryweather so sharply by the elbow that Merryweather knocked the lamp over, shattering the glass, releasing the oil in a slow drip from its belly, catching to flame as Merryweather's pipe fell from his open mouth as he was shoved to one side, falling so hard to his knees that he cracked both patellae. Not that he felt it, for he'd been overtaken by a pain far worse and tried to blink against the awful obstruction that had been thrust into his eye socket, severing his optic nerve, ripping right through it and going on up into his brain, the job finished by a boot coming down on Merryweather's neck that jammed his face into the packed-earth floor, pushing the obstruction as far as it could go; Merryweather gasping as he went, the pool of burning oil spreading out to one side of him, licking at his jacket, at his trousers. Merryweather aware of the flames flickering in the corner of his only functioning eye, trying to figure out what was going on, drawing in one last breath, letting it go again, seeing the flames jump and flicker on his horizon, but a horizon that was getting darker, darker, quick and fast, like the sea running over the sands from Hestan to Auchencairn and nothing he, nor any man, could do to stop it.

Chapter 12

The Nightjar Flexes Its Claws

Gilligan and Hugh were settled comfortably in their new surroundings of the Tuleys' home. Charlie Stirling had hobbled through on his crutches to join them. It took him a while to get used to this new way of moving, a kind of hopping jump necessitated by Hazel commanding him not to put any weight at all on his bad leg, not for the first few days at least.

'We'll get Gilligan up at the carpenter's again tomorrow to get you a clog made,' she informed him. 'But until then, you're not even to put that foot on the ground.'

Charlie had grimaced as he'd edged his way off the hospital bed with his crutches shoved beneath his armpits, grabbing at the handles put at elbow height down its length, toppling back to the bed the first few times he tried it, unable to get his body to put into action what his head was telling it to do, but eventually he had it.

'Well now,' Hazel commented, once they were all sat together on sofa and chairs. 'So we've two new patients needing care. What d'you think about that, Bill?'

She smiled warmly up towards her husband who was standing a little shakily by his drinks cabinet, pouring out several glasses of

wine, his own notably better filled than the rest. He took a large swig, swiftly uncorked a second bottle and refilled his glass to the brim before turning to hand the others their own tipples. Hazel's smile wavered as she watched this sleight of hand, but Bill was standing taller and stronger than he'd done for a long while, and when he gave Hazel her own glass there was a steadfastness to his expression, a determination that he squeezed into a small smile.

'I think it's grand,' he said, and must have meant it, for he left the newly opened bottle on the cabinet and came and sat down with the rest. 'In fact,' he went on, 'I've been thinking about what we can do for Hugh...'

Hugh beamed, and Gilligan knocked an elbow against his friend's arm.

'Soon have you riding racehorses and winning the girls' hearts,' he said, making Hugh blush.

'Well, I'm not sure about that,' Hugh replied, looking up hesitantly at Hazel as if this might really be the case.

'Odd you should mention horses,' Bill went on, standing up again, finding it hard to keep still in company, his usual practice being – as both he and Hazel knew – to come down late to his surgery in the morning, stick it out for as long as he could before going back up again to his room with a couple of bottles tucked under his arm and a tray of whatever food Hazel had prepared for him.

'Why horses?' Hugh asked, fixing his eye on Bill Tuley as he roved the room, went from one end of it to the next before coming back and sitting down again.

'Well, because horses,' Bill said, left leg jittering as he sat, Hazel wincing to see her husband becoming aware of it and placing a hand upon it to try to keep it still, Bill ploughing on regardless, 'even trained ones on the hunt, don't usually like to leap ditches,

jump fences, run through thickets. It goes against their innate sense of danger…'

He forced both hands down on his legs to calm himself, that single word 'danger' setting his nerves jangling, his heart racing, feeling ridiculous and weak in front of these boys, aware of his failings like never before. Quick drink, and everything in his world was right again, for a while at least. But couldn't do that now, didn't want to show himself up, let them see the shaking in his hands, in his body, the tremors leaking out from the very core of him.

'They have to learn those skills,' Hazel broke in to give her husband time to collect himself. 'Go against their natural instincts headlong into what appear to be dangerous situations. They have to learn to trust their sight, their reflexes, and the input from their riders.'

'Exactly,' Bill added quickly, casting a grateful glance at Hazel, Hazel not having missed the swift slant of Bill's eyes towards his glass, the twitch of his hand going the same direction, proud that he'd resisted. 'Anyway,' he went on, 'what I think we could do is this: Hugh needs to re-educate his brain to the fact that he only has one eye and not two, and it's the second eye that allows the brain to make the calculations of what is near and what is far, what is shallow and what is deep.'

'We're to train him like a horse?' Gilligan asked, perplexed, seeing Hugh in his mind's eye saddled up, and not liking that one bit. 'But how're we to do that?'

'Well…' Bill started and then stopped, looked down at his feet, fists clenched as they lay upon his thighs, Hazel recognising the signs and that Bill was about to give up at the first hurdle. She decided to take a chance.

'Didn't you develop that obstacle course, Bill?' She was about to add 'back in the Crimea', but stopped herself just in time.

'Remember the one? You had me putting out barrels and all sorts...'

Bill closed his eyes and shuddered, Hazel fearing she was pushing him too far for one night, but Bill lifted his face a moment later, fists loosening as the idea took hold.

'That's right,' he said, eyes bright and feverish, 'I did, didn't I? We put out barrels and odd shapes of metal and canvas, marked out walkways with string and put up a few small fences...and it worked a treat. And that's what we'll do tomorrow, boys. By God, yes! That's what we'll do!'

'Why don't you start sketching it out,' Hazel wanted to stretch the moment, 'while I fetch us something to eat?'

She stood up and motioned everyone to the table, fetching paper and pencils and laying them down, pleased to see that Bill was helping Charlie move from one seat to another, kicking a small stool along with him so Charlie could rest his leg.

'And I've not forgotten about you, lad,' Bill said, as he settled Charlie, 'though there's not much we can do for you for a while, not until that plaster's off, which will be...when will that be, Hazel?'

Hazel was already on her way out to the kitchen beyond, but she turned at the words and shook her head.

'Not for three weeks at least. Then we'll cut it off and take a look.'

'Cut off his leg?' Gilligan froze, looking from Hazel to Charlie, his face white with consternation. Hazel laughed, and Bill felt a tickle rising in his throat, but laughing was too much of a leap all in one day.

'No, Gilligan,' Hazel assured him, shaking her head, 'until we cut off the plaster.'

'But it's hard as rock already, miss,' Charlie frowned, tapping at the plaster with his knuckles. 'How're we going to get it off again?'

'One thing at a time, young man,' Hazel tutted, though in truth she'd not quite thought that far. She certainly hadn't got the expensive specialised, heavily strengthened scissors advocated for the job when she'd bought the bandages, never really believing she'd ever have the chance to use either.

'Some of them clippers they trim horses' hoofs with?' Hugh offered, seeing the problem and trying to figure out an answer.

Hazel dipped her head, impressed.

'Maybe so, maybe so. But we've three weeks to think on that particular solution, and right now I've to get some food on. So get sketching, see what you can come up with while I'm gone.'

There was a quick flurry of movement and a chatter of young voices as she moved away.

'So what barrels and stuff have you got that we can use, Mr Tuley?' Hugh was asking, Gilligan cutting any answer off.

'Mind that young pup one of the ratters had back at Solveig's? That thing he did of making him run through a tunnel of wattles?'

'I don't think Hugh's going to need to be trained to run down tunnels,' Bill said.

''Course not,' Gilligan laughed, such an easy sound, so out of place in the Tuley household that Hazel paused a moment and looked back. 'Point is,' Gilligan went on, lifting up a pencil, licking its end, stabbing it down on the paper. 'Point is he started it off real simple. Built a little corridor that got lower and lower so's the pup didn't get alarmed.'

'And I'm going to get alarmed by a few wattle fences?' Hugh sounded offended but wasn't, was in fact smiling.

'No, I get it!' young Charlie put in. 'He means we've to start easy and move on to harder things later. Isn't that right?'

'That's right!' Gilligan and Bill said in unison, the two swapping a quick glance, Bill feeling that small tickle in his throat again. He

mightn't be ready to laugh yet, but by God he felt it might not be that far off, and Hazel saw that in him too, in the way he leaned over the table and picked up his own pencil, started jotting plans down here and there.

'So we begin with a simple walkway that has a few humps and bumps in it,' Bill was saying, 'and then we move it up a notch. Stick in a few planked steps here and there, each one getting higher…'

Hazel left them to it. She moved into her kitchen, closing the door softly behind her. She could still hear them all talking, Bill's voice amongst them, and she pulled open a small drawer that held bits and bobs: stubs of candles, lengths of rolled string, squares of waxed paper, old corks; anything that might prove useful and didn't need throwing away. Right at the back she found what she was looking for: the small talisman Kerr Perdue had given her years ago after she'd fixed some minor ailment.

'But what is it, Mr Perdue?' she'd asked him back then, faintly disgusted by the clawed foot set in copper and on a cheap chain that he'd handed over to her.

'It's the foot of a nightjar,' he'd told her. 'Considered very good luck out in the East. Folk here call it the Devil's Bird, but not there. And luck can come from anywhere, don't you think?'

She hadn't, she really hadn't, not back then, and had shoved it away. It was beyond her to chuck any gift in the bin, and she pulled it out now and looked at it. The metal clasp and chain were green with verdigris, but the bird's foot seemed untouched by age. Luck had come knocking on her door at last and she wanted to hang onto it any way she could, so she picked it up and slipped it into her apron pocket, snug and close.

'Please God,' she whispered, 'please God, let this be a start, and let everything come to a good end.'

She'd never been God fearing, not before the Crimea and certainly not afterwards; no different from her husband on that score. You lived through something like that, you came out hardened, a brittler, tempered version of yourself like a brick comes out of a kiln, all square corners and sides, the softness you'd gone in with lost and needing to be found again. She went about her tasks – scaling and gutting the fish, stuffing herbed butter under its skin and crisping it in the pan before roasting it off in the oven, getting the potatoes boiling and then the kale – but every now and then, as she rubbed her fingers against her apron to clean them, she felt that small bird's foot in her pocket and wondered if Bill might finally be about to regain some of his lost vitality, if their luck was finally running true, if maybe the Devil's bird was really God's after all.

Sholto had been counting down the minutes until he could escape, but James Heron apparently had other ideas. The moment they'd slurped down their rather unpleasant dessert of cream whipped up with brandy, Heron was right back at Sholto.

'So, I gather you were looking at my father's library,' he stated, Skinner Tweedy hiding a loud burp against his sleeve, to Heron's evident disgust. 'Skinner, get off. You've no need to stay, and I've a few words in private needed with the Company man here.'

Skinner didn't hesitate, not wanting to be at this dinner any longer than was necessary.

'Righto,' he said, getting to his feet. 'Meet you over at the Thorn farm tomorrow morning?'

'That'll do, Skinner,' James Heron was dismissive, flapping his napkin in Skinner's direction. 'Said I'd be there and so I will. Ten sharp. Got to get that land down by the Ghost Trees sorted.'

'Ghost Trees?' Sholto asked, immediately wishing he hadn't,

that he'd not given the man another in to go on talking. Too late. James Heron was already off.

'Just a name. Few trees standing where once there was a wood. All manner of tales going on about it being haunted, all that kind of nonsense. Can't tell you how superstitious folk around these parts are. They've even gone to the bother of having the place exorcised on a number of occasions, for heaven's sake. Peasants.'

He wrinkled his nose, removed a silver box from his jacket pocket and took out a small cigar, offered another to Sholto, who refused.

'Stranger beliefs have often found themselves based in fact,' Sholto said, disliking the manner in which his host had dismissed the so-called peasants of Auchencairn.

'Is that so?' James Heron asked, snipping the end off his cigar and lighting it, leaning back in his chair, looking over at Sholto with evident amusement. 'Something you've read in your books?'

Sholto frowned, wished Brogar was here to drub this man into the ground. Heron saw his discomfort and held up his hands.

'My apologies. The last thing I want to do is offend you. Here, Esther, get some brandy for our guest.'

Esther reappeared out of nowhere, bringing two goblets liberally filled.

'Thank you, my girl. Now get you gone. Time's late, and long since you should have retired to your bed.'

Esther bobbed a curtsey and did as bid, Sholto smiling at her as she went, glad Heron had shown her a modicum of civility as Skinner Tweedy had never done.

'Your father's library is quite intriguing,' Sholto said, once Esther had left, answering Heron's previous question.

James took a puff on his cigar and rolled his brandy about in its glass.

'Never found it so myself,' he said, swirling the brandy one more time before taking a sip. 'Not really my thing. Father's father was a bookbinder, so I'm told, so naturally he took an interest, but farming's more my line.'

'Have you never wondered about all the foreign scripts he collected?' Sholto asked. 'Where he got them? What they're all about?'

James Heron put his fingers to his dapper beard with one hand, extracting the cigar from his mouth with the other.

'Actually,' he said, 'that's rather what I wanted to talk to you about. You're a linguist, so I gather…'

Sholto blinked in surprise.

'Well, yes…but how…'

'Your Company was very free with your details, at least when I pushed them. I always like to know who I'm dealing with, Mr McKay, and you're no different.'

James Heron eased his neck upon his shoulders, took another sip of his brandy, another puff of his cigar, and then put both elbows down upon the table and looked over at Sholto with undisguised curiosity.

'And it's just like they said. I can see it in you. That thirst for knowledge and taxonomy that will never leave you until you turn up your toes and are six feet under. And no use shaking your head, Mr McKay,' he went on, Sholto moving back in his chair, unsure whether he was more uncomfortable at the intensity of Heron's gaze or the fact that he'd used the word taxonomy so aptly.

'You're just like my father,' James Heron went on, a slight flush building on his cheekbones, 'and I knew him just as I know you, and you're just what I need. Someone to cut through all the crap that I've no time for. Someone to figure out what's worth money and what isn't. And it's money I need, Mr McKay, or rather this estate does.'

'But…selling off your father's books?' Sholto was shocked. 'Is that really the way to go?'

Heron laughed.

'Why? Because every grand house needs a grand library? What the hell's the point in that?'

'Well, I…'

'Well nothing,' Heron cut in. 'D'you know how many big houses I've visited that have even bigger libraries than here at Balcary? A lot, is the answer. And d'you know how many of those books are ever read?'

He gave Sholto leave to form an answer.

'Not too many, I'd guess,' Sholto admitted, seeing that the man had a point.

'Precisely!' Heron went on triumphantly. 'And wouldn't it be far better for all those books to be sold to people who would actually enjoy them? Value them for what they are? Read them, make use of them? Got to be better than them sitting unopened on their shelves for generation after generation, gathering dust, filling space that might be better used; nothing but a regiment of pretty spines lined up to be oohed at by some guest who hasn't got the curiosity or intelligence to open even one of them? No.'

Heron ended decisively.

'That's waste, and I despise waste, Mr McKay. Despise it, as should every right thinking man.'

Chapter 13

Libraries Lost, Libraries Found

Kerr Perdue came in and was ushered to the stove by Frith who vacated her chair for him, brought another over and sat back down. Perdue held out his hands to the fire and rubbed them together once or twice before settling.

'We've all tales,' he said, looking over at Frith, 'and there's one you need to know, about your mother and your father.'

Frith's eyes were gleaming in the firelight as she looked over eagerly at Kerr Perdue, reminding him of that sliver of green feather in the teal he'd found dead in the heather earlier that day.

'We did bad things,' Kerr said, closing his eyes, 'or rather, like your Kamyr-Batyr, we did good ones and bad, depending on how yous look at it.'

Brogar shifted in his seat, got himself comfortable. This day was turning out better than he could have hoped: the discovery of a new place, a scramble down a collapsed mineshaft, a daring seaside rescue and now a few stories about the fire.

'We're all ears, Perdue,' he said. 'Care for some of Merryweather's contribution, in the form of…well, I'm not sure what it is exactly, but he left a flagon of it behind.'

Perdue lifted a corner of his lip.

'Aye, why not. Hope you've not given Frith here too much of it.'

'Not at all,' Brogar assured Perdue. 'Just a drop while we were telling stories, so now tell us yours.'

Perdue dropped his head, pulled his blanket closer about his shoulders. He was still cold at his core, that ducking in the Solway not quite purged from him, as neither was his shared past with Merryweather, Stirling and Kheranovich.

'Aye well,' he began. 'It was what bound us all together, so to speak, 'cos no one does stuff like that without it taking an effect. We'd done hard things before, of course, what with us being in the wars an' all...'

'In Wola, for example?' Brogar asked, Perdue looking over at Brogar with cautious eyes, Brogar looking nonchalantly back, handing Perdue a mug of Merryweather's brew, Perdue taking it with a hand he wished didn't have quite such a tremor.

'So Gabriel's been here,' Perdue said after a moment and a sip.

'Not much gets past you,' Brogar replied easily. 'Not that he said much. Got a bit touchy when I was asking about what happened afterwards, which I'm guessing is where this tale of yours comes in.'

Perdue wiped his hand across his mouth, uncertain what to say.

'I wish you'd tell us,' Frith said. 'There's so much me and Charlie don't know. I mean, we know you was all over in Russia and that, but nothing much after. I mean how you and Mr Merryweather came back but not my da, not till ages later.'

Perdue couldn't bring himself to look at Frith, nor at Brogar come to that. He stared at his drink and then at the fire, watched the small flames leaping in the confines of the stove, saw the larger ones, the sky high ones, felt the heat of them on his face. He closed his eyes, exhaled, gripped his hands about his mug.

'What you don't know, Frith,' he said, 'is so much I don't even know where to start.'

Frith stretched out her hand and laid it gently on Perdue's own. Cold on cold. Small on large.

'Please tell me,' she whispered. 'Please, Mr Perdue. Please…'

And so he began, telling her how they'd gone to Sweden, signed up, defected over to Russia when the going got slow and them wanting action, how they'd hooked up with Kheranovich in the Russian army, him being in charge of any folk speaking English and not much else.

'After that,' Perdue went on, taking a deep breath, letting it out slowly to delay the moment. 'Well, it didn't go too good. Places we went? Things we had to do?' He shook his head. 'Them Russians don't like to lose, not one bit, so when the Poles started declaring themselves independent and spreading their revolution to other countries nearby, well. That was kind of it. Lot more Russians in their army than the rest of 'em put together, but that's not to say it was a walkover. Things was bad both sides.'

Perdue ground to a halt, much as Merryweather had done when talking about the same battles. Back at the bottom of the cliff, after Perdue had got Frith out of the cave, he'd thought seriously on giving it all up; but not back then, not back when they were all youngsters, barely pushing twenty. Jesus, the blood had been hot in their veins then, and they'd been close up in the fighting at Olszunka Grochowska in February '31, just east of Warsaw; two days of hand-to-hand combat, huge beasts of horses crowding in on every side, hard not to get crushed by your own lot never mind the enemy; mud and blood everywhere, hands so slick with sweat it was hard to grip your knife or your gun or aim either with any accuracy; and the noise had been something else, your ears thrashed and boomed so you couldn't get it out of your head, not for ages afterwards. And afterwards, no victory anyway for anyone. Thousands and thousands of men dead on either side and no one the winner, everyone – man and beast – withdrawing exhausted, stress in every sinew, every muscle, so fatigued all you could do was lie on your back in the shit and look up into the sky and thank your lucky stars you were still alive. No notion that worse was to come, like the massacre they'd perpetrated on the village of Ashmiany in Belarus, or the slaughter of the Poles at Ostroleka when eight thousand of the poor buggers were left littered over the battlefield at the end of play.

Bad times.

'Bad times,' Perdue said slowly. 'Bad times and bad battles you're not old enough to know about, Frith. But safe to say we was all sick of it. Sick of all the killing and fighting and nothing any of us wanting anymore but to get out and come home.'

'But you didn't come home,' Frith was puzzled, not understanding, Brogar stepping in to help her out.

'I think what Perdue is trying to say is that after their experiences in Poland they'd all have left there and then if they could've. But you can't just walk out of the army. Am I right, Perdue?'

Kerr Perdue took a swig from his mug and nodded, the firelight flickering over his face, enhancing the shadows, making his fifty-eight years of life look like he'd lived a whole lot longer.

'Aye,' he said. 'Right is right. Even Archie – your da, Frith – was a bit blown with it. But, like the man says, you can't just walk away. Kheranovich wangled us back from the front lines, an' that was when the two of 'em found themselns a new cause.'

'And you and Merryweather?' Brogar asked, wanting to push Perdue on.

Kerr Perdue let out a short exclamation that might have been a laugh, if he was a man inclined to laughter, which he wasn't.

'Would've gone if we could. Me and Merryweather was finished. All dragged up at the grand old age of twenty-one, but no place else to go. Had to tag along one way or another, and at least this new fighting was of a different kind and we didn't have to get our hands so dirty.'

'So you came back to Tatary lands in '32,' Brogar summed up, Kerr Perdue looking up sharply.

'Never said that, and what would you know about it anyway?' he asked, Brogar shaking his head, grimacing, his scar tightening down his face – a sure sign colder weather was coming.

'Just guessing,' he replied easily. 'Putting two and two together. Plainly the Russians got spooked by the uprisings in Poland and were fearing any others closer to home, and that'll be where Kheranovich got you. And Tatary is the obvious place, where nothing has ever been simple.'

'Simple!' Kerr barked again. 'That's a laugh and a half. Nothing simple about that place, you're right about that. Simple fact is we thought we'd all got out, and then we was dumped right back in it again. Bloody Tupikov,' Kerr forced the name out between clenched teeth. 'Like a goshawk he were, and ken how hard those birds are to train. They'll pick and peck you black and bloody afore they'll take any orders from the likes of you and me…well, that was what Tupikov was like. Not even Kheranovich and his clever words could get us out of that command, not for a while at least. Under his boot we was, right until…well, I'm getting ahead of meself again, still got to say the big say, an' no use you looking at me like that, Mr Brogar, Mr Big Man of the Company,' Kerr swept a vicious glance at Brogar who merely raised an eyebrow, took a sip of his drink and stared Perdue down.

'Aye right,' Kerr said in appeasement, lowering his head. 'You're right. 'Course you are. Get the feeling you're not unacquainted with what went on in them days.'

'Maybe not him,' Frith said quietly, 'but honest, Mr Perdue, I've no idea what you're talking about.'

Kerr softened, looking over at Frith, seeing in her face the same characteristics that had been in her father's; same look of bemusement that seemed the natural mien of his face at rest; the intensity of his gaze when he chose to focus on you, like Frith was doing now, like the world had fallen away and everything rested for him or her on whatever you were about to say next. Kerr found Frith's similarity to the young Archie unnerving and would have gladly called the proceedings to an end, pleaded exhaustion and a need to get back to his bed, but was pulled on by Frith, as he'd always been pulled on by her father.

'Well here's the nub,' he said, his skin slack and tired, that shake in his fingers taking hold again so he had to grip his mug with both hands, thinking on Kamyr-Batyr in his burning barn.

'Tupikov and his masters worried that the Tatars were getting too strong around the Azov end of the Black Sea, had a stranglehold on all the trade going over to Turkey, them being kin, so to speak, all of the other faith and a different language. They'd alwus been feared, what with them overrunning old Russia way back when and hanging onto the Crimea until that old Empress Catherine got it back from them in 1783.'

'You really know your history,' Brogar put in with a hint of admiration, thinking how much Sholto would love this, how much he missed Sholto's input, the simple truth occurring to him that what he was actually missing was Sholto himself. His previous assistants had come and gone without much care on his part, but if Sholto went…well, Brogar didn't even want to think about that. Chalk and cheese came to mind, but the kind of chalk and cheese that would sit well together on any slate or plate, each one advising the other on the alien circumstances they found themselves in.

Kerr let go his mug long enough to rub his nose with thumb and forefinger, thinking at first that Brogar was making fun of him, but apparently not, given the expression on his face.

'Aye well,' he continued, satisfied. 'Couldn't not, as it happened. Kheranovich was full of it, kept leaking out o' him like a burn from a lochan. And mind, come nights back then there weren't nothing else to do 'cept talk, and he and Archie talked. Oh my, did they talk. Two of 'em yackety yacketing like there weren't no tomorrow. So gist is, we got ourselves caught up in the Tatar thing, with Tupikov as our boss, and main job was to go from Tatar township to Tatar township, get the big men to chuck out all their books in the streets so we could set them burning.'

'But that's awful!' Frith exclaimed, straightening in her seat. She'd not a huge amount of learning, but the little she'd had made her revere books of every stripe. 'Why would they do such a vandalous thing?'

Kerr didn't answer and Brogar scratched the corner of his left eye where the scar scraped along its edge.

'Intimidation would be my guess,' he said, 'pull the power base down to its knees. Get rid of books, get rid of law and learning and social cohesion. I've a feeling they did it sometime before with excellent results.'

'Too right,' Kerr said. 'Can't remember the whys and wherefores of it neither, but Kheranovich said the same: Russians getting rid of some famous Tatar library hundred-odd years afore and thought they'd try the same again.'

'But what's it to do with my da? Or with you and Merryweather coming home?' Frith still didn't get it, and no wonder. Kerr cleared his throat. This was it then, this was the time to tell Frith how she came to be.

''Cos it was during one of them burnings that we came across your mam,' he said. ''Cos it was during one of them burning times that the Tatars got a wind of it and stashed everything from all around in some old peasants' barn, got them hid in the straw. And them peasants were your mam's grandparents, Frith. And it didn't end too well.'

Kerr hesitating; Kerr giving some of the details, but not all. Leaving out the part about the four young soldiers rubbing the dirt and straw off their hands; shovels and wheelbarrow hastily stowed at the very end of the barn in darkness where they'd not be seen to have been recently used. Telling instead of the four young soldiers looking off to the east, the sun still below the horizon but light enough to make out the band of men advancing: Tupikov on his horse, growing like an ogre as he came closer. In the house, a husband and wife wringing wet in their beds because they were sick, their granddaughter exhausted from a long day trying to look after them, weeping as they only got worse, fearing they'd not see out the night, no notion anyone else was out there who might be able to help them; a girl who mightn't have gone out anyway even if she'd known, because they were soldiers, and soldiers around these parts weren't folk you asked for anything. And quite right, given Tupikov's arrival and his orders to burn down the barn, and Frith's mother's grandparents going with it.

A horrible silence then, as they took it in. Frith breathing quickly.

'But not me mam,' she stated quietly.

'Evidently not,' Brogar agreed, studying Perdue's face, seeing there was more, wondering what it could be.

'It was the end of it for us,' Kerr sighed. 'The way we got ourselves out.'

He should have said more. Should have got to the end of it, but he was just too tired.

Couldn't bear the look in Frith's eyes.

Couldn't bear to say the last of it.

Needed sleep, needed to figure out how to say it all better than he was saying it now, especially for Frith. Aided by Brogar seeing that desperation in him and calling a halt, that the rest could be told in the morning.

Sholto was tired, tired of James Heron and his incessant need to talk, tired of James Heron's plans, tired to the bone. He wished Brogar was here to intervene on his behalf, shout the man down, but instead Sholto was being dragged into the library to be shown the wastage James saw on his father's shelves. Any other time than this, Sholto would have been ecstatic to burrow through its books, discover their secrets, worm out the hidden gems, but not with James at his side. The man was exhausting.

'He got most of them when he was over in the Crimea,' James was saying. 'God knows how, for he was in the Russian army at the time, but he got them anyway. Brought them over here. Bought this place with the proceeds from some of them, so I gather. And that, Mr McKay, is what I want you to do for me now.'

Sholto had given up trying to get Heron to call him Sholto instead of the more formal appellation of his name, and he was tired of trying to figure out what the man meant.

'We're not here to survey books,' Sholto objected quietly. 'We're here to take a survey of the mine before the sale, and if all is as you've told the Company, then that will be that.'

'But not at all!' James went on, undeterred. 'I told you. I know all about you, and if necessary I will petition your Company to allow you to stay long enough to itemize every single book on these shelves. I've sway, Mr McKay,' he added, turning suddenly back towards Sholto, 'and don't doubt I'll use it.'

Sholto sighed. Gave up. No use arguing, not tonight. He held up his hands.

'Very well, Mr Heron.'

'James, please!' Heron put in, as Sholto had singularly failed to do on his own side, James slapping a hearty hand on Sholto's back. 'Too late to start tonight,' he added, Sholto so relieved he didn't even glance at the books that were usually his greatest joy in life, merely turned and headed for the door and escape.

'Until tomorrow, then,' he managed.

'Until tomorrow!' James replied. 'I've to see to Thorn's farm early doors but after that? Well, we'll have all day!'

Not if I can help it, Sholto thought but didn't say, glad beyond measure that tomorrow morning would bring Brogar back into his ken, and if there was any man alive who could stand up to James Heron, it was Brogar Finn.

Sholto removed himself back to the room he'd been assigned and stood for a long while staring out the window towards Hestan, watching intently the faint light he could see over there, still watching when that light went out twenty minutes later, and only then did he disrobe and get himself to bed.

Chapter 14

Realisation And Retaliation

All was quiet in the Tuley household. Gilligan and Hugh had retired to their allotted beds in the small guestroom, delighted to find they had a bunk bed, Gilligan clambering up to the topmost pallet, ostensibly so Hugh couldn't miss his step on the ladder, but primarily so he could look out of the window and see the great darkness of Auchencairn Bay, the wavering white line of breakers on the sand, the stars up above; lying there, hands tucked beneath his chin as he gazed out of the window until he fell asleep. Down below, Hugh was having more trouble dropping off than he'd expected. He tried not to move too much beneath his sheet and eiderdown, not wanting to disturb Gilligan, but however many times he closed his eyes and counted back from one hundred to one to fool his brain into sleep with the task's monotony, his body was having none of it. One minute his toes were itching, the next his arm felt numb, and now his throat was scratchy with sudden thirst. He lay flat on his back, hands interlaced beneath his head. There was just enough light coming from the candle stub on the bedside table to see the round depression of Gilligan's body curled above him and the square jamb of the window framing the almost

full moon so perfectly it might have been a picture hanging on the wall. He concentrated on the oblate circle of light out there in the night, listened to the shushing of the wind in the trees grown as a windbreak to the west of the Tuley house, the gentle creaking of their branches, the calling of several tawny owls, or gilly hoolets as they called them back home. And he thought of home, and how the meaning of the word had shifted since he'd met Sholto and Brogar, men he would gladly have had as fathers, one or both, and how extraordinary had been the circumstances that brought them together, made of them a family. At least Hugh hoped that was what they'd all become. That was his perception of it, and he didn't doubt Gilligan felt the same.

He sighed, closed his eyes, turned onto his side. But it was no use. His mind was too busy, the stillness and silence usually so conducive to sleep serving only to make his imagination work all the more on what the next day might bring, of the obstacle course that they were going to build and how it might help him to adapt. He sat up, pushed aside his covers, put his feet to the floor, finding the slippers Hazel had given him tucked neatly by the side of the bed. They'd obviously been Bill's once upon a time and were far too large for Hugh's feet, but he snuggled his toes into them anyway. He'd never had slippers before, nor the pyjamas Hazel had conjured up for him and Gilligan. He rolled up the pyjama cuffs at wrist and ankle, both far too long for the likes of him, and stood up, lifted the candle in its holder, shielding the small flame with his hand so it wouldn't blow out as he shuffled his way towards the door, his intention being to fetch a glass of water from the ewer in the kitchen, or maybe some milk, if there was any there to be had.

Hugh went carefully down the short flight of stairs from attic room to landing to ground floor, holding out the candle stub

before him so he wouldn't trip. Stairs had become a little more complicated since he'd lost his eye, and the over-large slippers weren't making the process any easier. He had to keep flexing his toes to keep them on so they wouldn't slip away and trip him. He got to the door of the living room and nudged it open with his free hand, began to navigate his way between the furniture, when he realised he was not alone. Bill Tuley was still there, where Hugh and Gilligan had left him, head slumped on his arms, apparently asleep. Hugh sucked in a breath as he went about the table, but Bill was apparently not as asleep as Hugh had believed him to be.

'Who's there?' Bill asked suddenly, levering himself up to standing, hand scrabbling at his belt for a gun that hadn't been housed there for years.

'Only me, only Hugh,' Hugh said, pale face jumping in the small light of the candle that remained to him.

'Hugh who?' Bill demanded. 'Last name, boy. And why aren't you at your post?'

Hugh baulked, came adrift from one of his slippers, unsure what to do, the stone flagging cold beneath his slipperless foot.

'It's me, Mr Tuley. It's Hugh. I was here earlier, with Gilligan. Hugh and Gilligan. We don't have last names, nor numbers come to that.'

Bill Tuley remained erect, eyes darting about him, seeking enemies in the shadows, but all he saw was a small boy holding up the stump end of a candle, his memories shifting and clicking back into place.

'Hugh,' he whispered, slumping back into his seat. 'Hugh and Gilligan. I'm sorry lad. Didn't mean to scare you.'

'It's alright, Mr Tuley,' Hugh said, putting his foot back into his slipper, coming forward, placing his candle on the table, settling into the next door seat.

'But it's not alright,' Bill muttered angrily, tears caught in this throat, hands thrusting through his hair. 'It's not alright. It'll never be alright.'

Hugh sat by Bill and Bill sat by Hugh, until the candle threatened its final flicker, when Hugh moved and pointed.

'See that moon?' Hugh asked, Bill following Hugh's finger so both were turned towards the window. 'See that moon out there?'

Bill said nothing, but looked as he'd been told.

'Mr Sholto told me loads about it,' Hugh went on, 'how it's lit by the sun on the other side of the world; how it's always day somewhere else when it's night here. And that it's been there forever, that's what Mr Sholto said, or at least a lot longer than you and me, an'll still be up there when we're all long gone. Point being, it don't matter whatever you or I do down here, just that it's got to be done and done right, if we're able. No point fretting about it. And that moon? It don't care a jot, just keeps on doing what it's doing.'

Bill stared at the moon that was fitted to the top right of the window, just about to move out of view, just about to be lost to him, Hugh's hand dropping down beside his own, small and white on the tabletop.

'When did you become so wise?' he asked, throat dry. Too much wine again, like always.

'Thought I was going to die,' Hugh said simply. 'And then, when I didn't, it was like everything was new again, an' I just got so filled to the bubbling with questions I'd never thought on before. Like how long the moon's been up there and why it shines like it does, and how come it's one thing one night and different the next, and how some mornings it's still there in the sky for a bit when it's clear. Couldn't figure any of it out for the life of me. Just a load of knots in me head I couldn't get sorted.'

Bill blinked in the darkness, struck by the analogy, how closely it mirrored his own frame of mind now it had been said, how he felt just like that – knotted up from the inside out. So hopelessly tangled he'd given up trying to start the unravelling, the sorting out.

'You still got knots in there?' he asked, Hugh's small hand lifting as he laughed quietly.

'Oh crikey yes! Knots upon knots. Mr Sholto's going mad with it! Soon as he answers one of me daft questions there I go asking another…never going to end! But Mr Sholto, well. He's right kind. Never gets grumpy with it. Says that's how it should be, but that one day I'll have to find out all the answers by meself.'

'And it was your Mr Sholto told you about the moon,' Bill stated.

'He knows everything,' Hugh said, so earnestly Bill found with surprise that he was smiling.

'No one knows everything,' he said, not to dampen the moment but to lift it.

'Well ha ha,' Hugh was quick enough back, catching the mood. 'Ken that,' he added, with a smile of his own, before going on to qualify his statement. 'That's what Mr Sholto says too. But honest, he knows absolutely loads. Never known someone to know so much.'

'Like what for instance?' Bill asked, captivated by this midnight encounter, this meeting with a seeker in the darkness of the night. 'I mean, apart from the moon.'

He glanced up at the window but the moon had gone, a dark frame left behind framing a darker night.

'Hmm,' Hugh said, taking the question seriously. 'Where to start's the thing.'

He tapped a finger on the table and clenched his toes in his slippers, wanting to come out with something good,

'Aha!' he announced with jubilation after a few seconds. 'Like

when I asked him why you never see a plant with black flowers. And what d'you think he said?'

Bill frowned. Such an observation had never occurred to him, but certainly it was true, at least in his experience, because never in all his life had he seen a black petalled flower, not even on the shores of the eponymous Black Sea where so much blood had been spilled and decayed that the whole of it in his head was black from north to south, east to west.

'Well, I'm not sure,' Bill began, shoulders twitching with the effort of switching from one thought process to another, forcing his mind to go down other tracks – logical ones, instead of dark memories. 'Maybe to do with bees?'

'Bees!' Hugh chortled. 'Well, yes. Mr Sholto did say something about them, about how loads of experiments have been done on their eyes and that they see everything different to what we do. But that wasn't it,' Hugh leaned forward. 'Know what he said? Kinda obvious when you really thinks on it, like he did.'

Bill was flummoxed but intrigued.

How he'd been catapulted into this bizarre conversation was moot, but all the same here he was and he wanted the solution, and wanted to come up with it by himself, wanted to captivate this young boy as his Mr Sholto so evidently did.

'Clothing,' Bill said, the idea coming out of nowhere, but then not nowhere at all. Out of something he'd witnessed, experienced, the first of several small knots beginning to unravel in his head. 'I know it, I know it…' he went on, a man on the brink of an idea he couldn't quite grasp but knew intuitively he had the answer to, if only he could tease it out.

'Nearly there,' Hugh encouraged him. 'Nearly, but not quite… think, Mr Tuley. That's what Mr Sholto always says to me. Just think on it long enough and it'll come.'

And come it did, all of a rush, the revelation making Bill hold his hands down flat as he worked the idea through to its conclusion.

'There's no black flowers...' he began, 'because, of all the colours Descartes demonstrated in his spectrum, that we see in a rainbow, black isn't there because it's not a colour. It's the absence of colour, and it's not a colour because it doesn't reflect light at all, it absorbs but doesn't reflect. I have it!'

Bill beamed at Hugh and Hugh beamed back.

'Black takes in the light but doesn't let it out again, so any flower that's black would overheat, shrivel and...'

Out went the last lick of candle, not that either of them cared.

'The absence of colour,' Bill said, rather gaily. 'We're surrounded by it!'

'Up to our necks in it!' Hugh replied.

'Over our heads in it!' Bill said, the two of them laughing at their own paltry wit.

'Got any water in this absence?' Hugh asked, once he'd subsided. 'I'm absolutely parched.'

Frith was bedded down by the stove in Kerr's workshop, Brogar and Kerr having gone to kip in Perdue's tiny box of a bedroom below the light to give her privacy. She was glad to be alone, mulling over what Perdue had told her, wishing Brogar had allowed Kerr to say more, and there was more. She was certain of it. It had been terrible, what she'd been told, that the monster Tupikov had ordered innocent people to be burned to death. But it seemed distant, a story about people she didn't know, like Kamyr-Batyr in his own burning barn.

But what about her mother? Had she hidden? Run away? Been spared because she was so young? Because obviously she'd got away, or she and Charlie would never have been born.

Running the story over and over in her mind, half dreaming it, filling in the blanks Kerr Perdue had so studiously left.

Kerr Perdue was dreaming the same dream as he lay in his bed.

There was the old farmhouse, and nearby the tumbled down barn that had been stashed top to bottom with books, before Kheranovich and his men got there.

'They're coming,' Archie said, eyes blue as the sky, bright as a wren's.

'Too bloody right,' Merryweather grumped. 'Best measure our necks for the rope, 'cos there's no bloody way we're going to get away with it.'

Kheranovich stamping his feet to rid himself of cramp, rubbing his thighs with his hands before easing them back into his leather gloves.

'Take it easy, Gabriel. Say nothing, do nothing. Just follow my lead.'

'Easy for you to say,' Merryweather retorted.

'And easy for you to do,' Kheranovich replied sharply. 'Remember who you are. I'm your commanding officer and you will follow my orders, whether you like them or no.'

Merryweather growled in his throat but didn't say more.

'He's just nervous,' Kerr Perdue put in. 'We all are. This stealing business is…'

'We're not stealing, we're liberating,' Kheranovich cut him off. 'Would you rather see the combined libraries of this entire region burned to the ground like we did to the Khan's archives a hundred years ago?'

'We didn't do anything,' Merryweather couldn't stop himself, Kheranovich swerving towards him, held back by Archie quickly and forcibly gripping Kheranovich's arm to a halt.

'Let's just all calm ourselves,' Archie said. 'We've done a good thing, and let's not forget it. And we don't want Tupikov seeing us argue.'

Kheranovich backed down, though his left eyelid ticked with anger and Merryweather was flushed right up to his ears.

'That child's greeting again,' Perdue put into the silence that followed. 'Hope everything's alright within.'

'Let's concentrate on what's without and with us,' Kheranovich said, taking a deep breath, rolling his shoulders. 'They'll be here in a few minutes.'

They all looked up then, those four young soldiers, Tupikov bearing down on them with sudden speed, his men running to keep up with him on his horse.

'Just keep your nerve, boys,' Kheranovich muttered, 'and we'll be out of here in no time.'

In no time, Kerr mumbled in his sleep and was suddenly awake, listening to the darkness, to the night.

Brogar had rolled up in a blanket on the floor beside him, having absolutely refused Kerr's offer to swap places, asleep a few minutes later; Kerr listening to Brogar breathing deep and easy, like he'd not a care in the world.

Which maybe he hadn't, unlike Kerr.

What he'd told Firth hadn't been a lie exactly, more like an outline, a sketch waiting for someone to load the brushes with paint and fill it in. He'd told her how Tupikov had arrived and sent his soldiers into the barn to check on the information they'd been given, how they'd been more diligent than Kheranovich had expected and discovered the ruse within a few minutes. Tupikov, barbarous leader of the massacre of Ashmiany, called fearless because of it by his supporters, merciless by those who were not.

But either way, a bureaucratic arse of the first order. They should have known he would be thorough, leave no box unticked. His men going into the barn and overturning the two pallets Kheranovich had left in full view, sending their books scattering to the floor, stamping on them as they hammered their way into the rest.

'It's just straw, sir!' came back a foot soldier. 'The rest is just straw, and nothing more.'

Kerr Perdue not needing dreams to see it all again.

Tupikov glaring at Kheranovich.

'I thought you said you'd checked.'

Kheranovich wincing, hanging his head, letting out a deep breath.

'It was late when we got here, sir,' he mumbled, 'and dark. Just took a quick peek at the top ones…no reason to think our information was…'

'Well it *was* wrong, you idiot! How many times have I told you to double check everything?'

'Very often, sir; I'm sorry sir…I take full respons—'

Tupikov striking Kheranovich smartly across the face with the handle of his whip and turning to his men.

'Get those folk out of the house, right now!'

Kerr Perdue's fingers and feet twitching as he saw those men kicking down the door of the dilapidated farmhouse, dragging back out with them an elderly couple in their nightclothes, and a young girl who couldn't have been more than fifteen who kept yelping and pulling against her captors.

'They're not well! Please, they're not well!'

Even Perdue recognising the Russian words, mouthing them now as he stared into the darkness; he saw the girl in her thin shift, the soldiers pinioning both her and her grandparents by their arms, keeping them still, the two old folk lolling in their restraints,

hardly conscious, certainly not understanding what was going on, Tupikov leaning his big stomach down over the neck of his horse.

'Into the barn with the lot of them!'

'We've got to tell them,' Kerr whispered urgently to Kheranovich, Kheranovich's arm hard as stone against his own, Merryweather jiggling at their backs.

'Keep yer mouth shut,' Merryweather urged, punching Perdue hard in his left kidney, which had the merit of doing precisely that.

'He's right,' Kheranovich added quietly. 'Can't do anything for—'

'Something going on I should know about?' Tupikov barked, turning in his saddle towards them, hand on his whip, ready and eager to strike again.

'No, sir,' Kheranovich stepped smartly forward. 'Just saying we don't know how we missed it, just saying—'

Bam! That whip once more struck at Kheranovich, felling him, Perdue and Archie quick on their knees beside him.

'You've always been weak, Kheranovich,' Tupikov stated, wiping the blood off his whip, 'you and your band of turncoat foreigners. And don't think I don't know they all started against us, and would still be now if the likes of you hadn't taken them under your wing.'

He pulled at his reins, turned his horse with impressive speed, spitting out orders to his men, Kheranovich and his turncoats insignificant, immediately forgotten.

'Get those bastard traitors in the barn,' Tupikov shouted, his men doing exactly that, and easy done, with two of them being sick and the last a child who'd no more strength in her arms than two twigs of birch, and as easily broken. Shoved in they were, and Kerr could hear them going, their feet dragging through the mud, the several muffled bumps of them as they were pushed through the door, the screech of the plank shoved down into its iron holdings to keep them in.

'Time's now,' Tupikov commanded, sitting up in his stirrups, a general ready for action. 'Kheranovich. You and your men get it burning. Time to send those upstart Tatars round here a message they'll not quickly forget.'

Kerr staring up into the night, thinking of Frith over in the workshop.

Frith always a clever child, just like her father.

Knowing he'd got to tell her all, before she figured it out for herself.

CHAPTER 15

A CHARM OF GOLDFINCH

Brogar woke, yawned, threw off his blanket and was up. The room was dark as moleskin but it didn't take him long to feel his way to the door and push it open, breathe in the cool morning air. The snow had gone, melted by the salt and spray of the Solway. He was about to take a step outside when he stopped, saw the ground a few yards away moving and shifting, matted over with a twittering mass of birds like he'd never seen before.

'They does that sometimes,' came Kerr Perdue's voice, thick with sleep and last night's drink and bad nightmares, but recognising the sound. 'Them sees us like they sees boats, a stopper off point. Heard sailors tell of how a load of goldfinch or buntings come down on them when they're out at sea, so chock-a-block on the riggings they can't pull in the sails. Sign of good fortune, so they say.'

'Can well believe it,' Brogar commented, smiling widely. 'There's like a hundred thousand of them out here!'

And truly there was: a sight to behold. Every hummock, every inch of heather and wilting grass covered over with tiny birds chittering and chattering, wings flittering and fluttering as they

went up and down an inch or so to confuse the gulls that were swooping and diving on them from the air above.

'Best give them a few minutes,' Kerr advised, levering himself up on his elbows. 'Soon as sun's risen a bit they'll all be off again, and we've time afore tide's deep fallen.'

Brogar did as bid and withdrew, settling himself on the bottom of Kerr's bed, leaving the small door open so they could witness the spectacle, never mind the cold draught that was coming in because of it.

'Does this happen often?' he asked, Kerr swinging himself to sitting, pulling up his braces, tying on his boots.

'Sometimes,' Kerr said, clearing his throat. 'But only in winter. Had a load of pink foot here once that wouldn't go. Kept on leaving off for the gleanings in the fields and coming back again every night. Gulls didn't like that, not at all, but me and Merryweather kinda got used to the sound of them going on through the night. Peaceful, they were. Real peaceful. But a coupla weeks later they were up and never came back.'

'Good pickings for you, though,' Brogar stated, 'with your trade, I mean.'

Kerr yawned, scratched his beard.

'Aye, right enough. Always net a few afore they go. Call it a tithe, if you will. Always make good eating. Specially the geese. Had swans too, once or twice, and even woodcock in hard winters. All the lot of 'em together like you never see them otherwise. And the flocks of fieldfare and redwing we got a few years back? Don't sing so good as larks but taste just as good in a pie.'

Brogar laughed, and then was quiet, him and Kerr holding themselves still as the sun detached itself properly from the horizon when, just as Kerr had predicted, the whole lot was up in a one, some signal given that Brogar had been looking for but missed:

two hundred thousand tiny wings vibrating in the air, a hundred thousand throats giving voice as the flock rose and swirled a yard or so above the ground for several seconds before every last one of them was up and flying like a million leaves blown from the ground by an unexpected wind.

'My God,' Brogar breathed, exhilarated, leaping to his feet, stepping out the door, watching the sky darken with the exodus and then become clear as all those tiny birds merged into a cloud of their own making, taking themselves up and away, disintegrating and regrouping several times as they went landward with astonishing speed; finally dispersing as they got to shore, flitting themselves into familiar groups known only to themselves as they sank themselves down onto the gleaning fields and were at rest again.

One more sight to add to Kerr's list.

Frith awoke stiff and cold, unaware of what had woken her, only that she was awake and the stove needed feeding. She wriggled her toes in her socks, the unpleasant dampness of the wool making her want to itch and scratch. She lay on her back and placed both stockinged feet against the belly of the stove, wrinkling her nose against the acrid steam that immediately rose up and, more particularly, the smell of sweat that came from the fast drying wool. Fresh in her head was all Kerr Perdue had said the night before of his and her father's experiences in the army, the farmhouse, the books, her mother's family...

She lifted her feet smartly from the stove as she caught the scent of burning wool in the offing, got herself off her backside and up, shoved her feet into her boots that had thankfully dried out overnight. They might be old and cracked – Charlie's hand-me-downs – but she liked them better than the clogs most folk around here wore.

She went to the small stack of wood by the workshop door and selected a few of the smaller logs, returning to the stove, opening the door with the tongs and carefully placing them inside. She shivered as she clanged the door shut, rubbing her hands and holding them out to the warm metal before filling the kettle and placing it on top to boil. She hunted about the small kitchen area for some food she could get ready before she and Brogar went back over the Rack, a smile coming involuntarily to her lips as she thought on Charlie and all she had to tell him of her rescue from the cave and Brogar and Perdue's stories, and what Charlie would in turn have to tell her about almost being crushed to death. It occurred to her only now that it might not only have been Kerr Perdue keeping secrets. The plan to get something of their da out of Hestan – before the Company who'd bought the island moved in – now seemed weak, as Charlie's plans often were. Always about the goal, and never about the details leading up to it. Not to mention macabre. For what had they been supposed to find? A few bones?

They'd never known their da, not directly; toddlers when he'd arranged to send them back to his homeland from overseas, and not much older when he'd followed a year or so later. All they had were scattered memories: him pushing them around in a wheelbarrow down a cobbled lane; a visit to the carpenter's one time to fetch a cradle for the brother or sister who never came to term, the cradle standing empty all their childhood in the corner of the living room; her and Charlie laughing as he showed them how to roll eggs down a slope to celebrate Easter, how hers had been the one to get closest to the marker he'd set in the grass and him giving her a bag of sugared plums she'd immediately split with Charlie.

She'd a clearer memory of the patterns their mam had helped them paint on those eggs than she had of her da's face, because, not long after that Easter Day, he'd vanished.

Simply gone.

Up and left them, and them none the wiser about him going, right until they'd got that lawyer's letter a couple of weeks back. A letter stating several facts up front:

That it should not be sent until the Stirling children had turned seventeen;

That it should not be sent even then unless their mother, Nairi Stirling, had died;

That if Nairi Stirling was still alive when the children turned twenty-one, then it should be sent to them only at Nairi Stirling's discretion;

That it should be sent to them when they were twenty-five, with or without Nairi Stirling's approval.

The older Heron had tried to factor in all the odds.

He knew Archie's children were like Archie in so many ways, had been watching them growing up, expanding themselves, and by God he wanted the best for them. The very best. And this letter was going to give them that, when it finally reached them, at whatever age.

What he couldn't have factored into his odds was that his own son might put Hestan up for sale; that Nairi had died the year before Archie Stirling's children turned seventeen; that Archie Stirling's children had turned seventeen two weeks before the sale of Hestan was due to be stamped as done and dusted. That he'd addressed his letter to Charlie Stirling instead of both children, putting Charlie in charge. Heron dismissing Frith, assuming Charlie would naturally be the one who would be most like his father.

But that wasn't the case. Not at all.

Sholto was up not long past six thirty, still dark outside, up and dressed and down the stairs before Esther had time to even think

about bringing him any tea. He found the girl in the kitchen, riddling out the stove.

'Sorry to disturb you,' he ventured, Esther surprised by him again, just like in the library, clattering the riddling rod to the floor and standing up, knees cricking, apron smattered over with soot.

'My, but you're an early bird,' she said, straightening her bonnet, Sholto smiling, aware he'd intruded and wishing it was not so.

'Not so early as you,' he said, Esther taking the compliment as it was meant.

'Always got to be up before the master,' she said. 'Work to do and all that. Though not usually expecting guests down here, not in the kitchen anywise.'

Sholto shook his head.

'I'm not a guest, not exactly. I mean I am, of course, but it's for work, nothing more. And I'm wondering, Esther, about your master, the present one and the one before.'

Esther looked at her unexpected visitor with suspicion, even more so when he made a move towards the kettle, Esther nipping in before him, grabbing up a teapot on the way.

'I'll do that, sir, if you don't mind.'

Sholto took a step back, chided, and dragged a chair out from the table and sat down.

'A cup of tea would be just the thing,' he said, unwilling to leave. 'And the Herons? Why don't you tell me about them?'

'What exactly are you wanting to know?' Esther swilled some hot water around the teapot, ejected it, replaced it with a few generous spoonfuls of loose tea from the caddy.

'Where they came from, for example,' Sholto began. 'I mean, are they an old family from around these parts?'

Esther snorted, bringing the water in the kettle back up to a roiling boil before pouring it into the teapot, placing a trivet onto

the table and the teapot onto the trivet and covering both with a snug, fur-lined cosy.

'Hardly,' she said, fetching milk and putting it in a jug and placing it beside the trivet. 'You'll always be a newcomer if you ain't been here a couple hundred years.'

'And the Herons haven't been?' Sholto asked mildly.

'Bairns to milk,' Esther said dismissively, bringing over a bowl of sugar lumps and a pair of ornate silver sugar tongs. 'Before my time, mind, but I'm thinking the old Mr Heron came here sometime in the fifties. Place was empty for a while afore that.'

'So he maybe bought Balcary House earlier?' Sholto asked, more to himself than Esther, though Esther answered anyway.

'Maybe, might be,' she equivocated, cup and saucer deftly placed to Sholto's left, along with a tea strainer. 'Can't really say. Place was a bit run down, to tell the truth,' she added, 'before Mr Heron moved in. Some of the farmers was really complaining, what with no one being in the house since years. All estate land, see, all the farms tenanted, but no one there to run it proper, and no investment and all that.'

Sholto busied himself pouring a cup of tea, adding a couple of lumps of sugar.

'Will you not have a cup yourself?' he asked, Esther looking at him curiously, thin smile on thin pink lips.

'You're really not a proper guest, are you?' she hazarded, hands on hips, arrested momentarily by the strangeness of the situation.

'Not me,' Sholto said, with a small laugh. 'Told you before. Work only. Rather be out on that island with my colleague.'

'I think you probably would,' Esther said slowly, turning abruptly away from him as a small bell began to ring on a line of bells just to the left of the kitchen door. 'That's the master calling

for his breakfast,' she said, 'so best ask quickly what else you want to know because I'm soon to be away.'

Sholto sucked his tea down – and really good tea it was too, pleasantly fragrant.

'So the older Mr Heron came here in the fifties, but his son James? He can't be more than twenty-five, so…'

'Came here fully formed,' Esther supplied for him, busy now, getting out trays and more teapots, cups and jugs, checking the kettle on the stove. 'Man and boy. No hint of a wife. Talk was,' she went on as she bustled about the kitchen, started scrambling eggs, laying slices of bread on the range to toast, 'that old Mr Heron lived in Manchester afore he came here. A book trader, I think me mam said. And a really kind sort o'person he was, though a bit doolally in the end, poor old sod.'

The bell jingled again and Esther loaded up her tray and was off, leaving Sholto sitting at the kitchen table, sifting various bundles of information around in his head, trying to find meaning and provenance, sort all the dates he'd been given into order: Hestan, the property of Dundrennan Abbey for hundreds of years until passing into the Balcary Estate in the early 1800s; that inventory in the library alluding to some very valuable books being purchased in the Crimea in the 1830s, confirmed by James Heron's comments about his father's past of being there, and him wanting to sell off any more that had value; Perdue and Merryweather being granted licence to mine on Hestan since 1833 – according to that slip of paper he'd found the night before in the study, although if it hadn't been lodged with a lawyer it would be tantamount to being non-existent; Balcary House lying empty for years until the older Heron arrived sometime in the 1850s, after the purchase of Hestan, and presumably bringing James with him, around the same time the Crimean War ended in 1856.

There was a pattern running through all this. He could sense it as surely as a hound scents the tracks of a hare going through long grass. He needed more information. He needed to know precisely when and where the Heron family came from and exactly how long they'd owned Balcary; and he needed to know the nature of the older Heron's connections to the Crimea. He also wanted to find out when James had taken over the running of the estate from his father; and what Merryweather and Perdue's connection was with the latter, or Hestan, or both. Ostensibly his need to know was only in order to protect Merryweather and Perdue's livelihoods – as Brogar had directed – but curiosity was his driving force. Something hidden was at work here, an unspoken and unacknowledged objective he couldn't yet fathom, but with Hestan – and maybe the Crimea – right at its heart.

Chapter 16

Curlew Beaks And Bad Apples

Brogar was delighted to be out in the day, wanting to take another walk around the island before he left. Kerr stayed behind to prime his lamp, pleased Brogar had been able to use it so functionally the night before. It got him thinking how much greater he could make it, how he could adapt it to contact ships about to flounder, send out warning signals instead of being a mere speck of light in the darkness indistinguishable from any other specks. What he ought to do was set up two more lights on the points of Almorness and Balcary, a triangulate that could surely not be mistaken for anywhere else once it was entered onto navigational charts, a certain warning that ships should not go any further in towards the sands. And if he set them to dual purpose – both as warning lights and Morse code senders – he'd need to redesign the shutters, get the whole operation running more effectively, have a couple of helpers landwise. He figured Brogar might be able to help with the practicalities of design. He seemed a man who knew a lot about a lot, and maybe together they'd be able to come up with workable solutions to make the lights brighter and bigger. His head was so busy with all these new possibilities that he completely forgot he

might not be on Hestan in a few days' time. His list of things not to be forgotten was forgotten, his feet firmly planted on the roof of his box-bedroom next to his lamp, both standing tall and strong.

He finished refilling the lamp's chambers, stoppered the bottle of water and the container of calcium carbide, trimmed the wick, closed the hatch, began rubbing his fingers through his beard as he straightened his back and gazed across the bay, picking out the best spots on Balcary and Almorness for new lights, checking the line of the tide, calculating they'd a half hour yet before they needed to move and another hour or so leeway after that. Plenty of time to run his ideas past Brogar before Brogar left. All this he was thinking as he took the few steps across the roof towards the ladder down, his attention diverted by the sight of someone small, jumping and tripping over the heather and up the path that led from Merryweather's cottage to the workshop, a gleaming halo around her head as she ran, backlit as she was by the rising sun. He smiled to see Frith so, leaping like a cricket in her too big boots, exactly as she'd done when she was a nipper on the rare occasions Archie brought her and her brother over to Hestan.

Good days, he was thinking, as he launched himself over the edge of the roof onto the ladder. Not such a good day when he got to the bottom and turned to find Frith launching herself the last few yards towards him, cheeks red but no smiles or dimples now, face tight, eyes bright with panic.

'It's Mr Merryweather!' she gasped, hammering her hands to her side to stop the stitch caused by her running. 'He's really bad, Mr Perdue. Not even sure he's still alive.'

Down by the sands beyond Balcary House, Sholto put a hand up to his eyes to shade them from the rising sun, looking over at Hestan for signs of life, eager for Brogar's return so he could sound out

his theories, see if Brogar found them as cogent and compelling as he did himself. He'd rummaged a little more in the library after Esther had left to see to James's breakfast, intrigued by her belief that the older Mr Heron had been a book trader in Manchester before he came to Balcary and the possibly related statement by James that many of the books in the library were purchased in the Crimea. With these notions in mind he'd studied the layout of the library as he'd not done the night before, becoming aware how unusual this library was. James was certainly right that there were valuable volumes here. Sholto was able to pick out several at the merest glance, so there would undoubtedly be far more, given the diversity of topic, title and language groups represented. How James Heron knew that too was a mystery, but James had certainly been right about Big Houses and their wasted libraries. It had been a common frustration back in Trondheim to his fellow members of the Linnaean Society who spent months – years sometimes – tracking down one specific volume or another of importance to their work, finally tracing its provenance and whereabouts, only to be denied access by the owners informing them curtly that they'd no idea of such a book's existence and to please not bother them anymore. There was no law compelling private owners to divulge details of their collections to the public and so, short of someone physically going and banging on their doors and pleading entrance, those works disappeared from possible consultation by the researchers so keen to make use of them, drag them out of the anonymity they might have fallen into for tens, maybe a hundred, years. An intellectual crime of the first order in many people's minds, including Sholto's. And yet if Heron really had been a book trader in a former life then it stood to reason he would have itemised his library volume by volume, and given his son some notion of their value.

Sholto went back to the handwritten catalogue he'd seen the night before and scanned the shelves for others with a similar binding, finding three more, all demarcating certain categories of books, and all three undoubtedly scribed by the same hand, though these latter were far neater and more precise. Which fact meant nothing in itself, for there could be any number of reasons why that should be so. Still, it struck Sholto there was an ordered mind at work here and one whose order he would like to explore further, given the perfect opportunity by James Heron appearing fortuitously on the scene.

'So, you're accepting my offer,' James stated rather than asked, his threats of coercion the night before apparently forgotten, Sholto looking up to find James leaning easily against the jamb of the library door, neat in his tweeds, his high leather boots, wondering how long he'd been standing there.

'I'm...considering it,' Sholto said, not wanting to sound too enthusiastic. 'I'd like to spend a few more hours here, looking through...'

'You take your few hours,' James cut him off, pushing his body away from the door frame, readying himself to go. 'But by the time I get back from Thorn's this afternoon I'll expect your final decision. I can get any number of traders here from Manchester, Mr McKay, but chose to give you first crack as you're already on the spot. If you're not up to the job, or don't want it, then I need to know. Time's a-wasting, as they say, and I've never been one to waste time for anyone.'

And no more did he, James away, heels clicking up the corridor, no looking back for the likes of James Heron, leaving Sholto on the cusp of his dilemma – as was undoubtedly the intent.

'He's dead,' Brogar pronounced, levering Merryweather's body over and away from the slick of blood that had coagulated about

his head into a dark and greasy pool next to the broken lamp that had singed his clothes but had been too weak to set him burning. 'And been lying here a while,' Brogar went on, placing his large fingers to either side of Merryweather's head and lifting it a few inches for a better look. 'Blood's all settled in his face, and something else under here.'

Kerr Perdue retched, took a few steps back out the door of the cottage and retched again, body bent double, cold sweat on his temples, putting out a hand by reflex to stop Frith going in any further, shoving himself between her and the door to keep her from the sight.

'But he was fine last night,' Frith was whispering. 'Honest he was. Brought him his stew and that, and he can't have just died. How could he just have died?'

Brogar gently placed Merryweather's cheek on the floor, interested in what had been plunged into his eye socket – not that much of it was visible – Kerr, looking in at that moment, almost throwing up again, Brogar noticing.

'Get Frith back to the workshop,' he commanded, Kerr Perdue glad to go, pulling Frith on after him, though Frith was no easy person to pull on, digging in her heels.

'No,' she began, 'I need to...'

'No, you absolutely don't,' Kerr was stronger, a lot stronger, almost whipping Frith off her feet as he saw the tail end of what Brogar was fingering, the vomit in his throat burning and foul as the oil the fulmars spat at anyone approaching their nests. But Frith was stubborn, mule-headed and widderwise, as her father had been before her, twisting her body back around so Kerr almost pulled her arm out of her socket as he forced her away.

'Frith, please,' Kerr Perdue sounded so exhausted and so patently close to choking up the hot regurgitation in his throat that Frith

subsided, went along with him and away from Merryweather and the cottage, allowing herself to be taken into Perdue's workshop and comparative warmth.

'Sit down, Frith,' Kerr asked, closing his eyes, putting out a shaky hand for a chair and lowering himself into it. 'Please sit down.'

Frith sat, but was not meek, was like a terrier told to wait at a rabbit hole before being put into use, muscles straining for the off.

'I'll sit, Mr Perdue,' Frith said stiffly, 'but I'm not a child and I'll not be shielded from what's going on, not by you, nor by my brother, nor by that Mr Brogar, come to that.'

Despite his fear and anxiety Kerr Perdue let out a small exasperated laugh.

'You Stirlings have…always been thrawn and…contermacious,' he said, swallowing convulsively as he got out his words. 'Used to be said of your…da…long…before I'm saying it of you. Like a sea eagle,' Kerr went on easier, breathing and bile under control, the abnormality of the situation more bearable now that he was somewhat distant. 'That's what Kheranovich used to say of him,' he coughed, cleared his throat, remembering Kheranovich saying the words like it was yesterday and repeating them for Frith. 'Like a sea eagle, he said, that glides over mountain and dale for miles and miles and days upon days, until it spies something down below that it wants and then down it goes, talons out, and God forbid you get in his way.'

Frith didn't reply. Her father was to her a picture painted by other people. She laced her ankles together between the chair legs and thought on what Kerr had said: *like a sea eagle*; well, that was something, and not all bad, she supposed; magnificent even, if you forgot that mostly what sea eagles did was murder birds smaller than themselves. And in the forgetting came the good: someone who crosses miles and miles of country until they find what they

want, and if that's what her da had done then that was alright with her. She could forget the bits that didn't fit.

'So how'd you all get out?' she asked. 'You never really said.'

Kerr not answering immediately, looking over at Frith: the small embodiment of her father in some ways, completely different in others. Pretty looking too, just like Archie, he realised and then blushed because he'd realised it and didn't want to, not in any way.

'A friend,' he said. 'A good friend to all of us. Got so much more to tell you, Frith, about me and Merryweather and...'

His head lurching forward of its own accord, the thought of Merryweather too much, gagging up what he thought he'd swallowed, Frith leaping to her feet as Perdue vomited all over the table and over his hands the early morning coffee he'd drunk, the undigested hunks of bread and last night's stew he'd had for breakfast, scraped from the pot and warmed by Frith herself minutes before he'd gone out to see to his light.

'I'm so sorry...' he whispered, trying to wipe himself clean on his sleeves, making things worse in the process, Frith shocked but all the more quick and efficient because of it.

'Don't be,' she said, going at him with the cloths she'd previously set to drying by the stove, and a slop of water from the kettle. 'Don't know if you ken this,' she added as she poured more water on the cloths, laved him like he was a baby who'd spat out its milk, 'but Mam was pretty bad last few years and more than one mess. She'd pain in her like you wouldn't believe, and we didn't even know the cause of it until she was dead.'

Too much for Kerr Perdue, strong man that he was, and the sound that came from him was like a ewe separated from her lamb: desperate and undone, a lamentation for the lost that might never be found again; and no matter that he heard the keening and knew it was coming from himself and was shamed by it, he

couldn't stop it; the past become a snake that had swallowed him whole and wouldn't let him go, everything constricted and dark: no way forward, no way back.

And that was how Brogar Finn found the two of them: Kerr Perdue hunched over the table whose wood was busily soaking up his watered-down vomit and would never smell the same again, Frith by Perdue's side wiping first his face and then his hands with her dampened cloths, lifting Perdue's fingers one by one to clean them before placing them away from the table and onto Perdue's lap, and Brogar – having a good idea how Merryweather had died – finding it impossible that either could be so vicious, and yet logic telling him it could not be otherwise. Only three other people on the island when Merryweather had been murdered, and he knew he wasn't the guilty one. And as he watched Frith and Kerr Perdue he knew on whom he'd place his money, and that was the girl who didn't believe in good endings to folk tales for, just like in those folk tales, the prettiest apple was usually the one to hide the most poison within its skin.

All that was left was to slice the damn apple open and see what came out.

CHAPTER 17

DEFINING ENEMIES, FINDING FRIENDS

'Everyone ready?' Hazel asked, looking critically at the little group gathered before her on the grass: Charlie heaped uncomfortably in a handcart with Bill behind him at the helm, Hugh easing Charlie's broken leg onto a pillow and shoving another in at Charlie's back; Gilligan already running on ahead, the coins Hazel had given him warming in his clutched fist: his mission to hire the first horse and cart that would take them all the few miles from Auchencairn to Balcary. Hazel's initial plan had been for them to wait at the house until Gilligan returned, object achieved, but no one else was in agreement. She'd not wanted Charlie to go anywhere at all, but he'd been insistent he would be there at Balcary to greet Frith when she got over from the island, finding an unexpected ally in Bill who'd at once gone to the shed to retrieve the handcart that was cracked in three places along its base, the vulcanised rubber clinging to its wooden wheels in the merest shreds. She doubted they'd get the half mile to the village without Charlie falling through the planking, dreading the further damage he might do to his leg if he did.

'Surely that wondrous plaster of Paris will protect him,' Bill put in when Hazel objected, Hazel looking quickly at her husband,

certain she was being mocked, but all she saw on his face was grim determination as he gripped his hands about the cart's handles.

'I'll be fine, Mrs Tuley,' Charlie assured her, easing his leg against one pillow, his back against the other.

'Well, I suppose it's not far,' she acceded, though she gave Charlie a second dose of laudanum to ease the pain of being shuggled along a bumpy track; and then she gave the command to be off.

'A motley crew we must be making,' she commented, as they made their way from their track and onto the little lane that led to Auchencairn.

'I disagree entirely,' Bill said, smiling a little manically as he fought to keep the cart going in a straight line. 'Motley means many-coloured, spotted even, and we're about as drab as we can be.'

He was right about that, Hazel thought, all of them dressed in garbs the colour of mud. She thought on the gay hat she used to wear when they first came here, its felted wool the colour of pumpkin skin and made all the more garish by Bill planting into its red ribbon band a few pheasant feathers.

'Brings out the colour in your eyes,' he'd said, Hazel blushing like the young bride she was as he placed his hand against her cheek, thumb beneath her chin, lifting her face towards him. 'And prettier eyes I've never seen.'

A long time since he'd ever said anything like that to her and probably never would again, the thought so depressing that Hazel sighed, looked away, those early years together so lost to them both they might have belonged to other people. It seemed inconceivable now that they used to sit together in the living room at night, her with her fiddle, the two of them singing ballads to keep themselves awake in case one or other of their patients in the tiny hospital next door called out for aid.

All about Yule, when the winds blow cold...

The tune ran through her mind unbidden.

And the Round Table begins;

When there is come to our king's court many the well-favoured man.

One of Bill's favourites, the one he said best fitted him on seeing her for the first time.

Oh, I've seen lords and I've seen lairds, and knights of high degree,

But Young Waters is the fairest face that ever mine eyes did see.

God, there'd been nights when he'd sung that song to her and afterwards they'd run up the stairs together, peeling off their clothes as they went, the urgency to get to the bedchamber so strong they couldn't have cared if the whole universe outside of themselves was collapsing, as long as they got there in time, got there together, laughing and singing and kissing all at the same time. And she'd do it again tomorrow, if only she got the chance.

It never seemed to matter that at the end of the ballad Young Waters was deprived of wife, child and head with one blow of the axe.

Brogar had more practical matters on his mind. He needed to separate Frith and Perdue; interrogate – or talk to, as Sholto would no doubt have split the issue – and get both their stories on record. For the most part, he could account for each of their movements the previous night, but there'd been time-gaps when both were alone, and during those time-gaps it was equally possible for either to have murdered Gabriel Merryweather. The how was not in question: one of Perdue's copper-clasped curlew beaks had been rammed straight through Merryweather's left eye and a lot further, and both were strong enough to do the deed if they'd caught Merryweather unawares. The big problem for Brogar was the why of it, but once again it was Frith who came up tops. Her

explanation of her and her brother being on the island to pull out the bones of their father from shaft number three didn't ring true. It didn't explain why Frith hadn't been helping her brother, why she'd stayed hidden, why she'd opted – or been co-opted – into hanging out in a cave while her brother did the dirty work; for Frith didn't strike him as one to take a backseat, not if she'd the chance of doing otherwise. The sight of Frith cleaning up Kerr Perdue so efficiently only strengthened Brogar's suspicions; the smell of vomit was strong in the air and it was unusual to find someone so unmoved by another person's throwing up that they didn't shortly afterwards start throwing up themselves. All part of the body's method of defence: you see someone bowk, you do it yourself in case whatever infected them has infected you; a mark of social cohesion, same as someone yawning makes you yawn and someone laughing makes you laugh – no idea why you're doing it, just a reflex that is hard to stifle.

But not Frith.

Frith's calm, as she tended to Kerr, was unnerving; not that Brogar was discounting Kerr, not by any means, but for him Frith was the stumbling block, and a stumbling block he meant to get over, meant to get solved before either of the two of them got over the water to disappear into the maze of lanes and farms that were spread along the length of the Solway and far beyond.

'There's a few matters we need to discuss, Kerr,' Brogar began, his broad bulk filling the doorway. 'But first, go and get yourself a change of clothes. Me and Frith can finish cleaning up here.'

Kerr didn't argue, getting up on shaky legs, face pale and clammy as a boletus that has grown up in the woods without much light. He didn't look at all well, but guilt could play havoc with a person's physiology. Nevertheless, Brogar slapped a companionable hand on Perdue's shoulder as he came within reach.

'We'll get to the bottom of it,' Brogar said. 'Things like this don't happen without consequence,' he added mildly, 'not while I'm about.'

Kerr conjured a small quiver of his lips within his beard, the closest he could get to a smile. He nodded, but could get no words out, stumbling off through the door and away to his shack, seeing the square solidity of it stark against the sky, thinking how like Brogar it was with its certain strength, its lack of frailty, its ability to face anything that was thrown at it.

Brogar closed the door.

Frith was swiping at the table with a scrubbing brush to whose coarse bristles she'd first applied the large bar of grey soap she'd found by the sink.

'Not bothered by the smell?' Brogar asked, watching Frith's efficient movements, the hard knots of muscles beneath the sleeves of her rolled-up shirt, her coat slung over a second chair, presumably so as not to get it besmirched.

Frith snorted.

'Used to be, long time ago,' she said, wiping a fresh cloth over the table surface before moving to the floor by Perdue's recently vacated chair, it not escaping Brogar's notice that she had as yet refused to meet his eyes. One more mark tallied against her.

'That sounds mysterious,' he said. 'So what's the what with that?'

Frith scrubbed hard at the floor, rinsed her cloth in the bucket and swept away the meagre soap bubbles left by her cleaning before pushing herself up from her knees with the supple ease of youth and going to the sink to empty her pail.

'Not so mysterious when your ma used to chuck up every morning for the last six months of her life.'

Frith rattled her pail, put her hand to the pump to bring in more water. It was salty, straight from the Solway, and didn't mix

well with soap, leaving a grimy line of muck and bubble against the stone of the sink that she went at with her brush.

Brogar raised his eyebrows. Not an answer he'd been expecting by any means.

'She was ill, your mother?' he asked, moving further into the room, tarrying by Kerr's wooden line of beaks, trying to recall how many had been there the night before, if any of them were missing.

Frith finished her splashing but didn't turn around, scrunched up her nose, rubbed the corners of her eyes with fingers and thumb, this seeming too private a matter to discuss with a complete stranger. And Brogar Finn was a complete stranger, that was clear to her now as it hadn't been yesterday when he'd seemed dependable, trustworthy, a man to side with the angels as her mother would have said.

'You could say that,' Frith replied, unwilling to divulge too much. 'In a lot of pain at the end, and all the stuff the doctor put in her just seemed to make her worse.'

Brogar didn't reply. It was certainly an adequate explanation of sorts, and one he didn't dismiss. He held out his fingers to the beaks that were on display, certain they'd not changed their order: curlew, oystercatcher, gannet, puffin, fulmar, some kind of duck he couldn't remember the name of…all were there in their rack, and not one of them had yet been set into a clasp. There could, of course, be any number of finished talismans in the drawers liberally built into the workbenches, but nevertheless his suspicions about Merryweather's murder were beginning to shift. Frith and Perdue were still the most obvious suspects – no getting away from that – but he was casting his mind back over everything that had been told to him on Hestan by Perdue, Frith and Merryweather himself, having the vaguest notion of some common denominator lingering in the shadows of what each had

said. His daily work consisted of looking and finding, of making reductions and deductions, figuring from what had gone before what might be possible in the future. All to do with minerals and metals, of course, but the way those minerals and metals moved and behaved weren't so far off from how people lived out their lives. All on a very different timescale perhaps, but minerals, metals and men had a history they weren't in control of, pressures and events squeezing them, moulding them into what they would eventually become.

'I need to talk to Kerr Perduc,' Brogar said. 'You alright to finish up here?'

''Course,' Frith said shortly, scrubbing the brush unnecessarily hard against the sink, glad she wasn't being asked to divulge more details of her mother's illness, glad that once Brogar left she would be alone, knowing that the second he went she was going to start blubbing like the stupid little girl she was, but absolutely didn't want to be seen to be. Not ever. Not like her mam had been: the unnecessary stupidity of her keeping everything to herself for all those years and not a word about it to her children. And Charlie... well, he was going to get a bloody good earful when she got over the way, and she was going to get that letter sent from old Mr Heron and read it top to bottom, side to side, see what Charlie had been hiding from her, and she didn't care a damn if anyone else saw it, long as it was out in the open, thinking that it might be for the better if they did.

Kerr had changed his shirt and trousers, would have changed his jacket and boots if he'd had others to replace them with, but he didn't. The smell and taste of vomit was strong in his nose and throat and he glugged at the water the bottle on his nightstand to try and rid himself of it. The water was stale, sitting for several

days untouched; him and Merryweather dependent on fresh water brought over from the mainland to keep them supplied with what they could drink and not the salt water pumped in from the sea that was good enough for cleaning, a bit of cooking, but not much else. He scratched hard at his forehead, so hard he brought forth blood without noticing it. He'd no idea what was going on. He just couldn't fathom that Merryweather was dead; could find no reason, no why nor wherefore, his sole and completely unfounded conclusion being that he would be next.

He was sat on his bed, water jar in hand, when Brogar came knocking on his door and next came in, the only sounds being the slight creaking of the mattress beneath Kerr's weight and the harsh keeks and calls of the gulls as they moved in the morning on the roof above.

'We need to talk,' Brogar said.

'Talk away,' Kerr said, one hand brushing over his bed, no need for engagement, not with this man, not with anyone.

'First things first,' Brogar went on unabashed. 'Merryweather's body. Will you bury him here?'

Kerr shook his head and let out a breath.

'Nowhere real suitable,' he mumbled, 'though that's what he'd want. Him and me both, come to that. But even if we found somewhere soft and deep enough, your lot will soon be tramping over the place and digging up every last inch of the island from the inside out. Gutted like a herring it'll be, and not even Merryweather would want to be here when that happens.'

His words were bitter as the bile lingering on his lips but he didn't care who heard them, Company man or no. Brogar rolled his shoulders and looked at Perdue hunched on his bed, a man defeated.

'Well, you're probably right about that,' Brogar conceded, 'assuming they come.'

'Well of course they'll bloody come,' Perdue said with certainty, though no lift to his words. 'Nothing to stop them now, especially with only me here. One down, one to go, wouldn't you say?'

The implication of this statement caught Brogar off guard.

'You think the estate or the Company somehow engineered Merryweather's murder?' he asked, Perdue looking up suddenly, his eyes wet and shining in the dim light coming through the door.

'And you don't?' Perdue accused, jumping to his feet, stabbing his finger in Brogar's direction. 'You think it was me? Or Frith? Don't make me laugh!'

Brogar pulled his head back in surprise, taking a couple of seconds to get to the end of Kerr's logic, finally getting out a few words.

'You think…it was me?'

He couldn't stop himself; he began an almighty laugh that rattled with the gulls up above, pattering about the place at the noise, Kerr lunging forward the two yards that lay between him and Brogar with every intent of strangling the life out of him; Brogar, still laughing, pushing Perdue easily away, keeping him at bay with one hand held flat and hard against Kerr's chest.

'God's sake, man, stop!' Brogar said, wiping his eyes with his free hand, the situation so amusing he was almost crying with it. And then it was Brogar who stopped and Kerr who was crying, collapsing onto the end of his bed, holding his head in his hands, sobbing silent and wretched, shoulders heaving, body racked, and nothing amusing about that. Brogar stilled, Brogar softened, and up on the roof the gulls stilled too, as if they were neighbours with an interest in the affair.

'I'm not your enemy,' Brogar spoke slowly into the sudden quiet. 'I was mad as hell when I heard folk were still here on Hestan and

I've Sholto over at Balcary right now, trying to find a way to stop you getting chucked off.'

Kerr covered his face with his hands, fingertips hard against his eyes to stop the tears, a tremor in chin, mouth and throat as he fought against the urge to let go again, swallowing and sniffling, hating the humiliation.

'And I've an idea that might help,' Kerr heard Brogar's words falling like rain, like he was somewhere else entirely, like he was out on Hestan at its topmost point where Baliol had built his manor, like he was holding out his face against the spray coming off the sea, like he was one of those lines on his list of things to remember, like he was on Hestan's list, if Hestan cared.

Sholto glanced up at the clock on the library wall and hastily gathered all his notes together, re-shelved the books he'd been looking at with such intent, excitement tingling in his body with his discoveries. But discoveries were nothing until you could tell them to someone else, and that someone else had to be Brogar – due back any minute from the island. He'd tarried a little too long and went out of Balcary House on a run, getting to the beach by the house just as Hugh and Gilligan were spilling from the back of a wagon, Hazel and Bill behind them lifting Charlie down in his barrow – that hadn't split during the journey to Auchencairn, though might have done if Gilligan hadn't returned so promptly with his hire.

'Well met, fellows!' Bill shouted exuberantly on seeing Sholto, Sholto immediately caught up by Hugh and Gilligan coming rushing at him and throwing their small arms about his waist, surprised all over again by how much they'd missed him and how much he'd missed them.

'Well now,' Sholto said, once the greetings were over. 'Any news?'

He was thinking of Brogar, but Bill apparently had other things on his mind.

'In fact, yes,' Bill butted in before anyone else had the chance. 'Me and Hugh were talking last night about black flowers.'

'Black flowers?' Sholto repeated, not seeing the relevance.

'Precisely!' Bill went on. 'Hugh says you're the fount of all knowledge, so tell me this, Mr Sholto. If black flowers don't exist because black sucks in the sun and doesn't reflect its light, then why do all the women in hot countries habitually wear black?'

'For the exact same reason,' Sholto replied, creasing his brows, bemused but not lost for words. 'The black cloth sucks in the heat and holds it so – theoretically – their skin stays cool beneath.'

'Aha!' Bill exclaimed. 'I knew you'd have an answer!'

Sholto shot a glance at Hazel, but Hazel was busily ignoring the situation and seeing to Charlie.

'Leg alright?' she was asking.

'Fine,' Charlie replied easily, though the pallor of his face was saying otherwise. 'But might take you up on your offer,' he added, 'of stopping here rather than taking off across the sand.'

Hazel smiled, glad for it, and glad that Bill was interacting so eagerly with other people, if a little madly. Maybe it was time to exhume the fiddle from the cupboard where it had been mouldering for years, get it cleaned, restrung and tuned. It had been an age since she'd attempted to play it, but it was a skill thoroughly learned in her youth so maybe it would come back to her, if she tried hard enough.

'There's Mr Brogar!' Gilligan shouted, all on the landward side turning their heads to look.

'And that must be Frith,' Hugh added, for Charlie's benefit, as they saw a smaller figure running along behind Brogar's impressive profile to keep pace along the Rack, the two of them veering off

and starting across the sands towards Balcary, waving their arms at the folk waiting othersides, Hugh and Gilligan unable to be stopped and charging off to greet them halfway.

'I thought the entire bay was riddled with quicksand!' Sholto was alarmed, holding out a useless arm as if by doing so he could bring Hugh and Gilligan back to him.

'It'll likely be fine,' Bill said, lowering Sholto's arm with his own. 'Only mudflats. Nothing dangerous unless you're out there when the tide's coming in and it's not coming in yet, not by a long while.'

'But should they be running like that,' Sholto argued, heart hammering in his chest, 'not knowing where they're going?'

'They'll be fine,' Bill reassured him again. 'Certainly there's soft places that might suck them in, but only to their boots. And boots can be replaced. And not to worry, I'll be there to pull them out.'

He grabbed up a stout piece of driftwood and then was off, an ungainly runner, legs a little bowed, but he caught up Gilligan and Hugh without trouble, made them slow their pace, take their time, stabbed his stick into the sand before they trod on it further, for which Sholto was grateful. Still, he worried all the while they were out there, watching with every anxious second as they went on towards Brogar and Brogar strode confidently towards them, Frith running on his heels; but everything fine, the two parties meeting and turning in the same direction, everyone coming back with skin and boots intact, everything alright until Sholto saw Brogar's face clearly, when he knew that everything was not alright, not at all.

'So I'm guessing that Frith and Charlie's father is in number three,' Brogar had stated to Perdue earlier that morning in the dim square room beneath the gulls and the light.

'Aye,' Perdue answered dully, his rage spent and gone, no longer believing Brogar had murdered Merryweather any more than

he'd murdered Merryweather himself, unsure what to believe; the downside of this conviction leaving only Frith culpable, and that tide of events just didn't bear thinking about. 'Been in there a long time, though we never said it. And no idea how the kid knew about it. We all swore we'd never say.'

'And by all, who'd you mean exactly?' Brogar persisted, that notion of a common denominator popping up again, this time with more clarity, with more facts at his fingertips, facts he knew Sholto would take hold of and command once he was apprised of them.

'Only me and Merryweather,' Kerr said, a moment's hesitation too late, same monotone to his voice as before his outburst, Brogar irritated, wanting the truth, regretting stopping the man last night, even though Kerr had been practically falling asleep where he sat.

'All is not two,' Brogar stated flatly. 'All means more than two. All means not just you and Merryweather, so why the hell can't you just spit it out?'

Kerr Perdue flinched on his bunk. Secrets kept for so long, but what the hell was the point anymore? If young Charlie knew – and patently he knew some of it or why would he and Frith have come here in the first place? – well, there was the nub of it, how much young Charlie knew. Kerr Perdue took a chance.

'You said before you'd an idea that might help. Might help me, might help Hestan.'

Brogar took his time, pushed wide the door from Perdue's sleeping shack and stepped aside so the light flooded in on Kerr Perdue and his miserable stance on his bed, laid bare to the sights and sounds that Hestan afforded the early waker.

'I know you don't want to leave this place,' Brogar said, 'and I understand it. I also understand that with Merryweather gone you might feel the need to do exactly that. But hang on in there, Mr Kerr Perdue, because I believe there's something running

underneath this course of events that I haven't got to the bottom of yet. But I will. Believe me when I say that I will.'

'And Gabriel?' Kerr asked quietly, trying to quell the small grain of hope that was edging its way into his carapace of despair. 'What are we to do about Gabriel?'

'Gabriel,' Brogar stated, turning back towards Kerr, Kerr sensing his gaze and looking up, meeting Brogar's eyes. 'Gabriel,' Brogar repeated, 'will stay exactly where he is for the now. But tell me this: where is it he comes from? Where do you come from? You obviously knew each other before you went over to Sweden.'

Kerr put a hand to his face, rubbing thumb and forefinger into his cheeks and down into his beard.

'What did he tell you?'

'Not a lot more than you did,' Brogar parried. 'So we know you all joined up – together with Frith's father – went over to Sweden and then to Russia, that you all went back with Kheranovich to the Crimea, burning books and people and all that.'

Kerr lowered his hand, scratched his neck, opting for the simplest answer, which was the truth, but the truth without embellishment.

'Dundrennan,' he said. 'We all came from Dundrennan, or as nearby as made no difference. Me, Gabriel and Archie too. Few miles west of Auchencairn. We grew up there together. Started apprenticeships in Auchencairn together. Left from there together.'

'Well, that's fortunate,' Brogar said, Kerr watching Brogar closely, wondering if he shouldn't get the rest of it said right now, as he'd been unable to the night before. Brogar breaking the moment, giving him leave to think it over one last time.

'Either way, I'm going over to Balcary,' Brogar stated, 'get a coffin organised for Gabriel. But while I'm gone, there's something I need you to do…'

'What's happened?' Sholto asked Brogar immediately Gilligan and Hugh had departed with Frith to go see to Charlie, and the two were alone upon the sand.

'Merryweather's dead,' Brogar said.

Sholto was shocked.

'Dead? Dead how?'

'I mean dead as in despatched,' Brogar went on, 'as in someone helping him on his way.'

'Oh, for God's sake,' Sholto sighed. 'I thought we'd done with all that. What are we? Some kind of precursor to death coming in and sending his sword arm singing?'

The reference to the Eddas was lost on Brogar, but he got the gist, clapped his arm around Sholto's shoulders.

'You can't think of it like that,' he consoled. 'It's more that we keep getting shoved into situations where tempers run high. Mind what I once told you about tigers?'

Sholto did, and Sholto shuddered. The tale Brogar had told him about the man who'd been devoured in the snowy forests of Siberia, his two feet in his two boots found yards apart being the only sign he'd ever existed, still gave him nightmares.

'So who's the tiger in all this?' he asked, Brogar pulling Sholto close and then letting him go, sucking the air in through his teeth.

'I'm not sure it's that simple,' Brogar said. 'I think there's a lot more going on here that we don't know about.'

'Well, I can second that,' Sholto added. 'What do you know about the Crimea? And I don't mean just the war, I mean about the region itself.'

Brogar turned and placed his hands on Sholto's shoulders, pulling him around so the two were facing one another.

'Do you know what I like about you? Why we rub along together so well?' Brogar asked, his smile wide and infectious,

Sholto taking the question seriously, knowing how badly some of Brogar's previous assistants had met their end.

'That we're two halves of the same equation?' Sholto suggested, Brogar releasing his hold on Sholto's shoulders, some kind of laugh growing in this throat and coming out as a series of short barks.

'Priceless!' Brogar exclaimed, amidst his mirth. 'Absolutely priceless! And yes, you're right, Sholto. You're exactly right. You do your thing and I do mine. But right now,' Brogar dropped his voice, all humour gone, 'right now we need to get our heads together, pool our resources, because I'm telling you something is wrong here. I don't know how or what or why, but I can feel it. And it's a mystery, Sholto, and you know me. I've always liked a mystery.'

Chapter 18

Into The Burning Barn Goes The Hero

They had a lot to do, and not much time to do it in. Heron would be back from Thorn's farm that afternoon and would need an answer from Sholto. That part was easy, Sholto and Brogar both agreeing it would be a resounding yes, Sholto writing a quick note to that end and leaving it in Esther's care to pass on to Heron in case they weren't about when he returned. After that, they piled back onto the Tuleys' cart, everyone squeezing up together to make room for Brogar and Sholto. They could have waited, arranged their own transport, but Sholto pointed out to Brogar it might be illuminating to put a few questions to Frith and Charlie while they were together and in plain view, no chance to concoct answers or disguise their immediate reactions to those questions. Bill had kept up his frenetic pace and eagerly started reorganising everyone to what he deemed the best advantage, until Hazel stepped in and suggested he sit up front with the cart boy and keep him right, not that he could possibly go wrong, there being only one track and one direction back to Auchencairn; Bill acceded without hesitation, feeling in charge and on top of the world.

The pony was slowed by the extra weight, but it was nothing compared to pulling half a ton of spuds or a precarious mountain of neeps or straw bales and plodded on regardless, puffing every now and then as it strained the wagon wheels through ruts and holes in the track.

'So Frith,' Brogar began casually, 'have you told your brother yet about your near death experience?'

She had, but only in garbled form, and Gilligan wasn't about to let such excitement pass from his grasp.

'What happened?' Gilligan asked, eyes round and bright with expectation.

'Got stuck in a cave when the tide came in,' Frith answered shortly, not really wanting to go over it all again, but Gilligan was not to be deterred.

'Ooh,' he intoned, leaning forward. 'That sounds bad. Hugh fell off a pontoon into the water not long back and was nearly drowned.'

Hugh smiled as Frith looked over at him, brief introductions already made.

'It wasn't that bad,' Hugh said breezily, 'getting shot at was much worse.'

Frith raised her eyebrows and studied Hugh with interest.

'How your eye got done in and you got them scars?' she asked, Hugh nodding assent.

'Don't miss the end o' me nose,' he said lightly, 'but got a few problems with me eye, though Mr Bill and Mrs Tuley are going to help me on that score.'

Brogar looked over at Sholto, for this was news to him.

'Hazel and her husband were out in the Crimea,' Sholto said, slightly emphasising the last word for Brogar's benefit. 'Did a lot of work with wounded soldiers during the war. And if they can help Hugh, well, we'd all be glad of it.'

'Absolutely!' Brogar agreed with enthusiasm. 'And by the way, Mrs Tuley, did you ever meet Frith and Charlie's father out there? I'm sure Merryweather mentioned he was there around when you were.'

A bit of gamble on his part, Merryweather having clearly stated that he and Perdue were long gone when the war had started, but nothing about Archie Stirling, so no harm chucking it out, just in case.

Hazel continued tending to Charlie, keeping his plastered leg as still as possible, but she looked up at Brogar Finn. Over on the island he'd been swift and capable, decisions thought and made almost the same moment, but once back on the mainland she'd not given him a second thought. Not until now, not until she caught his hard stare, recognising she'd seen that kind of look before, mostly in generals giving out bad commands with no thought of how they would affect the men who came back several hours later from battle, broken and bloody, if they returned at all.

'I don't think so,' she said stiffly. 'But then we didn't know the family.'

'You didn't treat his wife in later years?' Brogar persisted.

'Well…no…' Hazel hesitated, adding quietly, 'I mean, I think Bill may have made up some medications…maybe visited a couple of times…towards the end.'

Charlie clicked his tongue.

'I knew I'd seen him before, your hubbie, like. Just couldn't place him. And by the by, that stuff he gave her? Didn't do a damn thing.'

The accusation in his voice was unmistakable and Hazel glanced towards her husband's back, hoping he hadn't heard the slight. Not that she was surprised by it. It wasn't the first time folk had complained. Financially they were on a knife edge because of it; Bill tried to be a competent doctor, but the truth of it was that he

wasn't. Not anymore. Getting worse down the years. She'd found him more than once cutting the wrong pills for the wrong people, getting dosages completely out of kilter – either far too much or far too little. If it hadn't been for her, they'd've been out of business a long time ago and folk knew it, tending to go to her if they could, at least if they could stand to be treated by a woman.

'And you Frith, and your brother,' Brogar asked, with one of the swift changes of subject that caught people on the hop. 'What exactly were you both doing on Hestan that was so sneaky you couldn't tell Merryweather and Perdue you were there? And before you answer,' he added, shooting a narrow-eyed stare from brother to sister and back again, 'let me remind you that you both nearly died in the trying.'

Frith's cheeks coloured and her mouth dropped open as if about to speak, but Charlie was quicker.

'Frith,' he warned, 'don't say anything. No one's damn business is what,' he added defiantly, looking up at Brogar, trying to stare him down and not succeeding, lowering his head, clearing his throat.

'So you weren't trying to drag your father's bones out of the mine?' Sholto put in, to general surprise, Sholto affecting not to notice and carrying on smoothly. 'For that would be entirely natural, given the circumstances, though perhaps not the way you went about it.'

'How d'you know about…' Charlie started and then stopped, grinding his teeth, realising his mistake, an angry red rising in his neck that he'd been so easily caught out.

'We know all about it, Charlie,' Brogar said loudly, 'so you may as well come clean, and you may as well tell us why the hell you made a plan so half-arsed it was damn near certain to get the two of you killed.'

Brutal, Sholto was thinking, but it had the desired effect.

'Because I don't think it was just Da we was after,' Frith murmured, her brother levering himself up, shaking off Hazel's hands, his leg dropping to the floor of the cart, the hard plaster thudding audibly, making Charlie wince at the pain, but not enough to stop the next two words wailing out of him, though they came as from a whiny child instead of the shout against the universe he'd meant them to be.

'Frith, don't!'

Frith looked over at her brother, understanding his urgency, his need to keep secrets, but angry he'd chosen to keep one of those secrets hidden from her of all people, and making her own deductions. She saw too the clamminess to his skin, his slender hands shaking as he tried to pick up his leg, get it comfortable, the wretched swipe he made as Hazel tried to intervene, Frith shaking her head, meeting her brother's gaze.

'You've got to tell them, Charlie,' she said, 'and me too, come to that.'

'Tell us,' Sholto said, placing a gentle hand on Frith's shoulder but looking over at her brother. 'Believe me when I say that all we mean to do is give you help.'

'Help, is it?' the pain in his leg had receded, Charlie regaining his belligerence. 'An' where was you all when we needed it? Where was everyone when me ma died screaming like Daft Annie when she went beneath the waves? Nowhere near is what, and no way we needs anybody's help. Not then, not now.'

The contradiction implicit in his impassioned plea completely passing Charlie by, but not so Frith, who was the more sanguine of the two, and left him in doubt of it.

'God's sake, Charlie,' Frith whipped her brother with her words. 'Can't you see it's all gone now? You've got your leg all smashed up

and I nearly drowned in that blasted cave you told me to wait in and Mr Perdue almost froze to death trying to haul me out, and he was Da's friend! Didn't I say we should have gone to him first, before we got into any of this?'

'Which rather begs the question why you didn't,' Sholto intervened quietly, smiling encouragingly at Frith, 'for you must have known that both Merryweather and Kerr Perdue knew your father's remains were left in that shaft. Something to do with his pension, maybe. Brogar?'

Brogar nodded.

'That's what I reckon. Army pension paid out long as everyone thinks he's still alive. Everyone keeping their mouths shut precisely to that end.'

'So when did you find out?' Sholto asked Frith. 'I mean that your father had died and not just run off again on one of his wild adventures?'

'We got a letter,' Frith said, biting her lip, quieter now.

'Frith…' Charlie closed his eyes, Frith shaking her head again, remorseful but utterly decided.

'We've got to say, Charlie,' Frith went on, 'you know as well as I do that when they starts digging Hestan up they're just going to chuck whatever it was you was looking for into a pit along with our da. At least this way we've a chance to get him out.'

Hazel had been listening intently to this entire exchange, at first bewildered, then curious, and now beginning to comprehend.

'So your father, Frith,' she said, summing the situation up as she saw it, 'died in that shaft where we found Charlie yesterday?'

Frith nodded, Charlie sighing, leaning against the backboard of the cart. He could hear Bill Tuley chatting animatedly to the wagon boy, telling the lad some anecdote about how years and years ago he'd trained a bird, a merlin, used to be called the Lady's

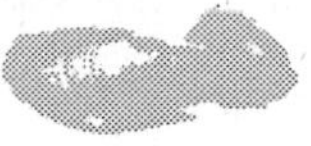

Falcon, on account of it being a favourite of the ancient kings of Scotland when falconry was more of a sport than it was now.

'The female is bigger, you see,' Bill was saying, 'and far better at hunting than the male, or at least hunting on command. But they're always difficult to train, those merlins; only the size of blackbirds pluffed up in the winter. Just like women, I always said, pluffed up and always difficult to train…'

Charlie stopped listening. He was weary, a little bleary, and his leg hurt like a bitch. He sighed, knew he was defeated.

'Just tell them, Frith,' he said, and Frith did.

Kerr Perdue was alone on the island, or at least the only living person here, he reminded himself, since Frith and Brogar Finn had left. Brogar had told Kerr that Merryweather had been attended to, that Brogar had lifted him onto his bed and covered him, left him decent – if dead – doused the stove to keep the cottage as cold as possible; not hard this time of the year.

'No need for you to do anything more for him just yet,' Brogar had said.

Just as well, for Perdue doubted he'd have been capable. It was hard enough to grasp that Gabriel was really gone, and far too hard to imagine having to see to his body. Back in the old days, when they'd been in Olszunka Grochowska and Ashmiany, seeing bodies was commonplace. They just kept on piling up, heaped together in bloody cairns, all twisted and torn, but all nameless and not really real somehow. That was what war did to you. Hollowed you out, made you believe that no one else except you and your mates were proper people with their own families, their own histories and stories. Made you think you were in a fairy tale; but even the good fairy tales – as Frith had reminded him – didn't always end well, at least if you looked beyond the obvious, which Frith – like her

father before her – seemed somehow able to do. But now Gabriel was dead, and not in wartime, not in fighting. Dead for no good reason Kerr could think of; just like Archie surviving all the battles they'd ever been in, and Archie surviving more than either Kerr or Merryweather had because he'd stayed out there so much longer, sticking to Kheranovich, the two of them bound together until the very end. And all because of those books they'd chosen to save and those folk herded into that barn in the middle of nowhere.

Kerr closed his eyes and then opened them again swift as he could. He was lying on his bed in his little square room below its light, thinking back on Merryweather asking him years before why he didn't share the cottage – plenty of room, and no reason why Kerr wouldn't take him up on the offer, except that once Kerr had built his lighthouse he found he enjoyed the experiences of waking in this square blank darkness better, it serving in some obscure way as penance for what they'd done way back, reminding him of the lack of sound coming from the old man and woman as they'd been shut into the barn, the beseechment on that young girl's face as the soldiers threw the bolt, locked them in, Tupikov loud at his back.

'We've to make an example,' he'd said, as if it was the most natural thing in the world to do such a terrible thing, and them doing it, Kheranovich agreeing, the look on his face saying *well, they're going to do it anyway; no point us chucking ourselves into the darkness with them.* And he'd been right. Kerr understood that. No point at all. Why not three people dying that night instead of seven? But such logic hadn't stopped any of the guilt or the nightmares, and it hadn't stopped Archie. Not Archie, who was never one to be stopped since he was a bairn.

Kerr lay on his bed fully dressed. He'd taken off his boots, but nothing else. He'd done everything Brogar had asked of him and

felt besmirched because of it. By adding a few more props and going quiet and gentle, taking his time, Kerr had managed to excavate the fallen roof at the end of the shaft, taking it out stone by stone by stone and removing all that remained of Archie – wonderful, glorious Archie – bone by bone by bone. All that time in the shaft, and never had Kerr thought on what Archie must have become because if it. He'd just been Archie, lost to the past, the same Archie who'd battered his way through the back of the barn in Genichesk, who'd waited until Tupikov and his men had turned to go wherever it was they were holed up, making certain their point by spreading the news as they went: that the blasted Tatars hadn't got the better of them, nor of Russia, and bow down boys, or we'll do it all over again. But they'd not got the better of Archie, who'd ripped his arms and legs to shreds as he tore at the wood at the back of that barn and forced his way inside, not even Kheranovich able to halt him, Gabriel stamping and swearing and saying they should all be long gone, Kerr agreeing and then changing his mind, thinking he should go and help but far too feart, far too caring for his own life; stuck, like the others, in the quandary of their cowardice. And then out came Archie, smoke billowing all around him, black as tar, dragging the girl with him, her back on fire, her singlet melting into her skin, and Archie ripping Perdue's coat off his shoulders and throwing it over her, rolling her about on the ground.

'Where the fuck's your humanity?' Archie had croaked, would have yelled only his throat was closing up against the smoke and the heat and the effort of his rescue, Kerr having no answer, standing like the spectre at the feast, shocked into immobility, only thoughts being that he was cold now his coat was gone, and that Archie was a far better man than Kerr could ever hope to be.

Chapter 19

To Be The Better Man

Once back at the Tuley household, Brogar bullied the wagon boy into returning to Auchencairn to drum up a couple of horses to take him and Sholto on to Dundrennan. They could have walked the few miles there in less than a couple of hours, but horses would be quicker and they'd much to do.

'But the boys must stay with me,' Bill insisted, meaning Gilligan and Hugh, completely unaware of the conversation that had gone on during their ride from Balcary to home, and no one wanting to apprise him of it, least of all Hazel.

'Righto,' Hugh agreed immediately. 'We'll get this testing of my eye going. Mr Bill made a right good plan last night, so might as well put it into action.'

Enough for Gilligan, never eager to let Hugh out of his sight these days.

'What Hugh said,' he added. 'Though maybe leave all the building stuff to me and Mr Bill. Don't want Hugh losing the other eye too.'

Hugh smiled, always easy going, but that wasn't the only reason he wanted to stay. It was obvious to him that Bill Tuley wasn't

exactly right, that by Bill helping Hugh, Hugh would also in turn be helping Bill, and Hazel too, if by proxy. And he liked the two of them, and would have done anything he could to make them both whole again.

'They're like clocks what've lost their time,' he said to Sholto in a quiet moment, when Brogar was away stamping about somewhere, the others off with Hazel to get Charlie back into the infirmary where she could keep an eye on him and his leg. 'Them just needs a little time together,' Hugh went on, 'to get all their stuff worked out, like.'

Sholto smiled at Hugh, resisting the urge to pat him on the head, knowing the boy would hate that – take it wrongly. But God's honest truth, he wondered how Hugh kept on being so caring after all he'd been through, how he still believed that people could be saved. Sholto wasn't sure he'd be so sanguine, given the same circumstances.

'I don't know how you do it,' Sholto said. 'But keep on doing it. You're an example to us all.'

Hugh looked up at Sholto, puzzlement his only reaction.

'How d'you mean, Mr Sholto?' he asked, and Sholto, like Kerr before him, already knew the answer.

No better man than you. Not that he said it out loud.

Brogar and Sholto could see the ruins of Dundrennan Abbey in the distance long before they got there. Frith was perched up behind Brogar on his horse and had been giving them a bit of a running commentary as they made their way along the thin lane leading out of Auchencairn and its up and down way across and around small hillocks and bends.

'That there's Drungans, and Blackford Burn, and Culnaughtrie. And over yonder is Over Hazelfield...'

'Any relation to our Hazel?' Sholto asked at Frith's back, not that she heard him.

'And up there's Suie Hill and Feltcroft Loch with Henmuir Burn coming out of it, and Kirkcarswell, and see that? That's Fagra Hill over to your left. The Abbey's at the foot of it and our house is just along towards Gillfoot.'

Brogar took in all the names and places as they went, making a map of them in his head: houses, hills, burns and tracks, for you never knew when such a thing could come in handy. Snowdrops were thick on either side of the track, the dark green of ramsons coming up by every overflowing stream, the scent of them strong in the air.

'And what do you do when you're at home, Frith?' Brogar asked, as they neared their goal, Frith slow to reply, not that Brogar minded, knowing how to wait when needed.

'Well,' she said eventually, 'Charlie's been apprenticed at the leatherworks coupla years. Comes home stinking. An' I mean stinking. Whole place is nothing but one big stink, like the bricks were made of it.'

Brogar smiled. He knew all about leatherworks. Useful stuff for all sorts of reasons: boots, saddles, scabbards, thongs, laces, book covers, gloves, belts, liquid containers…

Too many to name in a single sentence. He also knew how right Frith was on the stench of the places that manufactured it: the raw hides they took in with the flesh still clinging to one side, come straight from the butchers; the build-up of detritus on the banks of the streams they usually dammed up for soaking; the hides coming out of the water once soft enough to fold onto staves to properly rot so the flesh could be pulled off and the hairs fall out of their own accord; the dung they used to speed up the process of softening. And that was before they got onto the tanning proper.

'Not a pretty trade, not by any means,' he commented wryly. 'And you?'

'I've sort of taken over Ma's part of looking after the chapel and the Minister,' Frith replied. 'Doing his cooking and cleaning an' that. Not that I'm real good at it, not like she was. Specially the sewing. I'm real bad at that. Gotta learn to get better.'

'Mother gone, when was it you said?' Brogar asked, no hint of pity, for which Frith was glad.

'While back, no one to help, like Charlie said. Which kinda brings me back to that letter we was talking about earlier...'

Brogar said nothing. Another man might have prompted, turned a little in expectation, but not Brogar. He didn't move except to shift in his saddle in unison with the horse as they rounded the bend at the top of a short incline, Frith a small warmth at his back.

'It kinda took us by surprise,' she went on, as they looked down on the tiny hamlet of Dundrennan laid out before them: a single street, a few ramshackle cottages, the ruins of the Abbey a bit further down, its tiny chapel the only building still extant in its grounds. 'Got it from Mr Heron. He'd died too by then, quite a few years back, but left instructions for it to be sent when we turned seventeen. Came right out of the blue. An' honest, I don't know exactly what it said 'cos Charlie never told me everything. And he always tells me everything,' Frith added, ignoring the contradiction.

'But it told you to get over to Hestan,' Brogar said, 'bring out your father's bones, bring them home and not tell anyone.'

Frith nodded.

'That's what Charlie said. And I don't know why,' she answered, voice quiet now. 'I mean why we couldn't tell Mr Perdue or Mr Merryweather. Didn't make no kind o' sense to me, but Charlie insisted, although now...well, I've kinda got an inkling.'

Brogar didn't reply, for he had an inkling of his own. A posthumous letter sent from one old friend to his dead friend's son when he was deemed to have come of age; natural too for a Russian to send it to the son and not the daughter. Content of letter: the truth about how his father had died and where his body could be found, and something more. Add in Sholto's suspicion that whatever was going on had its roots in the Crimea, and Tartary in particular, Perdue's coming in at the end of Brogar's tale of Kamyr-Batyr with his doom-laden words.

'You think there's something else in that shaft,' Brogar stated casually, 'apart from your father; maybe to do with your family, with your mother' grandparents and that farmhouse in Genichesk.'

Frith didn't reply, because that was precisely what she thought. *Something about your mother and your father*, Kerr Perdue had said last night, though never finishing his tale; Frith distracted as they reached the lane going down to the Abbey and her home.

'Left here,' she commanded, and left Brogar went.

Kerr Perdue had lain down for a nap, but despite his hard labours his body was having none of it. His little room was dark, but it was far too early. He put on his boots, went up and primed the light ready to switch on as soon as it turned dark. He could have gone to his workshop, got the copper alloy melting, set a few more beaks and claws, but he'd not the heart for it, not at the moment, not with Merryweather dead just down the road. And it was Merryweather he was thinking about now. It didn't seem right that he was alone, and it didn't seem right that what remained of Charlie was lying outside shaft number three, jumbled up in the mealy sack Kerr had procured for the purpose following Brogar's request to get him out. Not right at all, not right for either to be treated as if neither meant no more to anyone than the pile

of stones Kerr had excavated from the mine during Charlie's disinterment. Time to change all that, but not until he'd taken a walk to free his head from all the clutter that was going on in there, get his thoughts straight and true, thinking too that it was maybe time to come clean to young Heron about the source of his wealth – or rather, the source of his father's wealth, the means with which he'd bought Balcary. Most likely he wouldn't care; most likely result being Kerr getting heave-hoed off of Hestan soonest, but that was going to happen anyway, no matter Brogar Finn's assurance to the contrary.

Time, Kerr told himself, to be the better man, no matter the consequences.

There was nothing to Dundrennan but the ruined Abbey and, on the opposite side of the lane leading to it, a line of labourers' cottages towards one of which Frith led her visitors.

'Is there no village here then?' asked Sholto, having expected a lively conurbation as Auchencairn had been, populated by all the usual industries of blacksmithing, carpentry, butchering, bakery, church and school.

'Just us few here,' Frith answered, slipping down from Brogar's horse, 'what takes care of the immediate Abbey lands, but there's loads of farms hereabouts and they comes in from time to time when we bring in a load of supplies and when Minister's here to do a service.'

'It seems awfully…sparse,' Sholto replied, dismayed for anyone growing up in such evident isolation. 'Where did you go for your schooling?'

'Like I said,' Frith explained, 'Minister's over from Auchencairn coupla times a week an' we used to go down there, when the weather weren't bad. And we gets by.'

Sholto looked about him. It was a pretty place, no doubting that, sheltered by being that bit further inland than either Balcary or Auchencairn and much brighter for it: hedgerows green with holly and enlivened by the yellow tails of catkins, bright aconites at their feet, the spears of daffodils coming up in clumps everywhere a bit of grass could be seen. Even the ruined Abbey was picturesque, the buildings dark and sombre in their dilapidation, stark against the fields and trees behind, a stand of ancient grave stones at their centre along which a line of sparrows stood chattering and bobbing. More recent burials had been made outside the Abbey's tumbling walls, though being outwith their protection they'd been so scoured by wind and rain it would be a miracle if any of their inscriptions could be deciphered.

Their ostensible reasons for coming here were to ascertain permission for Merryweather to be buried alongside his already gone relatives, and to get hold of the letter sent to Charlie and Frith. Sholto was doubting the first of these missions could be achieved, not realising Dundrennan had no minister of its own. Nevertheless, they hooked their horses to an iron ring set into the Abbey wall and followed Frith along the way to her home, past a distinctly untidy allotment with cabbages, kale and leeks up to their necks in mud and weeds; next to it were their animals: a scatter of chickens clucking and plucking at random in hedgerow and byre; one sow, one milk cow in a fenced paddock, and two mean looking goats Sholto would not have cared to go a round with.

'This here's Esmerelda, Lily, Maisie and Mabeline,' Frith introduced them to her livestock, 'and that's where we grow our veg. Not much to look at now, but we've still kale and skirrett and we've already got the spuds in and that, and come summer we'll have a right load of carrots and neeps. Anyway,' Frith said, opening

the cottage door and taking her visitors into the kitchen, both men having to stoop to get themselves in, 'I'll get kettle on once I've the fire going, an' summat on to eat. Mind, I'm not that good at it, not like Mam was.'

She knew she was talking too much, but didn't seem able to stop herself. First time she'd ever had visitors of her own – apart from the wake – and even the simplest things were seeming hard, only a few square yards of living area and these two men filling them to the brim.

'Minister will be over in the chapel,' Frith said, hoping to get at least one of them away.

'In the chapel? How so?' Sholto was surprised, if relieved.

''Cos it's Finan's saint day, big converter of the Celts from Iona,' Frith looked over at Sholto as if Sholto was an idiot. 'Didn't think I'd bring you all the way up here for nothing, did you?'

Frith smiled to see Sholto colour slightly because yes, that's exactly what he'd thought and she knew it.

'Well, I'll be gone then,' Sholto said, 'speak to him about Merryweather. Do you know if he's any family left hereabouts, Frith?'

Frith chewed her lip. In all honesty it hadn't occurred to her. She knew the place had been more buzzing years back, but the last few years there'd only been the few of them: the labourers who looked after the immediate Abbey lands that were only in purview because the chapel was still functional, a few of the old women who still spun wool, and her and Charlie. Certainly no one by the name of Merryweather.

'Pretty sure not,' she said. 'But Minister will know better. Name's Edward Fitch an' he's a bit, well…a bit stiff you might say,' Frith putting it the politest way she could of a man who had a stick shoved so far up his arse it would be hard to find either end.

'Righto,' Brogar agreed. 'You go on up, Sholto, and I'll stop here. Take a read through of that letter.'

'If we can find it,' Frith reminded him, Charlie having changed his mind, and been completely averse to the plan once they'd got back to the Tuleys' and not about to make it easy for them by telling them where it was.

'Oh, we'll find it,' Brogar said. 'I'll bet you a month of Sundays I'll have hold of it within half an hour.'

'A month of Sundays? What on earth sort of bet do you call that?'

Sholto heard Frith's bright words as he went back out the door, heard Brogar's easy reply.

'Means I'll bet you any damn thing you like. Name your price, but be certain I will extract my winnings by whatever means I deem necessary. And win, Frith, I shall do.'

Frith laughed a short 'ha!' to counter Brogar's certainty.

'Bet you nothing,' she retorted, 'but bet I'll find it when you don't. An'what'll you do then, Mr Big Man, who don't know nothing about my brother at all and me knowing him inside out?'

Good comeback, Sholto was thinking as he left them to it. One way or another that letter would be found, and like them he already had an unsubstantiated idea of what it might say, had conflated a couple of names, constructed a back story that might account for why Frith and Charlie had really been over on Hestan.

But it could wait.

Other things to be doing now, namely to secure a plot into which Gabriel Merryweather's body could be laid to rest.

The wind was coming up behind Hestan, straight off the sea, strong and sharrow, about as bitter as it could be, absent one minute then right at your back the next, aiming to knock you off your feet. And

so it would be at Balcary and maybe Dundrennan, Kerr alert to the fact that it might mean Brogar would choose not to come back over to Hestan when the tide was down, just as the sun went with it. And who could blame him? When the wind came up like this the rain wasn't far behind, and getting across the sands and onto the Rack would be the worst of work, visibility almost nil. But that would leave Kerr on the island with two dead bodies, and that feart him, never mind they were the dead bodies of his friends. Maybe more so because of it.

He pulled his coat about his shoulders and soldiered on; went up the track towards Daft Annie's Steps and stood a moment, baring his face to the oncoming wind, looking at the dark yellow heft of clouds coming towards him, knowing he was right. Rain on its way, probably snow too, judging by the weight of those clouds; either way they'd soon shroud Hestan from view of the mainland. Bad enough getting over in good weather, let alone in bad, even if you were in the know, and Brogar wasn't in the know. Brogar's plan was still stood good, though – get a coffin over and put Archie's bones in with Merryweather so no one would be any the wiser apart from them, Frith and Charlie. They'd always been two sides to the same person those two, not that he'd seen either in years, not since Archie died and they lied to cover it, and yet it seemed impossible he'd not recognised Archie's son the moment he'd been dragged out of the shaft, never mind all the dust and grime. But no point regretting things now. The lad was alive, as was Frith – thanks to Brogar's intervention – and that was good enough for him.

He reached the westernmost point of the island, leaning into the wind, daring it to take his weight or push him back on his heels, exhilaration raw on his face, eyes dark with it, lips curled in an involuntary smile. This was what being alive and on Hestan was

all about. None of that war crap, that stink of blood, of burning barns, burning books, burning bodies. The waves crashed against the rocks to the westward side of the island, booming in the caves that stood either side of what would have been Daft Annie's Steps if they hadn't been two foot under, water brown with up-churned sand, waves rebounding from rocks and caves and crashing against the incomers so they collectively flung out huge surges of spume and spray like dancers throwing up their hands even as they bowed low to take their applause. The water was wild and broken, and now here came the rain, moving like a ragged veil from Rascarell over the Balcary Houghs, waves climbing and bashing into the short sharp cliffs beyond Balcary House and deep into gullies and geos, and Kerr knew then there was no way for Brogar to be back. The wind was just too strong; the outgoing tide was already being pushed back against itself towards the shore, and would hardly keep the waters from Hestan long enough for a few oystercatchers to pull up a couple of cockles from the sodden sand before it was back again, surging about its edges, taking Hestan into its maw like a cat closing its claws about a mouse.

He gazed down on where Daft Annie's Steps would be if they'd been allowed to surface, saw the tip of the anchoring stave jammed between the rocks, once used by smugglers to pull themselves in when the water allowed, saw it shine in a brief shaft of sunlight that had forced its way through the advancing clouds; and Kerr frowned, for that anchoring stave hadn't shone in years, too encrusted by barnacles, rust and weed. It was almost as if…the thought took hold and then was gone as another surge of breakers crashed in and covered the rocks, sending a great spray of spume up the short spurt of cliff, Kerr turning quickly so it spattered against his back even as he strode quickly away and around the end of the island, heading for Copper Cove and Merryweather's

cottage beyond. But it snagged at him, that shining tip, hinting as it did of the bad old days when Hestan had been a haven for the Free Traders over the water who brought in whisky and lace and whatever else would fetch a price, when Balcary House was the headquarters of Manx men with no conscience. A bad trade Heron had gone out of his way his way to stamp out once he'd installed Merryweather and Perdue on the island and himself in Balcary House.

'Can't have that sort of thing going on,' Heron had said to Kerr, 'got a name to protect, a new business booming.'

The irony of Heron's words hadn't escaped Kerr Perdue at the time, but home was home, and Hestan had become home as far as he and Merryweather were concerned, and so they'd let it pass. Just like everything else.

Brogar had the letter before Frith's kettle had even boiled. He'd made a quick circuit of the tiny house – one room for cooking and living in, two bunked beds built into the wall by the fire, a smaller room off to the right that had been Frith's mother's sleeping quarters and was now Frith's, and a stabling room tacked onto the rest, divided by a door split at its middle so it could be opened – top or bottom, independently – into which the animals could be brought for safekeeping during winter nights. He immediately discounted the living room – there wasn't much in it: a table, a few chairs, a large wooden blanket box, a roof-high niche set with hooks and shelves at the opposite end from the fire on which to hang game or herbs, store vegetables and preserves. He walked swiftly into the tiny bedroom. Again, nothing much here bar the bed, a skinny wardrobe, an even skinner chest of drawers whose drawers didn't fit too well – judging by the dark gaps at their corners and the fact that the handles were loose from too much

pulling – a wash-set on top of its uneven surface comprising water jug and bowl, another blanket box at the base of the bed. Looking under the mattress was beneath him, and Brogar swiftly came out of the bedroom and opened the divided door and went into the stable. Not a lot here either – some fresh straw scattered for the animals, several lines of nails hammered into the wooden walls on which to hang necessary tools: saws, forceps, a few coils of rope, several glass jars suspended by strings about their necks in which were nails and tacks of varying sizes; a water trough and, in the corner, a neat stack of straw bales. He put his hand between numbers two and three and had the letter out in a moment.

No hiding from Brogar Finn, not anyone, nor anything, at least not for long.

Sholto unlatched the metal grille that guarded the ruins of the Abbey and entered into its peaceful sanctuary. As he'd seen from the track, most of the place was in ruination and so it was startling to see the little Abbey chapel still intact, hidden as it was by the main thrust of the ruins, it seeming to him a minor miracle it had survived at all. He knew nothing of the history of the Abbey itself but presumed it must have fallen into decline after the Great English Reformation in the 1560s and, as he approached the chapel, it was obvious that it too had at one time been in as bad a state as the Abbey proper but had been laboriously rebuilt – large parts of the upper walls being differently stoned and coloured, far less neat than the lower layers, and the roof being a curious mixture of wooden planking and thatch. There'd been, he recalled, huge swathes of reed beds at the lower end of Auchencairn Bay and he presumed they were farmed, as he knew such reed beds were farmed elsewhere, and was no doubt the source of the thatching.

He was about to enter the chapel when he was met by a man coming out, and had no doubt at all this was Edward Fitch for – just as Frith had described – he was straight as a staff from the base of his boots to the beak of his nose and had a face as thin as it was long, creased at the edges as if he'd been caught frowning into the wind. Not a face that invited confidences, and hopefully one well-hidden when folk came to him to confess their sins.

'Mr Fitch?' Sholto asked with some diffidence as the man noticed Sholto and came up short.

'That is myself, sir,' Fitch replied, voice clipped and restrained, 'what can I do for you?'

'Ah, I'm wondering if you know of any members of the Merryweather family buried near these grounds,' Sholto began, 'and if another plot next to them might be vacant.'

Edward Fitch looked at his visitor with less interest than he might have watched a shrew running across his path.

'I may and I mayn't,' his reply terse and formal, 'but first I'd need to know the nature of your asking.'

Sholto ground his back teeth together, fighting an immediate and visceral dislike of the man.

'It's Gabriel Merryweather over on Hestan. He's…died.' Sholto didn't want to add any details, finding this man as cold and uncaring as an icicle dropping from an eave, surprised when Edward Fitch creased his brows and looked directly at Sholto with something like concern.

'Gabriel Merryweather is dead?' he asked.

'He is,' Sholto agreed. 'Last night, we think. We've a coffin arranged in Auchencairn, and his friend, Kerr Perdue, thought this might be a fitting place for him to lie, given that he came from hereabouts.'

Edward Fitch said nothing for a moment as he studied his visitor.

'You…think?' he asked slowly. 'Was no one with him at the end?'

Sholto raised his eyebrows. He'd not expected this level of interest, yet obviously something needed saying.

'It was…somewhat sudden,' he offered, Fitch narrowing his eyes but saying nothing more, merely motioning Sholto to follow him as he went from the chapel to a gate leading out from the Abbey to the small cemetery that lay on the other side of its walls.

'Here's where the Dundrennan Merryweathers' are buried,' Fitch said, sweeping out his hand to indicate nine or so plots marked with headstones, the same headstones Sholto had previously observed as being so shrouded with lichen they were unreadable.

'And somewhere Gabriel can be buried too?' he asked, Edward Fitch nodding briefly.

'But how are you, a stranger, so concerned with this?' Fitch asked, catching Sholto off guard. 'For certainly you're a stranger new come, for I don't know you, and I know everyone around here, near and far, far and near.'

Sholto interlaced his fingers and stretched them in their interlocking bonds, alerted by this curiosity from Edward Fitch in Merryweather's death, certain there was more to the man than Frith had apparently appreciated, weighing up what to say, wanting to keep the man on side.

'You're right,' he admitted. 'Myself and my colleague are here to oversee the negotiations between the Heron family and our Company about the sale of Hestan Island and, while I'm here, what can you tell me about them? About the Herons? How they came here and when, for example.'

Edward Fitch leaned his straight body back, rocking on his heels, croaking quietly.

'Oh, but aren't you the arch one,' he said, fixing Sholto with a

gaze that was not exactly malevolent but was certainly getting there, 'and I suppose that any minute now you'll be asking about the locked library and where it went and how it was supposedly spirited away by my forebears? Well, good luck, sir, with that, for I'll say only what I said to old Mr Heron a hundred times before and that I really don't know. Possibly it was taken over to Manx land and possibly it wasn't. Possibly it's hidden on Iona or Hestan and possibly it isn't. Either way, take my word for it. That library and every book it once harboured is long gone from here, and no way to recover it.'

Sholto kept his face still, his curiosity indicated only by a slight twitching of his lips. First he'd heard of any locked libraries, missing or otherwise.

'Well, that's certainly an interesting fact,' he replied neutrally, 'but really nothing I was going to ask about. Was it connected to the Heron family, then?'

Fitch was quiet for a few moments, eyes narrowed, looking at his visitor with suspicion.

'Only by means of Dundrennan and Hestan,' he volunteered, 'for the two go back a long way. So you're really only here because of Merryweather's demise?'

'I am,' Sholto replied. 'And this is his only family? No one else alive?'

He gazed over the forlorn graves and was sad for Merryweather, sad for anyone that their last resting place be in such sad repair.

'Well, yes,' Fitch answered, seemingly unbothered by the fact. 'Gabriel was the only son of Elias, his father, the blacksmith down in Auchencairn. Now, of course, their grave plots have gone into the McTavish family who bought them up just before Elias died, long before Gabriel came back from Sweden or Russia, or wherever it was he ended up.'

'The Crimea, I believe,' Sholto filled in a gap, Fitch cocking his head.

'Is that so?' he asked. 'Well, that's news. He never spoke about where he'd been or what he'd done once he and Perdue ensconced themselves on Hestan. So what was he doing out there? Surely not involved in the war, came back long before that had even started.'

Sholto smiled, aware this Fitch character was fishing for information and wanting to take advantage of it.

'So who's the arch one now?' he asked, injecting a little humour into the conversation, a humour Edward Fitch did not take well, Sholto's smile gone as quick as it had come.

'That, sir, is entirely inappropriate,' Fitch said curtly, stiff and straight as a curtain rod, apart from his hands which he was bunching into fists.

Sholto held up his own hands and then put them together as if in supplication, realising his error.

'My apologies, Mr Fitch,' he said quickly, 'it's only that I'm rather interested myself in Gabriel Merryweather's past. Certain… questions…have arisen to do with their connection to the Heron family, and Hestan itself, as it seems the sale of the island means them having to leave it – or rather only Perdue now – but we're trying to find a way to prevent that. It's not the policy of the Company to depopulate the parcels of land they buy, not if the folk there have a moral right to remain.'

This, Sholto knew, was stretching the truth, for the Company had no scruples whatsoever about depopulating anywhere they took a fancy to, but that had never been Brogar's stand, and no more was it Sholto's.

Edward Fitch took the apology with little grace, but began to unbend, if only slightly.

'Well, that's good of your Company,' he said, 'for every man needs his home and needs to feel it secure, even if Merryweather and Perdue chose to live outside the place they actually belonged.'

'So does Perdue still have family here?' Sholto asked, wondering what had made the two men live out such a lonely existence in such a lonely place when they were so close to the home they'd been born to and belonged. It struck him as odd, particularly having only recently visited the very sticks and stones his parents had come from, and where they would have returned to in a heartbeat if it had been possible.

'No, sir,' Fitch shook his head. 'Both last sons of last families, but the Perdues have been here a long, long time. See over there?' Edward Fitch moved, pointing his finger to another small clutch of graves not far from the Merryweather plot. 'That's the last of the Perdues, apart from Kerr; but inside the Abbey walls there's graves going right back to the Dissolution.'

'When the English monarchs made war on the Church?' Sholto asked with interest. 'May we see the older ones?'

Fitch nodded curtly and led them back inside the Abbey grounds, taking Sholto to that ancient collection right at its heart, Sholto noticing that one amongst the rest was somewhat different, the words etched into it scraped back to the bone. He read the words out loud, beginning first in the French they'd been scribed in and then translating into English, to Fitch's evident surprise:

Ambrose Finan Perdue, 1621 – 1667, parti de la vie mais pas oublie,

All that you were & held, knew & cared for, all gone to our Brethren over the water.

'That's a very odd inscription for a gravestone, and Finan – isn't that the same name as your Saint's day?' Sholto commented, unbending his back, standing up, finding the angular frame of

Edward Fitch standing too close at his shoulder, making Sholto take a step to the right, almost bumping into the neighbouring stone.

'An old Abbey name,' Fitch said, 'come from their connections to Iona, although the place was built by Cistercians brought in from their Yorkshire holdings by King David, men originally from Reivaulx in France. Only thirteen of them at the start, plus a few local lay brothers picked for their expertise.'

'Hence Perdue,' Sholto commented, 'for that's a French name, surely.' Fitch nodding but adding nothing more, except to invite Sholto to his meagre manse.

'We need to get back to the main topic of Gabriel Merryweather,' he said as they went, Sholto agreeing, following Edward Fitch as he swept his swift way out of the Abbey and over towards the tiny cottage that served as his manse when he was here in Dundrennan. Sholto had a whole line of questions he wanted answers to, links forming in his head between all the disparate pieces of information he'd come across since he'd been in Auchencairn, Balcary and Hestan. And that gravestone – the inscription on it was nagging at him, as was the name Perdue, and Fitch's previous statement about the missing library. And hadn't Heron been a book dealer before he came to Balcary? If so, the suggestions of a lost library would have been tantalising in the extreme. And if Heron was the man Sholto believed him to be then there were yet more questions needing asking of his son, and of Frith, Charlie and Perdue. But what of Merryweather? Sholto couldn't for the life of him figure out why the man had been murdered, for who was Gabriel Merryweather to do another such harm that he had to be eliminated in such an appalling way?

Questions, and yet more questions.

He hoped Brogar was having more luck finding out answers than was he.

CHAPTER 20

GENICHESK 1833

The girl Archie had dragged out of the barn fell to keening, like the sound buzzards make whilst circling their nests, but on and on and on, her suffering evident, excruciating and desperate. It was all Kerr Perdue could do not to put his hands over his ears and walk away, not to be witness to the result of what they'd all four of them put into motion.

Kheranovich was not so moved.

'What the hell do you think you're doing?' he hissed at Archie, whose face and clothes were covered nose to tail in ash, and the length of his sleeves singed right back to his collar. 'Stop her squealing, or we'll have Tupikov back on our tail and all will be up.'

Perdue had never heard Kheranovich so angry, certainly not at Archie who, until that moment, had been his bosom pal and nothing anyone could say against him. Kheranovich's voice was coarse and bitter, Archie staring up at him, eyes bright as pools of iced water in that blackened face of his.

'That's a bad thing we done,' Archie croaked, throat thick with smoke, mouth and palate scorched by the heat so his words came out like tar dropped from a burning barrel. 'An' she's too young to

die, not like anything, and certainly not like that.'

Kheranovich tutted and strode away a yard or two, face grimaced, hands twisting at his back, Gabriel a dark shadow to the left of him, Kerr a dark shadow to the right.

'Seems only right,' Kerr ventured, voice soft, unwilling to speak up against Kheranovich and yet wanting to take Archie's corner.

'Right for who?' Kheranovich suddenly swinging round on his heel and looking daggers at Kerr Perdue. 'It's none of it right! We knew that from the off. But she's seen us. She'll know us and she'll name us, and then what the hell has any of this been for?'

'She'll not name us,' Archie said quietly, unwrapping the girl from Kerr's coat, lifting her gently onto his knees, her cries subsiding into pathetic murmurs as he fetched a pot of grease from his pocket – used for oiling his weapons – and slathering it with the utmost care over her nakedness, over her bloody and blistered back that was seared right back into the muscle and – in places – to the bone.

'How's she to name us?' Archie went on. 'She's just a girl, and how's she going to know who we are and what we've done?'

'Because she must have known about the books,' Kheranovich insisted. 'How else to explain how they'd all been cached together in that barn? Think the Tatars managed to stockpile them without her knowing it? And someone else knew it too,' he added, 'someone tattled – maybe even her – else how to explain Tupikov knowing? And he knew, boys, he knew long before he got here, before he sent us on their path.'

'I'll keep her on track,' Archie was stubborn, blue eyes cold as the moon that sifted itself out into the night above the cloud of smoke, cinders and ash that was still guffing up from the burning barn. 'I'll keep her right,' he went on. 'She's no notion of anything at the moment, 'cept that her folk are gone and she's so pained she's

past screaming. And I'll look after her, do what needs doing. You get what you're wanting an' I'll stay here with her while you do, so she's no notion of it.'

Kheranovich looked down on his companion, his jealousy of the burned girl Archie was so assiduously caring for vital and visceral, appalled at the bitter tears forming in his eyes because of it.

'Well, just make it so,' he commanded, voice harsh, but acceding, moving away as Archie lifted the girl with such tenderness, such a wrapping around of his arms, Kheranovich couldn't help but wish it was himself in her place, wishing too that he didn't wish it, angry and ashamed that he felt for the blue-eyed boy what he did, wishing the attachment away; not that it went, not then and not ever, not even after Archie had looked after the girl day and night for a full week, whispering to her, tending her wounds. And not after Archie had deposited her outside the mosque in Genichesk, not even years later, just before the Crimean War, when Archie came back to check on her, found her, made her his wife when he learned no one else would take her, not like she was.

Such a terrible longing he'd had for Archie all the time he'd known him, a longing never had for anyone or anything else, one so strong it frequently left him breathless; like when Archie was telling his stories as they sat about their camp fires, stitching in details of the place he'd come from, of Dundrennan and the Abbey and all its history, of Auchencairn where Archie had been apprenticed; still remembering all his days Archie's recitation of the place as if it had been a poem of the highest worth: over forty thousand people in the Stewartry and Auchencairn a hub within it: a village built upon a hill that led down to a reed-thick bay; two churches, one school, one leatherworks, one bakery, four public houses, one hotel, three blacksmiths, seven grocers, two tailors, one stonemason…

A paean of a place Kheranovich vowed he would see one day, breathe the same air Archie had breathed as a child, see that orchard he'd pilfered fruit from, buy bread from that baker's, buy gloves from the leatherworks Archie had been apprenticed to. But not for now that vision, not in the immediate aftermath of the burning down of the barn; only bitterness and rage that Archie had gone against him, and hate for the girl Archie had chosen to risk his life to save; and a terrible, unwanted admiration that Archie had done it, which only made Kheranovich burn at his core, like the fire in the barn had taken hold of him and got into his guts, into his sinews, running through him like a mole through its tunnels, blind to the world outside.

He left Archie, Perdue and Merryweather and went to the place they'd buried the books, stood looking at it, wondering if it had been worth the price, if he might have lost Archie because of it. But it had to be worth it; it could be the making of them all, and especially of Kheranovich who knew the value of books, folios and manuscripts, what they could fetch in an open market. And if ever he was to get over to Scotland, see those places Archie had been and come from, then this was his chance. Merryweather and Perdue would be no problem. He'd offer them a few volumes they could hawk for their involvement in this escapade – theft seemed too strong a word – but doubted they'd take him up on it. All those two wanted was out, and he could certainly arrange that. Sell a few books, buy them out of their commission, get them repatriated. He'd need to keep them close even then, for he knew that the longer people lived the more likely they were to regret what they'd done in their youth, and they'd done many things they weren't proud of – this stuff at Genichesk probably being the worst.

No harm making certain.

No harm stacking the deck.

And he had the ability, for he had their freedom hanging from his fingertips. His word and his money whether they should come or go, lock them into their remaining army servitude or send them packing.

But Archie was different. He didn't really believe that Archie wouldn't go. Archie was addicted to the life of a soldier, and Archie – with his ideals of loyalty and fealty – would probably not leave Kheranovich, even after all this.

One bright spark in a black night.

But a probability he couldn't count on.

So the most of the books would have to stay buried and safe where they were until all the politics had simmered down, which they would. Always had Russia had problems at its borders, with all those non-Russian tribes rejecting the dominance of the Tsar and the infliction of the Russian ways and tongue that were so alien to them; always had Russian troops had to put up arms against those minority populations in Armenia, Chechen, Georgia and the Azov, always worrying they'd invite in the Turks or the British who, in turn, were always eager to hammer on Russia's doors, challenge its dominance over the Black Sea ports – Russia's only frost-free way into to the rest of Europe and the Mediterranean.

Always so complicated, Kheranovich knew, this to-ing and fro-ing, this shifting of allegiances, and nowhere worse – or better – for it than the Crimea, where they now were.

So he came to his decision.

He'd offer Merryweather and Perdue their way out, buy their silence about Genichesk on the promise of it; and Archie, well for Archie he'd do something more, something stupendous. No notion then that Archie would stay as long as he did by Kheranovich's side, that Archie's forgiveness was wide and easy come in as the sea. But either way, Kheranovich would vouchsafe his future once

their fighting days were over. And already he knew how he would do it. Just one book, taken from that pile dug into the ground in the copse outside the barn. He'd known it immediately he'd seen it. One book, worth half the world, and he'd make Archie take it, tell him to treasure it, take it home, provide himself a good life, however he chose to make it.

And so he did, telling Archie about it that very night, wanting to win back his affection, his friendship, and Archie laughing because of it, making Kheranovich laugh too because Archie was saying what he most needed to hear.

'I don't want no book, man, for how's it going to add to what I've already got?'

Archie's face alive in the night, dancing in the firelight, them all toasty in the house; Merryweather and Perdue sat on their own to one side, the girl upstairs, stowed away and forgotten for the moment, the barn a smouldering giant slain outside, and everything back to how it should be.

'Got everything I need right here,' Archie said, bringing a bottle of wine to his lips and taking a slurp before going on. 'Got you, got Merryweather and Perdue, so how much better can it get?'

Archie slapping a hand on Kheranovich's shoulder, Archie refusing to countenance leaving when Kheranovich put his plan to Perdue and Merryweather to pull them out – and Archie too if he chose – out of Russia, out of war, out of everything.

'Might take a year to get things organised,' Kheranovich told them, Merryweather and Perdue content with that.

'But I'll not go,' Archie had said, smiling broadly, blue eyes dancing, no matter the previous disagreement, as if all had passed and nothing to do with him. 'Love it all, I do. Love this life,' he said, looking over at Perdue and Merryweather. 'Can't think why you'd want to leave it, but good on you if you do.'

And so it had happened: Kheranovich getting shot of Merryweather – whom he'd never liked, and Perdue whom he had – soon as he could; him and Archie going on and on into one skirmish and then another, the girl long forgotten, going on right through the next twenty years and the Crimean War, by which time they were so much older and even Archie had had enough.

And all that time Kheranovich had been looking to the future, going back first chance he got and digging up those books and getting them safely stored once Tupikov was long away, selling off a few volumes here and a few volumes there over the years, amassing the money he needed to put his grand plan in action. He'd bought up Hestan almost straightaway, which had been the easy part, for nobody had wanted it. Well and securely his by the time Merryweather and Perdue returned to take up residence, no one questioning them or asking what they were doing there, those in the know about its sale having been told to expect them. Kheranovich using his father's lawyers, his family's influence and the money from the books to buy up the rest.

It took well over a decade after that night in Genichesk, but in the end he had it all, Hestan just the start, Balcary House and its estates the real prize.

The keys to the kingdom.

Good on you if you do.

Perdue was thinking on Archie's words as he sat the dark night through in Merryweather's cottage, Merryweather shrouded beneath a blanket, Archie's bones in their sack tucked in beside Merryweather's knees, like they were all just bivouacking out the night on the shores of the Azov or the Black Sea, or any one of a hundred different places.

But mostly he thought on how everything had changed after Genichesk, how Kheranovich had got him and Merryweather out a year or so afterwards as promised, arranged them away, for them to be on Hestan. It had seemed a miracle at the time, Kheranovich explaining blithely.

'Always said it would be worth it. Sold some of the books off, made enquiries, had a lawyer look into sales about your parts and bought up Hestan, lock, stock and barrel.'

Kerr and Gabriel exchanging glances, not understanding how mere books could have such worth, but wanting it. Lord in Heaven, both wanting it more than anything. Knowing their silence was being bought, but they could live with that and – if truth were told – were glad to have this price put upon it, for neither ever wanted to hear mention of Genichesk again.

They'd got home, or home at least to Hestan; a place that became their sanctuary, kept them apart, kept them safe and not having to talk about anything they'd done during the long wars over in Russia. And better still when Archie turned up a couple of decades later, having sent a wife and two bairns on before him, Archie sauntering over the Rack to Hestan declaring himself home too.

Friends reunited, Archie working with them at the copper when he wasn't at Dundrennan with his unexpected family. All quiet and calm, all settled back into the norm, until Kheranovich turned up the following year and declared himself the owner of Balcary House. Different name, same person, and with him a son but no sign of a wife, like he was challenging Archie, like he was saying *look you, I've got one too.*

Like he was tagging Archie's life, trying to mirror it.

That the boy hadn't been Kheranovich's own was obvious the first moment Kerr clapped eyes on him, for a boy more unlike Kheranovich would have been hard to find: blond-haired, blue-

eyed – just like Archie. Unsettlingly like Archie. Kerr not dwelling on the reasons, just glad they didn't see much of him, that the boy was sent to school in Dumfries soon as Kheranovich could arrange it, after which he and Archie were as thick together as butter whipped with cream, like they'd always been; started working on yet another of Archie's mad plans, like Archie had never grown old at all, like Archie had come back unscathed from the Crimea whilst men like Bill Tuley – who'd never lifted a finger in the fighting – returned all frayed at the edges, as wrong on the inside as the men he'd treated over there had been wrong on the out.

A bit like Kerr when he'd first got back to Hestan, except he'd worked it out of himself like Bill Tuley had never done. But then Bill hadn't spent all his days hacking at the rocks down a pit shaft, hauling out the ore, sweat drouked into every crease of his skin, every fold of his clothes, being so knackered by the end of day he'd no energy left for thinking, talking to Gabriel only about the work, about the tides, about the weather, about the birds, until he forgot all that internal turmoil had ever been there at all.

Until now.

He looked over at Gabriel who, like Archie, hadn't appeared substantially changed by their experiences, remaining the same grumpy man he'd been when they were young: always the pessimist, always chiding, pointing out what might go badly with Archie's plans, and usually proved right. They'd been like the three points of a triangle back then: Archie at the apex – no other place for him – Kerr and Perdue at the base trying to ground him, Gabriel pointing out the bad, Kerr always giving the middle way, saying Gabriel was right about this and Archie right about that. He couldn't understand how it had all come to this, to the two of them lying together dead on Gabriel's bed, and only Kerr alive.

It seemed all wrong, the architecture of his life collapsing in around him.

The wind outside was loud and inconsistent, a gale – like so many others – that huffed and buffeted, then slowed and gathered before coming on in even stronger blasts fit to fell trees, flatten the reed beds at the base of Auchencairn.

The lamp flickered and Kerr glanced out towards the night, anxious for his light, torn between going and tending it and staying here on his vigil. He was fidgety, never one to sit still for long, liking to be doing: to be knitting, to be darning, to be patching, to be at his copper work and his beaks and feet. Anything to keep his fingers moving, his mind working, filling his head with inconsequential details. But what struck him as not inconsequential was his earlier thought about the twins and what they might really have been doing over here on Hestan, and of what Brogar Finn had asked him to do and, more specifically, of what Brogar might have actually expected him to find, Charlie's bones not the end of the task.

He hesitated, he worried, and then he stood up.

'Godammit,' he muttered beneath his breath, getting to his feet, snatching up the lamp, going to the door, heading off into the afternoon, the wind as ferocious as he'd known it would be, almost pushing him off his feet, the lamp only saved because he'd sheltered it beneath his coat. It could have waited until morning, but he couldn't bear to stay the long night through with two dead friends and a question to which he had no answer. And down the shaft there'd be no wind at all, not the way it was coming in, and so he stamped his way across the path, body bent with the wind at his back, coat tails flapping, blown up and slapping him intermittently about the back of his head.

'Goddamit!' he said again, louder this time as he slipped down the track into Copper Cove, immediately glad for the shelter it

gave him from the wind, heading for shaft number three, slotting in the pieces, suddenly grasping what Brogar suspected might be there, what Charlie had patently suspected too, that was worth so much more than his father's mouldering bones.

'Got it!' Brogar announced, as he came back into Firth's kitchen, brandishing the letter Frith had sworn he'd never find. 'And an interesting read it is too.'

He plonked himself down on a chair by the table, Frith whirling round at Brogar's startling announcement, sending an arc of boiling water from the kettle as she did so, narrowly missing Brogar, who was swaggering at the table like a lord, never mind Frith's sudden shifts of expression from anger to exasperation and then to a certain kind of hope.

''So what does it say?' she asked, abandoning the kettle and the making of tea, too intent on the letter Brogar had now flattened on the boards before him.

'Quite a lot, as it happens,' Brogar answered easily. 'Good job you never took me up on my bet.'

'Good job, indeed,' Frith retorted, before quietly repeating her question. 'So what does it say?'

Sitting herself down, trying to take the letter from him, Brogar keeping it pinned down with a finger.

'Tells me you weren't just over on Hestan for your father's bones,' he said, serious now, leaning in, looking straight at Frith. ''Tells me that quite something else was going on. Like what we spoke about before?'

Frith bridled, removed her hand from the letter, crossed her legs primly beneath the table, fingers laced in her lap.

'Think it's something to do with me mam,' she whispered, looking up at Brogar Finn, seeing in his face all she'd seen before:

the trust he invoked despite the violence implicit in his scars, weighing up her previous misgivings and shifting them all over again.

'Can you read it me?'

Frith's words so polite and meagre Brogar burst out a smile that had Frith blushing, even as she read upside down the first few words of the letter:

There's things you don't know, Charlie, about your mother and your father…

Almost the same words Kerr had used.

'I can,' Brogar said. 'It's from one Danislav Kheranovich, and addressed only to your brother, mind, not to you, so you can excuse Charlie's lack of veracity.'

Frith frowned, leaning back in her chair, slighted, belittled, hating that she'd been left out, that Brogar might yet leave her out, tell her she'd no right to know, Brogar putting her right.

'So it was sent to your brother,' he said lightly. 'Usual stuff. Man to man and all that. But I think we can make an exception.'

Frith smiling, Brogar going on.

'Talks of the place your mother came from, like you thought. Genichesk, over by the Sea of Azov, heartland of the Tatars. So what do you know about it already?'

Frith twitched her nose, remembering the book she'd cajoled her teacher down at Auchencairn into getting for her when her mother had infuriatingly refused to give any details of her past.

'Some,' Frith admitted. 'Not about Genichesk exactly, but a bit about the whole, like how Russia wasn't really Russia until the Scandinavians sort of stuck it all together and gave it a name…'

'The clan of the Ruiriks,' Brogar chipped in, mightily impressed. 'Well now, that's a grand start, Frith. So tell me more.'

Frith smiled, dimples back to the fore, sucking at her lips,

leaning in, trying to recall everything she'd read.

'Well,' she went on, seeing the pages of that old book laid out before her, 'they was going real strong, got all sorts done and founded cities and loads of trading posts and that. Got it going real good, and then the Mongols started steaming in and taking over, but them Mongols didn't last too long and got pushed back to the edges, and at the end of all that they got the Tsars and a load of new lands and made a load of new cities, and that was when they first started down to places like where me mam came from, but...' she hesitated, running out of words, out of history. 'Well I don't really ken after that 'cos my book stopped. It was real old and didn't get past what happened after they'd finished their war with Turkey in...well, I don't know when, but there weren't nothing after that to go on.'

Brogar beamed. This new aspect to Frith was a revelation, her having put the entire history of the Russian Empire neatly into one short paragraph, stopped at the critical juncture – as far as she was concerned – by the fact there'd been nothing more in the book she'd evidently read and absorbed like a sea sponge does water, at the precise moment her own mother's history would have kicked in.

'We're talking about the end of the 1820s,' he continued for her, 'when Russia made a peace treaty with the Turks over access to the Black Sea. But Frith,' Brogar put his elbows on the table and gazed at the girl, 'like you guessed, it's what came afterwards that has to do with your mother and this letter, and what your brother was trying to do over on Hestan. And now I think I know the why, at least in part.'

CHAPTER 21

STEP BY STEP, STONE BY STONE

Sholto followed Fitch into his small cottage, the two of them having to duck below the lintel and fold themselves inside a single dark and barely furnished room.

'So I assume Kerr wants the service held in Auchencairn? The coffin then brought on here to bury?'

Fitch was brisk and businesslike, the two of them sitting down at the small bare table, there being hardly enough room to stand.

'Well, yes,' Sholto replied with some hesitation. 'That's the assumption. In truth we haven't spoken details, there not being much time, Kerr stopping on the island, and everything come through my colleague.'

'Has the doctor been called in to view the body?' Fitch asked, all angles as he sat on his chair, attuned to the details of burial as Sholto was not.

'Not as yet,' Sholto replied, shaking his head, admitting this was something he'd not thought of. 'But you're right. It will have to be done, though in truth there's little doubt as to the way Merryweather died.'

'You've seen him yourself, then?' Fitch deduced, Sholto rubbing

the corners of his mouth with his fingers, wondering if it was time to come clean, if it would serve any of them to say what Brogar had told him. He opted for reticence.

'No, I haven't. Like I said, you know yourself the window getting over to Hestan and back is short, but Brogar Finn is not a man to make mistakes, not in situations like this.'

'In situations like what, exactly?'

Good Lord, the man was like a dog after a bone. Sholto was sincerely pleased he'd never to face Fitch in the confessional. But he supposed the truth was going to come out one way or another, and sometime soon someone was going to ask difficult questions about how a man had been murdered on an inaccessible island with only three people there for suspicion to fall on, never mind that it seemed inconceivable any of them would have reason to do him in.

'It's like this,' Sholto began, spreading his long fingers out on the table. 'Gabriel died very suddenly, and perhaps not altogether due to natural circumstances. There's a few...odd happenings been going on over on Hestan that haven't yet been satisfactorily explained, but myself and Brogar mean to get to the bottom of it.'

Fitch fixed Sholto with a penetrating gaze, a twist on his lips that was approaching a smile.

'So not only arch but mysterious,' he commented wryly, 'but Hestan has always been a place for the mysterious, not least why Gabriel and Kerr chose to barricade themselves out there at the whim of the tides.'

He drummed his fingers on the table for a few moments then stood up, expertly dipping his shoulders to avoid banging his head on the rafters, Sholto getting up after him, not so practised, knocking his topknot with an audible thump, Fitch cackling deep in his throat like it was funniest thing he'd seen in years, which indeed it was. An old trick, but one that never ceased to amuse.

'Come on, sir, time to be getting back to Auchencairn.'

'I'll need to fetch my colleague,' Sholto said as he followed Fitch out, wincing as he palped the bump forming on the top of his skull.

'The more the merrier,' Fitch replied, sounding anything but merry, stepping out of the door, not bothering to lock up after the two of them were away, not so much an act of trust as of there being no point, no one actually living here anymore except the several weaving women – three widows living in the last serviceable cottages in the village – a few labourers and one old crofter on the outskirts who had nowhere else to go and would stagger on tending his vegetable plots until he croaked in one or other of them. And of course the Stirling children, and them probably not for much longer, not now their mother had died. It was, Fitch reflected as he led his visitor away, a bit of a surprise the two had stayed on as long as they had, most likely only because they paid no rent, were allowed to stay gratis on the terms of old Heron's will. But that wouldn't last forever and soon, he thought with sadness, when the widows and labourers and the old man died, the Stirling children would leave for jobs and marriage and the last of its life drained away from Dundrennan. Hundreds of years of history left only to himself and the few visitors and pilgrims who came every year to gawp at an Abbey begun in 1142 by the monarch who did so much to give the Church in Scotland its independence, and whose founding stones could still be seen, and whose walls – everyone said, but perhaps only Edward Fitch truly appreciated – seemed imbued with a sacred religiosity rarely found.

He wasn't a man given to strong imagination or emotion but, as he left Sholto at the lane leading to Frith's cottage and started on before them along the lonely lane to Auchencairn, he wondered how many more years it would be until he too could hang on no longer, until he too would have to abandon Dundrennan to its

ruination, abandon the chapel he'd resurrected in his youth stone by stone, wall by wall, a sacred mission then – convinced of its importance, imbued with the spirituality of a place inhabited for centuries by his direct descendants, by the direct descendants of several other families of this place – the Perdues amongst them – feeling the weight of those centuries a burden he was not equipped to bear.

Hugh and Gilligan had been having a cracking day of it back at the Tuleys'.

They'd spent the morning, together with Bill and Charlie – who'd been wheeled up against a workbench to perform the simpler operations – putting together the obstacles as dictated by the plans they'd all concocted the night before, the boys picking up the rudimentaries of carpentry and metal-working as they went. Hugh was sporting a fine black thumbnail where he'd bashed himself with a hammer due to the very lack of depth perception they were ostensibly trying to correct, but after a couple of hours they had everything ready: the walkway with its humps and bumps, the steps made of increasing heights of planks, the more complicated obstacles coming next. They stopped briefly when Hazel brought out a light lunch, but the four of them could hardly get it down their necks quick enough before they were up again, eager to try everything out.

'You're to start at this end, Hugh,' Bill commanded, pointing the way, 'and what you're to do is walk through this first part slowly. Gilligan will lead the way, so watch his feet, try to match what they're doing with the cues you see. Once we've got the first part mastered we'll move you on, get you over the fences, past all the corners and angles; and when you're ready we'll speed you up, have you going through it at a trot and then a canter...'

'And then a gallop!' Gilligan chipped in.

'Quite right!' Bill laughed. 'But it's going to take a while. Gilligan and Hugh, you ready?'

'Ready!' the two piped up in unison, and then they had begun.

Charlie watched with waning interest as Hugh followed his friend slowly down the first part of the course and back again, thinking it a grand thing they were doing, but now he was no longer directly involved he was soon bored, twitching with inaction. The implications of his own situation were beginning to make themselves properly known: three weeks with this damn plaster on his leg, sitting around on his cart or hobbling around on his crutches. It was going to drive him mad. And he needed to get word to the leatherworks, tell them what had happened. They probably already knew – gossip whistling through the streets of Auchencairn like the wind – but still, it was a worry, and he needed to speak to his boss, make sure he'd be allowed back when he was fit enough. And they'd have no money in pocket until he got back there, only the small dribs of change Frith earned from Fitch for her occasional housekeeping and the maintenance of the chapel. No doubt the widows would look after them, offer pots of stew here and there, but the thought of being stuck out in Dundrennan on his own all day with nothing to do seemed tantamount to being in the wilderness like some damned hermit. He wished Frith was here now to look out for him. And he was worrying too about the shaft, about what he'd been unable to retrieve from it, that if the island got sold before he'd time to get back over, then that would be that; anything found becoming the automatic property of the Company that was buying it.

He couldn't believe he'd been so idiotic as to attempt such a task alone. He'd almost died; Frith had almost died; and all because

he hadn't gone to Mr Perdue for help. His father's friend. But he'd felt such a big man when he got that letter from Heron's lawyer, all of seventeen and the officially designated head of the Stirling household; had believed himself ahead of Frith – God forgive him, for in truth she was the stronger of the two. It had been Frith who'd got him the apprenticeship at the leatherworks, Frith who'd persuaded Fitch to take her on in their mother's stead, Frith who'd said they should ask Perdue for help, and Frith who'd said it didn't matter about their father's bones, that they'd be found soon enough once the new owners took over and only a few minutes work to find out to whom they belonged. But he'd been so spitting mad when he'd read about his father being out there all those years and no one bothering to tell them; spitting mad at Merryweather and Perdue and old Heron too. Precisely the reason he'd decided not to mention to Perdue what they were about – what he was about – on Hestan.

But everything needed reconsidering now that he'd bust his leg in two, Frith most of all. He'd told her about their da being on Hestan, but not about the other half of it, the best of it, the part that said the two of them could be set up for life.

He thumped his hand against the side of the cart, saw Hugh and Gilligan prancing through their damned obstacle course, Bill Tuley clapping them on. And what was that all about? Bill Tuley, the well-known soak, who'd hardly done a stroke of work down all the years Charlie had known him – which was all his life – suddenly resurrecting himself from his drink-laden days and bothering to care about someone other than himself. And apparently getting it right, judging from what he was seeing with his own eyes, getting it a lot righter than he'd done with their ma.

Tears of anger and frustration welling up even as he fought to keep them down: angry at Bill for letting their ma die so badly,

angry at Hazel for letting him do it, angry at himself for not doing anything about it at the time, angry at his stupid leg, and his stupid self; frustration at his own ineptitude, that he'd not shown Frith the letter immediately he'd got it and hadn't told her about it since; that he'd got everything wrong, misjudged the situation so badly he'd almost lost the one person in the world he never wanted parting from, namely Frith.

'Everything alright, Charlie?' Hazel appeared at Charlie's elbow like an accusing angel. He swiped at his eyes with his hand, ashamed to have been caught unawares, his resentment bubbling up in his chest like a ferocious pike breaking through the ice of its winter pond.

'No!' he shouted, not caring that everyone was turning their heads to look at him. 'It's not alright! I'm in this bloody cart and me leg's all busted up, and me ma died when she shouldn't have because of your shitting hubbie, and I can't get to me work to get us any money, and Frith almost drowned and everything's all wrong and…and…'

He stalled to a stop even he realised was pathetic.

'It's just not right,' he whimpered, tears leaking out the corners of his eyes as he slapped his hands against his cheeks to stop them, Hazel putting a firm hand upon his shoulder.

'Of course it's not, Charlie,' she said, no mollycoddling to her voice, only the surety the lad needed to shake him out of his self-pity. 'How can it be? Certainly not right at this moment. But it will be, believe me. It will be, and I've just come to tell you that Frith's on her way. Minister Fitch is only moments at our house and the others not long behind.'

'So, what've we got to go on?' Brogar was fiddling with a candle stub, rubbing its tallow into the cracks in his boots while he and

Sholto waited in the library at Balcary House to be summoned in to dinner. Brogar had been frustrated there'd been no getting back over to Hestan, but as soon as they'd returned to Auchencairn from Dundrennan and taken the wooded track up to Balcary he knew it would be an impossible task. The wind by then high and howling, rain and sleet whipping at them through the cover of the trees, seeing the water being driven in from behind Hestan – and Hestan already surrounded – a short bank of breakers advancing over the sands that no sane man would attempt to broach. He'd been to places like this before – Taganrog on the Azov not so dissimilar in its tidal habits – and understood that an incoming spring tide with a wind behind it could raise water levels by four or five metres in a couple of hours.

Treacherous places, both there and here.

They'd left Auchencairn a couple of hours before, the boys still with the Tuleys, Frith eager to reunite with Charlie, still bubbling over with all the letter had imparted and what it might mean for their shared past, their shared futures too. Brogar explaining briefly to Hazel, Hazel taking it all in.

'Exactly like a romance one might read in a fairy tale,' she'd said in response, 'though how they're supposed to end and how they actually end are two different things.'

'I've been studying some of these books,' Sholto said in answer to Brogar's question, a smile on his lips as he looked towards Brogar and saw him glancing heavenward, as expected. 'They're very unusual.'

'Let me guess,' Brogar sighed. 'A load of them are Tatar in origin, maybe linked to inventories come from grand houses in the Crimea at some point before the 1830s, books and manuscripts that were never seen again, at least not in their homeland.'

'Very good,' Sholto smiled, 'but what's really interesting is the pick and pike of them, the most I've seen so far being commonplace, only a very few being worth anything much.. Not what James Heron wants to hear at all.'

'Because his father sold off all the best ones,' Brogar stated, rubbing the last of the candle grease from his fingers and placing the tiny remnant of the candle back onto the table.

'Sold them off to buy this place, I'd guess,' Sholto agreed, 'and Hestan before it, but there is one exception, one very curious anomaly. A very valuable item listed in the earliest record, but absent from the later ones. I'd dearly like to get back into that study and take a better look through the estate's papers, locked drawers and all that.'

'I bet you would,' Brogar replied, lifting up his head in irritation as the dinner gong rang out through the halls of the house. 'So how d'you want to play this? I think we both know what this band of brothers got up to back in the 1830s – letter or no letter – and that time was brutal, Sholto. Brutal. But how are we to prove it? And how are we to figure it into what happened on Hestan?'

'We can't as yet,' Sholto said shortly, 'but there is one man who could.'

'You mean Kerr Perdue,' Brogar said, after a moment, not liking to throw the man to the wolves, but recognising the truth of what Sholto was saying and that at some point Kerr was going to have to tell his entire version of events. He'd seemed ready before, and given what Brogar had asked him to do, and what young Frith had figured out, confirmed by Charlie's letter, and what else was in that shaft, it seemed likely the time was nigh.

'I do mean Perdue,' Sholto agreed, 'but I also want to explore something Edward Fitch told me about, namely the locked library

of Dundrennan and a lost library at that. One the older Heron was apparently in search of, at least until his later years.'

Brogar clicked his tongue, standing up, impatient to be gone.

'What the hell is it with you and books?' he asked, looking down at Sholto, the sharpness of his words contradicted by the evident amusement on his crooked face.

'Only that all roads here seem to lead to them,' Sholto replied mildly to the accusation, 'as they've done in the past.'

'As they've done in the past,' Brogar repeated, shaking his head in overly dramatic fashion. 'Don't remind me. But if it's so, then it's so. And if you need to gain access to the office and its records then hell, let's see if we can't get you what you need.'

'Dinner first,' Sholto reminded his companion, standing up, ducking his head as if about to get a second blow from Fitch's eaves.

'Oh but such a joy that will be,' Brogar commented, rolling his eyes. 'But hey ho, got to get it done.'

'At least you'll get to meet the younger Heron,' Sholto added.

'Used to hunt them with hawks when I was a lad,' Brogar said wistfully. 'Damn good sport that was, and damn good eating afterwards.'

'Let's hope we don't have to hunt this particular one, with hawks or without,' Sholto replied amiably at Brogar's back, his words subsumed by a second, more insistent sounding of the dinner gong as they went up the corridor, Sholto hoping he wouldn't have to undergo another, more insistent repetition of the lecture on the wool trade once they reached the table.

'Well, I'll be damned,' Kerr whistled, as he got further into shaft number three. He'd been so concentrated earlier on retrieving Archie's bones that he'd not seen what he should have. 'You old

rogue,' he muttered, twisting out a smile, thinking fondly on Merryweather who'd patently made the connection long before Kerr, and hadn't wasted his last day on earth in speculation but gone looking. All that time he and Brogar had been walking over the island, then rescuing Frith, then getting warm, Gabriel must have been crawling over the obstruction of scattered rocks that hid Archie beneath them and gone on beyond, and quite a way. A surprise to Kerr, Gabriel being so superstitious, adamant he never wanted in – a grave being a grave and all that. But Hestan was about to be taken away from them, and them from Hestan.

Enough, presumably, for Gabriel to decide the prize worth the risk.

A way out from them both.

Kerr only wished he'd thought of it sooner.

Done it himself.

Admiration and bravery were not usually words associated with Merryweather, but both seemed applicable now. They'd always known what Archie and Heron had been up to, that Archie's shaft had been deliberately skewed from the copper vein for the purpose. But now Kerr was in it – swinging his lantern about as he shuffled along on his belly – he whistled again at the extent of the diversion, how it jackknifed sharply to the right at its farthest end, Kerr seeing its narrow darkness stretching off maybe another ten yards, looking more like a crawl space beneath a house than a working mineshaft. Plainly Archie had got much further into the heart of Hestan than he'd ever let on, had started burrowing into hard-packed clay and sandstone instead of harder, copper-bearing rock; and no wonder he'd such a sudden need of new props – green wood or no.

And green wood it had been, the evidence there for Kerr to see: the props badly made, bent in the middle, coming adrift from

their supports. Madness to go on, he knew, as Gabriel must have done before him. So far and no further. And the remaining length of shaft unnavigable for the moment, rubble-filled to its knees. Time to make a turnaround. Not easy given the confines, but eventually done. Taking his time now, sliding his hands against the walls as he made his return, finding what he was looking for – what apparently Brogar had known would be there – small irregularities in the shaft side, shifts in the shadows, the hints of niches like the ones all miners built in at certain points to stow lamp fuel, candles, a bottle of water, a meal piece; all handy so they could get what they needed without having to go the long crawl back into the light. Found one of them, found two, found the third.

But all empty, of course, for Gabriel had already come and gone. So how else was it supposed to be?

He got back to the cottage and looked at it with new eyes, for it had to be here somewhere. He paused as he closed the door behind him, regarded the hooks on which Gabriel hung his oilskins and caps, the box below in which he kept his boots and slippers, lifting its lid – but no surprise there. Boots still on Gabriel's feet, slippers there undisturbed. Nothing else.

He moved into the room, opened one drawer and cupboard after another, but nothing there either, not that he could find. He put his hand – with trepidation – underneath the various sides of Gabriel's thin mattress, but came up empty. Not many other places to look. He lingered over Gabriel's workbench – smaller than his own – where stood Gabriel's carvings, put out a hand to one of them – an otter, carved and sanded from driftwood, Kerr stroking the sinuous bend of its back. It was smooth to the touch. Gabriel must really have worked at this one. Casting his eyes over the few

others: the fox that lay at whelp, the two pups curled into her body, all stained red-brown by the pot of lichen paint next to them with the brush still in it; a sea-eagle, half-formed, the most of it growing by natural direction from the driftwood Gabriel had so carefully carved, dowelling holes marked ready to take the piece next to it: a wondrous outstretched wing, feathers neatly chiselled, and so precise. Kerr picking it up and holding it above the place Gabriel had obviously meant it to be set.

He'd been a master at it, this hewing nature from nature.

Kerr couldn't understand how he'd never seen it before, except that they'd mostly met in Kerr's shack and not Gabriel's cottage. But still.

And no sign of Archie's book, not that it was top of Kerr's list.

Kerr seeing instead how all might have gone.

'Oh Gabriel,' Kerr sighed. 'Whatever did you do?'

CHAPTER 22

ACROSS THE WATER

'Ah, our guests! Come in, come in, and get yourselves seated.'

James Heron shook Brogar and Sholto warmly by the hand as they entered the dining room and got themselves upon their chairs.

'I trust you've had a productive day?' he asked, flapping open a serviette and tucking it neatly into his collar.

'If by productive you mean laying out a dead man, organising his coffin and finding a place to park his bones,' Brogar said tersely, 'then yes. A productive day indeed.'

'Ah,' Heron said, nodding his understanding. 'Gabriel Merryweather. Yes, I heard about that. Was it his heart, do you suppose? He wasn't a young man, and that copper working is a hard business.'

'Not to mention the anxiety of fearing he was about to lose his home,' Brogar added sharply, pleased that the gory details of Gabriel's passing hadn't apparently yet trickled into the wider world. It would come out eventually, but for the moment the fewer people who knew about it the better.

Heron narrowed his eyes and looked hard at his foreman.

'What've you been saying, Tweedy? Been speaking out of turn again?'

He stressed the last word slightly and Skinner reddened beneath his collar.

'Nowt,' he pleaded his innocence with badly concealed truculence, "cept to say that once Hestan's sold they'll have to leave. Was I wrong?'

Heron chewed the inside of his lip.

'Well, was he wrong?' Brogar hammered the question home without a beat. 'Because we certainly weren't aware that would be the case.'

Sholto smiled a small smile. It was good to have Brogar back, not that Heron might endorse the statement.

'We understood that to be part and parcel of the agreement, yes.' Heron came back easily, rubbing his hands together. 'Let's get that soup ladled, Esther, if you please.'

'We'd like to take a look at that agreement,' Brogar was not to be put off. 'Speaking of which, any word on Fitzsimons getting here any time soon? Gather he was delayed.'

Heron smiled tightly as Esther went about her duties; taking advantage of the interruption to shift the course of the conversation.

'Not that I've heard,' he said. 'I gather there's snow up north, so no doubt he's found the Lowther Hills impassable. All the more time for you to spend in my library, Mr McKay. Have you come across anything of interest?'

Sholto thanked Esther as she filled his bowl with a delicious smelling haddock soup before switching his attention back to his host.

'I've really had no time to take a proper look,' he said, 'but it would help if I could look at all your father's correspondence, find out who he's been in contact with, if he had earlier inventories.

When was the last comprehensive one made, do you know?'

James Heron creased his brows, began spooning up his soup.

'Not really my area of expertise,' he said, between mouthfuls. 'Think maybe he had one made some time before he died, probably lodged with his lawyer. Is it important? Can't you just work with what you've got in the library proper?'

Sholto hesitated.

'I could,' he said slowly, 'but speed, I gather, is of the essence, so the more information I have about your father's past dealings the better. Maybe in the office?'

'Bound to be in there somewhere,' Brogar added casually, slurping down his soup, holding the bowl to his lips, eschewing the spoon, 'if I know lawyers. And I've known a few. And as we need to check the Company's correspondence regarding Hestan, why don't we look for both at the same time? Alright with you, Heron? Go at it in the morning? Get it done?'

If Heron took slight at Brogar's table manners or being addressed so casually, or his planning a foray into his private office, he'd no time to object, Brogar slapping down his empty bowl, already moving on.

'Business done, then,' Brogar announced, wiping his mouth with the back of his hand. 'So what's all this interesting stuff you've been telling Sholto about the wool factories down south? Always been fascinated with the trade, not that I know much about it. Fur is more my line. Had a lot to do with the Spitsbergen men back in the day. Went on a polar bear hunt with them once, not that they ever mention the bear by name, God forbid. Bad luck that would be. Treat him like a sacred relative, call him the Old Man in the Fur Cloak, if they have to call him anything at all.'

Heron's eyes had brightened at the merest mention of wool, eager to get started on his favourite topic, but he was immediately

entranced by Brogar's talk of bears, exactly – at least to Sholto's mind – as Brogar intended.

'Is that so?' Heron asked, leaning forward, impeding Esther's attempt to fill his wine glass. 'Is it true they can kill a walrus with one swipe of their claws?'

Brogar creased his face in a smile, rubbing his cheeks as he opened his mouth in a gesture Sholto knew was the precursor to one of his impressive stories.

'Partly,' Brogar began, 'but maybe not how you might think. Imagine Spitsbergen in the winter – an island just south of the Arctic Circle, stranded in the Barents Sea. Not that it's an island by then, nor a sea, only ice and snow stretching out to every horizon. Hard living for everyone: man and bear. And then comes the walrus, twenty yards in length, three times the weight of the largest ox and with overgrown incisors getting on for three foot long.'

His audience was enthralled, even Skinner Tweedy switched his gaze from the lithe form of Esther as she put before them pretty plates of rabbit loin flavoured with sloe gin and juniper berries, eager as the others to hear what Brogar would say next.

'Walrus breaks through the ice,' Brogar did not disappoint, 'ice so thick not even a man with an axe and strong arms can render a crack in it. Rumour has it a bear will wait behind an ice floe then suddenly fling itself onto the walrus's back, hanging on with teeth and claw until the animal is subdued. But,' Brogar waved an expansive arm, 'that's all nonsense. Both would quickly sink below the freezing waves and drown. But I've seen walrus hides that have bears' slash marks in them, and I've seen them fighting, though have to say it's usually the walrus – a mere overgrown seal with teeth almost as long as myself – who comes out on top.'

'You've seen this yourself?' Esther forgot her position and

spoke up, her voice taut with excitement. Brogar looked up at the girl and smiled.

'I have that, young miss, and I've seen too what happens to a dinner that's allowed to cool beyond its natural endurance. So shall we have in?'

Esther quickly obliged, putting the plate she'd been holding before him.

Sholto was impressed with Brogar. Not only had he negotiated them a way into the estate's papers but he'd also skewed James Heron off track, as far as the wool trade was concerned. And Brogar was about to do more, now that he'd caught Heron's attention, going on with his conversation as if it were a natural leap from polar bears and walruses to what he said now.

'So tell me,' Brogar went on easily, 'what's this locked library story I've been hearing about? Got lost, so I've been told.'

James Heron choked a little on his rabbit but was sufficiently put off guard to say more than he might have if he'd had time to think about it.

'An ancient tale,' he began, 'churned out by the monks when the Dissolution was in full swing, Henry VIII's men scouring at the Borders. Not that they spent much time in this neck of the woods, steering more to the east. But we were all taught about The Bloody Ledger they left of their doings – over four hundred men slain, double that taken as prisoners, ten thousand each of cattle and horses taken away as spoil, not to mention almost thirteen thousand sheep.'

'Well, that would have riled you if you'd been there back in the day,' Brogar commented, getting stuck into his meal. 'All that wool gone south over the border.'

Heron paused in his eating and looked over at Brogar, Brogar holding up a hand.

'I mean it, Heron, every word. Folk in power always know where to hit to make the people suffer the most. Take the Tatar lands in the Crimea, for instance,' Sholto perking up, watching Heron closely as Brogar went on. 'When the Russian Tsars feared they were losing control in that particular edge of Empire they did nothing so commonplace as stealing sheep or taking prisoners. Instead, they sent soldiers from town to town, village to village, demanding every last leaf of printed paper or handwritten folios from every last landowner and burned the lot, right before their eyes. Hundreds of thousands of books lost, and not a lick of them seen from that day to this.'

James Heron speared a piece of rabbit and swallowed, keeping his eyes on his plate.

'Effective,' he said, 'but if you're implying that the Dundrennan library was burned it doesn't seem likely. Most historians believe they got it over the water to the Brothers on the Isle of Man, and from there was taken into Royal custody.'

Heron went on a bit about Manx history, as was his wont, Sholto cocking his head at the few specific words embedded in it, but it was Brogar who carried the conversation on after a ten-minute lecture that took them through the main course of the evening, performing one of his wild skews, Sholto wondering if Brogar actually thought about what he was saying or if it just came naturally.

'The Isle of Man, is it?' Brogar asked, leaning back to allow Esther to remove his empty plate. 'Exactly where the smugglers came from who built this very house.'

James Heron smiled.

'Don't believe everything you hear, Mr Finn. That trade was stamped out good and proper in these parts and by my father, no less,' he said, removing his serviette, taking out his cigar case and offering it around, refused by Brogar and Sholto and snatched

back into his pocket before Skinner Tweedy got a look in. Skinner quiet all this time, but now speaking up.

'Them lads of yours were mighty impressed with the cellars.'

'As anyone would be,' Brogar stated, 'for didn't Gilligan tell me they could fit two hundred horses in side by side? And how many sheep would it take, Sholto, to fill that place wall to wall?'

It was a snipe too far, and Heron had had enough, Sholto feeling a giggle rising in his throat to see the man so baited, and was not without sympathy.

'Apologies for my companion,' he offered, swallowing his urge to laugh. 'But there is something I'd like to ask about.'

James Heron looked over at Sholto with something like supplication on his face, shrouded as it was in the smoke from his cigarillo.

'Ask away,' he answered, tapping the wasted ash into his unused water glass, taking a decent swig of his wine.

'It's back to Dundrennan, I'm afraid,' Sholto smiled meekly, wanting to explore those words *over the water* James had spoken, that had been on the gravestone Sholto had seen earlier in the day. 'Your knowledge of its history is impressive. Can I take it you had an interest in it? Maybe as a boy?'

Heron let out a short burst of laughter, blowing an almost perfect smoke ring on its tail.

'Oh no, my friend, not I, but my father. He always loved stories, always did, loved telling them, loved hearing them, went after any that interested him like a terrier after a rat. How I know so much about Dundrennan? Because he never let up about it. Was convinced that library was still somewhere hereabouts.'

Heron sucked at his cigar and looked over at Sholto, apparently mollified, for he began talking as voluminously as he had the night before, the spinning of tales apparently running in the family.

'The history of Dundrennan Abbey is an odd one, given what happened to others nearby, places that had lands the local owners wanted, taking advantage of the English army's pillaging to get them into their hands and away from the Church. Word has it that Allan Stewart, Commendator of Crosraguel up towards Glasgow, was stripped of clothes and basted in goose fat, set before a burning fire, eventually signing over the deeds of his Abbey to Gilbert Kennedy, Earl of Cassilis, or as much signing as a hand burned in goose fat can do.'

'But not Dundrennan?' Sholto asked.

'Not Dundrennan,' Heron agreed. 'It seems that Dundrennan was so lonely and insignificant a place that no one much bothered with it. The monks were told it was no longer to be treated as a monastery, but allowed to stay out their lives in the place; and most of them took advantage, went out into the world, married local women.'

'The Perdues amongst them,' Sholto put in.

'Quite right. And others,' James supplied. 'Can't hole men up in the middle of nowhere then give them their freedom and expect no consequences. Perdues, Fitches, Stirlings and Thorns, to name but a few.'

'But no Herons?' Brogar cut in. 'For I don't believe your family came from here at all.'

James turned his head slowly towards Brogar Finn.

'No Herons,' he agreed shortly, his voice rising in volume as it went on. 'But then why would there be? I think, Mr Finn, you already have suspicions of where my father came from. What you mayn't know is that he took me in when I had need of it, when my own family had been destroyed, lost and gone. Myself the only survivor. Took me in and brought me here, gave me a life, and a life I'm proud of and will do anything to protect.'

'Including selling Hestan?' Brogar asked.

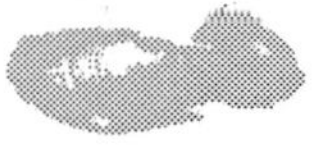

'Well of course!' Heron's voice was high. 'It's nothing but a bloody millstone! Always has been. Turnover from the copper is practically non-existent, not once everyone's taken their cut. Get your Company in and dig the lot of it up is the only way to make profit from it. And if Perdue and...well Perdue. If he wants to stay on afterwards then I'll not object, if you want to build that into your Bill of Sale. But it's got to be done.'

'Can I ask one more thing?' Sholto said politely, nodding at Esther as she went around the table with another bottle of wine.

'Be my guest,' Heron said, stubbing out his cigar, 'seeing as that is what you are.'

'It's just I saw an inscription on a gravestone at Dundrennan,' Sholto went on, noting the irritation on Heron's face that he tried unsuccessfully to hide.

'Which was what?' he asked, grasping his wine glass tightly in one hand.

'I don't remember it exactly,' Sholto lied, for he remembered it perfectly. 'It was in French, on a Perdue grave in the Abbey grounds. Something about all that they cared for going over the water.'

Heron shrugged.

'And?'

'And nothing, really,' Sholto went on, 'except that it struck me that maybe over the water might not have referred to the Isle of Man but to Hestan.'

Heron laughed loudly, taking out his cigar case and lighting another cigarillo, apparently finding the idea so humorous he was having difficulty holding it to the candle to get it alight.

'Oh my! Excuse me, but really you two are such a double act you should go on the stage! Over on Hestan? And by that I'm assuming you mean the mythical locked library? Should I build another clause into our Bill of Sale?'

'Mightn't be a bad idea,' Brogar put in, taking a swig of his wine and putting it back down on the table, 'for I've seen the way Archie Stirling was taking his shaft, at least at last reckoning, and it wasn't right, Heron. Going against the grain of the vein so to speak.'

Heron stopped mid-puff.

'You're not serious...' he said, his voice back to its usual timbre, looking first at Sholto then at Brogar. 'But my God, you are! I can see it in your faces. Do you know how ridiculous that sounds?'

On the other side of the table Skinner Tweedy cleared his throat.

'Was what your father thought,' speaking quietly. 'Mentioned it to me once, when I first started here. Banging on about Balliol this and that.'

'Oh for Christ's...' Heron lost his new found jollity, 'not you too, Skinner. Most grounded man I've ever met.'

'Don't know who Balliol was,' Skinner conceded, 'but found your father once in the office with all the maps of here and Hestan and that laid out on the desk. *Think it might be there*, was what he said, and there was a bit on the Hestan map that was marked as Balliol's Manor House, though didn't know then what he was talking of.'

'And now you do?' Heron spat. 'Several years later you think – right out of nowhere – that he was talking about some books a load of monks lost years ago?'

Skinner quavered, didn't speak, wouldn't look at any of them.

'So who's Balliol?' Brogar asked.

'Edward Balliol,' Heron supplied brusquely. 'King of Scotland for a couple of minutes way back in the 1200s. Big in Galloway, built a stronghold on Hestan because back then the island was more strategic, easy to land a boat on, not like now when the Solway has all silted up. But that's enough of history,' James declared, standing up, obviously sick of the proceedings, as forceful as Brogar could

be when he wanted to bring a conversation to its end. 'Long day just done, and long day ahead. And first thing on the morrow we'll get that Bill of Sale amended to allow Perdue's continuance on the island.'

'And the library?' Sholto asked, Heron misunderstanding, yawning widely, holding his fist across his mouth ostensibly to hide it, but intending the opposite.

'Well why not?' he countered. 'Hell, let's build it all in. Let's say if it's found, me and your Company will share the profits. Let's pretend Hestan is everyone's answer to everything.'

And then he was away, sudden and sharp, gone through the door and off down the corridor and up the stairs.

'No even man, that James Heron,' Brogar commented, pouring another glug of wine into his glass, Esther having already departed, buzzing with the conversation, gathering that dessert was not on the menu so all the more for her and cook down in the kitchen, nothing allowed to go to waste.

'You don't know the half of it,' Skinner grumbled, and then he too was out the door and off to his quarters, leaving Brogar and Sholto alone.

'Illuminating,' Brogar said, looking over at Sholto, Sholto smiling back at him.

'Very,' he replied. 'And you know those mysteries you were talking about? Well, I have the feeling they really are abounding.'

'Good job mystery is what we do,' Brogar fired back, 'apart from all the mining. And, by the way, ever seen stones like these in the vicinity? Found them on the beach just below the house.'

Brogar chucked a couple of pink pebbles from his pocket onto the table, Sholto picking them up, studying them with care.

'Barytes?' he asked, looking to Brogar for confirmation.

'Barytes; barium sulphate to be more precise,' Brogar confirmed.

'And if we can find the source of them, then it might turn this whole situation here upon its head.'

Chapter 23

Not So Lost Souls, But Still Lost Libraries

As James Heron had said: long day yesterday, long day today, things moving swiftly the moment everyone was up and at it, Brogar away soon as he could to Auchencairn to get the coffin over to Hestan; Sholto to the Estate Office, Heron handing him a bunch of keys and telling him to have at as many files as he chose, seek out any papers he needed relating to either Hestan, his father's books or anything else that caught his fancy.

'Just make sure you get back to the library soonest,' was James's only caveat. 'I need to know what's worth selling and what isn't. I want a crate ready for the off soon as your lawyer gets here so he can shift it with him back to Edinburgh, get the best prices I can.'

He and Tweedy away immediately afterwards, off to do whatever they did on a daily basis.

At the Tuley house, things were no less busy, Gilligan and Hugh eager to be at Bill's obstacle course again, Hugh convinced his depth perception had already improved and neither he nor Gilligan wanting to squander any opportunity to make it better still, not when they didn't know how much longer they'd be here

in Auchencairn. Charlie was in the infirmary, Frith off to the leatherworks to explain all that had happened, plead the case for Charlie's job to be left open once he was right again, Hazel heading out soon afterwards on some house calls, Bill leaving her to it, up miraculously early.

'Thought I'd go over to Hestan with Brogar and the coffin,' Bill informed his wife over their scanty breakfast, the others already finished and gone. 'Make the official mark about Merryweather being dead.'

Hazel was so surprised she pushed away her bowl of porridge, only halfway eaten.

'Are you sure, Bill? I mean, well, dead bodies…it hasn't exactly… are you sure you're up to it?'

Bill lowered his head, put his two hands over his face, rubbing his fingers hard at his eyes, down his cheeks, bringing them to rest below his chin, breathing deeply.

'I know I've been badly these past few years,' he said, words the bare minimum above a whisper, 'and for years before that. Have never been able to quite shake stuff off…been bad to you and to all the people who've depended on me…'

'It's not …' Hazel began, but Bill cut her off.

'But it is, Hazel. And I can't tell you how sorry I am. It's just I've always felt – since we got back, well, you know – since we got back, that nothing's ever been quite real again. Not like it was over there. Not after everything we saw.'

'It's been fifteen years, Bill,' Hazel sighed, unable to stop herself. 'Fifteen years of you skidding downhill, ignoring everyone who's tried to stop you getting to the bottom of wherever it is you've been going. And now you've suddenly seen the error of your ways? And what do you think I've been doing all the meanwhile?'

She hated the bitterness to her words, hated the scepticism

implicit in them; hated that she was doubting Bill might actually be seeing himself for what he had become and trying to do something about it, and her putting the brakes on.

Bill didn't move, then raised his head, looked at her directly, looked at her with a defiance that had her lacing her fingers together so hard they went white at the tips from lack of blood.

'I can't expect your forgiveness,' he spoke softly, 'and I truly don't expect it, but please, please let me try to do something better than I've done for a long time. That young lad Hugh? It's like he's pumped all the blood back into my veins, and I really think I can help him. And it would be the first good thing I've done for almost as long as I can remember. And then there's Merryweather. Who's to see to him if I don't?'

And there he was, the same man Hazel had first met, the same fire in him, the same goodness; and however this was going to play out she couldn't bring herself to deny him the chance, or deny herself the chance of getting back the man she'd so much loved when they'd begun together on married life. God, but it was going to be a hard road, hard to accept that if the Bill Tuley she'd known, loved and lost came back then she might be relegated back to the role of housekeeper, nurse and midwife; hard that she might have to deny all the knowledge she'd gained down the intervening years; hard to anticipate what would happen if Bill became a competent doctor again, when her services were no longer needed and her opinions no longer given any weight. A new start for her husband, perhaps, but the end of everything that had given Hazel's life purpose and meaning since they'd returned from the Crimea.

One happening, one arrival, one boy.

And now everything might be going to change because of it.

Hazel was finding it hard to bear.

Kerr was waiting on the other side of the Rack when Bill and Brogar arrived with the coffin. He couldn't figure out at first who was coming over with Brogar, the two of them quickly along the Rack with their light load, flabbergasted to realise – as the two came closer – that the second man was Bill Tuley, for everybody knew how that man had been slowly falling apart since he'd arrived in Auchencairn after the end of the Crimean War in '56. Good enough at first, but not for long. When Archie had got back a couple of years later he'd gone to see Bill, thinking they'd common ground, having been in the same war; but Bill had sent him packing before he'd barely got over the doorstep.

'Gone bloody mental,' Archie reported to Kerr. 'Can't think why. We all came out no bother.'

It was bit of an understatement, as far as Kerr and Merryweather went, but nothing had ever taken the shine off Archie, not when they'd last been with him in Tatary and apparently not after they'd gone; Archie like a piece of gold, untarnished when the rest had been rusting away with the weather of the years.

'We was young when we went,' Kerr said in Bill's defence, 'fighting fit and swinging. Got in gradual, like. But we wasn't working in surgeons' tents, hacking limbs off left, right and centre.'

'S'pose,' Archie relented.

'An' we had each other, when we was with you,' Kerr added, 'got to sit around a fire at night and talk our tales. Not like him. Gather they was at it night and day for all the time their war went on.'

Archie smiled with all the bright innocence of a celandine opening up in the sun.

'You're right about that, I guess,' he said. 'And speaking of tales, I stopped the night with Kheranovich after that, and you'll never figure what he told me. Ken we used to tell him all that stuff about the locked library?'

Kerr's turn to smile, though not so brightly – never so brightly.

''Course I do, and not so much the we as the you.'

'Well, some of it were true,' Archie came back at Kerr, 'least so my father said and his before him, an' all the way back. But that ain't the nub of it, the nub of it is,' Archie leant forward, fixing Kerr with his serene blue gaze, Kerr hanging on every word like he'd always done, 'Kheranovich reckons he knows where it's at.'

Kerr opened his mouth in utter astonishment, Archie holding up a finger.

'He's been busy since he's been here, been scuffling through the old graves and looking up some of the Abbey records that ended up in that Stewartry history place in Kirkcudbright.'

Archie tilted his head skywards, holding up his hands in mock reverence – an old joke, one Kerr joined in – as he began to recite the words Rabbie Burns had written in that town, Kerr joining in the prayer of grace they'd used out East to have got through another day, and still alive at the end of it, to eat a meal, no matter how paltry:

Some hae meat and cannae eat,

And some wad eat that want it,

But we hae meat and we can eat

And sae the lord be thankit.

Archie laughed, slapping Kerr on the shoulder.

'So you've not forgotten?'

'Not a word of it,' Kerr replied with a grin, 'still use it when I'm in the mood. But what about Kheranovich? You can't lay a trail like that and leave it lying.'

'Aha,' Archie said, tapping the side of his nose. 'He's found some old papers about the Balliol place…'

'Here on Hestan?' Kerr interrupted, excited despite himself, Archie able to whip up a storm from the calmest waters.

'Here on Hestan is exactly it,' Archie exclaimed. 'Reckons there was a well built right down through the island from the manor house that tapped into some underground offshoot of the Urr running below the sands.'

'Can't be right,' Kerr countered. 'I ken the sands were different back then, I mean they're different now even from when we were lads, but wouldn't we have found it?'

Recalling the days they'd spent as children running over the island like hares filled to the brim with March madness, exploring every inch, stopping out nights here even though they'd been expressly forbidden from doing so by parents who didn't want them to sink in the sands or drown trying to get out to Hestan or back.

'But that's just it,' Archie went on, more serious now, dragging out a sketch of what Kheranovich had shown him. 'Mind when the monks first used Hestan as a fishing place?'

Kerr nodded, knowing the history of the island as well as Archie, that Dundrennan monks had fished the waters around about it for as long as they'd been in the Abbey.

'Well look you here,' Archie said, pushing the paper across the table, Kerr seeing Archie's crude drawing of the Balliol Manor house as it would have been when standing, another smaller habitation to the south, a line going down from the second building straight through Hestan into the rocks below, a wiggly line joining its base to the tip of Almorness Point on the other end of the Rack.

'But even if this is right,' and Kerr was having a hard time believing it was, 'then such a well would have been filled in ages past.'

'Exactly,' Archie beamed. 'Ages past, but maybe not before the English came and shut Dundrennan down. Maybe just in time for the monks to stow something in there and fill it in themselves.'

'You're as bad as Kheranovich,' Kerr chuckled, 'you and your tales. You should never have told him about any of this. You know how he is with books.'

'But what if it's true?' Archie wouldn't let it go, Kerr keeping his fingers on the scanty sketch because, well, what if it were true? But he only believed it for a moment, the moment gone as soon as Archie switched his gaze from Kerr's face, as if he was some kind of enchanter of old.

'It'd all be filled in with rubble now,' Kerr repeated. 'And we never saw a whiff nor which of it when we was scampering over Hestan; n' hows we ever going to find it, even it's there? Balliol Manor's long gone, only grass and stone, and only this,' he tapped at the paper, 'to give us a vague clue 'bout where it's to be.'

Archie smiling again, Archie so certain, so alive with possibilities.

'But that's just it,' Archie said easily. 'Don't mean to come at it from above but from below. Kheranovich says I'm to skew my shaft, intercept it from the underlings.'

Kerr would have laughed out loud if he hadn't thought Archie was being serious, but plainly Archie was.

'That's insane, Archie,' Kerr said bluntly. 'If you get off the copper vein then there's no money to be made, and what then about your wife and children?'

Archie paused for a moment, but only for a moment.

'But that's why I'm going to do it, don't you see? If we find this library then we'll all be laughing…'

'But you'd be laughing anyway if you cashed in that book Kheranovich gave you back in Genichesk.'

Kerr spoke harshly, hadn't meant to say it – hadn't been meant to hear it that night, but heard it anyway – regretted it immediately, but no going back now.

'We all knows it's worth a small fortune, so why not just get it done? Why go through all these hoops and whatnots just because Kheranovich has told you to jump?'

Kerr could have bitten out his tongue, Archie looking at his oldest friend as if he'd been that last old woman strapped to the stake back when burning witches in Kirkcudbright was every day.

'Didn't know you knew,' Archie said, 'but thought I'd keep a hold of it.' Gazing past Kerr into some future that lay only in his head. 'Thought it'd do us all when we're old and grey. Kept it through thick and thin all the time after you was gone. Thought of it too when I went back for Nairi and she had the grace to hook up with me and we had the bairns. Thought on it a lot of times, Kerr, an' always thought on it as being ours, not mine. Told that to Kheranovich, too. Told him if I went after the library he'd to promise to see everyone right, me and mine, and by that I mean you and Merryweather too.'

A small jitter to Kerr's heart then, as he was swept out of the shadows and into Archie's light.

'Don't need to do that, man,' he said a little hoarsely, Archie brushing the words aside.

''Course I do!' like it was the most natural thing in the world. 'We was nigh on born together and we lived together and went abroad together, came out the other side together.'

Forgetting all the years that had separated Kerr and Merryweather's homecoming from his own as if they were mere pebbles on the path they'd started on together, a path leading right back to Hestan, to this single moment, to this declaration of allegiance so generous in its scope that Kerr had trouble getting in his next breath.

In the office of the Balcary House Estate, Sholto was busy burrowing through all the files and folders accessible now by means of Heron's

keys. He'd previously supposed the man had been keeping secrets from him and Brogar, but if he had it was not apparent. There was always the possibility Heron had been in before him and removed anything he'd not wanted Sholto to see, but Sholto doubted it. Nothing appeared disturbed, certainly not the older papers he found in the locked drawers of the huge wooden cabinet that went from the floor almost to the ceiling, taking up an entire wall.

Teetering on a stool to reach the topmost drawers, his deft fingers flicked through file after file, paper after paper, almost two hours gone now and still nothing of interest, it occurring to him that perhaps this had been Heron's intent – give him so much to get through that he'd lose interest and give up the chase. But if that was the case, then Heron didn't know Sholto as well as he thought he did and, after a further forty-two minutes of searching, Sholto had finally garnered several documents pertinent to his cause.

He swiftly gathered them together and left the office, returning to the library and the large rosewood desk that shone like a chestnut newly broken from its casing to greet the sun, experiencing what that chestnut might have felt – had it been sentient – and that glory was all about him, and much to be done.

'Well, well,' he muttered beneath his breath, a smile breaking across his thin face as he read through each document with care.

So, mysteries really do abound, he was thinking as he surveyed his cache:

One inventory of a book collection acquired by Heron's father in the early 1830s – similar to, but not exactly like, the inventory he'd already seen in the library before;

A copy of a letter sent out by the same, lodged with the Heron family's lawyers and only very recently dispatched – according to his instructions – to the son of Archie Stirling of Dundrennan on the day of his seventeenth birthday;

An elderly almanac listing details of the tide times in the Solway Firth and, more particularly, around Hestan;

Skinner Tweedy's application for the job of Estate Manager;

A topological map of the area around Balcary Houghs – the tall, sheer cliffs that surrounded the point – that gave a clue that might relate to those two pink pebbles Brogar had spilled out of his pocket the night before.

He'd not found any contract of agreement that Perdue and Merryweather be allowed to stay on Hestan for the remainder of their natural lives, but such a contract was now moot, given that Merryweather was dead and Heron willing to allow Perdue that right anyway – assuming Perdue would want it, once the Company moved in.

The bafflement to this whole affair was Merryweather's dying; Sholto sitting quietly at the rosewood desk as he constructed in his head a timeframe that could make sense of it; studying the inventories he'd access to, going back several times to the book shelves he'd earlier surveyed, pulling out one volume or another, obeying Heron's request that he amass all he found most valuable, piling them up at the far end of the desk as if building a wall to keep out the rest of the world. Only one book lay outside his self-made fort of profitable volumes, one he couldn't understand how he'd missed, the same anomaly he'd mentioned in passing to Brogar being now right in front of him: small, oddly cold, a little damp to the touch, but still perfect. Turning its pages one by one by one, willing it to give up its secrets, convinced he was on the path to righteousness, but not exactly where that path led.

Brogar and Bill arrived on Hestan and were taken straight away to Merryweather's cottage, though Kerr held Bill outside for the few moments he knew Brogar would need.

'Glad to see you on the out and out,' Kerr commented. 'Things better with you these days? Know what you went through. Went through similar meseln.'

Bill braced his feet against the wind, grateful Brogar had said to stay a while till he got things sorted inside, cleared his throat, a shivering going through his bones at what he was about to see and do.

'Been badly for a while,' Bill admitted, 'but trying to turn it all around.'

Kerr nodded, scuffing his boot into the dirt.

'Can take a time,' he said. 'Took me a time – things I seen an' did an' never wanted to? Takes a bit to flush out o' your head, and ain't never gone, not properly, nor ever should.'

Bill nodded, but remained mute.

'Mind when Archie went to see you, years back?' Kerr found himself saying, all those memories still wild and vivid in his head, Bill frowning, turning his body towards Kerr Perdue though unable to meet his eye, not that Kerr was looking at him, gazing instead somewhere over the sands of the Solway and way down the past.

'Can't say that I do.'

Though he remembered the occasion well enough, Archie Stirling come back home filled to bursting with all he'd seen and done in the Crimea, eager to chat to Bill about the war when all Bill wanted was to forget it had ever happened. Not that he'd even been able to.

'Aye, well,' Kerr went on. 'Just wanted to say that you mayn't've been ready for talking 'bout it back then, it all so fresh like, but if you ever do now, well. I mightn't be on Hestan much longer but I'll not be far. Travelling days is long done for me, and glad for it.'

Bill screwed up his eyes; *talk about it*; something he'd never done, not to anyone, not even to Hazel; especially not to Hazel. But Kerr was someone else entirely, solid as the island rock on which they stood, Bill finding the notion not so outrageous as it had always seemed, Kerr nothing like the bright bubble Archie had been – so eager to splash out his enthusiasm for all he'd taken part in; Bill recalling precisely the gleam in Archie's eyes when he'd stood on his doorstep and the nausea Bill had felt crawling in the pit of his stomach to know that the man had actually enjoyed being out there, proud of his part in the fighting.

Having too the strangest notion that Kerr was right.

That he really might soon have the need to talk about it, get it all out in the open – not the larks Archie would have wanted to chat about on idle nights, but the real down and dirty stuff that war had been: the filthy slip of mud the hospital floor had been churned into; the flattened earth transmogrified into black slurry by the addition of so much spilling blood; the gut-wrenching stink of gangrenous flesh, rotting limbs – a great pile of them thrown haphazardly into the pit dug outside the surgeons' tent. The awful truth the British public had learned through the reportage of William Russell about how most of the men Bill treated hadn't been battle-wounded at all, instead had been riddled with disease and malnutrition, abandoned by their ignoramus superiors who couldn't be bothered to keep their men fed and furnished. Bill going right back to the start of it, when he'd been so keen to do his bit, go out and help the lads, himself just newly qualified; all ideas of glorious empire wiped out in the few hours it took the SS *Arctic* to sink when he'd realised that the vast majority of men were mere animals at the core, only interested – at least *in extremis* – in saving their own skins. And what was more *in extremis* than war and the survival of it?

The experience had soured him sure as milk curdles in a thunderstorm, and the bitter taste of it had never left him since. Not until he'd met Hugh, and now Kerr Perdue, when it seemed to Bill that the thunderstorms that had blighted his life might at last be able to move on to other places, leave him behind; soured certainly, but perhaps not so sour he might not still have use.

Inside the cottage, Brogar moved swiftly. Straightaway to Merryweather he went, grasping the amulet at its base, the coppered skull of the curlew's head still apparent despite the beak having gone right in; fingertips touching the dry and clouded surface of Merryweather's dead eye as he wheedled the weapon out, leaving little evidence of it having been there at all – bar the pooling of blood in Merryweather's eye. Brogar's intent not so much to obscure the facts of Merryweather's death as not wanting Bill Tuley going into meltdown, on Sholto's advice, and to give them a bit more time to figure it all out. It had seemed as preposterous to Sholto as it had to Brogar that the three obvious suspects could be anything other than innocent, but no harm waiting until they could prove it.

He quickly placed the amulet into the leather pouch Sholto had provided and tucked it away in a pocket, hoping Sholto was right now finding something to explain this most inexplicable of deaths. Next, he picked up the bag of Charlie's bones and moved them to one side. He found it rather touching that Kerr had seen fit to cocoon the two together on Merryweather's bed beneath the blanket that covered the man head to foot, recalling the walrus he'd once glimpsed on the Kamchatka coast cradling its offspring in like manner, making it impossible to believe – as certain philosophers did – that animals were incapable of feeling loyalty, and maybe even love.

'Ready!' Brogar shouted, once done, and in came Bill and Perdue, Bill straight to the corpse to check for signs of life, though patently there were none.

'Dead,' Bill pronounced, 'as we all knew, but it had to be done.'

'Indeed,' Brogar agreed.

'But a strange blood clot here in this eye,' Bill stated, 'not usual at all. Does he have any relations? Anyone who might permit a partial autopsy?'

Brogar was surprised at this level of acuity; he'd been given to understand that Bill was rather shoddy at being a man, and a lot shoddier at being a doctor.

'No one immediate,' Kerr said, ''cepting me.'

'We'll deal with the details later,' Brogar cut the discussion short. 'Time now to be getting him back over. Perdue, will you assist?'

Perdue came forward, and together he and Brogar lifted Merryweather's corpse into the coffin. A neat fit, not much room for extras.

'Got a little bag here he might want to be buried with,' Kerr said, hiding his face from Bill, taking the line Brogar had told him, grasping up the sack of Archie and placing it over Merryweather's shins, there being so little left of Archie that he took up hardly any room.

'Fine,' Bill said, taking the hammer Brogar handed him, closing the lid, bashing at a nail. 'But that blood clot? It's most unnatural. I'd like to take a further look later if I may?'

'Later,' Brogar said, calling the conversation to a halt, casting a brief glance at Perdue. 'Got to get him over soonest.'

'Soonest is always best hereabouts,' Perdue agreed, eager to assist. 'Wind's bin strong last coupla days an' snow on its way, if I'm not mistaken.'

Perdue helped take the coffin over to Balcary – the quickest and easiest land point to be reached when carrying a burden such as this – acutely uncomfortable that, as he'd surmised earlier, by the time they got to it the wind had turned against them and no way for him to get back to the island. He looked with longing at the dark slump of Hestan, wishing he could be with it in its final hours before the Company arrived in force, knowing that tomorrow would most probably bring the lawyer Sholto and Brogar had been waiting on, who would put his name on the dotted line, make the agreement of sale legal and proper, sign everything away.

Having the dreadful premonition that he would never set foot on Hestan again.

He thought on his list of things he never wanted to forget, and top of that list was Hestan itself; not a lump of rock to be exploited but a friend, a living breathing entity with its own history and rhythms, maybe even a soul. He knew it would sound a nonsense to anyone who'd never lived there, but that was how both he and Merryweather had felt about it – that it had been a companion, a place to be a part of, a place that had absorbed them into its own, a place that would never reject them for what they'd done, would have kept on accepting them for as long as they lived, if allowed to do so.

He thought back on Dundrennan, the place his forefathers had come from; thought on how heart-wrenched those monks must have been the day they learned they were to be cast out from the Abbey's walls; or not cast out exactly, allowed to stay, but without the protection of Mother Church; isolated, abandoned, a choice to stay or go. Certainly they'd been luckier than their Brethren in other places, and most had chosen to stay in the vicinity, passing their names down through the generations, keeping the spirit of the Abbey alive as long as they could. Kerr not so different from

his forbears, a man who understood fealty and loyalty to his roots, the need to stay within his own self-constructed Abbey walls. What he couldn't properly comprehend or accept was that there'd be a day coming far too soon when he'd be the man kept outside those walls, would be a man who could see Hestan every day but not be allowed out there.

Last chance gone, like the Dundrennan monks of old; witness to the continued existence of the place to which they belonged but utterly denied the ability to be a living, breathing part of it. And for Kerr, maybe no last chance to stroll Hestan's small heights and lows, no chance to see to their kine in the paddock or the chooks in their moveable enclosure. Certainly no chance of Merryweather ever seeing any of it again. And the sadness of the situation caught in Kerr's throat as he shifted Merryweather's coffin onto his shoulders as they gained the shingle beach at Balcary, tried to think on the bigger picture but could not, still a part of Hestan and the gulls that he could see dipping and diving above and around its edges, as if he could still detect that white flash to their bellies as they came up and at you in the gleam of sunrise, and hear the raucous crawing of them dawn and dusk that would have you tearing out your hair until you got used to it.

All of it, all of it, Kerr was thinking, soon to be lost to him; symbol of what he'd known but couldn't articulate: of lives spent, but not necessarily wisely; the pennies of past years being shifted from hand to hand and you along with them – not that you'd any say in where you were being shifted; the marks those transactions left on you as apparent as the nicks on the beaks of the birds about Hestan, the raggediness of their wings where one feather or another had been torn from the skin and could not regrow. The past apparent in the present, and nothing you could do to make it right. Him and Merryweather there on Hestan trying to act out

atonement their own way. Trying, but not necessarily succeeding. His list surfacing again unbidden, maybe never to reach its natural end, wondering if Gabriel had the same list:

The seals that gathered on the sands and broke your heart with their singing;

The seals that bobbed up out of the breakers and looked at you like you were the only person left alive on earth, and how they seemed to beg you into the water to join them, save you from your own misgivings;

The first shoots of heather coming up from the bedrock in late spring, early curling buds still hidden, bees not yet from their burrows – not yet, but almost coming, and the first you saw of them being an exhilaration of the first order as they settled on the new sprung purple orchids that grew up in days as if they'd been waiting for that exact moment;

The dark caves, all clad in green, drip drip dripping, and the bats that rose so suddenly from the gloom;

The shaft down which he'd spent his later life – missing even that – missing the fug of it, the hardness and certainty of the rocks, thinking once again on Archie and how he'd skewed his shaft the wrong way;

Missing the camaraderie they'd had back in the east, the camaraderie that for Kerr had all come to an end with the burning of that barn;

And Hestan most of all; Hestan in the green in the spring, in the auburn it sank into in the autumn and the grey it was now, during the winter months.

So many regrets, Kerr was thinking as he, Brogar and Bill made their way out from Balcary Bay with Merryweather on their shoulders, Archie's hidden bones with him, about to be buried together – not that many people would know. His children would

be told to keep their silence for their own sake, for the sake of Charlie's paltry pension, especially now their mother was gone. And she too – Nairi – Kerr was regretting her too, that he'd never been to see her in all the years since Archie had brought her back to his home from hers, never going to her and trying to explain, because, in truth, what could Kerr ever have said to invite her understanding, let alone her forgiveness? Especially not after Archie had died, and there was so much more to regret on that front: that Kerr had never truly believed Archie would go along with Kheranovich's manoeuvrings to dig away from the copper vein into less stable rock; that he'd never actually checked; that Archie had shut Kerr out precisely because of his disbelief in stories shared; that he'd not insisted on going into Archie's shaft to make sure of the props; that the boat from Swansea hadn't been due for months to collect their ore, for if it'd been due earlier Kerr would have realised Archie hadn't been working the copper as he should and maybe would have gone in to see what Archie was really about, could maybe have stopped the shaft collapsing, could maybe have kept Archie alive.

But it hadn't, and Kerr hadn't.

Archie on the list of things to remember and miss ever since.

One thing Perdue hadn't been mistaken about was the snow.

Within an hour of them leaving Hestan it was all around them, all around Hestan, Dundrennan and Auchencairn, blown out of the north by a fierce wind that caused the few people still abroad to walk doubled over, or take their chance of getting punched in the back by the huffet and guffet of the wind that was bringing the snow in, had them holding out their arms to keep their balance, keep it from their eyes, take small, silly running steps to ensure they weren't blown over by the strength of it.

By that time, Brogar, Bill and Kerr were depositing Merryweather's coffin in the cool and empty cellars of Balcary House, Kerr's eyes wide with its immensity. Archie had told him and Merryweather about it but they'd never set foot in the house, let alone the cellars, their bonds of friendship with Kheranovich dissolved the moment they'd left the land of the Tatars behind them, happy to kick the dust of that past away from their boots, happy to be gifted Hestan on Kheranovich's say so but neither party having the urge to renew earlier acquaintance after Archie had come back and Kheranovich turned up from nowhere, hot on his heels.

'You could fit about half of Hestan in here,' Kerr said, whistling softly. 'My oh my, who'd ever have thought it?'

'And perfect for stowing a corpse. Same kind of cool as a cave,' Bill added pragmatically, though equally impressed by the size of the cellar and the complicated vaulting that held its ceiling in place above their heads.

Kerr shuddered at the mention of caves, that thought flashing through him he'd had back then about chucking himself into the water and having done with it. He shivered, his body recollecting the coldness, the utter inability to think, to act or react, his instinct to get things over with, however it went; realising, with unexpected certainty, that he'd have gone through with it if Brogar hadn't been there to haul him up the cliff and out. He'd no notion how things would go the next few days, of how his life would go, but looking on Merryweather's coffin – and Archie with him – and at the enormity of this cellar in which they were to wait out their final hours before being interred into the earth, Kerr Perdue had the strongest conviction that he'd been saved for a reason, and that single reason had to be himself: the only one left to bear witness, like the old monks of Dundrennan had borne witness to the Abbey's destruction.

Archie, Nairi, Merryweather and Kheranovich all gone, and only himself to say what needed to be said, to set the record straight.

Whether anyone would care to hear it was another matter entirely.

CHAPTER 24

TAKE A BOATHOUSE, TURN IT INTO A CASTLE

'Cor! Look at all that snow!' Gilligan was kneeling on the window seat in Hazel's living-room, face up to the glass, hands held like a visor about his forehead to cut out the reflections from the lamps Hazel had lit in the quickly darkening room.

'Cor, indeed,' she said at his back. 'Pretty stuff, but hard to get a way through. Think you boys might be stuck here for the while.'

Her words were light and a little disingenuous, liking having company other than Bill, wondering too how Bill had fared over on the island. They must have been away hours since, long before the wind had come up and the snow came down, presumably now at Balcary, far from that gloomy hunch of rock with water swirling in on every side, racing inward with the wind, the short-stuttered waves swallowing the snow like hungry fish swallow minnows: there one second, gone the next, never able to compete. Her mood, though, was buoyant, having not one, nor two, but four young persons in her care, Frith coming in at that moment to remind her of the fact, Charlie hobbling behind his sister on his crutches.

'We've got to get to Balcary,' Frith exclaimed, 'afore the snow gets too bad!'

'Why on earth, child...' Hazel began, Frith cutting her off.

'We've been talking, me an' Charlie, an' if we don't go they'll come and arrest me, think I killed Merryweather, that I did it!'

Hazel was caught on the hop. Why anyone would think Merryweather had been murdered was beyond her, let alone why anyone would believe that Frith – of all people – had killed the man, but Frith was insistent.

'There was only me and Kerr and the Company man out there,' Frith went on urgently, hands squirling through her smock, 'an' me who was the last person to see him. Took him stew, so I did. But I saw him, Mrs Hazel, that morning afterwards, an' he didn't die natural 'cos I saw blood and that, and when I said it to Charlie he said what I didn't think on before and that they're all going to think that it was me!'

'Now wait just a minute,' Hazel tried, but Frith was not to be put off, and by now Gilligan and Hugh had jumped up from their seats, eager for the in.

'Murder, is it?' Gilligan sounding too jolly for his words, but Hugh was already on it, taking over.

'We knows a bit about murder, Mrs Tuley,' he said, words calm and clearly spoken. 'I know it don't seem likely, but we do.'

'An' they'll all say it was Frith,' Charlie said at his sister's back, 'but it weren't, it really weren't!'

Charlie couldn't get any more words out, not the quickest thinker at the best of times, and certainly not in times of crisis, as this plainly was; terrified Frith would be taken from him and him from her, the only family each other had left.

'But that's preposterous,' Hazel intervened. 'A bit of blood means nothing at all. Could have slipped or had a heart attack, hit his head on the way down, or cut himself doing...well, that carving he sometimes does.'

Frith was shaking her head.

'There was summat there,' she whispered, 'couldn't see it much, and didn't think on it till talking to Charlie, but summat was sticking out his eye, keeping his head just off the ground.'

Hazel frowned. This was news, and she wondered why no one had mentioned it before, although perhaps – now that she thought about it – precisely for the same reason Frith was so perturbed.

'Mr Perdue wouldn't kill him,' Frith said, finding it hard to speak coherently, too much going on in her mind: a small pool suddenly overtaken by newly hatched worries like tadpoles bursting from spawn, 'and no more Mr Brogar. So who else is left? Only me is what, and I didn't kill him, honest I didn't. But who's going to believe that?'

'Well, me for one,' Hazel retorted.

'An' me,' added Gilligan.

'And that only means one thing,' Hugh stated with sensible certainty, 'that someone else was on the island between Frith taking the stew to Merryweather and Merryweather being found dead in the morning.'

'But how are we to prove it?' Frith pleaded, threading her fingers together, looking to Hazel for an answer, not that Hazel had one.

'We won't need to,' Hugh said brightly, 'because Mr Brogar and Mr Sholto will work it out. They always do, Frith, honest they do.'

Tears sprang from the corners of Frith's eyes.

'I don't know how,' she said, misery in every syllable, in every crease and shadow of her small face, her brother subsiding onto the nearest chair trying to snuffle back a sob.

'Then let's go find out,' Hugh said, that calmness, that absolute trust, making Hazel catch her breath as she looked from Frith to Charlie and then back to Hugh, resting her eyes on his damaged face.

'You're sure about that?' she asked.

Hugh nodded briefly, Gilligan hopping from foot to foot at Hugh's side, their optimism infectious and not to be stalled.

'Well then,' Hazel decided, not immune to Frith and Charlie's suffering and seeing too a chance to find out how Bill had gotten on. She cast a brief glance out of the window and didn't find the weather so bad and made a decision. 'Then so be it. Let's be gone.'

And out she went into the newly fallen snow, into the fast falling afternoon, bringing the donkey from its shed, harnessing it to the cart and piling everyone on with a load of blankets scooped up from the hospital cupboards before launching herself into the driving seat, feeling a small warmth at her side as Hugh snuggled himself alongside her.

'Alright, Mrs Hazel? Hugh asked, Hazel smiling despite the drama of the moment.

'Alright,' Hazel agreed. 'Let's get at it.'

And get at it Hazel Tuley did.

Never had she pushed her stalwart donkey so hard as she was doing now, heading up the track from home to Auchencairn, stopping briefly at the ostlers, swapping the donkey for a couple of ponies and some extra tack, and then they were really flying, heading up to Balcary, driving them all through the snow, trying to figure a way out of Frith's dilemma as she went, cheeks burning with the cold, scarf pulled close about her head, hands hie-ing up the ponies one second, brushing snow from her eyes the next. The urgency was in them all, Hugh beside her – unflinching, determined, leaning forward to meet the wind head on – Gilligan behind, Hugh's friend as easily excited as always, sticking out his tongue to swallow the snow; Frith a ragged mess in the back seat, clutching hard at Charlie's hand as they swung and swithered from side to side, hardly daring to hope, hardly daring not to; Charlie

quailing at her side, son of his father but so unlike him, defeat already in him, feeling the world slipping away with every yard, with every bend.

Not so Hazel, come alive in the moment, legs aching as she braced her body to push the ponies onwards, exhilaration in every muscle, in every movement, a queer flash of understanding burning up from inside that some kind of end was near, was almost in sight, if only she could get there in time.

'So, what've you got?' Brogar asked Sholto the moment he got through the library doors to find Sholto standing by a vast rosewood desk, moving one bit of paper here, another piece of paper there. Sholto looked up distractedly.

'Quite a lot, I think. You?'

'Got what you asked,' he said in answer, bringing out the pouch, spilling onto the table the object that had been thrust through Merryweather's eye and up into his brain.

Sholto frowned at the dried blood smears on the beak and coppered skull of the amulet.

'You didn't think to clean it?'

'Well, no,' Brogar smiled broadly, 'but hardly had the time. Didn't want Bill Tuley taking a fit. Which, by the way, seemed far less likely than you gave him credit for. Came on pretty level headed about it all to me. Even mentioned doing an autopsy.'

Sholto looked up.

'Is that so?'

'It is,' Brogar took out a large handkerchief and picked up the amulet up by its coppered skull before handing it over to Sholto. 'And he noticed the blood in Merryweather's eye. Thought you said he was damn near having a breakdown. Can't say he seemed that way to me.'

'No?' Sholto asked, taking the handkerchiefed amulet, studying it carefully. 'And nothing missing from Perdue's shack?'

'Not that I could see,' Brogar replied. 'But then again, he tells me he sells them by the dozen in the local shop, not to mention the amount he sends over to Swansea with the copper merchants.'

'I think we can rule them out,' Sholto said. 'But in the shop? That's hardly going to narrow it down, and not enough to take Frith out of the equation.'

'It's a problem,' Brogar said, rubbing his fingers over bristly chin. 'But the more I see of her, the more I like, and although the evidence points to her possible involvement' I don't think it likely. She's resourceful, and not squeamish, but can see no reason on earth why she would do it. No reason why anyone would, come to that.'

'Ah,' Sholto held up a finger and looked from the curlew beak that had done Merryweather in to Brogar Finn. 'I think I might be able to help with that, but it's going to take a bit of believing and a lot more yet to prove that it was so.'

Brogar raised his head and closed his eyes.

'Hallelujah!' he intoned. 'The master speaks! But what's the where of it?' he asked, serious now, liking Frith Stirling and not wanting the girl to hang. 'And the why of it? I can't see the beginning, let alone the end.'

'Like I said, I've an idea,' Sholto looking up at Brogar, 'but it's a bit of a stretch. Three people on an island in the dead of night when a man is murdered? And murdered so oddly?'

He shook his head.

'No one's going to dismiss the obvious, when all I have in exchange is so far-fetched. But we do have this.'

He handed Brogar a small booklet, Brogar reading the title, looking over at Sholto with creased brows.

'An old tide table? I don't get it. What does this prove?'

Sholto sucked in a breath.

'Nothing,' he admitted, 'not for the moment. It's a problem. But we need a quiet word with Kerr Perdue, and a lot more words with Skinner Tweedy after that.'

Hazel Tuley had her own problems.

The wind was strong and the snow so fast come that drifts of it were accruing at every small turn in the track, piling up between the high bank on the landward side and the trees that lined the shore, the ponies struggling to drag their load through the uneven depths, no matter how hard Hazel swerved the trap towards the shore where the snow was thinnest, the trap wheels skidding and free-turning as the drifts soon accumulated to the height of several feet against the bank. She urged the ponies on, but it wasn't long before they ceased their struggle as the wheels lost purchase, got stuck, the wood of the trap groaning, tipping dangerously over to the shoreward side, stopping of its own accord.

'Got to take the last mile on foot!' Hazel yelled, the scream of the wind through the trees whipping her headscarf away as she loosened her grip on it to speak. She watched it take flight, the slim colour of it slapping against a tree bole before it was up and away again, dipping and diving, like a snipe taking fright, quickly disappeared from view.

'Everyone down!' she urged, leaping from the trap, attempting to uncouple the ponies, fingers too cold to manage the task, Hugh and Gilligan immediately by her side to complete it for her, noses and cheeks red with the cold.

'But what about Charlie?' Frith wailed, as she got Charlie down and he stood there wobbling like a teetotum that had lost its momentum, would have slipped into the snow if Frith hadn't been holding him up.

Hazel stood in that snowy wasteland, some of it compacted into hail that hit against her face like shrapnel, skirts billowing up from her legs into her face, unsure, uncertain, a captain in charge of troops without having updated orders.

'Can wrap him up and stick him on one of the ponies,' Hugh advised – such a comfort, this boy, Hazel ashamed of her earlier scepticism of Bill's self-appointed resurrection because of him, a glimmering now of how that could be. Her leather boots were sodden, fingers frozen to the core, trying to get them back into the wet leather of her gloves, headscarf gone, ears tingling, face stinging with snow and wind.

And yet here was Hugh, urging her on. God bless the lad.

'Do it,' Hazel tried to say, her words lifted up into the wind and away, Hazel repeating them, shouting them, heart thudding in her chest, aware that if they couldn't trudge through to Balcary House they'd all be lost. But done it was, Gilligan and Frith quick to their task, binding Charlie head to foot in blankets and flinging him like a side of beef over one of the ponies' backs, Hugh leading the way with the ponies, Gilligan behind him coaxing the animals on, Frith and Hazel to either side to make sure Charlie didn't slide off.

And away they went, like pioneers, trap abandoned, pushing against the wind, against the snow, tramping their way through the drifts, rounding one bend and then another, no lamps with them and no lights to be seen and the darkness draping all around them – a bad companion – one yard taken as thirty might be taken on a fine spring day, battling through as vicious a snowstorm as Hazel had ever experienced; half a mile covered in half an hour, and then down to fifty yards, past the fishing kiddle that strode out into the bay like a half-built pier, a slim line all were thankful to see; fifty yards down to ten and then to five, and then – thank God – there was Balcary House; Hazel dragging herself up to its

doors in tangling skirts and pulling at its bell like there was no tomorrow.

'So what's your thinking?' Brogar asked Sholto as Sholto gathered up his evidence, scanty as it was, from the table.

'I'm thinking it may not have been so impossible,' Sholto supplied, tugging at the bell pull to summon Esther, 'for someone to get over to Hestan, kill Merryweather and get back undetected.'

Brogar bared his teeth, loving this part, the hiatus before revelation.

'Something to do with that weird boathouse buried by those trees just up the way?'

Sholto smiling, looking over at Brogar.

'Might've known you'd spot it. Obviously built to be hidden, looking just like a folly, like a miniature castle, but those doors that open onto the shore?'

'Could only be for boats,' Brogar went on for him. 'No doubt fancied up by the smuggling brothers who built this whole place.'

'No doubt,' Sholto agreed, 'but we know that no normal boat can get over to Hestan without being grounded. But a coracle? Or some kind of flat-bottomed rower? Different scenario altogether. Ah,' he added, 'here's Esther.'

Esther came in on cue, bobbing a curtsey, asking what was needed, Sholto replying that what was needed was a word with Skinner Tweedy.

'Waiting in the dining room, sirs,' she obliged. 'Won't be but a few minutes fore I can get him here.'

She went on a run down the corridor, not oblivious to the fact that a dead man had been stowed in the cellars and that nothing so exciting had happened in years, agog with what would come because of it. She was back within five minutes, Skinner Tweedy

lurching on her heels, his face all ascowl, unliking to be summoned, and by his master's guests at that.

'What do you know about the tides hereabouts?' Sholto asked without preamble.

'Not a lot,' Skinner said. 'Only been here a few years and tides is tricky things. Best you be talking to...'

'We're not talking to Heron, we're talking to you,' Brogar overrode him, Skinner's left eye twitching, lips pulling back from his teeth momentarily as he realised he was under interrogation and not liking it one bit.

'You're from Lancaster, or thereabouts?' Sholto put in, easing the moment. 'Grange-on-Sands, it says here, in your letter of application to work for the Heron Estate.'

Skinner hesitated, not seeing where this was going.

'And tides on the Solway,' Sholto pushed on, 'are not so unlike those in your neck of the woods. I'm thinking on Morecambe Bay, to be precise – shifting sands, fast tides, channels appearing here and there at random?'

'Well, aye,' Skinner was uncomfortable, shifted his weight from one foot to the other. 'But I don't know where—'

'I'm going,' Sholto interrupted, 'with the fact that you know exactly how the tides on the Solway run because you've grown up with them, in a different guise maybe, but grown up with them all the same. And so I'm going to ask you this,' Sholto thrust the ancient copy of the tide tables over to Skinner Tweedy, 'and I want you to explain something. I want you to tell me how a man could get out to Hestan and back on the recent tides with very little chance of anyone knowing they were doing exactly that.'

No sooner had Esther delivered Skinner Tweedy to the library than she was summoned again, much to her chagrin. She'd hovered a

couple of minutes outside the door, eager to hear what was going on inside, when the bell of the main door of the house began ringing, and ringing so insistently she couldn't ignore it. Pattering off down the hallway she was irritated not to know what the two Company men wanted with Skinner Tweedy but, on opening the door, was instantly overtaken by a newer, more exciting drama.

'We've a boy in trouble,' Hazel Tuley informed her, immediately the door was pulled away from its jamb, pushing at it with her hand, forcing herself in. 'He's a broken leg and is frozen stiff. We've had to abandon our trap in the snow and we also need to speak to Misters Finn and McKay most urgently...'

Hazel shuddered to a stop as the wind at her back pushed her forward a step and brought in a guffet of snow that showered both her and the girl who'd opened the door. Esther's cheeks went pink with this new development, peering beyond Hazel into the storm, making out – through the shifting screens of snow – the forms of a couple of ponies being led away to the stables at the back of the house, and two folk struggling up to the door with what looked to be a rolled-up rug.

'Come in, come in!' she bade them, Frith and Gilligan tripping over the threshold like skinny animated snowmen with their burden.

'We need to be before a fire,' Hazel announced, as Esther put her hands to the door and shoved it back into place against the determination of the wind.

'Library's the best place,' Esther decided, killing the proverbial two birds with one stone, eager to be a bit part in this play, see how it went, and no place better than where she'd just come from, with the Company men getting Skinner Tweedy on the bob. All good, as far as Esther was concerned, until she saw the boy's face lolling from one end of the rolled up blankets, skin grey and lifeless as an

undercooked breast of goose, a sight to shock any further ideas of snooping right out of her mind.

'Down the way,' she indicated with her arm, Hazel taking the girl at her word, commanding her troops in that direction, Esther watching them for a couple of seconds before cantering off to the kitchens to get some water heated, fetch some towels, fear and pity quickening every movement, loudly cursing the kettles that could not boil fast enough.

'Come on, come on, come on,' she kept muttering, fingers laced together, thumbs going round and round one another as she waited with horrible impatience, Pernel the cook coming in from the pantry at the commotion, spilling down a load of neeps and tatties on the table next to an entirely unusual pile of towels.

'What's the what?' she asked, irritated to see what Esther was at. 'Why've you shifted me pans for them kettles? We need to be getting the dinner…but whatever's the matter, child?'

Interrupting herself when she saw Esther's blank white face, the tears slowly trickling from their corners as she stared at the kettles, urging them on.

'Think there's a boy dying upstairs in the library,' Esther got out in a hiccupped whisper, 'and really think it. You should ha' seen him. Cold as anything he was. Ain't never seen anything like it.'

'Well get you gone,' Pernel commanded. 'Take them towels up soonest. I'll fetch water up when it's done.'

'Don't need that,' Skinner was saying, pushing away the tide tables, doing one of his quick switches, anxious now to please and not aggravate the situation, realising he might be under suspicion. 'Can tell you right enough it's possible, but you wouldn't want to try it. See the way the tides were yesterday?'

He took a step forwards, eager now at the puzzle, thinking back.

'High water fell around half past two, and I guess someone could row over from Balcary if they was strong enough, but they'd need to be strong 'cos they'd have to go in by Daft Annie's Steps across the current, tie up on the mooring stalk and let the water push their boat in by the big cave at the back.'

'Not the one we found Frith in?' Brogar asked, because if that was the case then this theory had more holes in it than pumice.

Skinner shook his head.

'Dunno who that is or which 'un that was.'

'The cave along the front of Hestan, going due left from Copper Cove,' Brogar supplied the necessary information, Skinner inclining his head.

'Not that 'un, but the one right around almost to the other side of Hestan, seaward side of the steps. Gets washed right through by the water, so if anyone'd been there any time after tide had turned they'd've been a gonner.'

'But there's a way up the cliffs from there?' Sholto asked, thinking this theory might really have legs.

Skinner rubbed his fingers through his hair, making it stand up like the crest on a skylark, wrinkling his nose.

'Dunno about that, but I'd guess so. Folk have a thing about caves and if there's anyways up or down someone would've found it.'

'Got that right, Tweedy,' Brogar agreed heartily, had never been any place the world over that had caves no one bothered about.

'*And out of the mouth of Cruachan*,' Sholto chipped in, knowing the legends about them being secret places, magical portals to the underworld, '*come the white birds whose breath will wither men to empty shells*. Old Celtic myth,' he added, a little shamefaced as Brogar and Tweedy scrutinised him, the first with curiosity, the latter with undisguised disdain at such fancy.

'Aye, well, don't know about that,' Skinner scorned, Sholto about to tip the conversation back to the right path when they were all arrested by the sound of people moving hurriedly down the hallway and, when the door was thrown wide open, in came Hazel Tuley, wild as one of the witches Sholto could have gone on to mention nested in other Irish caves than Cruachan: bare headed, hair whipped about her face, skirts wet and plastered to her legs. On her heels came Gilligan and Frith, just as wet, manhandling a length of blanket roll covered top to toe in melting snow, the small blond head of Charlie Stirling poking out one end with lips as blue as the Mazarine butterflies that clouded over the Caucasus on a sunny day.

'Get him to the fireside,' Hazel commanded, ignoring the three men who were startled into making way for her.

'What's going on?' Sholto began, Gilligan looking up as he scuttled past with his part of the burden.

'Got stuck out in the snow,' he gasped, 'an' Charlie here got the worst of it.'

'Lay him down,' Hazel interrupted, dragging over a rug and dropping it right by the hearth, grabbing up a few clods from the peat stack and chucking them into the grate, poking the fire to get it hot and fierce. 'Heat's what he needs, and get him out of those wet blankets.'

Frith and Gilligan obliged, kneeling on the rug, peeling Charlie from his coverlets and rolling him gently onto his side, Frith trying to keep his plastered leg still, though it was plain it hadn't fared well, was going soggy at the edges and not nearly so rigid as it should have been.

'Anything we can do?' Sholto asked, appalled at Charlie's stillness, his body tine thin beneath his wet clothes, the knobbles of his elbows looking like throwing dice, fingers drained of blood,

white as bleached cotton, only the faint trembling of their tips indicating he was still alive.

'Steer clear,' Brogar said, suddenly appearing at Sholto's side, a swath of velvet curtain in one hand as he sheathed the knife that had just slashed it away from its fixings with the other, going down on one knee and ripping away Charlie's jacket and shirt, tugging them off the boy, covering him instead with the curtain, rubbing it over the lad's chest with his capable hands.

'What are...' Hazel began to protest but Sholto held her back.

'He knows what he's doing,' he said. 'Everyone move back.'

'Oh Charlie,' Frith whispered, hands over her mouth, Gilligan beside her, steering her back a step to give Brogar room.

'Dinna fear, never fear,' he said softly, 'Mr Finn's done this a thousand times.'

An undoubted exaggeration, but enough to assuage Frith who watched Brogar's practised movements with awe as he silently went about the business of bringing her brother back to life, rubbing first at his chest with the curtain until Charlie's lungs began to work again and take in breath, then massaging Charlie's fingers with his own until they came back to normal colour, moving on then to Charlie's uncovered leg and repeating the procedure, though the toes on Charlie's broken one remained white as pigeon eggs, no matter Brogar's ministrations.

Esther came in then by the door, stopping short, dropping the pile of towels she'd been holding, Sholto over to her and scooping them up, bringing them to Brogar who nodded, chucked away the curtain, grabbed up a towel and repeated his applications.

'Will he be alright?' Frith breathed, speaking through the hands she'd not removed from her mouth, guilt-ridden, knowing this was all her fault.

'Got hot water,' came another voice no one had ever heard

before, Pernel coming in with two large, steaming kettles.

'Get it here,' Brogar commanded. 'And get the water on those towels and let's get them on him.'

And so it was done, Pernel quick at the job, seeing the problem, quick at the solution, spreading out first one towel and then another on the hearth stones, liberal with her kettle on the first three, less liberal with the fourth, leaving the last ones dry, admiring Brogar Finn going at his work, applying the hot compresses one by one just as she would have done, and for just the right amount of time.

'Gotta think you've done this kind o' thing before,' she commented, not at all put off by Brogar's face as he smiled up at her.

'As I think have you,' Brogar said in reply.

'Aye, indeed,' Pernel answered. 'Been cook here for years, and don't live in a place like this without mishaps occurring every now and then. But I'm thinking that foot there?'

She pointed to Charlie's toes, to the translucent whiteness of them that hadn't lessened despite Brogar's workings. 'Thinking them needs something more, scrutinised 'cos he's gonna to lose scrutinised 'em otherwise. Thinking warm goose grease to be exact. Can heat some up and get it to you?'

'That would be very grand of you,' Brogar replied, and was truly grateful. The last thing a lad in Charlie's situation needed was frostbite, and that was exactly what Brogar feared for those toes. Warm goose fat could pull it round entirely

'Not going to spoil your dinner plans?' he asked.

'Oh my, yes,' Pernel supplied, 'gonna shoot them to hell. But better that than wake up the morrow morning with a boy dead from the lack of a bit of grease.'

'Well hail Mary!' Brogar exclaimed, Pernel quick to reply, and with vehemence.

'You'll hail no Mary on my account. Don't hold with no Catholic stuff like that. Stick to the Lord we have, is my creed.'

Esther sent her eyes heavenwards, but not so Brogar.

'Well, let's hail good doctoring and strong women in her stead,' he said, Pernel taking him at his word.

'Fine by me,' was her only comeback. 'Esther, go make a room ready for the lad. And get the fire piping, and warm a couple of pans for his bed. I'll get blankets,' she said as she retreated on Esther's heels, jutting her chin at the torn away curtain as she went. 'Dunno what the master's gonna to make on that,' she commented, 'no sir, don't know at all.'

Her lips puckered in a tight smile, for she cared not a hoot what James Heron would make of it, thinking instead how extraordinary it was that a day could start off so ordinary and end up tit over heel.

Chapter 25

Bad Meals, Bad Judgements

'What the hell's been going on?' James Heron asked as he came into the dining-room on a fast stride, Hugh hopping along behind him, the two having not long met in the stables as Hugh was seeing to the ponies and Heron returned from Balcary Heights and the farm that lay just beyond.

'Where to start?' Sholto murmured, catching Brogar's eye, Brogar winking and taking the conversational reins.

'Got a body in your cellars,' he began, hands behind his back, staring at James Heron who flung aside his cloak on to the back of a chair and started brushing the excess snow from his clothes, regarding the gathered company with unconcealed annoyance.

'And this here's Dr Bill Tuley,' Brogar went on unperturbed, 'whose wife is away upstairs to garb herself in something dry after this lot...' he swept his arm towards Gilligan, Frith and Hugh, who'd rubbed themselves down with towels but refused to be otherwise re-clad, and had clumped at Sholto's side by unspoken consent, 'got themselves stuck in a snowdrift on the way up from Auchencairn to protest the fact that we might think Frith the murderer of Gabriel Merryweather, who is, by the by, the dead

man in your cellar. And this here,' he indicated behind him, where Kerr Perdue stood miserable and adrift, 'is Kerr Perdue, last living inhabitant of Hestan Island, for the while at least. Miss anything out, Sholto?'

Sholto coughed politely.

'The curtain in the library?' he suggested.

'Ah yes!' Brogar smiled, happy to be reminded, rocking on his heels. 'Had to slash it away to save a boy's life. Didn't think you'd mind, given the circumstances.'

'And what exactly are the circumstances?' Heron asked, not put off by Brogar's declamatory bravado, glaring briefly at Brogar before shifting his attention to all the other persons in the room, his eyes settling on the last. 'Tweedy. Explain. I've been gone what, three hours? So I'll repeat my question. What the hell has been going on?'

Skinner Tweedy shuffled his feet, red around his collar, fingers pulling at the skin at the base of his Adam's apple.

'Not rightly sure,' he admitted, 'but seems that some of these folk are thinking that Merryweather's dying weren't quite natural…'

'Not natural at all,' surprisingly it was Bill Tuley who spoke up before Brogar or Sholto could state their case. 'I've been examining his body down in your cellar and there's no doubt about it. Had a weapon thrust through his eye socket and up into his brain. Lacerations suggest the weapon was short, curved and sharp. Popped his eye out to make certain, but certain it is.'

No one spoke for a moment following this pronouncement, all staring at Bill Tuley, vision in all their minds of someone capable of doing such a thing.

'Put it right back in again,' Bill said, uneasy at the scrutiny, Heron narrowing his eyes, recognising the man, trying to equate this perspicacity with past performance.

'You're Dr Tuley,' he stated, with undisguised disgust. 'Same Dr Tuley who diagnosed my father with heartburn when it was nothing of the sort. Who gave him sugar pills when what was needed was digoxin.'

Bill blanched, closing his eyes to shield himself from his accuser, the second in so many days, for he had heard it: *Didn't do a damn thing*, was what Charlie Stirling had said of Bill's treatment of his mother. And he'd been right, as was James Heron now. Bill's throat went dry, couldn't get a word out in defence; indeed had no defence, as he was only just beginning to realise. He shook his head. Wasted years. So many wasted years.

'And I'm supposed to take your word on it?' Heron demanded, when Bill gave no reply. 'How is anyone to believe anything that comes out of your mouth?'

Sholto winced at the vitriol, despite it being deserved – given what he'd learned of Bill's failure to practice competently for years – but still, it seemed unnecessarily cruel.

'You may not believe Bill,' Sholto spoke up, 'but both myself and Brogar have seen Merryweather's body and there's very little doubt about the manner in which he was killed. And he was killed, and this,' he added, producing a small pouch from his pocket and from the pouch the curlew beak set in copper, 'is what did the deed.'

Everyone was brought up short by Sholto's dramatic revelation of the coppered beak, James Heron the first to speak.

'Well then, it seems we have matters to discuss. Esther, take these children down to the kitchen to dry out and get some food. Everyone else, please sit.'

Frith was about to object that she was far from being a child, but Hugh pulled her on.

'Might be able to find out something on our own,' he whispered, Brogar's love of mysteries having rubbed off on him, Esther leading

them away, Pernel passing them on her approach to the dining room bearing the not quite so perfect meal she'd hoped to provide.

'Mutton's a bit dry,' she announced, 'and veg is a little underdone, but given the circumstances...'

Heron nodding, cutting her off, bidding her serve what she could; Pernel obliging, getting out extra cutlery and place settings, everyone soon sat rather tensely around the table, all hurriedly getting up again as Hazel joined them a few moments later, badly clad in some of Esther's spare clothes that neither fitted nor looked well.

'What've I missed?' she asked as she gravitated quickly to Bill's side, Hazel acutely aware that he'd lost his shine and had crumpled back into his seat as if someone had dropped a sledgehammer on his head.

'That rather depends on what you knew before,' James Heron said, affable now he'd got his earlier confusion off his chest. 'Mrs Tuley, is it?'

'It is,' Hazel replied, sitting down.

'How's Charlie doing?' Sholto asked.

'Very well,' Hazel said. 'Toes back to normal, so no chopping to do tonight, except possibly of these potatoes,' smiling tightly as she regarded the meal in front of her, which didn't look good: the meat dry and overcooked, the boiled tatties half bashed into mash and obviously not cooked enough. But the kale was fresh, smothered in butter and pepper, and the smell of it made her realise she was absolutely ravenous – battling through snowdrifts can do that to a body – and without waiting to be invited she picked up her fork and tucked in. Heron raised his eyebrows but picked up his fork and followed suit, as did everyone else, and for a few minutes nothing could be heard but the desultory scraping of knives and forks on china as everyone cleared as much of their plates as they found edible.

All except Bill, who pushed the food about but ate not a morsel.

'So,' Heron announced, once he'd shovelled his bad meal down his throat, swallowing a couple of burps as it sat heavy in his stomach. 'You're definitely thinking murder?'

'It certainly looks that way,' Brogar said, 'although I suppose we can't rule out the possibility of a freakish accident, as wildly improbable as it seems.'

Heron sat back in his seat, glancing about the company as Esther cleared their plates and filled their glasses, eyes settling on Bill's huddled form.

'And what's your professional opinion, Doctor Tuley?'

Slight inflection on the word *doctor* not lost on anyone.

Bill shuffling his feet beneath the table, but looking up.

'If you really want my opinion,' he began, Heron interrupting.

'Oh but I do, I do. My apologies for my earlier remarks. I was caught rather…unawares. It's not every day a man is murdered in my bailiwick. And I know how hard your war was. Don't forget my father was there too, even if he was on the other side.'

A small spasm twitched across Bill's face but he made the effort, straightened himself, encouraged by the soft touch of Hazel's hand on his thigh, a touch he'd not felt for years.

'Well I can't believe it was an accident, however freakish. There were certain serrations on the lower eyeball and socket that strongly suggest the weapon was twisted as it went in.'

'What weapon?' Hazel moved her upper body suddenly forward. 'And eyeballs? You've been looking at dead people's eyeballs?'

'Not a question you generally hear around the dinner table,' Brogar commented, somewhat amused. 'Show her, Sholto.'

Sholto moved his arm to reveal the copper amulet on the tablecloth.

'That's what killed Merryweather?' Hazel asked, removing her

hand from Bill's leg and leaning across the table to look more closely, never minding the dried blood. 'This little thing?'

'Not so little when you know how minimal is the distance between the eye and the brain, and that a little wiggling around can do an awful lot of damage,' Brogar supplied.

'Well, no,' Hazel said, 'but even so. It seems a very strange weapon to commit a murder with. How could anyone be sure it would have the desired effect?'

Brogar cocked his head.

'Now that, Mrs Doctor Hazel Tuley, is a very interesting observation. Answers, anyone?'

'Maybe a crime of opportunity, then,' Sholto quick to explication, wondering why he'd not thought on so obvious a deduction before. 'Maybe the only object to hand. Maybe meant only to incapacitate while something more…effective could be found.'

'Or maybe someone who had medical knowledge,' Heron joined in, obscurely jolly, enlivened by the proceedings, liking the mental agility needed to solve such conundrums. 'But who was there on Hestan at the time? And when exactly was the time?'

'Well, you've rather put your finger on it there, Heron,' Brogar smiled, impressed by his host. 'Only three, far as we know, being myself, Kerr Perdue and young Frith Stirling.'

'Is that so?' Heron said slowly, returning Brogar's smile. 'Such a small pool of suspects, and what are we to make of that?'

'Make of it what you will,' Brogar was undeterred. 'But to your earlier question about the when. We've rather a wide timeframe at the moment, but Bill? Any thoughts?'

Bill shuddered as if stung, breathed deeply before answering.

'It appeared to me, when I saw him on Hestan, that he'd passed through rigor and come out of it.'

He quickly held up his hand as Hazel looked over at him.

'I know what you're going to say and yes, normally rigor begins within a few hours and lasts a lot longer, sometimes up to thirty-six hours; and in cases of sudden death in healthy adults rigor can often be delayed for the same amount of time, especially in someone of such well-developed muscle mass. But I don't think that was the case here.'

'You think he underwent some sort of cadaveric spasm,' Hazel said for him, seeing the light. 'Very rare, but we saw it a few times in the Crimea, when soldiers were so catastrophically overtaken by death they went into immediate rigor. Some still clutching their rifles.'

'But it's not true rigor,' Bill strove to explain. 'More like a reaction to an overwhelming stimulus. The body suddenly shutting down. So you get false rigor that then precipitates proper rigor with rapid onset and of short duration, lasting only the few hours that it normally takes to set in.'

Heron was bemused.

'I don't understand what you're telling me. Do we or do we not know when Merryweather died?'

'We do not,' Bill admitted. 'The most we can say is that he must have been dead for a minimum of seven to eight hours; but we could pinpoint it more accurately by looking at his stomach contents, at least if we knew what he last ate and when.'

Skinner turned a little green and Kerr coughed repeatedly into his napkin at this statement, finding it particularly hard to take. Not so Brogar Finn.

'Well, that we can,' he said. 'Frith took him some stew around… well, not entirely certain,' glancing at Perdue, 'not much use for clocks over there.'

'Before or after we sent the Morse code?' Sholto asked.

'Definitely after,' Brogar supplied, 'which would make it what?'

'That was just after sundown, so around five thirty, then thirty-odd minutes of signalling, so say let's say six, half six...'

'Good,' Brogar agreed, rubbing his hands. 'Something to start with, then. So we finished signalling around six, went back to the workshop, Frith well into cooking when Merryweather came over, brought us some home-made hooch that wasn't half bad. Talked to him for maybe ten, fifteen minutes before he left. Then me and Frith ate, talked a bit, felt bad Merryweather hadn't had anything, Frith taking him down a bowl, back not long after.'

'The perfect opportunity to kill Merryweather!' James Heron sounded jubilant. 'Who'd have thought it? Just a slip of a girl she seemed.'

Waving his arm at Esther, signalling they needed more drink, the first bottle barely wetting their lips.

'An accusation easily disproved if his stomach holds any stew,' Brogar protested, 'and if that's the case then there's only me and Perdue in the picture.'

'She could've done it during the night,' Heron put in. 'Assuming you slept in different quarters?'

'Or unless someone else was over on the island,' Hazel pointed out quietly, cheeks flushed with this talking, the medical challenges it was putting her way – or rather Bill's, assuming he was up to slitting open Gabriel Merryweather's gut and studying what lay within.

'Someone else?' Heron asked, taking out his cigarillo case and handing it around the company, Brogar and Tweedy accepting, lighting up, blowing smoke into the air, Kerr Perdue standing up sharply, excusing himself, vomit hot in his throat.

'Sign of a guilty conscience?' Heron asked mildly, as Kerr retreated on a rush, straight to the front door and out into the cleansing purity of a snow-clad, wind-whipped night, managing

only a few running steps before he chucked up all he'd eaten and drunk, wishing he could chuck up everything else that had happened the last couple of days, wipe it away like he wiped out his vomit with a kicking over of fresh-fallen snow, as if it had never been.

Down in the kitchen, Hugh, Gilligan and Frith were being well looked after by Pernel. From the pantry she'd retrieved a haunch of smoked venison, sizzling slices of it in a pan, serving it with a sauce made from sloe jelly and cream and the remnants of the kale. All in all a far better meal than the folks upstairs had received, her new charges tucking in with a hearty enthusiasm that Pernel appreciated.

'Seems to have hit the spot,' she commented, as she began washing up her pots and pans.

'Hit it bang on!' Gilligan smiled up at her, a liberal dose of sauce about his lips and on the tip of his nose that she swiped away with her tea towel as she passed him by.

'Must've been mighty hungry,' she went on, Frith collecting their empty plates and slipping them into the sink, taking over washing duties while Pernel saw to the kettle and made a large pot of tea, brought out a plate of shortbread and raspberry jam, sitting herself down with them about the table, kicking off her clogs and swapping them for a pair of comfy slippers.

'So what's the what with you lot?' she asked, pouring everyone a cup of tea, looking critically at Hugh. 'You looks like you been shot in the face by a load of wasps.'

'Musket,' Hugh replied shortly, picking up a biscuit and slathering it with jam.

'Fighting smugglers,' Frith added, remembering what she'd been told earlier.

'Smugglers, is it?' Pernel asked, interest piqued. 'Used to get a lot of them beggars round these parts, 'specially after they started up the Temperance Movement in Auchencairn in the '40s, what didn't go down too well with most of the locals. Thinking on Reverend Murray just now, a name I've no thought on in years; but he was strong in Auchenleck, just down the road. Didn't like that the iron workers there were spilling away their wages on the booze, including my hubbie, God rest him.'

'And the smugglers, are they still at it?' Hugh asked, still perturbed that Frith might be a suspected murderer, trying to find a way out, other people to blame.

Pernel croaked out a laugh.

'Lord no, boy. Them's long gone. Old Mr Heron saw to that.'

'But wasn't this whole place built by smugglers?' Gilligan got in, still full of the tales of the cellars and all the men they'd once hidden within their walls.

'That, my lad,' Pernel explained, 'is ancient history. Built by smugglers, but no longer ruled by them, not since a long while. But let me tell you this. Ever hear of our great poet Rabbie Burns?'

'Never,' Gilligan answered truthfully, Pernel frowning, a little annoyed that because of it her next pronouncement might not carry as much weight as it usually did.

'Well, you should. He's our biggest sale around here. Get loads of people visiting on the back of it, 'cos he was stationed right here at Balcary,' Pernel went on, 'when he was with the Excise. Called a Revenue Cutter back then; an' he wrote a song for a Miss Kennedy what lived in Back Street, and I can tell you right now that was me mother's mother. Imagine that!'

'Ooh, what's the song?' Gilligan was quick to appreciate the anecdote. 'Can you sing it to us?'

Pernel shook her head.

'Nobody can; bit of a ladies' man was that Rabbie Burns, if ye ken what I mean. And me gran was only just married so it was all on the quiet, so to speak.' She dropped a couple of cubes of sugar into her tea and stirred it with vigour. 'Sometimes thought me mam might be the bard's bairn, and some kind of fame in that, but if it were true it didn't follow down the family, for me mam couldn't read nor write a word!'

Pernel laughed, smiling widely, her party piece going down well, everyone laughing.

'But gave me a love of the singing,' Pernel went on when the merriment subsided. 'Used to be grand back at home when we was gathered round the fire, all setting off at different speeds and notes but getting into tune with each other in the end. Grand days, them were. Real grand.'

A look of true regret settled upon her face with the words, and Hugh took the opportunity to launch in.

'Kinda what Mr Brogar and Sholto do,' he said, looking over at Frith, 'coming at a thing from different speeds an' angles, but getting it all together in the end.'

Frith raised a small smile, but didn't look convinced.

'Not sure if they can do it this instance,' she said. 'Gonna take a lot more than singing a few songs.'

'But they'll be at it right now, Frith,' Gilligan put in, leaning towards her. 'They'll not waste a moment trying to figure it all out.'

'Figure what out?' Esther asked, coming into the kitchen at that moment, fetching a couple of bottles of wine from the crate brought up earlier from the cellar.

'Who killed Merryweather,' Frith spoke quietly, ''cos if they don't they're all going to think it was me, and it weren't; it really weren't.'

'Well of course it weren't,' Pernel bridled. 'Who could think such a horrid thing of a nice lass like you?'

'Mr Heron does,' Esther said, for that was the last of the conversation she'd heard before being sent on her errand.

'Well young Master Heron can go hang, if that's what he thinks,' Pernel was not persuaded. 'That lad's aye been as smart as a needle in some respects and as sluthered as a pile o' sand in others. Take you no mind, love,' Pernel went on, patting Frith on the knee. 'Used to knock himself black an' blue when he was a bairn, always tripping over stones, trying to get on too fast an' not seeing the ground he was trying to fly over.'

'That's a wee bit unfair, Ma,' Esther said, as she took her two bottles away with her to the door. 'Ye ken he could hardly speak a word of the English when he first got here. Bound to make mistakes.'

'Aye, right enough,' Pernel conceded, 'and a prettier boy you'd've been hard to find. An' always clever with his fingers – always pulling stuff apart and putting it back together. Mind one summer when he was home from his school in Dumfries when he went and builded himself a boat. Can you believe it!'

Esther departed with her bottles and Pernel chattered on, glad of the company, breaking into a few songs later on, Frith encouraged, Gilligan entertained, Hugh storing up everything she'd said in his head, hoping it might prove useful later on.

CHAPTER 26

AFFABILITY ABOUNDS, AND THEN IS GONE

'There has to have been someone else over there,' Hazel was saying with adamant conviction. 'You can't truly believe that Frith or Mr Finn here murdered Merryweather. And Kerr Perdue? What possible reason could any of them have to do such a deed?'

James Heron was leaning back in his chair, smile wide and infectious, relishing the conversation that so rarely came his way.

'I'm not saying anything of the sort, merely throwing up conjectures. Ah, Esther. Welcome back. Please, rejuvenate everyone's glasses.'

Esther did as bid, Hazel putting her hand over her own, not wanting more, casting a brief glance at Bill's, but his was still full, untouched; Esther missing out Kerr Perdue's, the man having apparently disappeared into the night.

'I'm aware the last few days have thrown up oddities,' Hazel went on. 'But there has to be another explanation. One we've not yet considered. What strikes me as very peculiar is the confluence of all these events. Why they've come clumped together as they have.'

Bravo, thought Sholto, who'd been piecing together his own confluences in accord with her rationale, for it was long past time

they came to some conclusions, hating to be in the dark. Always hating it: that moment when his mother snuffed out his bedside candle at night being the worst.

Make you stronger, she'd always said, *make you realise that the night is not your enemy but your friend.*

He'd never understood that amity his mother felt for night fallen, not until he'd come over to Scotland and started to appreciate how hard it must have been for his parents in the bad old days, the decisions they'd been forced to make, the choice between taking him over the water and abandoning that other family they'd been a part of back then, how they'd allowed the sun to set on the past: that particular darkness not an enemy – just as she'd said – but a mechanism of survival and, in the end, a friend.

'Exactly what I was thinking,' Brogar took over from Hazel, taking a liberal gulp of his refilled glass. 'So let me summarise. Gabriel Merryweather is dead. Murdered. Lying in state now in the cellar below this house.'

James Heron began tapping his fingers in fast sequence upon the table, looking over at Brogar, a slightly amused – if tired – expression upon his face, Brogar raising his eyebrows before continuing his analysis.

'Then there's the letter received by the Stirling children that purportedly came from your father, Heron, that sent them racing over to Hestan.'

Heron stopped his tapping, looking over at Brogar with suspicion and surprise.

'What letter? And how could he...'

'From your lawyers,' Brogar interrupted, 'evidently to be dispatched to them on their seventeenth birthday, telling them what had really happened to their father and where his remains

could be found. Surprised you didn't know, a copy of it being amongst your father's papers.'

'His remains?' Hazel asked. 'What remains?'

'He died on Hestan,' Sholto explained, 'got caught in a shaft collapse.'

'A shaft that Archie Stirling was skewing off in entirely the wrong direction,' Brogar added, 'very likely on your father's say so, Heron, always in charge like he was back in the day. And guilt can be a powerful motivator.'

It was obvious the swerve the conversation had taken had neither been anticipated by their host, and no more was it appreciated.

'My father,' Heron muttered through clenched teeth, 'was a better man than the lot of you put together. He swept me out of a war zone, brought me here, gave me a chance at life and a good one, not to mention giving his old army pals a free pass on Hestan. How dare you vilify his name.'

All graciousness dissipated like a flake of snow on a dirty pond, Heron staring at Brogar so hard his eyes began to water at their edges, his cigarillo dying an unconsummated death as he stubbed it out angrily directly onto the tablecloth, leaving a circular hole whose edges burned away a few further threads before petering out. He stood up abruptly, dislodging his wet cape that fell in a crumple to the floor.

'Never did a damn bit of harm in all his life,' Heron stated, shifting his gaze from Brogar to the rest, moving from one to the other as he declaimed his case, daring them to defy him. 'Never did anything but look after the hangers-on who clung to his coat-tails out there and who hung on even harder afterwards. Like your blasted Kerr Perdue and your precious Mr Merryweather. And what did either of them ever do to deserve it? You answer me that!'

James Heron turned his head away from the collective company and spat on the carpet, an act of rage that made even Skinner Tweedy baulk, and him a man well aware of his employer's propensity to quick temper when things didn't go his way.

'Let's start again,' Sholto attempted to smooth the situation over, but Heron was having none of it. Brogar had touched a nerve and touched it hard; add in a few glasses of wine and Heron was not about to be deflected.

'Let's start at bloody nowhere!' he retorted, kicking his chair away as he went for the door. 'I'll not stand for anyone slandering my father's name and you'd all do well to remember it! And before you say anything more,' he stared first at Brogar then at Sholto.

'But that's not—' Sholto started to say, cut off before he'd properly begun.

'I'm telling you to go no further,' Heron stated. 'I can bring the sale of Hestan to its knees if I have to, and be sure I will, if only to get rid of you two. And be damned certain you'll not come out of it well. I've your names and I'll use them. Make sure you never work for your Company or any other company ever again.'

He took two long strides, Skinner Tweedy rising in solidarity only to be dismissed summarily as Heron reached the door.

'And you can go to hell as well, Tweedy. Don't know what tales you've been tattling to these...people,' Heron paused to cast a last glance on the company about his table, 'but I can tell you this. Come the morning, you can pack your bags and be gone with the rest of them. Noon tomorrow, snow or no snow, storm or no storm, sick boy or no sick boy, I want every last one of you out of my house and gone. And that includes you Company men. Business concluded, however I see fit to conclude it.'

And off he went, not bothering to close the door behind him, Skinner standing distraught in the silence left by Heron's sudden

departure, hands to his cheeks, no one speaking, everyone clearly hearing Heron's last denunciation out in the corridor as he bumped into Kerr Perdue, who had the misfortune to come back into the house at that moment from whatever he'd been doing outside.

'And you! You, Perdue, can forget any notion whatsoever of staying on Hestan. You've twenty-four hours to get your stuff together and clear out, no matter what little piece of paper you produce from my father. Get yourself as far away from me as possible.'

Sound of Heron's boots thumping up the stairs, quick, hard and angry; sight of Kerr Perdue hanging at the door of the dining room like one of those ghost trees at Orchardton: still alive, last man standing, only thing keeping him upright being the sudden shocked reality of absolute despair.

'Want to take the rest of them biscuits and that jam up top?' Pernel asked, getting out a little bowl of cream they could take with them, Gilligan, Frith and Hugh eager to oblige, to find out what – if anything – had been going on since they'd last been apprised of the situation. Which appeared to be quite a lot, as they discovered when they arrived a few minutes after Heron had so precipitously made his exit: Hazel leading Kerr Perdue to his seat, Skinner Tweedy on the stand, Brogar and Sholto exchanging conspiratorial glances.

'Welcome to our young companions!' Brogar said jovially, on seeing the three of them emerge from the servants' doorway at the back of the room. 'And welcome too to what you're bringing,' snatching up a piece of shortbread and dipping it into the bowl of cream as soon as it was put down.

'Missed much?' Hugh asked, grabbing Heron's vacated chair, pulling it back to the table.

'Missed a lot,' Sholto commented, 'like how we've all been sacked, all to clear out by midday tomorrow.'

'Wooo, that's something alright,' Gilligan whistled, Hugh nodding, apparently unconcerned, interrupted by Skinner Tweedy inching back onto his seat.

Esther picking up her master's discarded cape and giving it a shuggle out before heading back down to Pernel and the kitchens with all she'd heard, gossip abounding.

'You've only gone and lost me me job,' he bleated. 'See what you've done?'

'And what exactly have we done, Tweedy?' Brogar countered, leaning back in his chair, fingers interlaced about his neck, taking an easy breath.

'You've gone and buggered me bloody livelihood, is what,' Skinner repeated, bitterness in every word, 'and for what? He gives me a bad reference and I'll get nothing either side of the border, from Lanarkshire to Lancaster.'

'Quite,' Brogar commented, tipping his chair back down to base, Skinner looking daggers at him, Brogar holding up his hands. 'But stand fast all. And you, Skinner, are included in that. Heron might be mighty offended that we brought up his father's name, but now he's left us we can maybe get to the bottom of what's been going on. Nothing like a deadline to sharpen the mind.'

'I don't see why he took such extreme offence,' Hazel Tuley frowned. 'Did he think we were blaming his father for Archie Stirling's death?'

'His father? But how?' asked Frith, excited by yet another revelation coming on the back of all the rest. 'Thought he died in a shaft collapse?'

'He did,' Sholto said, 'and best to tell you all now that we've your father down in the cellar with Merryweather,' holding up his hand

to forestall Hazel's questions, Bill too looking up, for as far as the two of them were concerned there was only one body in the cellar. 'I'll explain all shortly,' he went on, 'but,' he turned back to Frith, 'what we didn't find was what your brother was really in that shaft for, what that letter from Heron senior sent him to find.'

'But I don't know what that was,' Frith's voice was tiny, 'and I'm not sure Charlie knew either.'

'*Something to vouchsafe both your futures,*' Brogar quoted, 'the letter unspecific, maybe assuming Frith and Charlie already knew. Any ideas, Perdue?'

Perdue didn't move, everything slipping and sliding around him, no idea what was going on except that twenty-four hours from now he was to be off Hestan, never to return, the certainty of it far worse than he'd imagined now it was actually coming to pass. He shook his head, couldn't get out a word.

'Let me see if I can help,' Sholto said kindly, disturbed by the events of the evening, aware that his and Brogar's interventions had not made anything better for any of these people, but indeed had worsened them in a manner completely unanticipated. 'I suspect that object your father left for you, Frith, was a book, and a very valuable one.'

He cast a quick glance at Brogar, ready for raised eyebrows, a sardonic half-smile of amusement, some snipe about everything coming back to books, but there was nothing of the sort, Brogar merely waving a hand for Sholto to go on.

'Remember that anomaly I was talking about in the library?' Sholto asked him, Brogar nodding shortly, Sholto rubbing the corners of his eyes with his fingers as he sought to get everything straight, get it in order. 'Well, I believe it all goes back to that part of Heron's father's past that James is so eager we not find out about, beginning with the fact that his father, back in the day, was called

Danislaw Kheranovich, posted in the part of Crimea that was, in the 1830s, a Tatar stronghold...'

'Oh, but I know about this!' Hazel intervened. 'We heard about it when we were over there. Remember, Bill?'

Bill didn't answer, Bill still halfway down the narrow tunnel he'd dug for himself, a fact noticed by all except Skinner Tweedy who'd only stayed because he was afraid to leave, starting to dig his own tunnel, head hanging low, not really listening.

'So what do you know?' Sholto asked Hazel, hoping to take Hazel's mind off her husband, who could be dealt with later.

Hazel brushed a few strands of hair back from her forehead and attempted a smile.

'Well over there, in the Crimea, I mean, we didn't have much spare time, what with all that was going on. The cholera was terrible early doors, never mind anything else. And in what time we had left to us after working in the hospital there wasn't much to do by way of amusement,' a bit of an understatement, but she wasn't going to dwell on it, 'anyway, when we were in Eupatoria we met Lord Raglan...'

'That man was an idiot!' Bill broke in loud and unexpected, uncurling himself, words spilling out of him that he'd played over and over in his mind, wishing he'd said what he was about to say right to Raglan's face. 'Forbade us from using anaesthetics during amputations; forbade us basic necessities of medicating them afterwards; same bastard who insisted that Private Frederick White – ten years earlier – didn't die from the hundred and fifty lashes he'd ordered from the cat, despite all the evidence to the contrary.'

'Enough, Bill,' Hazel chided sharply, knowing all about Bill's opinion of Raglan; Lord knew, she'd had the same misgivings herself – especially after his disastrous misjudgement of sending the Light Brigade in at Balaclava – but the fact remained he'd been

kind to her, and she'd not forgotten it. 'This is not about you or me,' she went on without remorse, 'this is about Frith, and Gabriel Merryweather losing his life.'

She took a breath, looked over at Sholto.

'Raglan lost his sword arm at Waterloo,' she explained. 'Came to us occasionally when he'd infections or sores on his stump. And he was always generous with his books, talked to us about the war and how it had come about and such.'

'Very interesting,' Brogar said, not sounding very interested. 'Point being what?'

'Point being,' Hazel sat up straighter in her seat, squaring her shoulders at the challenge. 'Point being, Mr Finn, that those who listen are those who learn.'

'Not that Raglan ever did,' Bill muttered, Hazel and Brogar ignoring him.

'Point taken,' Brogar replied, lips twitching. 'Please, go on.'

'Very well,' Hazel nodded. 'So it's like this. From him and his books we learned that Tsar Nicholas took over from his brother Alexander when Alexander died in Taganrog by the Azov Sea of some unspecified fever...'

'Taganrog and the Azov!' Frith interjected. 'Weren't they some o' the places you said of, Mr Brogar, when you was speaking on me ma?'

'Indeed they were, Frith,' Brogar agreed.

'Oh, do go on, Mrs Hazel!' Frith was jubilant, eager as a dog waiting beneath the table for scraps, Hazel just as eager to provide them, recalling the conversation she'd had previously with Sholto about Frith's family arriving in Dundrennan and nothing known about them until Archie came home a year or so later.

'Well, it goes like this,' Hazel continued. 'Nicholas wasn't as educated a man as was his brother, and not nearly so clever; started

dismantling a whole lot of what his brother had done about dealing with the West, with us: with Britain and with France. Reverted to type, I'm afraid, became a bit of a despot, as so many Tsars before him, at least according to Raglan's books. Result being the war we had with Russia – which was awful enough – but before that he'd waged his own private war on the tribes around Taganrog, around the Azov. Awful, awful things.'

Hazel tailing off, Sholto going on for her.

'Like the burning of the Tatars' books; the entire collective memory and history of a people wiped out within a single year, and I've no doubt,' Sholto added, 'that despite James Heron's posturing he knows fine well that his father was involved in it, that he's the same Kheranovich implicated in some of those burnings – given the details of his service records in the estate office – and that he likely bought this place on the back of them. No doubt why James doesn't want us looking any further into his father's past. But if we do exactly that, if we can make some sense of its bearing on what's been going on here and on Hestan, then I think it needs doing. And it needs doing now. Letters from Heron's father's lawyers? Archie Stirling's shifting of his shaft? Merryweather dying as he did? They're all connected. I know it. I can feel it, even if I can't prove it.'

'But maybe there's someone here who can,' Brogar put in, 'and time he stopped feeling sorry for himself and put in his bit.'

Sholto winced, finding this too confrontational, but apparently Brogar's ploy worked, Kerr Perdue shrugging his shoulders, breathing out a long breath.

'Always set to come down to this,' he murmured. 'Knew it back then, know it better now.'

Kerr as quiet on the outside as the snow that was settling on the roof and grounds of Balcary and on Hestan – if the salt from the

sea spray would permit it – but not on the in; on the in he was in turmoil, everything coming back to bite him, as he always knew it would.

'Aye well,' Kerr went on, head down, unable to meet anyone's eye, skin pale as a shorn sheep beneath his beard. 'Seems you already ken the most of it. Mind what I telt you over on the island?'

Brogar nodded and Frith leaned in, abashed to realise she'd not thought about it since, curiosity shocked out of her by finding Merryweather and the speed with which life had jogged on ever since.

''Bout me ma's folk, you mean? And them burning with the books?' she asked softly.

Kerr sighed, closed his eyes, stretched his neck.

'That's it, lass. What I never told you was that it weren't just them. Your ma was in there too. Just a wee thing she was then, but Tupikov got his men to stick 'em all in the barn with the books. Told us to set it alight. And we did, with them in it. God forgive me…'

An audible intake of breath from Frith, who put her hand to her mouth, shaking her head, Kerr's words descended into whispers, but he had to get it out.

'An' we all went with it: me, Merryweather and Kheranovich. But not your da, Frith. Not Archie. Never Archie.'

Eyes damp. Never Archie.

'Went back in for her, he did,' Kerr ground on with difficulty. 'Went back in the minute Tupikov was away up the path; smashed in the door at the back and brought your mam out, and her burning like a side of beef stuck in a fire pit.'

Frith hiccupping, Frith crying silently, Frith remembering her ma's laying out, her shock at seeing those scars, more shocked now she knew how they'd got there and hardly able to imagine how her ma had lived with such a terrible tale and never spilled it out.

'Can't never excuse it,' Kerr said, eyes wet as Frith's with the telling. 'Still see it now, I do, still watch them cinders flying up into the sky not knowing which of 'em come from the books or from your mam's gran and grandad's bits and bones. Still feel them cinders falling back down on us all, on our hair, on our shoulders, still with a smoulder left in 'em. And them cinders been on me shoulders and me conscience ever since.'

He knew he was saying it all clumsy and wrong, not like Archie would have said it, but it had been in him too long for it to come out in a straight line. Only yesterday, back on Hestan, he'd been figuring how it would go if he came to James Heron and said all he could say about how his father had come over to Scotland, bought up Hestan and Balcary. And now here he was telling it to people who were practically strangers, it all tumbling badly spoken from his lips, and James not even here to hear it.

He shook his head, looked down at his fingertips that were splayed lightly on the white edge of the tablecloth, unable to meet anyone's gaze as he got himself together enough to go on, aware of the silence his words had left, no one willing to speak, not even Brogar, all aware there was more to come, that the wind had dropped, that the sea was whispering its own tales across the sands out there in the darkness, aware the time had come for Kerr to unburden himself and get the last of it out.

Which he did.

'And all for them books,' he said, 'cos we'd already got the most of them out afore Tupikov arrived, stashed 'em in a trough we dug between the trees. And he knew it, Tupikov. I mean, not that we'd done it. Tupikov didn't think that at all. But he knew most of 'em had been taken, crates of straw left in their place. Thought it were Frith's ma's folk or someone they knew, and that's why he shoved them into the barn and got us to set the lot of them alight. *We've*

to make an example, is what he said. *A message they'll not quickly forget.*'

'But you could've stopped them!' Frith wailed, unable to keep silent any longer. 'You could've told them! You could've told me folks to get away, or that you were the ones what pinched the books! Why didn't you tell them?'

Kerr Perdue wretched, right back in Genichesk, as undone a man now as he'd been then, because in truth they could have done all of that. Should have sent the family away, but not one of them had thought on it, not even Archie, none of them thinking on how badly things might go. And when it had started, they'd be torn between doing the right thing and knowing that doing the right thing would end up with no right thing being done at all, just more people dying – including himself and Frith's father – Kheranovich's words as plain today as they'd been then: *They're going to do it anyway; no point seven people burning instead of three.*

'It weren't no use, Frith,' Kerr croaked through the bile in his throat. 'They was going to make an example one way or another, and us chucking ourselves into the flames weren't going to make one change on that. And I ken you can't know this, that you'll think us all cowards, but we was all just young, trying to survive, get ourselves out of a bad situation. And them books we buried? Well, they was what saved us all in the end: me and Merryweather bought out of the army on the proceeds, Kheranovich wangling Hestan and then Balcary a while later; and your da, Frith. If it hadn't been for that day, for what he did, he'd not have gone back years later to check on your ma and you'd not be here, breathing air upon this earth.'

Everyone about the table taking all this in, this awful tale, even Skinner Tweedy minded that no matter how bad things were

looking for him at this moment, they were never, ever going to be that bad.

Brogar whistled through his teeth, after the air had settled.

'That's a story and a half,' he said.

'Which means there's still a half missing,' Hazel added a few moments later, creasing her brows in concentration.

'Which would make it more than one tale,' Brogar pointed out, logical as always, summing everything up, 'and in fact far more than two. First, the saving and later selling of the Tatars' books; second being Archie's rescue of Frith's mother; third being him going back and marrying the woman what, twenty-odd years later; fourth being Kheranovich settling that old band of brothers here; fifth being the book Sholto thinks Kheranovich gave to Archie because of that night,' all eyes swivelling to Sholto, but Brogar wasn't finished. 'Sixth being that Kheranovich meant for Charlie to find that book in Archie's shaft, that he assumed Charlie already knew what he'd be looking for, which patently he didn't. Seventh being,' pausing for dramatic emphasis, 'that he and Archie were pursuing Dundrennan Abbey's missing library on Hestan, which caused Archie to swerve his shaft, a course of action that very likely led – if indirectly – to Archie's death.'

'He used bad props,' Kerr added quietly. 'Told him not to. But he weren't for the telling. Never for the telling, wasn't Archie.'

And no more was Archie's daughter.

'What book are you on about?' Frith asked succinctly. 'And if Charlie didn't find it then where is it now? And what's all this about a lost library?'

'Think Merryweather must have got it first,' Kerr said quietly. 'The book, I mean. Think he got it, and thinking now it's maybe what got him killed, though can't figure out the how or why.'

Chapter 27

Something Springs From Bill, And Bill From Spring

And there it was. All laid out clear and bare.

Skinner shaking his head, growling out a few acerbic words as if he was standing on the gallows, saying his last.

'Makes no matter on all these stories. Fact remains Heron's kicking us all out the morrow and nowt more to be done about any of it.'

'That is what he said,' Brogar agreed calmly. 'But nowt, as you so eloquently put it, Skinner, well. I'm not so sure about that. Heron's a businessman, and from what I gather this particular business of Balcary is in trouble. Sale of Hestan to our Company a part of the way out. He's bargained before and, despite his wild words, I'd put money on it that he'll bargain again, and I have something might swing it. Ever seen more of these?' Brogar asked, taking those two pink pebbles out of his pocket and laying them on the table.

'Place is littered with them, man!' Tweedy scoffed. 'There're all about the bay and there's a load more up the heights. Ain't got no more worth than the rest of the shite that rolls up on these shores.'

Brogar scooping the pebbles up, clacking them like a stonechat a couple of times before putting them away, speaking to Perdue.

'How'd you know Merryweather had been in the shaft?'

Pouring himself some more wine, taking a goodly mouthful – it really was fine stuff Heron stocked his cellars with, never mind the odd body or two.

Kerr shrugged.

'Well all the rubble'd been shifted – must've taken him a couple of hours.'

'This was after you'd got Archie out?' Brogar asked.

'Long after,' Kerr admitted. 'Was sittin' in the cottage thinking on what you'd said. Thought occurring you didn't just mean Archie, so went back in.'

'So you did know about the book,' Sholto commented. 'And if you knew where it was, why on earth didn't you get it out before?'

Kerr grimaced.

'Couldn't,' he said simply, though nothing about any of this was simple. 'Not with Archie being in there. And he'd to stay there, else Nairi and the kids would've lost the pension.'

'But if you'd got the book out and got it sold they wouldn't have needed the pension in the first place,' Sholto pointed out a flaw in the logic, Kerr setting him right.

'Aye well. 'Spose you might've. But what were we to do with it in Auchencairn?'

'Go down to Dumfries or Carlisle and get it sold?' Hazel suggested.

Kerr sighing, rubbing at his beard.

'Coupla copper miners from Hestan? Don't make me laugh, missus. It'd've been snatched off us afore we'd hardly got through the door, and into the clink with us both. Either that or we'd've been given a pittance for it, made some other bugger rich, but nothing for Nairi and the bairns.'

Sholto nodded, for yes, he thought, that was exactly how it would've gone.

'But how are you so sure it's not still in there?' he asked, though he had his own ideas about that.

'Knew he kept it safe and close in one o' the bowalls,' Kerr answered, thinking on Archie's words about how Kheranovich's gift would look after them all when they were old and grey.

'A bowall? What's a bowall?' Brogar asked.

'Little ledge built into the wall,' Gilligan shot up a hand and an explanation. 'We use 'em to keep candles in an' that.'

'Ah!' Brogar exclaimed. 'Well yes, you would. A niche then, what I know as a hulning. But all empty? Couldn't there have been more further up you didn't know about?'

'No,' Kerr replied, with certainty. 'Knew it were in the main section. Archie'd said so once or twice. Checked 'em all, an' all empty. But one had to've had summat in it not long since 'cos the stone were dry,' lowering his head, lowering his voice. Wishing Archie had just taken the damn thing to Heron like Kerr had once advised, told him to get it sold in the first place. Keep the money safe.

'Not as safe as Hestan,' Archie had replied, as if it was the most obvious thing in the world. 'Our looker-afterer, our kinship-keeper, for me and mine. An' we've plenty time,' Archie had added. Except the following year he was dead.

'But how could Merryweather finding it lead to him being murdered?' Hazel asked, perplexed, Sholto catching Brogar's eye, Brogar giving a slight shake to his head. They'd their own theories about this, but Brogar wanted to keep them close for a while yet. Both surprised when someone else answered for them.

'Seems kinda obvious,' Skinner said quietly – not a bright man unless he was talking yields and fields, but seeing a path through

the grass when it was staring him right in the face, seeing now why Sholto had asked him about the tides. 'Seems to me someone else knew all about this history yous all been on about, heard about the young fella getting dragged out o' the mine and figured what he was onto. An' afore someone starts on with the suggestion,' Skinner added in a garble, pushing his fingers through his hair, 'absolutely weren't me.'

'So Frith's in the clear!' Hugh stated in delight. 'Not that we ever thought you weren't.'

'Have to say I did,' Brogar stated. 'Of the three of us over there, you were my best candidate.'

He looked at Frith, getting a scowl in return, but a scowl that soon shook itself into a smile.

'It's odd you should say that, Skinner,' Sholto intervened, 'because myself and Brogar...'

Interrupted by a loud thump and scrape from the room directly up above, as if someone was dragging furniture about and making a bad job of it.

'That'll be Heron,' Skinner interpreted, 'getting ready to flit back to the city once he's shot of us lot. Look for a new foreman, for one, maybe a new buyer for Hestan for another.'

He cast an ill glance at Brogar, but Brogar was not put off.

'Good luck with that,' Brogar said, 'but don't despair, Skinner. All is not yet done.'

Brogar shot a look over at Sholto who understood, went on for them both.

'Can I ask, Mr Perdue,' Sholto obliged, 'if you know what Archie's book looked like? Might it have been small? Bound in white calf skin, with gold lettering on its cover and spine?'

Kerr's skin – so pale before – taking on the dark pink hue of a daisy just about to open to the warming sun.

'How'd you ken...'

'In a shagreen pouch stamped with Kheranovich's initials?' Sholto went on, needing absolute confirmation. Kerr nodding dumbly.

'*For me and mine*,' he whispered. No notion how Sholto knew what the book looked like, no longer caring.

'Your anomaly,' Brogar stated, Sholto smiling his assent.

'What anomaly? What are you saying?' Hazel put in, fingers in a fiddle on her lap, feeling she was missing a piece of the puzzle, and not liking it at all.

'Sounds like he's seen it, and maybe knows where it is,' said someone everyone had forgotten was there, Bill dragged from his tunnel by the talk of Archie Stirling, by the memory of Archie standing on his doorstep, that light brightness in his eyes even as Bill slammed the door shut in his face. Bill listening quietly all this while, slotting one piece in here, another piece in there, focussing on someone else's story for a change, because he was sick to the marrow of focussing in constantly on his own.

James's harsh words kicking in and kicking hard.

How's anyone to believe anything that comes out of your mouth?

Harsh words, but true...except perhaps for now.

'He's saying,' he went on, 'that the night Gabriel died someone else was on Hestan, like you said before, Hazel.'

Hazel placing a hand on her husband's arm, Bill gently lifting it off again; no more need for pity, swearing internally that from this second on he would abjure it until the end of his days.

'Probably went over in a flat-bottomed boat as the tide was dropping,' he went on in a monotone. 'Tied it to the old moor post on Daft Annie's Steps. Probably dragged it into the cave towards the south end on a long painter so it couldn't be seen. Dug out the shaft, took the book, killed Merryweather – who must've seen

him doing it – then went back over the sands at low tide in the dark, either cutting the boat free or carrying it on his back if he was strong enough.' Shaking his head. 'Must've known those sands right well.'

Bill leaning back in his chair, raising his eyes, roving them over the cornices and fancy plasterwork above the picture rails that framed the room: so elegant, and yet so inconsequentially useless, so exactly like men like Tupikov and Raglan, responsible for slaughter and barbarity; and down came his eyes again, dismissing such men. Down from them to the actuality of real people sitting about a real table with real lives, zeroing in on that small burning James Heron's unspent cigarillo had left behind on the blind white expanse of the tablecloth, and then away to the windows that were winking back the light from the lamps within, and away beyond the glass to the snow that had gathered out there in the darkness – snow that might have done for Hazel and the three young folk sat here about him. Worlds colliding, and thank God for it: collision being what he needed.

'Precisely what we deduced,' Brogar said, no point hiding their suspicions now, two and two already out there, and plenty of people here to add it up to four, nodding over at Sholto.

'Which rather begs the question,' Sholto obliged, 'how it came to be that Archie Stirling's book is right here, in the library of Balcary House.'

CHAPTER 28

KAMYR-BATYR MAKES HIS MOVE

Everyone up in a flurry – swirling out the doorway and down the corridor towards the library like leaves on a stream – all except two.

'Kinda makes you a bit dizzy with their talking,' someone spoke, breaking Bill from his internal monologue, Bill looking up to find only one other person in the room: Kerr Perdue, sat at the opposite end of the table.

'Ken what you should do?' Kerr went on. 'What might do you well?'

Waiting a moment, Bill tipping his head to one side in anticipation.

'Come back over to Hestan with me the morrow,' Kerr continued. 'Only one day we've got, but you'd like it out there. Naught to bother you, only the gulls and the sea. And no talking, not if you don't want it. Could stay in Merryweather's cottage. He'd no mind. An' he's enough home-brew to give us a right good hoolie, if we fancied it.'

Kerr smiled, rubbing his beard, meaning every word.

Last night on Hestan – it hardly bore thinking about – but a last

night on Hestan spent with someone who'd been where he'd been, and seen what he'd seen – if a couple of decades apart – would be a fitting send off.

'Can't tell you how much I'd like that,' Bill's voice quiet and low, a quiver in his throat at the generosity of the offer. 'Should've come long before,' he whispered, closing his eyes. 'Should've come over and met you and Archie when I first had the chance.'

'Ain't nobody ready afore they're ready,' Kerr said pragmatically. 'And ain't nobody kens that better than me.'

'I don't understand where it's gone,' Sholto was saying, as everyone gained the library. 'It was right here,' he pointed at the large rosewood desk. 'Right here!'

No sign of the shagreen pouch containing Archie's book. Nothing but a blank space where'd he'd placed it earlier that evening.

'Think we've got our last answer,' Brogar growled.

'James Heron,' Sholto sighed, had been hoping it hadn't been true, but was casting his mind back to that first dinner spent with the man, how his hair had been so unruly and damp, like he'd just come in from the rain, or maybe just run over the sands, maybe back far earlier from Manchester or Lancaster – he couldn't remember which – than he'd let on.

'James Heron,' Brogar agreed. 'And I suspect he knows we know,' thinking back over the conversation at the table, at Bill's insistence on the manner and method of Gabriel's dying, his idea of fixing the time of it by examining Gabriel's stomach contents, of Sholto producing the murder weapon; the possibility that something about it could link it directly to James Heron, of Heron throwing in that maybe the murderer had medical knowledge – as any competent farmer and stocksman would.

'In fact,' Brogar went on, 'I'm sure of it. Hence that engineered tantrum to get him out of the room. Maybe out of the house altogether.'

'And that single book able to set up him up for another life, if he knows where to sell it,' Sholto added.

'And he knows where to sell it,' Brogar stated, James undoubtedly having all his father's contacts in the book trade as he'd made quite plain. Plan A to have Sholto stumble on the book and declare it a find of great worth, Plan B being to scarper with it if it all went wrong; Brogar turning on his heel, off out the library on a run, bumping into Skinner Tweedy who'd not come in with them but had hung in the hall, unsure what to do or where to go.

'You seen him?' Brogar demanded, grabbing Skinner's shoulders.

'Seen who?' Skinner flinching as Brogar shook him roughly, Skinner still not really getting what was going on, only thing in his head being his dismissal and what the hell he was going to do tomorrow.

'Heron!' Brogar shouted. 'Did you see him?'

But the answer was there for all to see once Brogar opened the front door, revealing a giddy trail of deep footprints heading out into the snow.

'Sholto!' Brogar hollered, Sholto already there.

'Gone?' he asked, knowing the answer.

'Should've twigged it first time we heard him moving about upstairs,' Brogar angry with himself, had to have been a quarter hour since. Make a big noise to attract attention, then sneak down and away first chance you got. Snatch up your most valuable assets – and in this case only one was needed – and ready for the off.

He'd've done exactly the same.

'But where could he go in all this snow?' Hazel asked, running up beside them, Esther's badly fitting dress getting trapped between her legs as she rushed onto the scene.

'Gotta think he'd likely do as he did as a bairn,' came a voice from a completely unexpected quarter, Pernel appearing from the kitchen at the hullabaloo, her and Esther having listened at the servants' door to all that had been going on. For why wouldn't they? Most exciting thing to have happened in Balcary since Rabbie Burns visited their shores a couple of generations back.

'Boathouse,' she added. 'Alwus stopped out there when he was in trouble. Mind you'd best be moving 'cos he's a boat in there sails like the wind, an' tide'll just be on the in. He gets past the point an' the other side of Hestan?' Quick shake of her head. 'He'll be away down the water towards Dumfries on the bore, when the fastest man in the world won't be able to catch him.'

The fastest man in all the world, thought Frith, who had to tie his legs together to keep himself still.

'Gotta try,' she said, shoving past Brogar as she made for the door, Brogar fast on her heels, out into the snow; Sholto, Gilligan and Hugh not far behind, Hugh tripping over the door stopper, falling face-flat in the snow, picked up by Hazel, held back by Hazel from going any further.

'Plenty going after him,' she said, 'so let's you and me sit down and wait.'

'It's been a rather...uncommon night,' Bill was saying, sipping slowly at his wine. No need to gulp it down, not any more, the rage in him no longer needing fuel. Slaked and gone.

'For you an' me both,' Kerr agreed.

Neither perturbed by the events going on about them, the loud voices in the corridor, the sound of feet running out the main

door. No need to pursue it any longer. All done as far as they were concerned.

'You understand it all?' Bill asked, Kerr puckering his lips.

'Got the main pieces,' he replied, sighing. 'Just can't see why any of it had to happen. All seems such a waste.'

Main waste being Gabriel, and losing Hestan.

'Not so much for me,' Bill added quietly. 'Think it might have been my saving.'

Kerr nodding, understanding.

'Not all bad, then.'

'Not all bad,' Bill agreed.

'What's not all bad?' Hugh asked brightly as he and Hazel came in to join them, Hugh brushing loose snow from his front, massaging the bruises coming up on what was left of his nose.

Bill smiling at the two of them, no one else he'd rather have seen in all the world.

Brogar caught Frith up with ease.

'Know where you're going?'

Frith jutting her head along the track leading out past Balcary in the opposite direction from Auchencairn.

'Boathouse is along there. Can't miss it. Right down on the shore, an' looks like some kind o' fancy cake.'

'How far?' Brogar asked.

'Bout five minutes,' Frith panted, slipping in the snow, Brogar catching her arm and hoisting her upright.

So Heron had fifteen minutes on them, doing the maths in his head, grimacing. Enough time to get a boat out if you were used to it – if it wasn't too far from boathouse to water's edge – scanning the shoreline but the damn trees were all in the way. Sprinting past Frith, time of the essence and all that, glad for the bright moon

that glittered on the snow, showed him the way, following the trail of boot prints, Pernel getting it right.

Sholto in the rear with Gilligan, Gilligan soon outpacing him, catching up with Frith, seeing the dark bulk of Brogar racing on ahead, running like a man who'd just untied his feet.

'What d'you think'll happen if they catch him?' Kerr asked, as Hazel and Hugh joined the small party at the table.

'Guess he'll get tried for murder,' Hazel said, 'though the evidence is mighty slim.'

Reaching for a piece of shortbread and dipping it in the jam, still hungry.

'I don't think it's slim at all,' Bill countered, Hazel looking up, small lump in her throat to see him so relaxed, like he'd woken from the deepest sleep, the darkest dreams, to find the world better than he'd left it. 'Firstly,' Bill went on, 'there's the very fact that he's running; secondly he'll have that book on him when they find him...'

'If they find him,' Kerr put in.

'Oh they'll find him,' Hugh said with absolute certainty, the three adults swapping smiles, Hugh producing one of his own.

'You don't know my Mr Brogar,' Hugh putting them right. 'He'll swim the Solway if he has to, to catch him up.'

'I don't doubt it,' Hazel said and, now she'd said it out loud, realised she didn't doubt it at all.

'But I may have more,' Bill added, with far less certainty than Hugh, but he'd been having an idea, his eyes resting on the copper-set curlew beak Sholto had left lying abandoned on the table. 'I don't know if anyone has ever heard of fingerprinting...'

Hazel looking up in extreme surprise. She'd kept up with a couple of medical journals over the years – when she could afford

to subscribe – and had always passed them on to Bill, but hadn't for a moment thought he'd actually read them.

'Are you thinking of that article about Herschel?' she asked, holding her breath, not having to wait long for an answer.

'I am,' Bill said. 'I don't remember much of it, but I do recall that he'd been palm and fingerprinting his contracts with the natives when he was Chief Magistrate in Jungipoor.'

'India,' Hazel added, for Hugh's benefit.

'India,' Bill agreed. 'Not for scientific reasons, not at first. Merely to frighten them into thinking he could find them if they abnegated the judgements he'd imposed. But over the years, starting…Hazel?'

'Starting in 1858,' Hazel eagerly supplied, allowing Bill to go on.

'Right. 1858. Exactly two years after…well. That's not important.'

Hazel so proud of her husband she forgot all about the shortbread, hanging on his words as Kerr and Hugh were doing.

'He began to notice how different they all were,' Bill said. 'Began to see that each individual had individual prints. And then there was a study by…a Frenchman…'

Again his memory stopped him short, and again Hazel prompted.

'Coulier. Jean-Paul Coulier…'

'That's right!' Bill beamed. 'He figured out a way to preserve fingerprints by iodine fuming, and methods of identifying each different type, and thereby each individual.'

'So all we've to do is to…put the beak into…iodising?' Hugh asked, jumping up, grabbing the beak from the table, misunderstanding the principles.

'Well, not now,' Kerr said, having gotten the gist and realising that Hugh had just made the whole process moot.

'Was thinking more on the door of Gabriel's house,' Bill

advocated for Hugh, 'and the book. Was thinking that if we can isolate his fingerprints on either or, then we'd have a good case. Could easily get an exemplar from his room. Might take a bit of swallowing in the courts, but the principle is entirely demonstrable.'

'Oh Bill,' Hazel couldn't stop herself, leant over the short distance between them and kissed her husband quickly on the cheek. 'Welcome home,' she whispered, as she withdrew.

'More glad than I can say to be back,' Bill replied quietly, Kerr and Hugh smiling mightily, even as they shifted their eyes away.

'Not all bad then,' Kerr Perdue murmured, winking at Hugh as if he'd been present at that earlier conversation.

'Not all bad,' Hugh replied, as if he'd been there.

Two people, like clocks that had lost their time, just needing to get all their stuff worked out.

Brogar almost missed the turning down to the boathouse, had run on a yard or two before registering there were no more footprints in the snow. Went back, ran down the narrow opening between the trees, saw the boathouse and that its gates were open, saw the tracks made in the snow by a boat having being dragged out the few yards to shore.

'Heron!' he shouted out into the darkness; saw the sea, saw the dark slump of Hestan like a shoulder shrugged up from the Solway as the waters came in – not as raging as they'd been before but still quick and fast. Thundered down the last few yards to the shingle bay.

'Heron!' he yelled again, quick cloud across the moon blocking any view. And then the cloud away again and Brogar had it, had the small dark sight of a boat skewing off towards the south, towards the point. Only ten yards out, only seconds to make his decision, but Brogar had lived long enough in Sweden, Finland

and Siberia to have done the same before. Sweat yourself into a lather in a steam-house and then come out running straight into the sea, bollock naked. Off with boots and coat. Off with all the trappings that would have stopped a lesser man and into the water, into it with his sword arm swinging – as Sholto might have said. And as Brogar hit the water, there was Sholto at the top of the slope that led down to the boathouse, Sholto pushing himself on after hearing Brogar's shouting; him, Gilligan and Frith getting there just as Brogar launched himself into the water.

'Oh my God!' Frith was aghast as she stumbled down the slope and onto the shingle of the shore, snow swept away by the incoming tide. 'But he'll die! He'll die!'

Gilligan panting hard beside her, not able to get out a word, Sholto too finding it hard, finding truth in Frith's words, summoning up the last of himself, seeing Brogar struggling through the water as he attempted to close on his goal.

'James Heron!' Sholto had never shouted so loud, had to cough at the constriction it gave to his throat, but wouldn't give up.

'James Heron!' he yelled again. 'You're done for! That book's known and provenanced! Got it all right here, right here in your own father's inventory! Only way out is back!'

'Oh God,' Gilligan whispered, as he saw the boat going onwards, saw Brogar swimming on after it; saw Heron swinging his boat towards the Point at the base of the Balcary Houghs, trying to get level with Hestan and out the other side.

'Ain't no good!' Gilligan shouted, loud as he'd ever done in his entire life. 'And ain't no good because it ain't no good! Gotta come back, Mr Heron, so's we make sure you don't hang.'

Hazel picked up the curlew beak and studied it closely, Kerr being right. No hope of fingerprints on it now. Even if any had been

there Hugh would have compromised them completely. But was thinking on the nightjar foot in the pocket of her apron back in Auchencairn, and when Kerr had given it to her.

'I know it don't look none too pretty,' Kerr had said. 'But it's one o' a kind. Ain't nobody the whole world over ever gets exactly the same, no matter how many I makes. All part of the luck.'

'How many curlew beaks have you set?' she asked Kerr Perdue, holding the amulet up, Kerr's mouth twitching spasmodically at the sight of the dried blood.

'Dunno exactly,' he got out. 'Ain't my most common thing. Kinda rare, in fact. Spend most o' their time inland when not feeding on the mudflats, so don't get washed up dead a lot. Not like the cormorants and guillemots that get themselves snagged on the rocks.'

'But did you ever give one to James Heron?'

Kerr frowning, shaking his head.

'Never did. Oh but…wait on!' he exclaimed, eyes wide opened. 'Gave one to Kheranovich when he weren't long here! He liked the curve on it, said it were like the scimitars the Tatars used to use…'

'A talisman against the bad old days,' Bill added, wishing he'd had one of his own.

'And might it be this same one?' Hazel asked, proffering the murder weapon over to Kerr Perdue, who took it gingerly between finger and thumb, twisting it this way and that, studying the setting, the tool marks in the copper, squinting.

You wouldn't have seen it if you didn't know where to look, but Kerr knew, had been the one to put them there: two letters on the curved part of the setting immediately beneath the hole meant to take a chain. Only two letters, no room for more; letters degraded by Kheranovich wearing it about his neck all those years, and presumably also by James Heron since his father had died. A

weapon of opportunity then, just as had been surmised.

Kerr touched that James had bothered wearing it at all.

Two letters: *DK*.

Danislaw Kheranovich.

All begun with him and now ending just the same.

Brogar was battling with the sea.

The current was against him, the water coming in strong and fast, but he was closing on James Heron who was struggling to get the sails up on his boat, fighting with the wind, having to get back to the oars every couple of minutes to stop himself being swept inland on the tide and smashed into the cliffs.

Brogar having no choice but to keep moving.

The exhilaration he'd being relying on to keep himself going in the freezing water was waning, and he knew he didn't have much longer. Had to head for the boat. Had to get there or the jig would be well and truly up. But by Christ, he wasn't going to go down without a fight and was not long off. Arms still pumping, legs still kicking, nothing in him of the lethargy that had stilled Kerr Perdue after his ducking trying to get to the cave. Bigger goals on the move. Murderers to catch. Or one at least. And so Brogar went on, five minutes in the water turning into ten, only reason he was still alive being that his head wouldn't let him stop, that he was so far in now he couldn't have got back if he'd tried.

Sholto was distraught. Could see no happy way out of this situation. James Heron off and Brogar after him, only way for Brogar to survive being to reach the boat, but that occurrence didn't look too good at the moment.

'Think I have it, Mr Sholto!' Gilligan leaping at his side. 'Heading for the point, so let's get there first,' Gilligan off, Sholto

following, Frith a shadow behind them as they leapt over a fence and went off up the hillside, which was steep, Sholto gasping, cattle murmuring disconsolately as they went by. But Gilligan had the right of it. They reached a plateau halfway up the heights, the sheer cliffs of the Balcary Houghs going straight down to the sea, the three getting there moments before the boat did, and Brogar not far behind.

'One chance,' Gilligan puffed, looking desperately about him, Frith understanding, Frith picking up a large pink rock and teetering on the cliff edge, taking aim and hurling it out and over, Sholto grabbing her by the waist to stop her going with it. All three panting as they heard it hit.

'It's his da's,' Kerr said. 'No doubting it.'

'So he really did it,' Hazel stated. 'And now he's on the run.'

No idea of how all that was going.

No idea that Frith's well lobbed rock had hit its mark, no idea that James Heron's boat was quickly taking on water from the hole made in its boards, nor that Heron had stumbled over the side with the shock of that rock coming out of nowhere, nor that Brogar was dragging Heron up by his collar, the two of them by now clinging to the wreckage, letting the tide take them back towards the boathouse, Brogar expertly wielding an oar to keep them from smashing into the cliffs, like he did this every day. Sholto and his entourage racing back down the heights and grabbing up ropes from the boathouse, yelling as they chucked them out, Brogar releasing the oar, grabbing hold of the closest rope as the tide pushed them on by; Sholto, Frith and Gilligan hauling in their catch, depositing them shivering on the shore.

No more running for James Heron, who'd never been the fastest of men.

Feet soon tied, as were his hands.

Snow beginning to fall, as if Kamyr-Batyr's second companion had removed his hat and allowed the blizzards to fly.

No companions to save James Heron.

No more tales to end well, at least not for him.

CHAPTER 29

ENDGAMES

'They've been gone an awful long time,' Hugh was worrying, standing up, going to the window, seeing the snow coming down once more with abandon, hearing the faint whoosh of the sea as it swept on down the bay.

'You're right,' Hazel too stood up. 'Come on. Grab what lamps you can and let's go look.'

Bill and Kerr on their feet in a moment.

'But where to look?' asked Bill.

'Boathouse is what Pernel said,' Hugh supplied, jittering as he attempted to grab up a lamp and missing its handle.

'More training needed for you, young mister,' Bill chided, taking up the lamp. 'No need for you to...'

'Try and bloody stop me!' Hugh was adamant, although Bill's suggestion had been meant for Hazel, but she and Kerr Perdue were already at the door and no stopping them either.

'Off to the boathouse!' Hazel commanded, leading the way, another Light Brigade heading off into the unknown, Hugh clinging to Bill's hand as he lifted his feet with exaggerated care over the door lintel that had previously tripped him up.

The snow was thick and fast, but the moon still bright despite it, and no difficulty discerning the way previous boots had gone. Bill thinking on that bright square of light in the top corner of the window when Hugh had stumbled down the stairs in his too large slippers, how he'd thought that brightness was lost to him as it slid away.

But here it was, leading him steadfastly by the hand.

Down on the shore, everyone had taken shelter in the boathouse, Brogar and Heron too cold to attempt further passage back to the house. Canvas and tarpaulins had been found, Frith insistent they be used to cover Brogar up like a dormouse in its nest and, grudgingly, covering James Heron too.

'Shame of it all, Heron,' Brogar was saying through teeth that had finally ceased their chattering, 'is that it was all so unnecessary.'

'D…don't…t…take no risks…d…don't get…no gains.' Heron got out. 'And…n…needed…g…g…gains.'

'Father not much of an estate manager, then?' Sholto asked.

'F…father organised…men…not…'

'I think we've got it, Heron.' Brogar cut him short. 'So you thought selling off Hestan might stave off the worst, but things still bad. Seen what the Company were paying you for it and have to say, that wouldn't have taken you through much.'

'N…not much,' Heron agreed.

'Until you heard about Charlie's little foray into number three,' Sholto went on for him. 'Knew all about your father's legacy to Archie Stirling and probably knew about that letter to him. Figured what he was really in there for.'

'N…not much choice. Once…sold to your Company it w… would have been yours, not mine. And it's rightfully m…mine.'

Brogar raised his eyebrows.

'Can't figure that at all. Rightfully belongs to Charlie and Frith.'

James Heron swivelled his eyes onto Brogar.

'Best of…the…lot,' getting a bit warmer now. Getting a bit of righteous anger back into his belly. 'Best b…book in the whole lot. And I'm his son.'

'But not back then,' Sholto pointed out. 'And probably wouldn't ever have been if Archie hadn't managed to produce a couple of children of his own.'

Remembering Esther telling him how the younger James Heron had come here fully formed, not long after Nairi and the twins arrived.

Heron didn't reply.

Had guessed a lot of this a long time ago.

Had always wanted to make his adoptive father proud, but never quite seemed to make the grade. Packed off to school and taught to speak right, and even when he'd been at home it had always been Archie this and Archie that. And even more so after Archie had apparently disappeared, dead, he now knew, and most probably – exactly as Brogar had earlier surmised – because of his father's obsession with the missing library of Dundrennan. Forgotten after Archie, as so much was, until his father had realised he was going to die. When he'd told James far more than James had ever wanted to know.

He wasn't sure how much more he could take.

Plan A had backfired, as had Plan B, and he had nowhere else to go.

Through the blizzards and the rising wind came the rest, all heading for the boathouse. It was hard going, and very slow, but they came to the top of the slope leading down to the shore, saw the tangle of ropes on the shingle and feared the worst – until

they saw the small flicker of fire that Gilligan had rustled up, and several huddled forms beside it in the darkness; all of them heading down the slope, getting there in time to hear Brogar's final pronouncement.

'But that's not the greatest pity,' Brogar was saying, quite cosy now inside his coverlets, although the salt on his skin was beginning to itch as the flames warmed him up, clothes beginning to steam inside his blankets.

'How so?' James Heron asked dully, knowing all was up but finding this intimate situation oddly companionable, irritated when the group from the house came battering in from the shingle and piling through the door.

'You're alive!' Hugh gasped, going straightaway to Brogar and hunkering down beside him, dragging Bill with him; Bill reminded of wonky nativity scenes lit by flickering candles in draughty churches, this one life-sized and himself being brought in like one of the three wise men. Not that he was wise, nor had a gift to give.

Unlike Brogar.

'You got that right,' Brogar said easily, 'mostly thanks to Frith.'

Frith blushing in the meagre light brought by the newcomers' lamps, Kerr and Hazel easing themselves in from wind and snow.

'Glad to find you all well and good,' Hazel said for them all, although it felt to her – seeing the angry jut of James Heron's chin as it stuck out from the canvas in which he was wrapped – like they'd stepped in where they weren't wanted, at least by him.

Gilligan breaking the moment.

'You got here just in time!' he informed them, shifting to one side, making space for Hazel and Kerr by the fire, as if they were all out on a jolly picnic jape as the roof planks above them creaked and lifted in the snow-skirling wind.

'Brogar was just about to tell us something important,' Gilligan confided.

'That so?' Kerr smiled into his beard as he pushed himself into the circle, sat down, looked over at the pink-cheeked Frith, at that bright alive face that was so like her father's.

'Ooh, go on, Mr Brogar,' Hugh urged, Brogar obliging.

'Very well then,' Brogar said. 'Was just telling Heron here that the greatest pity of this entire escapade was that it needn't have happened at all.'

'How so?' Hugh repeating Heron's earlier words, Hugh eager where Heron had been resigned, though Heron found himself hanging on Brogar's every word as the rest were doing.

'Because of these,' Brogar announced, and out came those small pink pebbles again, that Skinner Tweedy had scoffed at. 'These are barytes, and you've a whole heap of them about here somewhere.'

Frith blanching, Frith looking closer.

'Just like that rock I lobbed over the cliff,' she said.

'Was it indeed?' Brogar asked. 'And where did you find it exactly?'

'Up the heights,' Sholto supplied. 'A plateau in the…oh hang on! Didn't I read once that barytes only occur in sedimentary rocks, and are sometimes associated with copper veins?'

'Hang on indeed, and yes you did,' Brogar said. 'Large deposits in Europe are very rare. Germany and Austria mostly. And you, Heron, from what I've seen, have the makings of an entire mine right here in Balcary. Heavy spar it used to be called, can optimise drilling amongst other things, and my Company would have paid you handsomely for the rights to have at them.'

General amazement from all about the fire, who passed the unassuming pebbles from hand to hand, finger to finger.

'That's a bit of a turn up,' Kerr said.

'About the biggest,' Sholto agreed.

'Indeed,' James Heron managed, lips twisted in an ironic smile. 'Although I suspect the only relevant word for me in your little summing up, Brogar, is hang.'

First thing James Heron had got right for quite a while.

Pleading guilty to the murder of Gabriel Merryweather soon as he was landed in Dumfries.

Bill Tuley – expert witness at the trial – acclaimed for first cited use of fingerprinting in Scottish law.

The Stirling children finding themselves suddenly very wealthy indeed: Archie's book clamoured over by collectors – particularly from Russia, Tartary and Turkey – and finally going at auction for a small fortune.

And more good news for the Balcary Estates – not that James Heron would see a penny of it – when the franchise for the barytes was sold to Lundt and McCleery's Pan European Mining Company, Brogar and Sholto getting a hefty bonus that year on account of it.

And over the heights, in Dundrennan, Edmund Fitch soon thanking his God for both those happenings, two opened letters lying on the table in front of him, his fingers flitting from one to the other, unable to decide which was the most miraculous. The first informing him that Lundt and McCleery's wanted to settle all their incoming baryte miners in the abandoned houses of Dundrennan, all cottages in the hamlet nominally in Edmund's see, still part of the Abbey's heritage. The second stating that a large, anonymous donation had been settled on the Abbey's overseer – namely Fitch – to completely renovate and upkeep the chapel within its walls.

New families soon to spring up about it, Edmund Fitch

upping sticks entirely from Auchencairn and settling himself in Dundrennan, devoting himself wholly to his new flock, his beloved chapel and his Abbey. Only sadness being for him that Frith and Charlie no longer lived here, finding he missed them rather more than he'd anticipated, not slow to realise that *anonymous* meant Frith and Charlie – given their recent good fortune – though he suspected Frith had the greater hand in the gift.

Always a good girl, and a wise one.

Fitch looking fondly on Esmerelda, Lily, Maisie and Mabeline, the animals he'd been bequeathed on Frith and Charlie's leaving.

'Alright girls,' he'd say every morning. 'Going to be a good day, I can feel it in my bones.'

Stick still there, perhaps, but more pliant these days, and not quite so far up as Frith had once described.

CHAPTER 30

AND JUST A LITTLE MORE

'Guess you'll soon be off, then?' Kerr Perdue was saying to Brogar Finn as Brogar came across the Rack one morning.

'Reckon around mid-April,' Brogar agreed. 'Sales all done, both for Hestan and the Heights, survey up there going well.'

Andrew Fitzsimons finally arriving a few days after the dramatic night that had seen the apprehension of James Heron. And none too pleased to be embroiled once again in one of Brogar and Sholto's exploits.

'Can you never make anything straightforward?' he'd sighed, as he'd unlatched his case, got out his writing implements, seals and papers.

'Not if it means giving you an easy ride,' Brogar quipped, which Fitzsimons hadn't in the slightest appreciated.

'So another day, another murder. Another change in circumstance. What is it with you people?'

Annoyed he'd also been burdened with a task that was not his own, but when no less a person than the Procurator Fiscal of Dumfries asked then even the likes of Fitzsimons felt compelled to jump.

'You're an impartial third party,' he'd been told, 'and so it's up to you to get everything about the Heron Estate drawn up and to scratch; at least if you want your Company to take the benefits of Hestan and the barytes mine.'

Hands tied.

As were James Heron's, when he was taken from the courthouse in Dumfries and condemned to a life of hard labour, with no hope of release. That James Heron had always considered his life one of hard labour, no one cared nor minded.

Except for Sholto, who visited the man after trial and judgement had been passed.

The only one who did.

'I'm sorry it's ended this way,' Sholto said, regarding James Heron – who was slumped in his cell, looking thin and defeated – Sholto trying to equate the man he was looking at with the exuberant raconteur who didn't seem able to shut up about all his plans of what the future might hold, about the possibilities of wool and flax, of harvesting hair from France.

'Don't be,' Heron said shortly. 'Always knew my life was on a lease.'

Sholto frowning. It was like he was talking to someone else entirely.

'How d'you mean?' he asked.

James Heron raising a small smile.

'You don't know what my father – I mean the man I called my father, Danislav Kheranovich, as he was then – took me away from.'

Sholto shaking his head, for no, he didn't. All James had said previously was that Kheranovich had rescued him from a war zone, brought him to a new land and a new life.

'Place I was in was hell,' James went on. 'Russians and English

ripped our village to shreds. And couldn't have cared less about it. Had their battles, cut everyone down and then moved on.'

'When was this? Sholto asked.

James shrugged his shoulders.

'Does it matter? Fact is, I was eating grass and drinking out of bloody puddles when Kheranovich came along. He went back down the lines – completely against orders – and picked me up. Said he wasn't about to let me die like a mangy dog in the dust.'

'And brought you out,' Sholto stated.

'And brought me out,' James agreed. 'But it doesn't ever leave you.' James shook his head. 'You can shift countries and languages, be moulded into something new like I was. But it doesn't ever leave, that beginning, that burn in you that tells you to survive, no matter what.'

And no wonder James had taken such measures to get hold of Archie Stirling's book, whether he'd got wind of it from his dying father or from the copy of the letter to Charlie. Sale of Hestan nothing compared to what that book would have garnered him. James doing what he had to do to protect his livelihood, obeying his instincts. Anything to survive, no matter the consequences. Sholto ashamed he'd not registered any of this before.

He'd been puzzled why James had acted so precipitously, choosing gamble over reason, why he hadn't just waited to see how events would turn out. But here was the answer: James Heron primed by his early life of eating grass and sucking water out of bloody pools.

James never wanting to be that boy again; James singled out for rescue by Kheranovich because of his superficial resemblance to Archie Stirling – a fact James must at some point, growing up in Balcary, have realised. James never the true object of Kheranovich's affection, for that was reserved for one person and one person only: Archie Stirling.

Sholto could only guess how much James must have riled and roiled as he got to grips with such a simple fact, such a huge betrayal. And now he was about to compound the cruelty. Sholto picked at his shirt cuffs, but there was no point keeping quiet. One way or another James was going to find out.

'There's something I need to tell you,' Sholto speaking quiet and slow, hating what he was about to do. James unexpectedly taking the burden from him.

'Let me take a wild stab at it,' James said, lifting his head, looking at Sholto directly. 'Now that I'm well and truly done for, now that I've been told the rest of my life is going to consist of breaking rocks, let me take a guess.'

Sholto remained silent, though he held James's stoic gaze.

'Balcary Estates to pass with immediate effect,' James stated, 'to the children of Archie Stirling.'

Sholto hesitating, James seeing it.

'Then I'm not wrong,' James said. 'And maybe that's as it should be.'

Sholto had expected outrage, argument, righteous anger.

But James merely closed his eyes and shrugged.

'Like I said before, always knew my life was on a lease, but I was glad for it while it lasted.'

And that's where they left it: Sholto going back to Balcary, leaving James Heron in his cell in the Dumfries gaol; Heron about to be projected into an existence most people – Sholto included – would consider hellish and of no worth, Sholto comforted by one fact and one fact only: that James Heron had come from worse. He'd survived then, and he would survive now. All the intervening years considered by James a mere hiatus, an extension of life not granted to any other of his kin.

It didn't sit easy with Sholto as he left the gaol, left Dumfries.

Troubled more by what he'd not asked, the farther he went back to Balcary.

What no one had ever asked either at Balcary or during the trial itself, Sholto writing several consecutive letters to the gaol addressed to James Heron.

'What's your name?' he wrote, in one. 'Your real name? Before Kheranovich found you?'

But the letters were returned unopened, informed that the prisoner James Heron had been moved on, and Sholto never got his answer, nor James the option to reply.

Which seemed to Sholto the saddest thing of all.

Strange days, and stranger to follow, Skinner Tweedy coming to the fore, taking Firth and Charlie step by step through the running of the estate: the tenancies, the livestock, the rotations of fields throughout the season, James's plans for making it all more profitable. Skinner Tweedy finding he knew a lot more than he thought he did and proving himself a good teacher; Skinner Tweedy undergoing a slight revision in character with this revelation, evening himself out, curbing those sudden swings of temperament, quelling them the second he saw the warning flash in Frith's eyes when he overstepped the mark or spoke too roughly. Skinner Tweedy liking that change, liking those dimples in Frith's cheeks when he got it right, adjusting his behaviour as he came to like them more and more.

'He's like a cat what's tumbled into the cream,' Esther remarked to Pernel one afternoon as they got the dinner ready, Pernel answering easily as she dried her hands on a tea towel.

'Don't knock it till you've tried it,' she advised. 'Everyone grows up in their own time, and seems to me it's maybe his time now.'

And right she was.

Skinner Tweedy no longer the unpredictable little shite he'd always been since he was a bairn who switched from good to bad on a sixpence; Skinner Tweedy realising that there was oh so much more to life than just himself.

Skinner Tweedy realising that he'd throw the rest of the world away as long as Frith Stirling was still there to notice he had use.

Frith to Skinner as her father had been to Kheranovich.

Love and loyalty.

Emotions not easily bound.

'You still poking down that shaft, then?'

Kerr standing on the topknot of Hestan where old Baliol had once built his manor, where he'd once excavated his well.

'Still at it,' Brogar called up from the pit he'd been digging down through the topsoil and then the clay and sandstone, trying to intercept Archie's skewed shaft; at it every free moment he had after surveying the heights. 'But the barytes have made the drilling easier.'

'A plus then,' Kerr observed, turning and heading for home, and home it was now: Kerr granted leave to stay on the island as long as he wanted, part of Brogar's bargaining with his Company for the barytes, and Hestan's copper no longer of equal use.

Kerr thought Brogar's venture fruitless, but was glad it had kept Brogar on the island these past two months, them spending companionable evenings together, Bill Tuley a frequent visitor when the tides allowed.

'Made our doctoring practice a legal partnership,' Bill had announced a while back. 'Hazel and me to share duties, work together. Some folk still don't trust me, and who can blame them?'

Brogar liking the idea, and saying so.

'She's a rare woman you've got, Bill. Best keep a hold of her.'

Bill agreeing with all his heart, Kerr congratulating Bill, pouring out some of Merryweather's hooch to celebrate.

'To partnerships!' he'd announced, the three of them clinking glasses and agreeing before subsiding back into general chat about what they'd been doing, how the Stirling children were coping with Balcary, which seemed well enough.

Almost like the old days, Kerr thought, but without the blood of battle in their nostrils.

Kerr and Bill often talking quietly, after Brogar had retired, of what they'd both seen and done in their respective days. No bitterness to it, and no anger. Just two men who'd been through the mill and needed to get it said in order to get it rid.

Bill and Hazel talking too, Bill finally able to retrieve his old and battered suitcase from beneath their bed and fetching out his journal from those days in the Crimea, Hazel soft and tender as he read the first few sentences from it…and then stopped.

'But you kept one too,' Bill said, hardly daring to meet Hazel's eyes. 'Why don't we read from yours instead?'

Hazel going one better, bringing out her ancient fiddle, getting it tuned – though not too well, given the age of it and how long it had been sitting unused in a cupboard.

'Going to be a bit of a screech,' she warned, as she flexed her fingers, did a few practice scales before she was ready. 'What would you like?'

Bill so astonished he could hardly speak.

'You choose,' he said, and Hazel did.

'Young Waters, then. Do you remember it?'

Bill's throat closing, because of course he remembered it. His favourite ballad, not heard for years, and how they'd used to sing it together and then go up the stairs in delighted abandon. Hazel starting hesitantly, violin and voice a little out of tune as they

attempted to find their previously well-trodden way:

All about Yule, when the winds blow cold, and the Round Table begins;

When there is come to our King's court many the well favoured man...

Bill breaking in suddenly and without conscious thought – even more out of tune than Hazel and her violin, if that was possible.

Oh but I've seen lords and I've seen lairds, and knights of high degree,

But Young Waters is the fairest face that ever mine eyes did see.

Bill suddenly choking up.

Bill suddenly standing and coming over to Hazel, taking the fiddle from her hands, wrapping his arms around her.

'And you're still the fairest face, and always will be.'

And for the first time in over fifteen years, up the stairs they went as one.

Brogar was as far down his shaft as he could go.

One more push and he'd have it.

Got the drill going one last time, braced his feet against the sides of the shaft as he did so, choking on the dust, pushing away the rubble, and then it was done; Brogar landing in a small cavern, a few yards on from where Archie's shaft had reached from down below, never quite getting to its goal as Brogar had.

Brogar finding what he'd never truly expected to find, but no harm looking.

'Kerr!' Brogar yelled. 'Kerr Perdue!'

Perdue on his way from the lamp over to his workshop, but the evening was calm, no wind, nor rain, nor snow, and he heard the faint call and cocked his head.

'Kerr! Kerr Perdue!'

He heard it more distinctly this time, retraced his steps, got to the top of Hestan and looked down the shaft to see Brogar Finn fifteen-odd yards below, face upturned and covered in dust, like the ghost of Hestan past.

'Send down ropes!' Brogar's voice coming up at him. 'Because I'm telling you, there's really something down here!'

A sea chest, kept safe and buried for three hundred years, a sea chest bounded in iron that held within it the lost locked library of the Abbey of Dundrennan.

Edmund Fitch was going to blow a gasket.

Over the water, brothers, over the water.

Just like on the ancient Perdue grave Sholto had read from.

Lost, but now found.

The tale for once, for most – if not for James Heron – ending well.

Kerr Perdue standing at the top of Baliol's Castle hearing Brogar's call; hearing Archie's bright voice in his ear as if he were standing by his side.

I told you! Didn't I tell you?

'You did, Archie,' Kerr Perdue whispered.

Kerr Perdue revising his list, though not by much.

For here were the birds, here the sea, here the sands, here the tides and the water and the Rack.

Here was Hestan.

Himself a part of it, and nothing – nor anyone – able to take him from Hestan, nor Hestan from him.

AUTHOR NOTES

The history of Hestan I've kept as true to as possible, its ownership by the Abbey, the copper mining extant since 1841 and the barytes mines since the 1870s.

Also adhered to are the details and dates of the book-burning in Tartary and the battles in Crimea, Poland and Russia, as well as the mentions of the Crimean War and Lord Raglan.

And what was said about Herschel's fingerprinting and Coulier's following up on his ideas about them.

It's also the case that Robert Burns was in Balcary when an excise-man.

Not to mention the locked library of Dundrennan Abbey that vanished after the Dissolution although, as stated in the text, most believe it went over to the Isle of Man and from there into the property of the Crown.

Believed, but never proven.

So maybe still on Hestan, waiting to be found.

Clio was born in Yorkshire, spent her later childhood in Devon before returning to Yorkshire to go to university. For the last twenty-five years she has lived in the Scottish Highlands where she intends to remain. She eschewed the usual route of marriage, mortgage, children, and instead spent her working life in libraries, filling her home with books and sharing that home with dogs. She began writing for personal amusement in the late nineties, then began entering short story competitions, getting short listed and then winning, which led directly to a publication deal with Headline. Her latest book, *The Anatomist's Dream*, was nominated for the Man Booker 2015 and long listed for the Bailey's Prize in 2016.

'Surprisingly,' Gray says, '*The Anatomist's Dream* - although my eighth published novel – was amongst the first few stabs I made at writing a book. Pretty appalling in its first incarnation (not that I thought it at the time!) it was only when I brushed the dust off it a few years ago that I realised there really was something interesting and unusual at its core that I could now, as a more experienced writer, work with. The moral being: don't give up. The more you write, the more self-critical you become and the better your writing will be because of it.'

Clio has always been encouraging towards emergent writers, and founded HISSAC (The Highlands and Islands Short Story Association) in 2004 precisely to further that aim, providing feedback on short listed stories and mentoring first time novelists, not a few of whom have gone on to be published themselves.

'It's been a great privilege to work with aspiring writers, to see them develop and flourish,' Gray says. 'There can never be too many books in the world, and the better the books the better place the world will be.'

Enjoyed the Scottish Mysteries series? Why not try one of Clio's previous historical adventures, ***Legacy of the Lynx***, available now:

Award winning writer Clio Gray has written a thrilling adventure story, steeped in historical fact and legend, that will keep readers gripped to the very last page.

1798. Three people, two brutal murders, and a single promise... Golo Eck is searching for the fabled lost library of The Lynx, Europe's first scientific society, founded in 1603. Fergus, his friend and fellow adventurer, is on the trail of the legend in Ireland when he becomes embroiled in the uprising of the United Irish against English rule. His only hope of escape is Greta, a courageous messenger for the United Irish cause. Following the bloody battles of New Ross and Vinegar Hill, Fergus is missing, and Greta is on the run.

Golo meanwhile suspects other forces are on the trail of the Lynx, and he heads to Holland in pursuit. When Golo's ship founders and he disappears, his ward Ruan is left to fend for himself, a stranger in a strange land.

Can Ruan pursue the trail to the lost library? Will Golo and Fergus be found? Can Greta escape Ireland with her very life? And will the truth of the Legacy of the Lynx finally be revealed?

URBANE